Agony

of

Being Me

Part One

Agony

of

Being Me

Part One

Dark Dramatic Romance

by

Victoria Valentine

writing as

January Valentine

Agony of Being Me (Part One)
Copyright © 2016 Victoria Valentine
All Rights Reserved Victoria Valentine

Printed in the United States of America

ISBN-13: 978-0692695951
ISBN-10: 0692695958

Book Design & Cover by Victoria Valentine
Edited by: Phaedra Valentine
Song lyrics by Victoria Valentine

Cover art: © Isabel Poulin | Dreamstime.com

Water Forest Press Books
PO Box 295, Stormville, NY 12582
waterforestpress.com

January Valentine Books

Love Dreams Contemporary Romance
Michael is in a wheelchair. Sienna has been emotionally damaged.
They keep having accidental run-ins, but can they find love?

Sweet Dreams in the Mind of a Serial Killer
He plants roses ... in dead women. A witness says: He doesn't
look human.

Fighting For You Steamy Contemporary Romance
Jewelia wants to work for the NYPD. Indigo is a medical student
with baggage. They come from two different worlds. Can they
beat the odds?

*Beautiful Experiment Paranormal Romance Book One of The
Island of Defiance Trilogy*

Six unruly teens are kidnapped, sent to an uncharted island.
Caretaker, Brook, is hot. Father is mysterious. Will they find a
way home before the island is overrun with demons?

Wheel Wolf (Werewolf Horror)

Don't stop at the lake! You never know what you'll run into. Jack
& Jenny are lovers sharing an unconditional love. Is there an
ungodly creature at Hosner Lake? Ask Jack.

All titles are available on Amazon, B & N and through other
booksellers in print and ebook format. Some as Audio books.

Find all of my books on my Amazon Author page
http://www.amazon.com/January-Valentine/e/B007Q28DFE/

Agony Of Being Me

In a matter of moments, an inhumane and hideous act all but destroys a young girl's life.

This story is loosely based on an actual event which has been expanded into fictional form. Names and locations have been changed to protect identities. This is the story of a young girl who survives a brutal attack in the boiler room of her school, and how the emotional aftermath affects the years to follow and the paths she takes while trying to cope with life and loss.

When life is too painful, you either suffocate in hell, or fight back. The violence in this book is not gratuitous, but necessary for readers to fully understand the physical suffering and psychological damage Zoe has endured, and why she behaves as she does. Contains mature content which may be too intense for some readers. Not intended for readers under 16. The opening pages contain the one sexual assault scene; although not graphic, it may be disturbing. What you are about to read is raw emotion turned into a character rich two part set:

Agony of Being Me (part one), *Finding You* (part two).

Available on Amazon in Paperback & Kindle

Dedicated to Victims of All Forms of Abuse. Don't bear the burden alone. Reach out to caring hearts and trained professionals.

Share the words of love and hope and
life can be good again.

For someone I owe just about everything to ... Thank you Tom, for your undying love, understanding, and acceptance of my many quirks and phobias. Some pain never goes away. A life may be haunted by terrifying events; It isn't easy to stop the demons from following, but it's possible. For me, it was a long journey.

Your wings have flown you into the sky,
but my love for you will never die.

Agony Of Being Me

Acknowledgements

How do I begin? So much has happened during the writing process of this book. First of all, I want to remember Tom Valentine, my incredible husband of almost forty years. I started *Agony* in 2014, right before Tom fell ill. During that time I wrote sporadically, when my nerves and time permitted. After Tom passed on May 6, 2015, I put *Agony* aside to deal with my grief and loss. As I couldn't think straight, there was no way I could write, although I desperately wanted to finish. So in January 2016, I started to pick up the pieces. Shortly thereafter I fell ill and was completely out of commission for almost three months. Another setback! Getting my brain to work again was not easy, but I was determined to publish *Agony* on my mom's birthday, June 1, 2016, as a loving memorial to someone who made such a difference in this world and mine.

The end result of writing intermittently produced a manuscript too long for one book, so I split it into two parts: *Agony of Being Me* and *Finding You*. I don't believe I could have completed this, or any journey, without my kids: Phaedra, Tom and Cindy. Their love and strength gave me a reason to live, and courage to go on. So here I am, pushing the publish button, which is never easy, especially when half your brain and heart are missing. :(

I also received the assistance of two Facebook pals who volunteered to beta read. A huge and endless thank you to Heather Freeman Chrisco and Michelle Nageldinger. Heather, you saved me from some embarrassing bloopers :D and Michelle, you proofread through an illness. This is dedication ladies, and I appreciate your amazing help from the bottom of my heart.

PHASE I

THE BEGINNING

I never figured on being part of the drama class in school. But when the club needs help configuring the set of the upcoming play, my art teacher volunteers my assistance. Grudgingly, I agree. I've been in the auditorium a hundred times, but never for this reason.

I walk backstage, which is like a scene of destruction rather than construction. Now I know why Mr. Cooper sent me. A rack of jumbled costumes is squashed against a wall. I step around slabs of plywood and a variety of tools that are strewn across the floor. These are the first things to hit me. She's the next.

A girl teeters on top of a stepladder, trying to reach the ceiling, where a string of glittering stars are slung from corner to corner. She's struggling to reattach one. Although her slender fingers work furiously, each time she releases it, the star unhooks and falls to the floor. I pause in the doorway, my shoulder against the frame, mesmerized. Up and down the ladder she stomps, and by the look on her face, she's getting pissed. The back pockets of her jeans are trimmed with sparkly studs, enhancing her rounded butt. The rest of the curves shaping her petite frame are impressive, to say the least. She's so damn adorable. I could stand here all day watching her. My sneakers are silent as I cross the room, where the air turns sweet, scented with floral perfume.

I'm not creeping up on her, and the last thing I want to do is scare her, so I call out a throaty, "Hey." A falling star aims for my head, so I grab it, extend a hand, and joke, "Here's the one that got away."

I must startle her because as she does a quick spin, one foot shoots off ladder, then the other follows. Not only is the string of stars falling, but the girl is tumbling, right into my arms.

I catch her like a baby, stunning both of us. Her, because she's obviously got no clue who I am, why I'm here, or how she's ended up cradled in my arms. Me, because she's the most beautiful girl I've ever seen, and embracing her is an unexpected pleasure. Long lashes frame her big blue eyes that stare up at me, questioning. For a moment, I just hold her. Light as a feather and crushed to my chest, she feels amazing. A perfect fit for my arms. Neither of us speak. My eyes move at will, cruising from the top of her lush blonde head, down the slope of her nose, lingering on her plump lips. I stare at the most amazing Cupid's bow I've ever seen. This girl is the portrait I've been waiting to paint.

My gaze dips to her baby-soft neck, to the Z dangling on a silver chain, and the fullness beneath her sweater registers; I'm not holding a baby.

Her lips purse, her brows furrow, forcing me to regain my senses, reminding me to release her. So I set her down slowly.

"Thanks for the save," she says.

I detect a hit of irritation in her tone. Her lids lower as she pushes her hair behind her ears.

"My pleasure." Hiding my amusement is difficult. Hiding my attraction is impossible.

When her gaze climbs from my chest to my lips, I offer an innocent grin. She rolls her eyes and with a few small steps, inches away.

"Let me give you a hand." I make a move for the ladder, but a sudden command stops me.

"I've got it covered." Delorese comes up from behind, acting as if I'm in her space. She nods in the direction of the teacher entering in the room. "Zoe, that's my job. You shouldn't have been on the ladder," she whispers. "Ms. Jordan will write me up if she knows I snuck out for a quick smoke. We can't have a fairy with a broken leg." Her laugh sounds forced.

While thinking, "Zoe," is a perfect name for this girl, I'm shoved off toward Hillary Jordan, who instructs me as to what kind of set decorations she wants me to build.

Twice a week, I watch Zoe rehearse. It's hard to work, even harder to concentrate on building the set. We're never alone. She's always deep into her role, making it impossible to get close to her.

No longer is being a stage hand a nuisance, I look forward to it. But all too soon, my job here is done, and since I really want to get to know this girl, I decide to give it one more shot.

Entering the room, I find Zoe wearing jeans and a pink shirt, sitting on a folding chair beside Delorese. Zoe is strumming an acoustic guitar, singing a song I've never heard before. But it sounds damn good. Like it could be a hit. Delorese appears caught up in her voice. I'm caught up in everything about her. The way her hair cascades softly over one shoulder as she tilts her head and inches forward in the seat. The careful way she holds the guitar, like I wouldn't mind being held, her delicate fingers moving expertly over the strings.

Make a move, my mind says, so I waste no time moseying up to them.

"You sound great," interrupting her song, I give her my warmest smile.

Her head snaps up, and she hugs the guitar close to her chest. "Thanks," she says.

I watch her cheeks turn pink, confirming she's sharing my vibes.

"Why haven't we run into each other before this?" The words I've been wondering for weeks finally have a chance to emerge.

Her hand moves from the neck of the acoustic to flip her hair off her shoulder. "It's my first year here." She bites her bottom lip. So tempting. I wouldn't mind nibbling a bit.

"Junior year?" I hold my breath. Don't be a freshman …

Her expression of interest seizes. She plucks a string. "Freshman."

Her reply surprises me. She looks mature for ninth grade. I'd take her for at least seventeen. Still, jail-bait. I'm bummed.

Her voice tests, "Senior?"

Hands stuffed in pockets, I nod.

Claudette calls out from the doorway, demanding her ride home. I'm not sure if Claudette's choice of timing is a good or bad thing. It certainly ends an awkward moment, but leaves me pondering a question. Would I want to date a freshman? Even if she's gorgeous and intriguingly angelic? Being with Zoe wouldn't be like dating the girls I'm used to. We'd need to take it slow. Would that be possible? *You're taking a lot for granted, Jesse. Would she even want to be with you?*

Claudette's voice rings out louder, closer now. "I'll be there in a minute, Claudette," I snap, without offering her the attention she's obviously seeking.

Zoe's eyes shift from me to Claudette. The modest smile that had begun to grow across her lips fades. She hops to her feet, drops the guitar into a case, snaps it closed, and before breezing away, says, "The set looks great. Thanks for all you've done." After a pause, she adds, "See you around."

"I'm Jesse–"

"I know," one dimple deepens, "I'm Zoe."

"Yeah," I give her a cocky grin, "I know."

Zoe

> *My prince rode in on a Harley*
> *Wearing nothing but tattoos*
> *Naked I sat guitar in lap*
> *Singing out the blues*

The stars are falling! Whirling, my eyes dart around the room searching for Dee, the person responsible for stage decoration. As usual, she's never around when I need her. So I proceed to drag the stepladder from one place to another, reaching up to fasten the hooks on the stars that Dee haphazardly strung across the room. I'm on the top step, straining to reach the corner star closest to the ceiling. "Should I be risking this?" I ponder aloud, to myself, because Ms. Jordan, my drama teacher, has stepped out for coffee.

I mumble a flat, "What the heck," and carefully lift one foot, then the other until I'm perched on the very top of the ladder. I dread heights; my limbs tingle with apprehension. The moment I reach the dangling star, the glitter begins to flake and the star slips from my jittery fingers. At the same moment my eyes follow the glittering trail, a hand comes up beside me, scaring the crap out of me. I lose my balance and feel myself falling faster than the stars, which are also tumbling, because I'm strangling the string they were secured with, pulling part of the sky down with me.

In that fearful moment my mind spins. Broken leg, maybe neck, definitely a concussion. But I make a soft landing, and am being held firmly by a pair of strong arms. Initially, I'm struck with, "Who the hell is he?" Then it registers. "Oh my God. It's Jesse Sinclair. The hottest guy in school!" I don't say this mind you, my brain does, and I pray that my eyes don't give my thoughts a voice.

He grins down at me. I stare up at him, unable to utter a word.

"Are you okay?" He chuckles softly. I don't believe there's humor in his eyes though, or his smooth deep voice. "You could've broken a leg. Or worse."

"Yeah," I manage to move my body, indicating he better set me down before I faint, because his gaze is drinking in every part of my face, which is making me weak. "Thanks for the save."

He stands beside me, arms straight at his sides. "You shouldn't be doing this alone. Don't you have stage hands?" He holds up a palm, and cocks his head.

"Volunteers aren't easy to find." I'm breathless as I push strands of hair from my face, securing long locks behind my ears.

"I'm here to help." His eyes close in on mine. Brown, kind, and delicious. His cologne is making me even dizzier than the movement of his lips, which I'm imagining the feel of as they come down on mine. His nearness, the way he's looking at me, gives the distinct impression he wants to kiss me!

Just then Dee breaks the moment. "Don't tell Hillary Dillary I left. She'll write me up." It must suddenly register what's going on between Jesse and me, because Dee gets a strange look on her face. "What did I miss?"

"I'm designated stagehand. And apparently, you could use the help," he replies to her, but watches me, his gold-flecked eyes examining my soul. Paralyzing. But for the adrenaline rush weakening my limbs, I'm unaware of the world around me … until Dee's voice breaks the spell.

"Sure can." Dee's eyes travel from me to Jesse and she grins.

"So what's the play about? What kind of props do we need?" Clearing his throat, he asks with authority. Just what I need. A take charge guy. Handsome, handy, and all around amazing.

So is my dad. Not that Jesse reminds me at all of my dad, but how would my dad react to me acting this way? Feeling this way? To him I'm Peanut. His little girl who's not permitted to date yet. Ugh.

The sensation of inadequacy snaps me back to reality, and I'm suddenly embarrassed to be playing something close to Peter Pan. "It's about fairies. I'm the lead." I stave off an eye roll. The last thing I want to do is appear immature, or nervous, although I'm both, and at this moment, I feel like I need a sedative.

A grin spreads across his face. His hand comes down on his hip, and he runs the fingers of his other hand through his gorgeous hair. "Cool." I'm sure he's just being kind. "I can come up with some great fantasy decorations."

"Sweet," Dee inserts herself into the conversation, "we've got Picasso on the team." She shoulder-checks Jesse. "We're gonna rock this—"

A heavy fragrance wafts across the room, followed by a sultry voice. "How about that ride home, Jess?"

Our heads turn to watch the striking brunette saunter toward us. In moments, Jesse is gone.

After dismissal, Dee and I discuss the most exciting moment I've had since I started this school.

"He was about to totally hit on you till she—"

My hand shoots up in protest. "Don't bother, Dee. My parents won't let me date till I'm sixteen. Firm rule." My face twists into a scowl. "Warning, actually."

Dee clips a thumb under the strap of her shoulder bag and lights up with a mischievous grin. "Jesse could always pick you up at *my* house."

After careful consideration, and although the concept thrills me to the core, I don't hide things from my parents, and I don't lie, especially to them. I haul in a breath, blow out my puffed cheeks, and drift into thought. "I'll just have to try to keep him interested, but hanging," my finger jerks up, "just till my birthday." Then my brows crunch and my heart sinks. "Technically, he never asked me out, Dee. And what about Claudette?" I sigh. "Plus, I'm a freshman. Seniors don't date freshmen."

Zoe's Flight of Fae

Fear not darkness
the Fae will light your way
sprinkling stardust cross her skies
brightening every day

her gestures and her whispers
calm the forests, charm the creatures
Listen closely and you may hear
her siren pleas and promises

trees not shed
the world needs your splendor
birds sing sweet and far
so the lost can find shelter

If you see a Fae you're forever blessed
She holds the lamp of kindness
purity and trust
Goddess of all treasure
wise beyond all measure

An intriguing bit of magic
with a drop of human tears
Once your eyes have brushed her wings
you'll fall in love for years

ZOE CHANNING

Dad guides our Mazda to the curb, pulls the gearshift into park and slings his arm over the back of the seat. "Tonight." The only movement of his poker face is the lift of one thick brow.

The engine idles smoothly. I swing my head around and scrunch my mouth to one side, matching the arch of his brow with the thin line of mine.

"Dinner," he chuckles in his deep, musical tone, "Italian or Chinese. I'll call Mom later and tell her what to order."

"Gah." My head bounces with a series of nods. "I forgot it was Friday. Takeout night."

His arm fills the air between us, and he tugs my ponytail. "So, what'll it be, Peanut?"

"Zoe." Arching my brow higher, I correct him. "Peanut went out with the Barbies. Remember? No I guess you don't," I lower my voice and try for wry, "since you just called me Peanut."

He belts out a laugh. "Your mother and I might have named you Zoe, but you'll always be my Peanut." His smile shadows. "Sorry for trying to stop the clock." His eyes go so soft, I'm afraid he's about to cry. *Don't cry, Dad. I don't know how to handle your tears. Dealing with Mom's was hard enough.*

My gaze slips over his pressed work uniform. "Don't be sorry. No one's perfect," I tease, indulging him with the side grin he calls *impish*. Maybe a silly face will bring his smile back.

"Except you," he replies, his face glowing with pride. "Someday my perfect little daughter is going to save the world." I watch his hard swallow, and my throat automatically tightens. "You'll never do the things I've done. Cause the pain I've ..."

I'm fifteen years old, Dad. I have no clue how to handle your solemn mood swings, so I'll joke my way around them. "Let's see if the polluters say that when I'm part of the EPA. I'll be causing them a whole lot of pain "in the wallet." I tap my backpack, adding a deep, "Oh yeah. I plan on making them pay big time." I flash him a double-dimple grin.

"Sometimes that's the best kind of poison, kiddo. Those fat-cats will see you coming and run the other way." He chuckles, his faded eyes hanging onto mine.

While vowing to never date a guy who favors alcohol over a relationship, I brace for his mournful reverie: *"If I hadn't screwed up, I'd still be an executive, making a good living with my brain, and not working for a moving company, breaking my back."* But his regret doesn't surface.

His fingers slide over the strap of my backpack, idly, tiredly. His hands are worn from lifting other people's valuables, his face from his past lifestyle. He's only thirty-five, but drinking and smoking have taken their toll. Even though he's been clean, as Mom calls it, for the past year, deep lines edge his once bright eyes, crease his forehead. Choking down bitterness, I remind myself: It wasn't his fault. He was sick. Still, if I don't block the images of Mom wringing her trembling hands as she paced the floor each time he went missing, I wouldn't like my father very much. There was a time I found it difficult to look at him. To call him Dad.

"Hmph," I grumble, escaping back into my plan to scrub the

environment clean: I'll be responsible for sparkling oceans, sweet air, rolling back time with the arguing skills I'm going to have to acquire if I'm really going to change the world, bring everything back to the way I imagine the world was when it was new. "I've got a long way to go." I roll my eyes, bump his shoulder with mine, and plant a kiss on his cheek.

Before hopping out of the passenger seat, my heart turns over in my chest. Not far from the Mazda's polished front fender, a circle of boys and girls congregate before the glass wall of the local hangout, a small cafe directly across from Jefferson High School. Now and then they glance my way, empty-eyed, which I'm thankful for. The last thing I want to do is make an impression on them. They can be cruel. Turn my life into a living hell. I've seen them do it to others, so I keep my distance.

They're the cool kids, or rejects, whichever way you chose to look at it. Either way, they're the ones a kid like me steers clear of. I'm not in their group. I don't want to be in their group. Maybe that's why they don't accept me. Try to befriend me. Maybe not. Before the first period bell rings, they'll stroll into the cafe and, without a care in the world, skip class, drink frappes till the bus 'or their wheels' takes them home.

My family is small, loving and demonstrative. Sometimes overly so. Still, I should have known better than to kiss my father's cheek in public. What was I thinking? My face flushes as I slide out of the car as inconspicuously as possible. *Don't slam the door! Gah.* I hear their giggles and snorts, while trying to ignore their condescending voices: "Daddy's little girl" ... "I wonder how she kisses him at home." I stare straight ahead and bolt around the car. Before I'm able to dash across the street, I hear the whine of Dad's window as it rolls down, the sound of his bellow, "Peanut! Your lunch!"

My body begins to shrink into the crack the tip of my sneaker dips into. I'm about to become part of the stiff, cold pavement my other foot feels glued to. My body lurches, but I catch my balance as gracefully as possible. Turning as if in slow motion, I watch in horror as he dangles the brown bag containing my tuna sandwich and apple out the window. He's smiling broadly, while I fight off a panic attack.

"*Peanut.*" Of course the gawkers can't let *that* go unnoticed. They mimic my father's endearment, his voice, and double up with laughter, as I snatch the bag and flee without another word to my father.

From across the street, I hear his car pull away and a stab of guilt cuts through my chest. Why didn't I thank him? He was kind. Thoughtful. And I was embarrassed because he showed his affection in public? Yes!

My father is handling life the best he can. Memories of him staggering through the front door of our small house, or missing from the dinner table for days at a time, flood my mind. I see my mother crying. Pacing. Yelling. I remember cowering when my father's drunken temper flared. Maybe I was born withdrawn, maybe it was the years of seeing him that way. Maybe that's why I take drama classes and plan on signing up for public speaking next year. Maybe I'll even join the debate team. I have to find some way to crawl out of my shell. I have the desire; I just need the confidence.

The angry rhythm of blaring horns collides with my senses like a jolt of electricity, slicing through my ears and down my spine. I spin to watch the commotion in the street. The *commotion* turns out to be Jesse Sinclair, who is crossing the street, and my heart skips a beat. He's snaking through traffic with one muscular arm slung around Claudette Fabre. She's a senior, and she's striking. He's holding his other hand out before him, like a traffic cop. At the same time, he seems to be joking with her. So casual, so confident. If it were me, I'd be stumbling over my feet, and apologizing for the interruption. They're practically strolling! I wish I had that much faith in myself. My stare glides from his forearm to his wrist, and my stomach seizes. His fingers are locked around her hip. Her very swaying hip that with each step, bumps his. His protective grasp is sexy, intimate. I'm dumbstruck and filled with butterflies, just watching them. My eyes fix on the spidery black ink scrolling from his wrist to his middle finger. I think it's a scorpion. Hmm.

Grinning, he guides Claudette around bumpers and fenders. I wonder if they're intentionally walking in unison: right foot, left foot. With legs aligned, they hop the curb and break into the line ahead of me. They're laughing. My eyes feel glued as I wonder whether or not his arm will remain around her, and if she's his girlfriend of the week, or will be after the intimacy they just shared. But, as soon as she's steady on her feet, his arm drops to his side. Then he runs a hand over his head of thick silky hair, gives his stubbly chin a quick rub, and he starts joking with a group of kids they've just displaced from the line of students waiting to enter school.

Using a tall girl standing before me as a shield, I continue to sneak peeks. I'm mesmerized. A sidewalk stalker. I can't help myself, or the way I feel.

Claudette is clinging to his side. The way she gazes up at him makes my seizing stomach knot tighter. I know how she must be feeling. It's obvious she wants his arms cemented around her. Only her. Forever. I'd feel that way too if he'd just touched me that way. A pang of desire replaces the jolt my spine is struggling to recover from. Even though Jesse and I have only been together on the school stage, sharing a few necessary words, I'm a believer in the heart knows what the heart wants. Needs. And I'm counting the days until my sixteenth birthday.

Watching them together is painful. My mind keeps replaying the day I fell off the ladder and into his arms, and envy builds. Our first encounter is embedded in my body, my brain, every single part of me. I close my eyes, reliving the feeling of his skin sliding against mine, and freezing on the spot with the tantalizing friction. I've had it with daydreams; I want the real thing. I wish he had asked me out. I might have broken the rules and let him pick me up at Dee's.

Jesse Sinclair would be so worth getting run over for, even by a truck, floats across my brain, making the lips I'm chewing break into a secret smile. He could cause a scene just walking down the street. He's one of the sexiest guys in school, with girls falling over at his feet. With all he's got going for him, add *nice* and you have a beautiful miracle wrapped up in faded jeans and form-fitting t-shirts.

Unable to remove my stare from his stunning profile, I sigh. *In your dreams, girl:* the words are like a slap in the face, sobering me. Still, my eyes are trapped by his broad, square shoulders, before daring a nosedive. His perfectly carved legs are mind blowing as my gaze inches up to his tight hips, masculine butt. His movements are expressive, precise. The way he runs his fingers through his hair while he angles his head drives me crazy. The way he grins, the curve of his lips as he speaks, melts every muscle in my legs that are beginning to shake. He's perfect.

Covered by goose bumps, I venture to wonder how it would feel to walk down the hall with his arm around me, as he gazes down at me, like he's doing to her now. Correction: I'd glide down the hall, because being near Jesse makes me feel lightheaded. Limbless. Imagining his plump lips working across mine makes me flush. *Dumb. Dumb. Dumb.* You're just a freshman, Zoe. Jesse's a senior who dates experienced girls. Beautiful girls. Like the ones hanging all over him as he breaks away and strides toward the doors. Envisioning Jesse making out with someone like Claudette, my cheeks heat to an intolerable level. I feel terribly self-conscious and touch my face with a palm. Do I look feverish? Sick? Can the people standing around me guess why I'm glowing like a neon tomato?

JESSE SINCLAIR

Coffee in hand, I elbow my way to the door of Moon Cafe. Even though the place is packed with school kids overdosing on caffeine, I've stopped wondering if I'll run into her here. Stopped hoping. She never sets foot in this place. Then again, after pushing through the bunch of degenerates slouching in front of the doorway, it doesn't surprise me that a girl like Zoe would shy away from a dive like this. *You'll never find Zoe Channing hanging out with this crowd.* She's so different from other girls. Don't get me wrong; she's a cool girl, and totally hot, but Zoe doesn't act like she's taken a good look in the mirror. That's one of the things that attracts me to her. She's small but determined. I can see it in her eyes when she's up on stage reciting her lines like a pro. When she sings. Damn, I could listen to her sing all night. Nightingale. That's Zoe.

The cardboard cup I carry in my right hand is hot as hell, too. The pads of my fingers burn. I gaze down, fixating on the tiny dot of grease stuck under one fingernail. No matter how hard I scrub, there's always a reminder of my afternoon commitment. Oil rinses off easy. Grease doesn't.

I take pride in everything I do, but there's a world of difference between handling car parts and capturing a sunset on canvas. I like having oil paint stuck to my fingertips. Under my nails. It reminds me of something I love. My brother Jamie laughs at my obsession. He says paint flows through my veins, instead of blood.

I'm a senior this year, and finished with classes by noon. Occasionally, I hang around and run track. Usually, I need to get my ass in gear, drive to the service station my dad owns. Without fail, Jamie is there to pounce on me the minute I set foot in the office. He's like a dog that needs to be let out of its cage because its bladder is about to burst, spouting off: "It's about time you decided to show, shitbag. I'm starved. Be back when I get here." The minute I walk through the door, his nagging starts. Then he's on his way out, laughing, cocky grin broadening. "Don't wait up for me, bro." Before I can object, his pickup roars to life and plows into the road. So, I'm left alone to man the register and do a break job or an oil change, while Dad is usually under the hood of a customer's car. Mostly he's standing beside the computer, doing inspections. Or cashing out the register drawer.

When Mom passed away, Dad took on sole responsibility for the business. Bookkeeping. Ordering parts. My brother Jamie put off college until Dad could get on his feet, or so he says. Neither has happened yet: Dad isn't on his feet, and Jamie isn't in college.

James, or Jamie as everyone calls him, is three years older than me. Yeah, it's a riot. Jesse and James: Jesse James. My parents could have been high, or just didn't realize they were setting their kids up for a lifetime of jokes. If I ever have a kid, I'll let him choose his own name. His own religion. Whether or not he wants to keep his foreskin. I have to laugh at my idiotic thoughts. You're an asshole, Sinclair.

My gaze travels to the road I'm about to cross on my way to

class. With the eye-opening scene unfolding before me, Jamie is tucked into the back of my mind so fast, I don't even remember I have a brother. A breath catches in my throat when I see her. My every thought focuses on the adorable girl who's dodging a car as she dashes across the street. "Oh shit," I mumble, watching her stumble in the middle of the road. "Zoe," I groan beneath my breath. "What the hell's wrong with you, girl?" She should wear a *Caution* sign, I muse. Her shapely body does this graceful wobble, then she reels around, races back to the car, rips a bag from the hand sticking through the driver's window and takes off like a bird in flight. A frightened bird. Her long blonde hair covers half of her face as it swings with the jerk of her head. But I am able to catch sight of one beautiful blue eye. Wide. Troubled. *What's up with you, Zoe?* This girl does not make approaching her easy. That's for damn sure.

I tighten my grip on the small white bag dangling from the fingers of my left hand. The bag containing my bagel with cream cheese. She hides her bag beneath her arm. Hell, if I still had someone thoughtful enough to pack my lunch, I'd wear the empty bag on my head. Funny. Girls I mean. The dumbest things set them off. Not that Zoe is dumb. Not by a long shot. She's an honors student. Star of the upcoming play. She sits backstage, practicing her songs, delicate fingers strumming her guitar. She's a hell of a musician. I wonder if being on a stage is her dream for the future. With grades like hers, she should be more. She should be with me. The thought chokes my gut with butterflies, proving guys do get butterflies. Before I set eyes on Zoe Channing, I argued the point with my buddy Christian, who insists guys are immune to those kinds of disabling attacks. Maybe his fingertips haven't brushed Zoe's, like mine did the day I handed her the wand I made for her character. Maybe if she'd fallen off the ladder into his arms, instead of mine, he'd feel like I do. The look in her eyes that day, that flash of bright blue, was startling, rendering me mute. All I could do was to grin like an idiot.

Her sweetness, gentleness is enough to throw me into another dimension. The memory of capturing Zoe in my arms makes my head spin. When I look at her, all I want to do is hold her, kiss her softly. It's crazy: I'm so damned attracted to her, yet not for the reasons I'm attracted to other girls. It's not the same. I hook up with other girls. Plenty of other girls. But Zoe. Zoe isn't a hit and run. You don't bag a girl like her. You make love to her, carefully, slowly. She's everything I'm not, so I doubt I'd screw her, even if I had the chance. It might be the end of me.

She disappears into the crowd, but hasn't left my mind.

The degenerates, or pretenders as I call them, are bugging out, making animal noises. They start yelling and I'm getting pissed off, because I have a feeling they're throwing shit in Zoe's direction.

I tell myself they enjoy taunting others because they're miserable in their own skin. Shrinking others stretches their failing egos. It doesn't take a rocket scientist to figure this out. Which is why I tagged them the *pretenders*. They hide their inadequacies behind bullshit. Deep down, it has to hurt though. I shake my head, trying to imagine what would make anyone be so cruel to another person. Maybe they're hurting. Maybe I'm giving them too much credit. Maybe they really don't give a damn about anyone but themselves. Kind of like Jamie.

Zoe's clear across the street, and the degenerates are still heckling her. Chanting shit that makes my blood boil. *Attack me, but not my family.* They seem to be trying to take her father down. They don't even know the guy and they're raking him through the mud. When I hear a guy say: "I wonder how she kisses him at home," I set my cup and bag down on the curb. I can't take their bullshit anymore. Jamie started with me first thing this morning, because he couldn't find a clean shirt to wear. Like I'm about to dig inside his closet for something clean? *Do your own fucking laundry, bro.* I roll the shoulder he slammed into the door frame as he shoved his way through the doorway. Yeah. I'm in the mood for a fight.

I shake my head, take a few steps forward and direct my voice to the douche who seems loudest. "Why don't you get a life, shitbag. Better yet, an education, because you look pretty fucking ignorant standing there like an asshole covered by a sweatshirt."

I have to laugh at my descriptive choice of words.

Their circle loosens. Two of them head straight for me. I slip my jacket off and lay it beside my breakfast. My blood is pumping through my veins. I'm so ready to face off. There's a lot of resentment burning inside me. And what better way to vent than by slamming my fist into some dumbass's jaw. Even if it's not Jamie's, it'll still feel good.

Zoe, this one's for you, sails through my brain, along with my fist as I block the jacked-up dude who comes at me first. I throw a solid punch that lands him on his ass. When the second guy comes up from behind, I twist his arm behind his back, spin him, bring my knee up to his ass and send him tripping across the sidewalk and back to his friends.

"You got nothing better to do than talk shit to little girls?" I growl.

He rubs his arm, mumbling, "Fuck off."

The first douche bag gets up in my face. A trickle of blood flows from one nostril. Before he can lift a hand, my finger that rhythmically pokes his hard chest pushes him back to his circle.

"Anyone else?" My face heats with anger, my voice gritty with irritation. "I figured as much." I shake my head. "Get a life, fucking losers." I'm theatrically sarcastic as I shake my head. I brush past the school janitor, who, instead of trying to break up a fight, seems to be enjoying the show. Another degenerate. Only this one looks like a kid-toucher. I stare deep into his seedy eyes:

He quickly shifts his gaze and takes off across the street, skimming around passing cars. Horns start blowing. Drivers shout. Yep, this is a typical Pleasantville morning.

When I return to my space at the curb, my jacket and coffee are gone. I run a hand over my hair, swiping the long front strands back into place. From the corner of my eye, I spot the brunette stepping out from beside the building. The first signal to hit my brain is the shape of her tight red sweater. Then my gaze washes over the short jean skirt barely covering her killer thighs. My jacket is tucked under one of her arms. She's grinning, looking sneaky.

"Hey Jess," sidling up to me, she purrs. "Here." She lifts my hand, fans my fingers, and presses the now cold coffee cup into my palm.

"Hey Claudette." I stare her down. "What are you doing with those losers? I thought you were better than that."

Her eyes slide to the side, then confront me. I figure she's feeling lost. Using me to get away from the misfits. Maybe she's trying to get back at my brother for dumping her after he graduated.

"Following in your brother's footsteps, I see." Trying for sarcastic, she shoots me a silly grin which comes off as sad. Desperate. Heartbroken?

"Never happen. Unlike Jamie, who enjoys a good fight, I was settling a score."

"Oh?" She angles her head, cuts her gray eyes into mine. "What kind of score?"

"Nothing you'd be interested in."

She pulls my cap from my jacket pocket, stands on her toes and reaches up, pretending to slide the NY Yankee cap on my head. "Try me," she says, slipping it over her head instead of mine.

Claudette's parents were born in France. She was born here, so she lacks the sexy accent. But the girl still has some assets.

My eyes scroll her face. Pretty. Heavily made up. Not my type at all. I shoot a grin at her. "I'm sure it's nothing you would understand."

I remember how she acted in the passenger seat of Jamie's truck. How her arm went around him possessively when other girls were around. Which was often. Jamie was bombarded with girls when he was in school.

We're far from outlaws, but the Sinclair name carries a stigma: one I haven't yet been able to shake. My mother kept us in line, but after her death, well, Jamie's record is proof. Even my dad went kind of nuts.

I remember when we were kids, and Jamie had my mother on the verge of tears of frustration. She'd look at me and say, "Jesse. Please don't grow up like your brother." Then she'd switch gears, and he eyes would fill with passion. "Or your father, for that matter. You know the reputation he had before we were married." She'd lift a brow, eyes glued to my gaping face. "Nah. You have no idea." She'd scruff my hair. "You're a good boy." My chest tightens with memories.

The warning bell rings. The losers file into the cafe. Zigzagging around the traffic we're jamming, I casually sling an arm around Claudette. We take our time walking toward the mass of kids dragging their feet into school.

Zoe

Hugging my backpack, I step carefully through the expanding crowd. I have a tendency to become lost in thought, clumsy, inattentive. I take my place at the end of the snaking line of kids waiting to pile into the building. Buses are unloading. Kids are shouting. A sweet breeze washes the fragrance of early morning rain across my face and I hold my nose high. Inhaling the scent of flowers, I mentally rehearse my lines for the school play. The song I've written for *The Flight of the Fae*, the musical we'll perform for the elementary students, and of course, all parents. Just thinking about standing on the stage before all those people causes my heart to flutter and my stomach to drop. Accidentally, I back-step and my heel crushes the toe of the girl standing too close behind me. To make matters even worse, I lose my balance and practically knock her over.

"Hey freak," she spits. She's so angry, her saliva literally reaches my face before she shoves me away. "Watch where you're going. Look what you did to my shoe." She tosses her head and her long hair flows from one shoulder to the other.

"Oops, I'm sorry," I stammer and stare up into the scary face of a tall, gum-chewing brunette wearing too much makeup. "I didn't mean ..."

"But you did," she speaks through gritted teeth, "how 'bout wiping off your footprint, asshole."

Under her scrutiny, my stomach hits the ground. *Bitch.* An odd time for thoughts of the play, but at the concept of performing before someone like her, a chill covers my skin. Before she can see my quivering lips, I swing my head forward and wrap my blue sweater tight across my chest. On the verge of tears, I strain to find Delorese, hopefully just a few heads away. Maybe I *am* the peanut, the baby my family treats me as. When I catch sight of the back of my best friend's thick black hair, I heave a sigh and my body relaxes.

Delorese, or Dee as I call her, has been my bestie since she moved across the street the summer before. I hang with other kids too, but I trust Dee the most. She's a sophomore. She's wiser. I wonder if we'd be this close had we not been the only teens living on the same street. I want so badly to be up there beside her, but in my school, line cutters get their asses kicked. Especially the lowlife ninth graders.

Just as the bell rings, a gust of caustic fumes burns my nose and eyes as the last bus empties bodies and rumbles away. The line moves slowly, the brunette behind me breathes down my neck as though that will make everyone's feet move faster. As I'm crushed with the crowd, I unzip my backpack, stick my lunch bag inside, and somehow manage to slip it between my back and the brunette's front. With thumbs tucked beneath the straps, I'm pushed through the door with the wave of other kids flooding the spacious lobby. Instead of rushing to homeroom by way of the staircase dead ahead of me, I duck down the hall to my left, into the silence of the bathroom for a quick pee. I must have stood before the mirror longer than intended, fussing with my hair, because when I emerge, the halls are empty, the silence eerie.

The bathroom door squeaks shut. *Now I'll have to walk into class like a loser, with everyone's eyes on me,* is the only thought plaguing my mind. I haven't taken two steps when I feel the ominous presence behind me. Before I can spin to confront the danger, one massive hand comes around my waist, while the other slams over my mouth. My lips are crushed against my teeth. My head is jerked up, the involuntary movement almost snapping my neck. *Bite!* My mind screeches. *Kick! Scream!* But my mouth is sealed shut, so the only sound I can manage is a grunt. I can't turn my head which is in a vice-like grip. I can't move my arms, as they are suddenly pinned tightly to my sides. *Oh God. What's happening to me? Help me. Someone help me!*

The taste of blood spills into my mouth, the drum of my pulse fills my ears. In the moment of sheer panic, with a blank mind I freeze, then reality sets in. The fleeting thought of a joking wiseass dissolves. I don't know who or why, but I know I'm being abducted. My mind spins, racing to reason. Thoughts crash inside my head. I'm in school. A place that's supposed to be safe. I'm surrounded by teachers and students, but they're all behind closed oak doors, hidden by impenetrable plaster walls. And they are safe. Their haven is protected. Mine is being violated.

My eyes roll back and forth in their sockets, struggling to search my surroundings. There isn't a monitor at this end of the hall, or security cameras, because this bathroom is nearest the teacher's lounges. *The quiet end of the hall. Desolate. Deserted.* And I'm locked in the steel-like arms of an unknown power I can only assume is male, being silenced, forced through a doorway and shoved down a flight of stairs. His body presses so firmly against mine, we could be one. The hardcover books inside my backpack cut into my shoulders, his strong fingers into my cheek. If his hand presses any harder, his sweaty palm will break my front teeth.

This is when I begin fighting for my life. Attempting to

separate us, I throw my body, twisting, kicking my legs out, up, down, behind me, to the side. I am unable to scream, but guttural sounds rise from my throat. My mule kicks connect with his shins, still, nothing works. We continue to make our way down the stairs. Somehow, the soles of my sneakers manage to grip each iron step without losing footing. Then I realize my feet aren't touching the steps at all. I am being lifted and hauled like a sack of flour. The struggling me is being carried like a pathetic nothing. A thing without value, moaning into my abductor's hand. While his breath heats the back of my neck, his saliva peppers the side of my face. His beard scratches my skin. His kneecaps dig into the back of my legs, causing a sharp pain with each communal step we take.

I'm certain he is going to drag me through a back door, throw me into a van with no windows, possibly shackles on the floor. Torture me. Skin me alive. Cut me into pieces. *Will my body be found? Will I be the next victim people read about in the news?* I want to scream at him: *If you're looking for ransom, you're kidnapping the wrong girl! My family barely makes ends meet!*

I think my eyes are open, but I'm seeing only shadows. Everything around me is a blur. Staircase, walls, a door which my body is being plastered against.

The metal door scrapes the concrete floor as our body weight forces it open. The odor of dust and fumes immediately enter my nose. A burst of heat burns my eyes which begin to tear. Then it hits me: I haven't cried. *Why haven't I cried? Cry? Scream you idiot.* The moment he lifts his hand I try, but I have no voice. I'm released and shoved across the room so angrily, my body slams against the cement wall of my prison.

Somehow, my backpack lands beside me as I slump to the floor, disoriented, desperate. Possibly momentarily knocked unconscious. *Don't open your eyes!* My mind screams. But before I can stop them, my lids snap up while I wish I hadn't awakened at all. The boiler sounds like a jet engine getting ready for takeoff;

the deafening sound fights the roar of blood in my ears. The smell of stale food mixed with dank air causes my stomach to roll.

I lower my head for protection, flatten my chin to my chest. Staring at the floor, my mind whirls. Think of an escape! When I gain the courage to lift my head, I have no choice but to stare in horror. He stands not more than two feet away, so I crane my neck to get a look at the man responsible for my agony. From my compromised position, he looks like a giant. He's taller than my dad. Six-three maybe. His hair is swept from his face, knotted behind his neck, and it's very dark. His eyes are even darker.

Like a ghost glowing beneath one hanging fluorescent light, his face is expressionless. But his eyes, his eyes hold rage, hatred, lust, pleasure: a lethal blend that makes my heart all but burst through my chest. I know I'm not dealing with a normal person. He is a soulless, emotionless monster. This is when I manage to let out a blood-curdling scream, and it doesn't stop. I keep screaming and screaming. If I cover my eyes, he might disappear. No. I should confront him. If I go down, it will be fighting.

I leap to my feet, eyes darting in all directions, fists balled at my sides, determined to fight my way out. I charge him, head down like a bull, my foot aiming for his balls. His bulging extended arms stop me before I can make contact. I'm still screeching as he flings me back against the wall. My shoulders hit first, followed by my head, knocking the sense out of me. But I'm still screaming, "Bastard! Let me out of here. I'll fucking kill you." My throat burns but I continue to scream. "Help! Someone help me!"

Closing in on me, he shouts, "Shut up! Or I'll kill you right now." He pulls a knife from his pocket, aims it at my throat, then smirks. "On second thought, if screaming makes you feel better, be my guest. It's kind of a turn-on." He winks. "We're in the basement, surrounded by soundproof walls. Nobody's gonna come running."

Now that I realize I can't fight my way out, and screaming won't get me rescued, I know I have to talk my way out of this. Try to reason with him. Convince him that I'm *human*.

We don't remove our eyes from each other as I pull myself to my feet. I gather my sweater so tightly around my trembling body, the cable knit rips at the seams. My first instinct is to back away, but there's nowhere to go. I want to sink into the cement chilling my back.

My petrified brain wants to shut down. I feel like I'm out of my body, watching someone else. It's the strangest feeling. My arms and legs contain no muscle, no bone, yet they are capable of movement, and are encased by a ghostly radiance. My mind is numb. My vision is cloudy, or are my eyes detached and floating all by themselves through a supernatural haze?

Once the boiler shuts off, I struggle for sounds of life, other than his and mine. But surrounding me, there are nothing but pipes, whistling steam, and the burly stranger who is sizing me up like I'm a free shirt on a store rack and he's about to take me down, try me on.

"I know you," I manage to whisper, my voice not my own. "I've seen you in the school. You work here." I try to make sense of why he brought me here. Make him realize I'm a student and not his to do what he wants with. I'm a person. My own person. *Not his!*

"I've seen you too," he growls, relaxing from his alert stance. "Up on the stage. Rehearsing. They made you a princess. You're a jezebel." He advances a step, his boots crunching the same grit that has skinned my hands during my fall.

"What are you talking about?" My mind floods with scenarios. My part in the play flashes across my mind. Grasping at straws, I level my voice as best as I can. "I'm a fairy. That's all I am." I'm a Peanut. My mind taunts me, painting a vivid picture of Dad's face as I snatched my lunch bag from his hand not twenty minutes ago. And now I'm here. Imprisoned by this lunatic.

Along with pictures, my mind fires off words that scroll through my brain in disjointed sentences. *Will I ever see my father again?* I should have been kinder. Told him I how much I loved him. *I don't hate you for being an alcoholic, Dad. I forgive you for everything you put me and Mom through. Mom!* Less than an hour ago, we were gathered around the kitchen table, enjoying breakfast, chatting, planning a trip to Vermont during spring break.

Mom is on her way to work right now. The thought hits my head like the stone wall behind me. My cell phone is inside my backpack. Can I reach it in time? Dial 9-1-1? Auto-dial one of my parents? My heart is pounding, fluttering, skipping beats. This brings my thoughts of escape and punishment to a close. I'm certain I am having a heart attack. *Good! Die. Die before this monster has a chance to touch you! You can't face this. But you can't get out of it. Oh God.*

He stands before me, runs his fat fingers over his slick hair. His fingers stroke his bearded chin, then fall to his belly to unbuckle his belt. In one swift motion, he strips the leather from the loops and his baggy pants fall to his ankles. I don't want them to, but my eyes instantly lock on him. At the sight of his thick, hairy legs, his tight-fitting underwear, the expanding bulge of his crotch, my head spins. Breakfast rises to my throat.

My stare narrows, swivels around the room, calculating. Searching for something I can use to defend myself. Something deadlier than my backpack, which my hand is carefully creeping toward. Other than a broom far beyond my reach, the only thing my stare finds is a cot, covered with crumpled sheets, positioned in dimness against the far wall.

His growl brings my eyes back to his. "Stand up and take your clothes off."

"No," I whisper, drawing my knees to my chest and hugging them, as though they'll protect me from this madman.

"Do as I say and you'll walk out of here in one piece. Cross me and you'll end up down there in the crawlspace." He hitches his head in the direction of a door, not the door we almost fell through, but a door to another kind of hell. By the look in his eyes, I believe he will kill me if I don't cooperate.

Slowly, I rise and stand before him, a shaking, hopeless wreck, my back pressed to the wall. Ready to pee my pants. Covering my face with my hands, I sob. "Please don't do this. I'm a virgin. I'm only fifteen. Let me go and I won't tell anyone." *Please, please, please.*

His laugh holds the same tone as his angry growl. "Yeah yeah. That's what they all say. The ones that are buried down there," again he motions with a snap of his head to an iron grid in the floor, "they..."

"I don't believe anyone is buried down here. I've never heard of anyone going missing."

"You want to be a first? Is that what you're telling me?"

My arms drop to my sides, then my fingers fumble with the button of my jeans. This action stops his tirade mid-sentence, which gives me a chance to think. I don't believe anyone is buried beneath me. I can't believe it. If other girls went missing, I'd have heard about it.

"That's a good girl. Behave and there won't be no rough stuff. Strip and put your clothes over there." He gestures to a folding chair beside the cot. "No one will ever know this happened if there aren't any bruises. And there won't be any bruises if you behave yourself."

My mind spins. *Buy time. Think. There has to be some way out of here, Zoe.* "I can't with you watching me. Turn around."

He shoots me a suspicious squint, but turns, grumbling, "Don't try anything stupid, you little bitch."

Without a plan, all I can think of is to use my backpack as a weapon, and carefully reach down, quietly as possible. *One, two, three, lift, swing, aim for the back of his head. When he's down, dig your fingernails into his eyeballs. Stomp on his crotch. When he's doubled over, stab him with the broom ... then run. Run like hell!*

He derails my plan by folding at the waist. His body is angled and his eyes are on me. Arms dangling, he fishes through the pockets of the pants he's just stepped out of. When he stands he's clutching a plastic bag. I watch him rip it open, slip his fingers inside, and pull out a rag! Then as though he can read my thoughts, he swings around, grabs my readied backpack and flings it across the room. Rage replaces the pleasure in his eyes. "Game over," he says as he lunges for me.

"No! No! No!" I struggle with every ounce of strength I can gather, but he restrains me with one hand, and with the other stuffs a disgusting rag he's pulled from the bag into my open mouth which is no longer capable of screams.

My fingers lock around his wrists, but he's so strong, and I'm growing so weak. A fingernail snaps when I claw his skin. Then another.

Whatever is on this rag makes me sick to my stomach, dizzy. I feel myself slump into his arms. I'm lifted and carried.

I'm not sure if it's the searing pain tearing through my belly that awakens me, or the rhythmic pumping of his body against mine. But my eyes fly open with a start. My arms and legs, bound to the cot, feel like lead. The feel of his body sliding over mine covers me with chills and sheer panic: I'm naked. A moan escapes my mouth as I attempt to focus my eyes. He's braced with an arm on either side of my head, and as I return to my senses, I watch his chest as he lifts himself partway off of me, taking note of his perspiring skin, curly, dark chest hair. It is then I am able to fill my lungs with air. Gazing down at me is not a face, but a horrid mask of passion and insanity.

I squeeze my eyes shut, turn my head to the side. My body

hurts so badly, I let out a series of groans. My eyes make contact with my modesty: my clothing which he has folded and placed on the chair, just a few feet away. Beside it is my backpack, on the floor. If I could only reach it, grab my phone. I'm almost certain, in his moments of passion, I should be able to dial the phone. Someone would trace the call and I would be saved.

With a rough hand, he snaps my head back to face him. "You're like a fucking corpse. Wake up. Participate."

Fear is replaced by anger, then anguish. There's no way I'm walking out of here. Not after this. "Get it over with." I'm mad as hell but I'm powerless. I hate the sound of my whimper.

With that, he lowers himself and begins to pound into me. I gasp, but my lungs are unable to fill with air as I am crushed by his full weight. With each thrust, his morning breath floods my face. My eyes are shut, but he refuses to let me turn away. He stops momentarily, and instinctively one of my eyelids unseals so I am able to peer up at him. Mistake! I'm sickened by the look of rapture staring down at me.

I can't take anymore. Death would be better than this. "Kill me," I mumble, tossing my head from side to side.

"I don't do corpses," he pants. "We've got a long morning ahead of us, girlie. Grow up. This is life."

"This isn't life! You're a monster. I don't want to be me. I don't want to be me anymore," I sob over and over until I am once more gagged and sedated. And this goes on, like an endless circle, as we change positions, as he assaults me.

The burning pain is so intense my throat closes. I cannot swallow. I'm choking. My body feels wet, torn to shreds. I'm certain I'm hemorrhaging. Dying from shock and loss of blood.

When his tongue swipes my lips, I catch the tip with my teeth and bite down as hard as I can.

"Bitch!" Wide-eyed he grunts, burying his tongue into the corner of his mouth. He bares his teeth, and the rag is jammed back into my mouth. Again my head is spinning, my body floating as I fall into a peaceful blackout.

Out of breath, he demands, "Do you have a boyfriend?"

"No," I gasp.

"I might just keep you here for myself."

"No," I mumble, almost out of my mind. "No more."

He hovers over me. The breath my deflated lungs inhale is his. The animal sounds I hear are mine. Between bearing his weight, and the vomit clogging my throat, I'm suffocating, sure the end is near.

What's it like to die? Will Grandma be waiting for me? Will I ever forget the horror of this day, or will it live inside me for eternity?

I'm limp. I'm hopeless. Finally he releases. Thank God. Thank God. It's over. I'm so weak, I can barely breathe, even after he lifts his body. He rolls to the edge of the cot, hops to his feet, and begins to dress, like he's waking from an alarm clock and is about to begin his day. Like nothing happened. Like he hasn't just destroyed my life, with no remorse.

Without blinking an eye, he throws my clothes at me. "Get dressed. I have to get to work."

My head is throbbing, spinning. I can barely focus my eyes, thoughts. My limbs are stiff, refuse to obey, but I am able to sit, dress, and stand on shaking legs. Ease myself toward the door.

"Hold it, girlie," he says, unzipping my backpack, digging into my lunch bag. "Let's see what Mommy packed for us today." He smirks. "How time flies. It's almost lunchtime. Care to join me?"

My stomach lurches, and I vomit my breakfast of pancakes on the floor at his feet.

He's at my side, his fingers cutting into my arm. His voice is eerily calm. "We have rules around here."

My stare is blank, but my heart stops again. *Out. Let me out!*

"Rules of silence. You don't talk. I don't throw you in the dungeon, take a drive over to Willow Lane and kill your family. Comprende?"

My voice is lost, but I nod. Not the same nod I gave Dad, runs through my mind and I almost laugh. My mind is on autopilot. Tonight is takeout. We never decided: Chinese or Italian?

My backpack is slammed against my chest, shoved into my arms so hard it all but knocks the breath out of me. My attacker pats me on the ass and sends me out the door. The outside world looks different. Fake. *Am I really here?* It's all surreal. The trees, the sky, the *me* detached from reality.

I don't remember dressing. Leaving the building. The fresh air hitting my face brings me back to life. *Did he really let me go? Shove me out the side door? Free his hostage?* This is too easy. He'd have to be crazy. Doesn't he realize I'm heading straight to the police? No, I mean my parents. I have no legs. I'm running on air. Sobbing. Longing. Longing for my mother's arms to come around me. To completely break down. For her to calm me. Hold me. Tell me everything will be okay.

No it won't be okay! I've been raped. Threatened. He knows where we live! How? I can't ever tell my parents what happened. A gruesome thought flashes across my mind: Imagining him doing what he did to me to my mother, I ... I can't even begin to imagine. This seals the deal. My mouth is shut. Sure, he's crazy. But smart enough to realize he's branded terror into my head, my heart, my body. Even my soul.

As my mind runs rampant, I run as fast as I can down the path behind the school, hugging my backpack for dear life. Steer clear of the road. This is a shortcut only Dee and I know. If I ran down the road, any moment he could step out in front of me, or appear behind me. Those arms could capture me again. My heart beats so wildly, catching my breath is impossible. My chest pains.

My heart will surely stop beating ... any moment now. *How much agony can a body endure before it falls and never gets up again?*

You're no longer Dad's perfect little peanut. You're not a virgin. He took everything from you. I don't want to spend another moment on this earth.

Tears stream down my face as I continue to run until the raised ranch comes into view. My mind fills with panic. Did he take my house key from my backpack? Is he inside, waiting for me? Holding my parents hostage? My fingers lock around my keychain, and my heart rate becomes somewhat normal.

I slip through the front door and slam it shut behind me. Back pressed to the door, I stare at the stairway that will lead me to safety. Take each step slowly, looking in every direction. I dump my backpack on the floor and collapse beside it. Curled in a ball, I shake. I cry. I want to stay here forever. Moving is painful. Getting up means returning to life. I have to clean myself up before my parents come home. If they ever saw me this way, they'd die on the spot. Call the police, and we'd all be dead by dawn.

In the bathroom I avoid the mirror as I brush my teeth and gargle, holding Listerine in my mouth so long, the inside of my cheeks and gums burn like hell. The more it burns, the better I feel, so I spit into the sink and take another mouthful, squishing the irritating solution through my teeth while I rip off the clothing I will never wear again. Spots of blood dot my panties, which are damp from his ... I'd rather choke than admit his semen dampens the crotch. I consider wrapping my underpants in a plastic baggie, for evidence. I want him arrested. Thrown into jail. Beaten. Raped. I want him to suffer every painful horror I felt. My head is about to explode with thoughts, fears, scenarios. I'm in a police car, on the way to the hospital. Doctors, nurses, rape kit. Prying eyes, hands. Noooo!!! I can't take anymore. *Bury it. You're a big girl. You can do this. Oh my God, suppose he got you pregnant!*

Examining my skin for bruises, I'm shocked to find the

restraint marks on my wrists and ankles have disappeared. Thankful though. Maybe they were never tied. Maybe fear held me to the cot. Fear and his body.

The inside of my thighs are streaked with blood. I shake my head. Hold my face over the sink and let the Listerine seep slowly through my lips. I lift my head and sigh, but still avoid the mirror. Standing beneath the shower, I cry. My fists pound the tiles. My chest feels so heavy, so tight, I find it hard to breathe. Exhausted, I slump onto the floor. I want to drown. Slide down the drain with the dirty water, bloody water. I'm filled with shame. Anger. Heartbreak. I hate what he's done to me. I hate being me.

I have no idea of the time of day, but the sun seems to be sinking outside the curtained window. Mechanically, I stop the pulsing stream of water, and my tears, and step from the shower. Like a zombie, I make my way to my room. Dry and dress, slipping a pad between my burning crotch and my clean white panties. I'm so worried, praying I don't have internal injuries. Maybe I need medical attention. Something to ward off the diseases he might have implanted inside me. Oh God! Pictures flash across my mind again: ambulance, police. My mother's face. My father's. I cover my body with a turtleneck and baggy jeans, my feet with wool socks. I'd wear a face mask if I could pull it off.

I crawl onto my bed, roll up in a ball, and thank God I'm home. For fifteen minutes I'm a zombie: then I check myself. Phew. The pad is dry. No blood.

I pick up my acoustic guitar from its open case on the floor and light at the edge of my bed. My fingers find the strings; they must have a mind of their own, which will come in handy, as mine is blown. My fingertips strum the perfect melody: *The Flight of the Fae*. With a raspy voice, I mutter the lyrics I wrote for the play: *trees not shed, the world needs your splendor, birds sing sweet and far, so the lost can find shelter...*

Surprisingly, I find the right key and sing the refrain until my body stops trembling. Until there is a knock at the door. I know it's Dee. She always stops by after school. For gossip. For a snack.

"Dee," I almost cry as I invite my savior into the kitchen. She's wearing the same green sweatshirt and inky jeans she wore to school. Before entering, she kicks off her Converse sneakers and pads across the floor wearing two different colored socks.

"What happened to you today? You never made it to lunch." She looks wired, but flops onto a chair and sprawls her long slender legs out in front of her. "Why didn't you answer my texts?"

"I felt sick so I left school early." I want to fall into her arms, but I can't. I want to fall apart, but I refuse to.

She runs a hand over her smooth caramel cheek, then straightens her windblown bangs. "You look like shit."

"Thanks." My voice bottoms out. And when I don't return Dee's chuckle, her expression tells me she's looking right through me. She knows me as well as I know myself. She knows I've reached the end of the world.

She cocks her head, lifting an expertly groomed brow. "What the hell's up with you, girlfriend?"

"Nothing." I try to stare her down but my eyes burn, then water.

"Don't try to bullshit a bullshitter. We've known each other for what, a year? We've spent time together almost every day since I moved in across the street. You're not yourself."

"Who am I?" I try to steady my voice, but now I'm doubting I know who I am. Will I ever feel like *me* again? Like a normal girl and not some half dead, defiled creature?

As we sit at the table, the room grows smaller. The walls tilt. I open my mouth to speak, and nothing comes out but ragged breath. I begin to hyperventilate. Dee is at my side, patting my back, her secretive voice telling me to, "Slow down. Slow your breath. You're having a panic attack." Her arm tightens around my shoulders. "Don't worry. Can't hurt you. I have them all the time. Just try to relax." She draws back and looks into my eyes. "Then tell me what's wrong, Zoe. You have to." Her eyes fill with compassion, then narrow.

Then all the horror spills out. It's as though someone else's voice relays the disgusting story of a stranger and an innocent girl who suffered terribly at the hands of her psycho captor.

The table rocks, because Dee's foot has slammed into one of the legs. "That fucking bastard." Her scream is shocking. Her face contorts. Her cheeks redden. From a pocket, she whips out her cell phone. "I'm calling the cops. He's gonna pay for what he's done to you."

"No! He warned me," I draw a quivering breath, "if I tell anyone, he'll kill my entire family ... after he kills me." I feel my eyes bulge. "He knows where I live." I panic. *I told!* My heart pounds so hard, it's got to burst soon. "Promise you won't tell anyone!"

Dee's mouth hangs open. If her complexion was as fair as mine, I imagine she would look as white as the flour inside the glass canister on the immaculate kitchen counter. Her face is burnished stone. Her golden green eyes are as glassy as the row of jars I'm trying to focus on so mine don't cross. So I don't faint. Or vomit. Or run from the room, out into the street, screaming like a lunatic. I'm so stressed I can barely stand it. Dead! Please come back, dead. Dead is better than this! Empty. I want to be empty.

"I can't fucking believe it." Breaking silence, she shakes her head. Her normally wide eyes are slits. I believe she's fighting to comprehend, as I am, what has happened to the girl named Zoe Channing. "I can't fucking believe this shit." She slams her fist on the tabletop. "I want to kill the fucking bastard with my bare hands!" Dragging her hands over her head, she catches a breath. "So what are you going to do?"

My eyes widen. I feel them plead. "Suppose I go to the police and they catch him before he gets to my family? Do you think it's possible?"

"For as much as I'd love to see that scumbag castrated and hung, I don't think telling is wise. Not now, anyway. We need to give this some thought. Moody is connected. Suppose he really keeps his promises? Or is involved with a gang? Oh shit. Suppose he puts a hit out on you. I couldn't stand it if something happened to you, or your family! Maybe it's best to do as he says." She's at my side, one hand stroking my hair, the other gripping my shoulder. "Try to forget it ever happened."

"Forget it ever happened? Are you fucking kidding me?" My head snaps up. "And how do you know his name is Moody?"

She shrugs. "I've heard some of the guys call him that. They joke behind his back, but never challenge him."

"So people talk about him? They actually *know* him?"

"Not really, I don't think. He's just a temp, covering for the regular guy who broke his leg, remember?"

"No. I don't. How could he work here? I mean, why doesn't the administration fire him? He said he watches me in the auditorium. Maybe he's done this to someone else? He said there are bodies buried in the crawlspace under the boiler room." My chest starts doing the crazy fluttering again, like it's filled with butterflies batting their wings around my thudding heart. "Have you ever seen him in the auditorium?" I draw a quick breath. "Because, I haven't. I mean, wouldn't I know if someone was stalking me?"

"Nah ah. Never seen him. But then, I'm not around there as much as you are. I don't have a starring role. I only work behind the scenes. Ya know?" She looks as bummed as I feel. As helpless. Her stare is unnerving. She sighs and shrugs. "Don't let it ruin your life, Zoe. You'll forget in time."

"I can't believe you're so matter of fact about this. So nonchalant. What the hell is wrong with you? Do you not get it?

I was just raped." Silenced by a stabbing pain, I double over, hugging my stomach.

She pulls a joint from the pocket of her sweatshirt and places it between her lips.

My mouth drops. "What the hell are you doing, Dee? You can't light that in here." Shock replaces the wimp in my voice.

"Sorry." She pulls the joint from her lips and sets it on the tabletop. "I figured a couple of hits might help. Maybe you can smoke it later, in your bedroom. Open the window ..." She slides it toward me. "I wish there was something I could do, but there isn't." As I rock back and forth, hugging myself, her gaze drops. When her eyes widen, they glisten. "What's wrong?" she gasps.

"It hurts. It feels like a knife is slicing me open," with a palm I sooth my lower abdomen, "down low. Inside ... and out."

She's not listening to me. She's cooking something up in her mind. Her frozen features spring to life. "We better get you a pregnancy test."

I draw in a painful breath, wondering if he broke my ribs. "I thought about that. Calculated the time of the month ..." I shake my head frantically. "That can't happen–"

"You never know. Better to be safe." She pauses, and her expression turns so calculating it scares me. "On second thought, tomorrow we're going to the Women's Clinic. Get you looked at. They won't ask questions. They'll give you a double dose of penicillin. You never know what that creep might have put inside you." She wrinkles her nose, and the disdain on her face compounds my pain.

Ready to vomit again, I hang my head, then peer up at her. "Can I stay at your house tonight? I can't face my parents," I mutter, "and I don't want to be alone."

She tightens the elastic band holding her thick dark ponytail. Studies me for a moment, then sucks on her wide bottom lip. Her tongue makes a moist click. She looks sad when she says, "You better not. The shit's hitting the fan again." She rolls her eyes. "Family drama is the last thing you need right now."

I feel my face fall. I know Dee feels bad. The muscles in her face are so tight, she looks like a plastic doll. Rounded features. No lines or creases. For a moment, my best friend doesn't look real. And I don't feel real. What a pair...

Another tongue click followed by, "I have no choice, Zoe. Family first. That's how I was raised. Do you understand?" As she rolls her eyes again, they water. "But listen, I'll call your first thing tomorrow morning and we'll figure everything out. It'll be fine." She drops a kiss on my forehead. "Don't worry, okay?"

She's acting odd. Is it my imagination, or is Dee distancing herself? Is she afraid to be seen with me? Maybe she's as grossed out as I am. Who wouldn't be?

After Dee leaves, I don't leave the kitchen. I'm stuck to the chair, my body stone, too heavy to be moved. My eyes touch the numbers on the clock. My ears hear a key in the lock and the opening of the door.

Mom walks into the kitchen carrying a green bag packed with groceries. "Phew. What a day," she groans. "There's a run on head colds. Sore throats. Even a mono outbreak in the elementary school, imagine that?" Her gaze meets mine head on. I sense her mind changing gears, and in the same breath, she asks, "How was *your* day? Everything good with school?"

Are her eyes scrutinizing? My heart skips beats. Her eyes are almond shaped and brilliant green. Dad calls them cat eyes, which deepens the pink of Mom's cheeks. They share a magnetism I wonder if I'll ever share with a guy. Like a hard slap, my mind cruelly corrects: *would have shared.*

"Is there anything going around your school?" Mom stands motionless when she asks, as though she's bracing for bad news. If she wants bad news, she's asking the right person. I bite my bottom lip as if the slight taste of blood will stop my nightmare thoughts. Stop me from flying off the handle, bursting into tears, blurting out the entire sordid account of *how my day was*. Yeah, there's something going around my school, I want to scream. And it's a rapist! I have to will my hands not to tremble, like my lips are trying to do. Lips? Hell, my entire body wants to convulse. I fight for control.

Thank goodness Mom doesn't seem to notice my agitation. Doesn't guess I'm about to fall apart. She's tired. I can tell. Her eyes leave mine to glance at the table, where she plops down the reusable grocery bag. I hold my breath, hoping she doesn't notice the joint Dee forgot to take with her, which has miraculously rolled behind the napkin holder. "The office was mobbed today with sick kids."

Now that her hands are free, she lifts me off the chair and pulls me into a hug, which almost breaks my heart. I've never kept secrets from her. Guilt washes over me. When she draws back, her lips scrunch with concern. She brushes some long strands of hair from my face. "Are you okay, hon? Oh, you smell sweet. Did you just shower? Your eyes are puffy. Let me see–" she runs a fingertip over the hollow beneath one of my eyes, "you have purple shadows." Her stare widens as much as a cat's can. "You're not feeling sick, are you? We've had a few cases of Mono ..."

Is my life going to be filled with lies from this moment on?

"I'm fine," I say with as much cheer as I can muster as I unpack the bag. Place the plastic container of the still warm barbeque chicken on top of the stove. The burst of pungent aroma would normally smell delicious, but my mouth is watering from nausea, not hunger. "Yum. This looks good," I chirp, drawing attention from me to the chicken. "Good choice for dinner."

Mom appears relieved. "Something told me you and your father would like it." She lifts a brow and grins. "I haven't heard from him all day. Guess he was busy. So I took a guess and brought

Chinese food, too."

"Oh yeah, he mentioned that this morning," I reply, pulling out two cardboard containers before mechanically washing a head of lettuce and three tomatoes for the salad.

"You're a sweetheart." Mom drops a kiss on my cheek. "I'm going to run and change. Dad should be home any minute. Starving, as usual." She leaves the room, but I hear her chuckle as she heads down the hall.

My parents spend an hour of catch-up during dinner, leaving me to pick at my food, while trying to act as normal as possible. From the corner of my eye, I catch Mom's glances. She looks confused. Concerned enough to break from their conversation about vacation plans. "I hope you're not coming down with something–"

"I told you. I'm fine," I snap. My immediate apology doesn't stop my mother's recoil. Or the shocked expression that grips Dad's face.

He cocks his head. "What's up, Peanut? Bad day at school?"

"Nope." I force such a broad smile, my cheeks hurt. "Everything's fine. I'm still stuffed from lunch. Friday is pizza day."

She frowns. "You threw away the lunch I made?"

The big bad wolf ate it, Mom. After he ate me. "Maybe I felt like pizza," bursts through my lips.

Mom blows my rudeness off with a small smile: her way of saying, *I shouldn't treat you like a baby.*

"As long as you're fine. I don't care if you threw your lunch away. That's the price you pay for having a mother who's a nurse in a busy pediatrician's office." She forces a chuckle, but I watch her eyes shade. "I don't want to bring my work home with me."

Dad laughs at her silly joke. "Good idea, hon. Leave the germs at the office."

Dear God, I silently pray. Make them stop joking for my

benefit. Make them stop asking questions. Make my mind stop playing this horror flick over and over. Make everything stop. Please.

Somehow, I make it through the evening. Attempting *upbeat* is painful. After a long week, my parents crash early.

"Don't stay up too late," Mom stands in the living room doorway, adjusting the belt on her robe. "I'm thinking about ... shopping tomorrow?" Her statement rises into a question as her face breaks into the broadest smile.

The first thing to pop into my mind is food? "Shopping?" I parrot, grabbing the remote to silence the TV. "You stopped today after work–"

"I have a Kohl's flyer," she interrupts. "Preseason swimsuit sale?" With pursing lips, she tilts her head. Right now, my mother looks as much a teen as I do. "They have a nice pool at the hotel we're thinking of staying at."

"Maybe." My mind races. Thinking about the Women's Clinic, I suck air in through my clenched teeth. "I ... I have plans with Dee tomorrow. Sorry." God, this is so hard. I feel terrible. I don't do lying well.

Mom fakes a frown. The filtering light from the hallway lightens her hair. It's soft, curling slightly around her ears. She's so pretty. Angelic. No wonder Dad is madly in love with her. I want to hug her. Tell her I love her too. Confess the darkest secret a daughter could shock her mother to death with.

"Sunday then." She yawns. "Night honey. Get some rest. You look worn out."

"So do you," I say softly.

Dad's bellowing voice breaks into our moment. "Night, Peanut. Sweet dreams."

Mom laughs, then rolls her eyes. "He's never going to let you grow up, or admit that you have. I hope you know that."

If my stomach sinks any lower, paramedics will be scraping

it off the floor.

I try for a light tone. "He'll have to someday."

"I wouldn't be so sure about that. He still babies me." She blows me a kiss before disappearing down the hall.

Falling asleep during a good movie normally pisses me off, especially if I wake up just as it's ending. Tonight there's a good show on, but I can't fall asleep. So I grudgingly move from the sofa to my room, crawl under the covers, and I think: What could I have done to prevent this? To stop it? What should I *not* have done? Is it the way I acted that made me stand out as a victim? Was it my clothes? I think back to the outfit I wore: jeans and tank top, covered by a sweater. Hardly sexy attire. From one side to the other I turn, trying to find a comfortable position. The covers are pulled to my chin the entire time.

"This is not working," I mumble. "I'll never sleep."

I tiptoe into the dining room where my mom leaves her handbag, on the armchair in the corner, and after digging around I come up with her bottle of Xanax. It doesn't take long for the pill to calm my body. But my head is a different story: My brain is filled with terror.

Sleep eventually wins. I don't dream about the attack, but have a horrible nightmare. I'm on a speeding train, and there's a guy in the next car who is shooting people. I know it's a guy because his angry face cuts through my pitch black mind. The sound of gunshots wakes me with a start. Heart pounding, I brace on an elbow, snap on my table lamp. I'm safe in my bed. No man. No gunshots. The sound is really a result of the blood pounding in my ears. My ears are popping. I must have been grinding my teeth. My stiff jaws feel like they've chewed a hard chunk of bubblegum for hours, nonstop. I move my mouth. Ouch. My jaw really hurts. I rub my cheek, run a finger over the sore inside of my mouth, the smooth front of my teeth that cut the inside of my lower lip. I grip my chin and work my jaw; I should check my teeth in the mirror. See how far I've ground them down.

Jesse

I haven't run into Zoe in a few days, so now I'm about to hunt her down. *Stop procrastinating*; the voice fires off in my head. You're into the girl. So, go get her. Now I feel like a caveman. Go get your woman, Sinclair. This is what I'm thinking as I yank the auditorium door open. The room is silent, dark. Like a massive tomb. Only there aren't any bodies inside. But for a centered microphone, the stage is bare. My eyes roll over the empty seats, and for a brief moment I feel excitement. This entire theater will be filled soon. Zoe will be on stage, doing her beautiful thing. I'll be right behind her, hanging onto every word she says, listening to every passionate note that comes floating out of her gorgeous mouth. The mouth I want on mine. Now. Well, soon. Which is why I'm here, hoping to catch her in an unplanned rehearsal.

No luck. So my mind takes over.

I envision Zoe on the stage, enjoying every move she makes. The way she holds her guitar. Cradles it as though it's something she loves. The way her delicate fingers strum the strings. I want to be the strings of her guitar. Screw the strings. I want to be that fucking guitar, with her arms around me. Cradling me. Gazing at me like I'm special, like she can't live without me. This is sick, I tell myself. You are one sick bastard, Sinclair. You barely know this chick and you're ready to jump hurdles for her.

The pissed part of my brain keeps browbeating me. Sissy. Asshole. But the damned sappy side fires back: She's not just some chick! She's one in a million. Win her over before someone else does. The breath I pull in is through clenched teeth. Shaking my head, I step from the room and the door closes quietly behind me.

When I wander into the gym, Mr. Bagalioni is standing across the room, tacking flyers to the bulletin board.

"Hey Mr. B. Getting ready for a game?" My shout echoes.

He reels. I've obviously startled him. He's glaring. "What are you doing in here Jamie?"

My hand taps my chest. "It's me, Jesse."

He stomps closer, straightening his eyeglasses, and before reaching me shakes his head. "The resemblance between you two is uncanny. And that's where it ends, Hallelujah Amen for that. He's gone. The school is safe and in one piece."

Hands stuck in pockets, I let out an uncomfortable chuckle.

"What are you up to Jesse?"

I can't seem to stand still. I shift my weight from one foot to the other. "Not much. Is it okay if I shoot some hoops?"

He cocks his head. "Free period?"

"Killing time, actually. Figured I'd mess around down here, maybe grab a slice of pizza before the cafeteria closes."

"Waiting for someone?" This is the first time he smiles.

"Kinda. I have something to do–"

"You don't have to explain." He nods. "Knock yourself out."

After hoops and pizza, eighth period still hasn't arrived. I think of Jamie and the garage and am filled with satisfaction. I'm surprised my cell phone hasn't rung yet. He must be taking his anger out on someone's car "oh shit" while he waits for me to relieve him. *Too bad, bro. Have a dose of your own medicine.*

I waste time in the library, then hang out in the hall outside drama class for ten minutes, waiting for the last period bell to ring. Listening to a love poem someone recites with gut-churning emotion. Feeling like some stalker dude. But when class lets out, Zoe doesn't walk through the door. And my stomach sinks.

"Damn," I mumble under my breath. After finally deciding it's time to ask her to Trent's party, I'm bummed she isn't here. I curse my perfectly memorized pickup line.

"Hey Zoe. You're looking pretty good up on that stage. You pull those lines off like a pro. I like your voice. Did you score that tune along with the lyrics? What are you doing next Friday night? Want to hit up Trent Holloway's party with me?"

I should have been spontaneous. Hit on her right after Art Appreciation when I had the chance. Had the chance? At the sound of the bell she's out the door like a ninja, disappearing before I make it out the door.

From the moment I grasped the true magic of crayons, I started doodling cartoon characters. Soon I began sketching nature and people. My sketchpad holds images of Zoe Channing. Her perfect profile: cute nose not entirely straight, but not too pushed up at the end. Round glistening eyes, plump lips. I like to watch when she spreads on lip gloss and blots her lips in the cafeteria after lunch. Yeah, she's turning me into a stalker. I've even sketched her tube of Burt's Bees lip balm.

Jamie is red-faced, perspiration-pissed when I stroll into the office, but I personally don't give a shit. I'm growing tired of my brother's tantrums. He's twenty and should act like it.

With his black snaked forearm, he brushes coal colored hair from his brooding eyes. "Nice of you to finally show up, douche bag. I'm fucking starving."

The drywall behind where he's standing has another crack in

it. Yeah, he likes to use his fists.

My backpack is in my car, but I carry in a couple of books, hoping to get some studying done. "The world doesn't revolve around you, dude. I had stuff to do." I dump my books on the desk, which is a mess. Like my brother. "Why don't you pack lunch like other people do? Oh, yeah. That would be normal. That would take time, patience. Brains."

I don't see his fist coming, but feel it. "Go fuck yourself," he says on the way out the door.

###

Hours later, my adrenaline is still pumping; if I had Zoe's number, I'd shoot her a text. What girl can't be found on social media these days? Zoe. Yeah, well, that would be too obvious anyway. An accidental run-in, spur of the moment invitation, is easier to deliver. Just in case she laughed in your face. Maybe she'd just have ignored you, strutting away with that cute little ass swaying from side to side, pegging your level of desire, sparing you the embarrassment.

Nah. Zoe's a kind person. She'd smile and make up some kind of excuse. Let you down real easy. What makes you think she'd be interested in you, anyway? Grease monkey wannabe artist. Yeah, right. Zoe Channing is at the other end of the food chain. High above the air you breath, pal.

The glass door swings open and my head jerks up, half expecting my brother to come strolling back in, apologizing for taking his frustration out on my jaw. Claudette saunters in instead. Her lipstick looks freshly applied. Her hair is half puffed on top, half hanging down her back, in one of those model-like styles. She's grinning. Silvery eyes flashing in different directions. Scoping out the office for Jamie, no doubt. Right now her eyes appear translucent, striking against her dark hair.

"Hey," she says as she zeroes in on the entrance to the garage where we work on cars. "Jamie around?"

Bingo.

"Nope." I finish my last sweep of the floor and rest the handle of the broom in a corner.

I feel her stare follow me as I move around the office. "Is he coming back?"

"Your guess is as good as mine," I reply, smacking dirt off my hands.

"Oh. So I guess I can keep you company then." She stands beside me, on tiptoes again, her fingers working through my messy hair. Then she pushes a lock away from my brow, tucking it behind my ear.

"Yep, you would be stuck with me," she's getting too close for comfort, "except I'm getting ready to close." My cold stare is deliberate, sending her back several steps where she pauses for a breath before speaking. I can't help but notice the rise of her chest. It's big. The breath I mean. Well, the chest too. I force my eyes off her chest.

She adjusts her red sweater around the curve of her hips, her eyes steady on mine. "Are you going to Trent's party next week?"

I swing my head to the side and stare at the *Miss April* page of the calendar hanging on the wall. The sexy model doesn't look much different from many of the girls I've known. Claudette could give her a run for her money. Zoe could bury both of them.

From what I understand, everyone's going to the party. Trent's gigs are always packed. Maybe Zoe will just magically show up. Without invitation. Or ... maybe she'll be there with another guy. Someone who isn't afraid to put himself out there. Someone like Trent. He's got money and a future in his father's lucrative business. A big mouth. A BMW. Yeah, he's got it all over me. He's a dork though. Also, I'm better looking. This all runs through my mind as Claudette taps the desk with the lead point of a pencil she's been rolling in her palms.

"Are you?" she repeats, her gray eyes growing anxious. She

drops the pencil, settles at the edge of the desk and dangles one tempting leg. Her skirt hikes up, giving me a great view of her red panties before she slowly closes the gap.

She's grinning. I'm swallowing hard.

I bite the inside of my cheek. Interesting ... but I don't take the bait. "I guess," I say, idly, then shoot her down by shrugging carelessly. Busying myself by organizing the cluttered desk, the heat of her stare is distracting. Her intake of air causes me to face her, and when I turn my head, our noses are inches away. Her breath hits my cheek: cherry candy.

She angles her head, runs a finger around and under the neck of the black t-shirt I'm wearing. "Who's the girl you stood up for the other morning?"

Without surrendering to the finger that is now being slowly dragged the length of my neck, I lift a brow. I know damn well she was part of the circus. She's just playing games. Like her finger which is now tracing my ear. "What are you talking about?" I've had enough drama for one day. I take a step back.

Her pursed lips gather and move to one side of her mouth. I notice their fullness, and can't help but wonder what parts of Jamie they've touched. How it must have felt. Hey, I'm a guy. Guys have these thoughts. Even if they have no intention of hooking up with a chick, there's no law that says they can't fantasize. Chicks do it too. I can tell by the way Claudette is checking out my jeans.

"The blonde girl that tripped across the street. You like them young and innocent, I see." The tip of her tongue parts her smirk. "Kinda like Jamie. He was a senior. I was a freshman."

"It's not my style to date freshmen. But if it was, it would be my business." Zoe is far from a kid. Still, Claudette has crudely opened my eyes. Stalker and jailbait slam me like an exploding bomb.

Claudette won't let it drop, maybe not until I do. "Zoe, huh?

So you know her well?"

"Not really. I've seen her around. Like I see you around. Same difference." *Not.*

"You're cuter than your brother. You know that?" Claudette giggles.

I smirk. "I've heard that one before."

Claudette huffs out an exasperated breath. "I bet you have. So, I'll see you at the party?" She returns her playful hand to the pencil on the desk, which is half buried beneath her ass. This I notice too.

She moves her body like a gymnast, every muscle flexing when she lifts and slides seductively off the desk. She poses at the door and hesitates. "What's Jamie been up to? I never see him around town anymore."

"I have no idea. I don't see that much of him myself." Which is a blessing, since he's a bigger pain in the ass than a nagging girlfriend.

The side of her head and one hip rest against the doorframe. The biting of her bottom lip is a dead giveaway. She's not as hard as she pretends. "Is he with anyone?"

"I wouldn't know. And I'd venture to guess, not any *one*." The look on her face softens me. "I'll tell him you stopped by, okay?"

She rolls her eyes. "Yeah, you do that" Her mouth turns down. She disappears somewhere in the lot outside. I didn't hear her car drive in, and I don't hear it drive out.

"You can do so much better, Claudette," I talk to the empty room. "Better than my brother. Better than me. Keep walking, babe. I'd probably fuck you over. My brother already did.

Talking to walls is something I do often. I have my share of friends, but no one I can have a heart to heart with. No one I really care to be close to. But then there's Zoe. My mood is destroyed, my stomach's knotting. How do you feel deprived of something you've never tasted? You can be told it isn't good for you, but that doesn't stop your mind from spinning crazy dreams.

The door flies open and I'm expecting Claudette to come bouncing back in. I swing my head to see Christian Jenkins, the best damn basketball center our school ever had, stride into the office.

"Hey bro," Christian says, rubbing the side of his nose. This has been a habit since a ball slammed his face and broke it. His nose is still slightly crooked.

"What up, boss?"

"Boss?" I shoot him a dark, sarcastic look. "That would be a stretch."

Christian laughs. "The first thing on your list: fire your brother." He takes a leisurely walk around the office, pokes his head in the garage and walks back. "You alone?"

"Yeah. Closing up."

He shakes his head. "Jamie doesn't hang around any longer than he has to, does he."

"My brother is a dick."

"How about grabbing a six and a pie. We can catch the game at my place."

"Can't tonight." I check my watch. "In fact, I have to get my ass in gear. I want to see my dad before visiting hours are over."

Christian puckers his lips and makes a whistling sound. Drops his hands into the pockets of his cargo pants. "That was some shit." He shakes his head. "Your dad's a young guy. When he rode with us, he was just like one of the guys. Crazy."

"Yep. Heart attacks are like that. You don't see it coming and next thing a paramedic is pumping your chest and you're having a double bypass."

"Is he coming back to work?"

"Sure. I'll be here to help as much as he needs me. And I plan on dragging my dead-ass brother with me too."

"Good luck with that." He smirks. "We miss you on the court, bro."

I shrug and shake my head. "What are you gonna do?"

"So I guess I'll take off and let you get back to counting your millions. Tell your dad I said hi."

"Will do."

"Catch you later, Jess," he says on the way out the door.

I count the receipts, stuff the cash in the safe, and lock up all the doors. By the time I leave the garage, dusk is fading into darkness.

I park my Mustang in the driveway and jog up the wooden steps leading to the back porch. Its overbearing whitewash is now a looming shadow pinned against a colorless sky. I enter through the kitchen door and shake my head. The sink is full. The tiled counter lined with beer bottles.

Christ. You're around all fucking day, dude. And you can't even put the dishes into the dishwasher?

"Jamie!" I shout, waiting for the silence or the cough.

If my brother doesn't reply, he's either not home or crashed on a chair, possibly the floor, halfway to his bedroom. If I hear him cough, I know to steer clear of the choking location. A coughing fit means either his dick or his head is buried between some chick's thighs. This has been our signal since Mom passed two years ago.

"In here," he yells back nonchalantly. So without another word, I stride into the living room.

"He..." The rest of the "hey" lodges in my throat, because I don't expect to see the naked back of the dark haired chick who is straddling my brother, who is sitting in an easy chair, digging his chin into her shoulder, flashing me a broad smile. Fluttering his smooth brown brows, he rolls his eyes.

The girl continues to rock her hips. Her jet black hair is

69

wrapped around the nape of her neck and pulled over one shoulder. A scrolling tattoo, in the shape of an arrowhead, dives toward the crack of her ass.

After taking a moment to recover myself, my hands drop into the pockets of my jeans. "Thanks for the warning, dude," I snap.

His fingers have been squeezing her ass. He drops one, and with the other, slaps one rounded cheek. "Say hi to my little brother."

Her hands leave his shoulders, as her bare ass slides from his lap. When she stands, she flips her hair to her back. A crucifix is buried in the deep valley between her plump breasts. She runs a finger across her chest, nudges the chain free, lifts the cross to her lips and let's it fall.

"Hey baby brother." She grins. Her eyes tell me she's high as fuck. So is Jamie.

"Jesse, Serena. Serena, Jesse," he says, eyes crinkling with humor.

My mouth refuses to close. I turn my full attention to Jamie, at least I try. "What happened to you this afternoon?"

He grins slyly and shifts his stare to Serena, who is in the process of bending to the floor to pick up her cell phone and check messages. Or so it appears.

"How about a beer, babe," Jamie says with another slap to her ass, which rocks her on her feet. "And get dressed. We're leaving."

My mind is still racing to process this scene. "To go where?"

"Lake Tahoe. I need the bike."

"No fucking way."

"I'm taking the bike."

He's referring to my Suzuki, the one I picked up dirt cheap because it had mechanical problems. Since I'm good with cars, I figured I'd try my hand at overhauling the bike's blown engine.

Shaking my head, my voice is firm. "Nuh uh. I'm still working on it."

A sardonic grin slides across Jamie's mouth. His chest and feet are bare. He's wearing pants, but they're pulled wide open. He slowly lifts his body from the chair, and as he adjusts his cock and pulls his fly up, he hitches his head in the direction of the den, which Serena has disappeared into. "Want a shot at that?" Checking out my crotch which must shout *I want to fuck your date*, as I can feel the throb, he bites his bottom lip and bursts into laughter.

This helps deflate my desire for Serena. But not entirely. I have no idea where Jamie finds these girls, but this chick is one of the finest yet.

I wait till Serena strolls back into the room, then toss my brother half grin, half smirk. "Claudette was around today. Looking for you." I poke a finger into his chest. "You know, you're girlfriend. Not sure if she's your ex as I don't believe you had the courtesy to break up with the girl ... formerly that is."

He ducks away to pull a Harley t-shirt over his head. "When you see her, tell her I'll get back to her sometime." Then stabs his finger into my shoulder muscle.

Jamie never fails to surprise. Shaking my head, I study him, wondering how we could have ever been born from the same parents. My mother was cool, but honest and caring. My dad too. Jamie though. He's like the one peg that doesn't fit any of the holes.

Any stranger can spot the resemblance. We've been mistaken for twins. Despite our age difference, we stand eye to eye. My eyes are dark brown, his are light. We both have Mom's dark wavy hair, though, and Dad's lean but muscular build and chiseled features.

"Tell her yourself."

A jab leads to a shove, and we're on the floor, brawling across the carpet, knocking over an end table. The crash of a lamp stops us on a dime.

"That was Mom's," I shout, swiping perspiration from my face with my arm. "You are the true meaning of ..." my voice hitches, "scumbag!"

Like a statue, Serena stands in the corner of the room. She's wearing cutoffs and tank top, thongs on her feet. I'm guessing she knows they're not taking the bike.

"Christ, Jesse. Shove the fucking bike up your ass already. We'll take Dad's pickup."

"You fucking will NOT. He's coming home tomorrow."

"I know. That's why I'm going to Lake Tahoe. He'll be back at the station, and you won't need me."

"Jesus H., Jamie. What the fuck?" I glare. "Dad's talking about retiring. If you don't kick your ass into gear, we could lose everything. Don't you give a fuck if we lose everything our parents slaved for?"

His mouth tightens. I could swear his eyes water. He drops to his knees and starts gathering the ceramic pieces of the smashed lamp. "You were always Mom's favorite. But you know that, right?" His voice cracks. "She only tolerated me because she had no choice."

"You drove her nuts. You were tested for every possible condition, and have nothing other than douche to blame for your behavior, so save the sob story for someone who gives a shit."

"When are you gonna stop blaming me, Jesse? I didn't kill Mom. Cancer did."

I run my hands through my hair, down the sides of my face. I'm still breathing hard. My balled fists relax, though. This isn't good for anyone. And I need to get the house in shape before Dad comes home tomorrow. But I need to get the last word.

I look down at my brother, who is still crawling around the floor, gathering pieces of lamp. "What are you gonna do, try to glue it back together?"

"Yeah. Maybe I am. So shut the fuck up, asshole."

"I can't believe you were about to take off on one of your vacations from life. When are you going to grow up, Jamie?"

That's when I hear the back door slam, and realize, Serena has left.

"You look pathetic. Get the fuck up off the floor. Your playmate just ditched you."

He's huffing, working his jaw, ass in the air, reaching under furniture. He looks like he did when we fought over Matchbox cars and hid them from each other. I can't help but burst out laughing.

Jamie doesn't stand. So I drop to the floor beside him and we both crunch over with laughter.

"You're a real asshole," I say, catching my breath.

"Takes one to know one, bro." His arm arcs through the air and lands on my chest.

"Remember what Mom used to do when we did this shit? Besides calling us raunchy puppies." Tears sting my eyes.

"Pulled out her water gun."

"Ice cold water. Who could ever forget that?"

"Or her." His voice cracks.

I force myself to look into the bathroom mirror as I brush my teeth. Other than pale with dark circles beneath my dull eyes, I don't really look different. No one would ever guess I'd been repeatedly raped. Tormented. Threatened. And now I'm running on empty, waiting my turn to see a PA at the Women's Clinic.

The door opens and a PA enters the room like peach scented tea poured from the spout of a China pot. Graceful and silent, she has a purpose. A place. A smile on her sweet looking face. *Is she that much older than me? Maybe twice my age. Maybe less.*

My heart rate picks up; it doesn't race, but it's faster than it was when I woke up this morning and made the decision to visit the women's emergency clinic. The walls are blue, the ceilings white. Fluorescent lights make the room too bright. Small, the room feels so small. I'm smothering in here. The only good thing about this place is you don't need an appointment. Just show up on their doorstep and a friendly face will sign you in. Then you wait. Thirty minutes can feel like thirty days when you know why you're here, but don't want anyone else to.

Dee couldn't come with me. She had family issues, or so

she said. I wonder if she'll still be my friend. Can someone who's never been raped even begin to understand the struggle of someone who has been? Will she dump me like a bag of trash? Because she thinks I might have something contagious? Or being seen with me could make her a victim! Is she frightened? As frightened as I am to return to school?

To make matters worse, the bus travels right by the service station Jesse's family owns. I turned my head as we passed, covering half of my face with my hand as I scrunched down low in the seat. Still, I couldn't resist the urge to peek through my fingers to see if Jesse was standing out front. I've seen him there before, working on his bike, or under the hood of someone's car. Imagine if he saw me get off the bus on the corner? Would he see me sneak into this building marked Women's Clinic? It's a free, state run clinic, not your average GYN office; the quiet place girls visit in confidence. What would Jesse think? What difference does it matter?

"Good morning," the PA's voice is cheerful. "I'm Maggie. And you are?" She's holding a pad of paper and is already scribbling. What, I wonder? Replaces my thoughts of Jesse.

"Zoe Channing." Oh crap, I shouldn't have given her my real name. If Dee had been here coaching me, I'd have made something up, like Mary Smith, or Jane Doe. Crap. I'm busted.

Our eyes meet. Hers question. Her skin is pale and her hair is dark, almost black, and tinted with wine. For a displaced moment, my mind wanders. She's really pretty. I imagine what I'd look like with her hair color.

Dee did coach me over the phone before I left my house and walked the few short blocks to the bus stop. "Tell them your boyfriend might have fooled around. And you're concerned he might have given you an STD."

So I begin to tell this to Maggie, who immediately knows I'm lying. I can read it in her warm brown eyes that draw the truth from me.

She moves to my side. When I shy away, the paper beneath my butt makes a crinkling sound. "Put this on." She hands me a pale blue gown. "You can tie it in the back, hon. Remove your panties. So, you're bleeding between periods?"

I nod, and in chalky white scrubs that look over-washed, she appears to float like a cloud to a small desk in the corner, settles onto the chair and scribbles more notes. I don't take my eyes from her as I walk behind a folding screen to remove my clothing and slip into the gown. When I'm ready, I hug myself tightly. I think it would take monumental strength to pull my arms from my chest right now.

I lie as close to the edge of the exam table as physically possible, trembling so badly, my legs won't stay still, my feet slip from the stirrups. Forcing my knees together makes my leg muscles shudder more. I squeeze my eyes shut. *Slow inhale. Slower exhale.* I'm recalling last night with my parents. How difficult it was to look them in the eye. Feeling like a liar. Traitor. But I could never be the cause of their deaths, so while I choked down vegetable fried rice, I smiled and tried to act excited about our trip to Vermont. The last thing I want to do is be stuck in a car for five hours. No. The last thing I want is to be here. No, wait. The last thing I want is to go back to school on Monday.

During the exam, she's silent. So gentle I barely feel her probing fingers. Then she's at my side again, eyes soft, wise. "Your boyfriend did this to you?" she says, her expression somewhat pained.

I'm too frozen with fear to move.

"You have vaginal abrasions and tears. Injuries that need to be treated. When was your last period?"

"I, um, about ... three weeks ago. What do you mean I have tears? Is it serious?"

"We can take care of that. What I need to know is what happened to you."

"You can tell just by looking?"

She nods solemnly. "Sexual abuse is every bit a crime as rape."

I suck in a breath which is quickly displaced by a sob. She puts her arms around me and all I can hear is the beat of my heart in my ears.

"I'm supposed to report all forms of abuse."

I jump down her throat. "No!"

"You're a victim. It's not your fault."

But I feel like a criminal. Just for being in this room with bare walls, shuttered windows. I keep shaking my head. "I'm fine. I'll be fine. I have to go."

Wrapping the robe tighter around myself, I begin to slide from the table. Her gentle hands stop me.

"You've experienced an emotional trauma and you're not sure how to deal with it. Some withdraw, others lash out. I know talking about it is very painful, dramatic, even humiliating. But I'm here to help, Zoe. In any way I can. I'm here to provide strength. I've been where you are. And here I am now. I know it's hard to believe, but you will get through this. Have you told your family? Friends? Are you close to anyone?"

"I think my best friend is distancing herself."

"It's sometimes normal for friends to, I don't like using this word, *abandon* you." Her jaw tightens. I imagine her to be clenching her teeth. Is she talking from experience? "Because they can feel uncomfortable, Zoe. Perhaps she feels helpless, and because she can't help you, she can't handle what has happened. Sometimes it's easier for people to withdraw. But in the long run, that's not going to help."

All I can do is nod.

"We offer counseling and self-defense courses."

Decisions spin through my overtaxed brain. "If I tell, I'll have to go to court, right?"

Now it's her turn to nod.

"Then I'll have to talk about it, relive it, in front of everyone. Suppose he denies it?"

She crams my head with facts. So many, I forget each sentence when the next one starts.

"Don't you have brochures?"

"Yes. You'll get one before you leave. Are you eating and sleeping? Exercise too. It's important. This was not your fault. You are not weak. Did you consider changing schools?"

"I can't do that," I snap. "It will look weird. And I have a life there. Friends, I'm in a play. He's there too, though. Suppose he–"

"This is why you need to consider talking to your parents, and filing a report with the police."

"I know you're right, but I ... I will. I just have to find the right time." The right time? Will there ever be a right time?

His face hasn't left my mind, not for a minute. I'm trying to close down, but talking about it makes it all too real, and when I consider the possibility of confronting him again, a chill runs down my spine. The thought of facing him in court is bad enough. But remembering his threats, how tall he stood, the width of his shoulders, the size of his hands, his wretched mouth, wild eyes. I want to bang my head against the wall to stop the memories. This leaves me no choice but to remain deaf, dumb, and blind.

"This can be a very lonely time. You feel isolated. You don't want to talk about it. You may feel friends are ... on and on she goes until all I want to do is cover my ears to avoid screaming "Shut up!" to her.

I walk out of the clinic with a double dose of antibiotics and the morning after pill. Maggie catches me at the door and tucks her card into my hand.

"Call me whenever you need to. Don't be afraid, or ashamed. This is not your fault. And don't let it haunt you. There is a life after rape. I'm living proof."

Christian is bouncing around on the lawn in front of his house, a clapboard two story, overpowering in this land of the low and sprawling brick ranches. He's waving me on like a landing signal officer on an aircraft carrier. Wearing khaki cargo pants and green striped shirt, he looks much like he does almost every day in school.

As my car rolls to the curb, "The Stang!" he sings out, palming the polished red fender. Gently. He knows better than to fuck with my wheels. "It's about damn time. Hit it. Quick. Before they get a chance to do a number on your paint job."

"Hey," I say as he throws the passenger door open and lowers himself onto the smooth bucket seat, drawing his long legs up at the knee so they don't collide with the dash. "Nice to see you dressed for the occasion." I chuckle. "Should I drop you at Jefferson?" I hit the console button to lower his window all the way, because he's just filled the interior of the car with a gagging burst of nose-stinging fragrance.

"What the hell, dude? Cologne instead of a shower?"

His head jerks toward me, incredulous. "No. Why?"

"I can taste the shit you're doused in. Don't light up in my car."

Easing into the seat, he laughs. "Tonight I am a chick magnet, my good friend."

"Chick repellent, you mean," I reply, distracted by my image in the rear view mirror. Checking out both sides of my head, I gather some loose strands of hair that have fallen near my eyes and smooth them back into the long top of my *undercut.*

"Your hair's the shit. When'd you get it cut?"

"This afternoon." I take another admiring look in the mirror.

Christian's hair is shoulder length and parted in the center. He hastily combs through the thick mess with his large hand, then plucks the collar of his shirt with two fingers. He shoots me a one-sided smirk. "Nice, huh? Old Navy. Clearance rack." He hangs his arm out the window, tapping the side of the door to the beat of the song on the stereo, which I've just turned down a few notches. "Holy fuckballs. I couldn't wait to get the fuck outta there. Insanity runs in my family. Did I ever mention?"

With my foot on the break, my palm cradles the leather shifter as I rev the idling engine, an ear tuned to the deep muffled melody my car is producing. "No. And I'd never have guessed."

He pulls out the joint concealed between his sandy hair and his ear and sticks it between his lips. "Not everybody primps like the Sinclairs. I'm digging your wardrobe." He rocks his head, and I assume he's referring to the " oh shit " probably too obvious new looking jeans I'm wearing, and perfectly pressed dark blue button down shirt with just a hint of a pin stripe if you catch it at the right angle.

Reaching through the air between us, his hand whisks by my headrest. "How long did it take you to create that pompadour?"

"Longer than it just took for you to destroy it." My hand goes to the crown of my head, taking a two second glance at him before putting the car into motion. "What's the chaos on your front lawn, bro?" I laugh. "Is that your mom and grandma?" Each time the screen door of his house flies open and bangs shut, another member of his family pours out into the front yard. I laugh harder. "They're heading this way."

"Aye. They're coming to get me, man. Hurry up. Get us outta here." He emits a loud, "Phew," as I slide the shift into first gear, then he continues his rant. "My sister's wedding plans. You'd think it was the Royal wedding. The house is in an uproar." He rolls his eyes. "If and when I go down that road, it will be what the wise man calls shacking up with a hot chick. And if she bitches, our possibly permanent commitment will be by way of a Justice of the Peace. Maybe. But only if she's hot enough. None of this million buck shit for me." He shakes his head. "Yep. I'm the lucky one who's been chosen to walk my sis down the aisle in some ten pound monkey suit. Pfft."

"And you'd rather wear cargoes and a hoodie."

"Why the hell not? Actually, I'd rather not be there at all. I don't see the big deal in all that crap. Weddings are a waste of cash that could help put my wheels back on the road. So my best friend wouldn't have to cart me around in his Stang."

After checking that the road is clear, I hit the gas, and the Mustang lurches forward, tires spitting gravel. "Not me. When the time is right, I'm doing the deal." Watching the tachometer, I smoothly shift into second, third, fourth, and we're cruising like a boat in fifth gear.

"Don't tell me you're thinking about getting hitched?" His deep voice lifts with shock. "Holy fuck. Are you nuts?"

"No. I'm not thinking about anything. I just mean, I have nothing against shacking up with someone, to see if you get along and all, but when the perfect girl walks into my life, then I'll do the deal the right way. Like my folks."

"I never took you for traditional." He cranks the radio and starts moving to the beat in the passenger seat. He lights the joint, drags hard, and offers it to me.

"Na ah. Not when I'm driving, dude."

"That's what I like about you Jess. You're one level-headed bastard. That's for damn sure. I almost wish I could be that way." He exhales and immediately takes another long drag. "But I can't."

The beat of drums pounds my head, with bass so intense it's impossible to hold a conversation without screaming. But then, I don't really feel like communicating. I'm concerned about Dad's health, which has been deteriorating. The station is a lot to handle. Especially when so much responsibility falls on one part-time helper. Me. I can help out, but hell, I'm still in high school, and Jamie is ... well, great at disappearing.

I'm also worried about the business we've been losing due to early closings the past few weeks. But I'd hate like hell to pass on college the way Jamie did. Although, I'm not sure my dickhead brother even thought about making anything better out of himself. Inside I'm torn. I feel selfish for not wanting to hang around to keep the business going. Is that how Jamie felt? Doubtful. I don't think even Jamie knows why he makes the senseless decisions he does.

Cooling air rushes through the windows, displacing Christian's cologne and the pungency of pot. As I drive, I watch an awesome sunset. Now that's something I plan on painting when I get home tonight. If I get home tonight. This is going to be an epic night. I can feel it deep down inside. Lately, I've been feeling a lot of things. Right now peace tops the list, followed by optimism, anticipation. I'm ready for something good to happen in my life. It's about damn time.

Radio blasting, we cruise through the center of town, then commercial lots roll into forestland. I snap the radio off while the car crawls to a stop at the side of the road, behind a long line of others. I kill the engine and consider whether or not my car will be safe here.

"The place is already packed." After rolling up the windows, I turn to Christian and extend my hand. "Got any more?"

"Do squirrels have nuts?" he deadpans, lights up another joint and hands it to me.

I take a pull and inhale deeply, savoring the smoke that's trapped in my lungs. Holding it there as long as possible. "What do you think of Holloway?" Emerges with dribbles of smoke through my lips. "Every time his parents leave town, it's party time. Not that I'm complaining. It's just his holier-than-thou attitude I guess."

"He's a douche," Christian replies with tight lips, then a band of smoke wraps his face. More disheveled than when I picked him up, he looks like he just climbed out of a wind tunnel. I laugh, and he pulls down the visor mirror and smoothes his hair. "That freaky, huh?"

"Yeah, you're a chick magnet, alright." My laugh is cut short. "Sometimes I'd like to shove my foot up his ass." The battle between sedated and edgy begins.

Christian shrugs. "Holloway is an ass, I guess. But he's got the booze and chicks, which puts the smart in front of ass."

An elbow braced on the interior door frame, my hands rest on the wheel, a bit too forceful. I decide to smoke more weed. "I think I'll get fucked up and sit here all night."

"For damn sure, this shit takes the edge off. I can't see through the fogged windows, dude. What's happening outside?"

"It's dusk, idiot. And looking like a short night for you." I study the area around us, feeling a twinge of envy. Not liking it. "Holloway would have a lot going for him if he wasn't such a douche," I say after releasing a brisk wisp of smoke. "He could seriously make something of himself, but chooses to behave like an asshole. He seems to thrive on attention. Negative or positive doesn't seem matter to him. He's the kind of guy who laughs his way through life, usually at someone else's expense."

"Buys his way, you mean," Christian's laugh, or maybe what he's just said, annoys me. "Either way, every asshole hits up his parties. Two-faced, dude. They'd rather pluck their ass hairs then hang out with him, yet they go to his blowouts."

I burst out laughing. "That doesn't say much for us. As we sit here getting high, waiting to join the other assholes."

Christian holds his gut with laughter, then, as if someone has poured cold water over him, he calms. Eerily so. "Hey. I got accepted in Pittsburgh."

"Duquense?"

"Yeah."

"That's awesome. I'm really happy for you."

"How about you? Anything yet?"

"I haven't thought about it."

"Bullshit."

I exhale a burst of smokeless air. "I'll be right here for now. There's too much going on to pick up and leave. Maybe catch the next semester."

"Sorry, dude. I know I fuck around a lot, but I mean that with all honesty. You're the best, bro. Sorry you gotta be stuck here. I'm gonna miss you. Stuff like this." He sighs. "Like tonight. And with graduation around the corner it'll be kinda like part of us will be dead and buried."

"Knock it off. You sound like you're getting ready for a funeral. Or worse, getting sentimental on me, Christian."

"Don't sink into depression, dude. I'll be back for Thanksgiving. Bearing gifts. Not turkey either. I'll be brewing us up some chemical goodies."

"Don't go getting your ass kicked out of school. You barely made it in."

"Yeah, I'm cool."

I roll down the window and gulp fresh air. Not far away, the sprawling three story structure, the size of a resort, glows with interior lighting. Music blares through windows, and the front door functions like a turnstile in Grand Central.

"Obviously, Holloway's parents aren't around." Christian yawns.

"Obviously. The fact that his old man owns this entire dead end street doesn't hurt the atmosphere either." I shake my head. "He thinks of everything. Look at the tents."

"Yeah, plenty of room for us to crash. It's good though. Nobody has to drive wasted. Maybe I should go into real estate instead of chemistry." Christian leans back into the seat, attempting to stretch his legs. "We have all the privacy we need to party, without interruption. No parents. No cops. Just coolness." He reaches for the door handle. "Let's rock"

Christian and I blend with the progression of other guys and girls heading toward the house. The air vibrates, drumming in time with my heart, and it feels as though I'm walking into a rock concert. Exciting. Stimulating.

I hear Christian yell, "Catch you later, Jess," but all I see is the back of his full head of hair. He lifts an arm, then another, and is flanked on either side by a girl.

I hear a series of "Jesse James" ring out as my body swipes others.

I make my way to a corner of the porch where cans of beer are buried in buckets of ice. I pluck one out, shake off droplets of water, and pop the top. The icy brew flows easily down my throat. Refreshing. Delicious. Delicious like the redhead handing me another. It's Amy from biology class.

"Hey Jess," she says with a smile. "There's a keg inside. And more booze too."

Before I get a word out, she's swept off her feet and thrown over some mammoth dude's shoulder. He's red-faced and perspiring. "Hey, Jess," he says. I have no idea who he is, but he apparently knows me.

So I untangle myself from the bodies hanging around the barrel, and shoulder my way through the crowd. Heading where, I don't know. I'm not sure what I'm looking for. A familiar face, maybe. Someone I'd actually enjoy spending the next five or six hours drinking with, getting high with, whatever. That's what I tell myself as my eyes scroll the face of every girl here. Who am I kidding? The stalker side of me confesses. I'm looking for Zoe, hoping she'll magically appear, but convinced nothing in this place would hold her interest. Myself included.

A body slam jolts me back to the party. My shoulder feels the impact as someone latches onto me. I spin so fast, my face almost crashes into Claudette's. Her eyelids bounce from half-shut to entirely shut. Steadying herself, her fingers dig into my chest.

Grabbing each of her arms, I hold her out before me. "When did you get here? This morning?" I say with sarcasm.

She mouths a kiss. "Why. You miss me? Waiting for me?"

"No. I'm wondering how much alcohol you've consumed."

She's giggles. "Enough to make me loveable."

I sling my arms around her waist and shove her toward the door, half carrying her because she's not moving her feet. "Come on, loveable. You've had enough party for one night. I'll drive you home."

She presents me with one or two options: let her sink onto the floor, or ditch the party to bring her home. My soaring spirits are suddenly nose diving. The only other option would be ... oh yes ... Jamie. My eyes search the room, hopeful, disappointed. If he were here he'd be buried beneath a pile of girls, or up on the bar making a spectacle of himself. I don't see either scenario.

"Hell no I'm not leaving," Claudette's lips barely move. But she's loud enough to attract attention and catcalls from nearby males, which we both ignore. Me, because I choose to. Claudette, because her face is now buried against my chest.

When she surfaces, tears gather in her lashes. "Where's Jamie? Where's Jamie?" Her lips quiver. The tears her eyes are producing are so big, for a moment I stare, then gently dab a thumb beneath each eye, because I've never seen such huge tears before. For some stupid reason, I feel the need to touch them, to dab until they're dried. She looks like a porcelain doll. A broken doll. I feel so bad for her. She shouldn't be bleeding out over my brother.

"Claudette. You need to pull yourself together," I whisper into her ear. "Get over him. You're so much better than this."

A guy named Finch passes by with a nod, does a three sixty and returns like a yoyo. He puts a hand on each of Claudette's shoulders, and the tug of war begins. "You've got your hands full." He laughs. "Here, lemme give you mine." Removing his hands from her, he slaps a palm on each side of my chest and leans in. So now, Claudette is crushed between us, her breasts plastered to my ribs. "I'll take her off your hands, Sinclair."

With one arm, I hold Claudette, with the other I shove him off. "No you won't."

He looks to the side, then back at me. Obnoxious. "Ah. Brotherly love?"

"Go fuck yourself," I reply. Gruff. Disgusted. If this is what the night holds, I'm out of here.

"Come on, man. I just want to dance with her."

"Seriously? She can barely stand up."

"She's not yours, man." He laughs. "She's your brother's leftovers. What the hell do you care?"

I haul in a breath. Let it out. My jaw begins to work in time with my flexing fist. "See that sofa over there?"

He nods.

"If you're not out of my face in five seconds, I'm dumping her and kicking your ass. Understand?"

"Six," he says.

"Asshole." I figure I can let go of her and land a fist in his surly face before she drops to the floor. Which is what happens. Sort of. I land a fist in his face, he stumbles back, but she drops like a lead weight.

"You can have her," he says, shaking his head as he walks away. "If I need a corpse I'll visit the morgue."

I scoop my brother's ex off the floor and into my arms and carry her like a baby. Her head falls onto my shoulder and rolls. She moans softly, and her arms go around my neck.

Her hair slips between my lips when I whisper, "What am I going to do with you?"

I consider lugging her to my car, dropping her onto the seat, driving her home. Then what? Dump her on her front porch? Like this? Ring the doorbell and present her to her parents? In the condition she's in, they'd not only want to kill her, they'd have me arrested. Pot and alcohol. Great. You shouldn't be driving anyway. A variety of scenarios circle my head. Then I remember how strict her parents were when she dated Jamie. So strict, they wouldn't let a loser like him pick her up. So I had to. This seals the deal. I'm not turning myself into Jamie for Claudette or anyone else.

Either I'm strong or she's light, because the two of us somehow make it up the stairs, past people sprawled on the carpeted steps, making out.

"Thank you, Jesse," her whisper is weak, but her lips brush my neck. "You're nothing like your brother. You're sweet." Then she passes out. I mean, out like a light.

I pick the first room I come to, check to make sure it's unoccupied, and lay her down on the bed, positioning her on her side in case she pukes. By now, her skirt is hiked up to her hips, so I tug it down to cover her bikini underpants, straighten her top which has twisted itself around her body, leaving one breast half exposed, and throw a blanket over her, pulling it up to her neck.

Her face is buried in her hair, so I lift her head, sweep her hair out from under, and spread the silky length across the pillow.

When I do this, she gives me a goofy grin and moans.

"There. Better now? Why am I even talking to you," I mumble. "You're so trashed, you can't hear a word I'm saying." I chuckle. Maybe because she she's still grinning, maybe because she looks kind of like an angel. But only now that she's sleeping.

She's so still, I lower my face to hers, checking to make sure she's still breathing.

A lazy, "Mmm," oozes through her parted lips. "Stay with me," eyes closed, she whispers, then all I hear is her light, rhythmic breath.

I stand beside the bed watching her. Thinking. "What the fuck do I do now?" Scrubbing my jaw, I pace. Mumbling to myself, I rationalize, "I'm not your babysitter. Dammit. But I can't leave you here like this." I stare at the ceiling, rolling my eyes. "Why do you do this shit, Claudette?"

Sprawled out like this, she's a sitting duck to be easily passed around without even knowing anything was happening. I wouldn't put it past some of the wasted assholes downstairs to wander up here and try.

I walk to the window, pull the curtain aside, and gaze down at the yard. Looking for what, I have no clue. As expected, the scene below is chaotic. Thoughtless. I have no idea what to do with this girl. I know one thing, I don't feel like sitting up here all night. Staring out the window. Or at her.

You can do one of two things, Sinclair. Maybe you'll end up doing both. Stand guard at the doorway. Or lay your ass down beside her so no one can touch her.

I let out a deep, annoyed breath when it hits me. "If you were ever around, please let it be now." I pull out my cell and hit the send button for Jamie. After five rings, my heart sinks. "Fuck. Shit ..."

"Hey shithead! You actually answered your phone?" I've never been so happy to hear my brother's nasty voice.

"What do you want? I'm busy."

"I'm here with your girlfriend."

"I don't have a girlfriend."

"You know damn well what I'm talking about."

"Claudette?"

"In the flesh and sound asleep."

"She's trashed, huh?" He laughs. "Good for you. You want my blessing? You have it. Now forget my number, dickhead."

Through the phone, a girl says softly, "No phone, my baby. Don't stop what you are doing." She has an accent I can't place, but she sounds sexy as hell. "Come back into da bed, Shames." I almost bust a gut listening. "You make me feel so much better."

"Shames?" I laugh into the phone.

Her voice grows louder, more urgent, "Come to Greshen, Shames."

"Where the hell are you, anyway? Norway?"

His voice is flat. "Jersey. And if you haven't already noticed by eavesdropping and heavy breathing, I'm busy."

"Trust me. I've got better things to do than listen to you have sex over the phone, jerkoff."

"Listen, bro, I really gotta go. Talk to you soon. Not."

"Wait! Don't hang up. Claudette is here. Right next to me. She's calling for you. Have a heart, Jamie. She's in bad shape."

"What do you want from me?"

"We're at Holloway's house. Come and pick her up. The place is mobbed. I'll meet you outside." My phone is plastered so close to my mouth, I'm practically kissing it, my voice disgustingly pleading.

"What am I supposed to do with her?"

"What the hell did you ever do with her? I don't give a shit, dude. Just get her the hell out of here, Jamie. Before something happens to her. I can't babysit her all night."

Jamie's pissed off sigh at the other end of the line is interrupted by Greshan, who is now moaning, begging him to finish her off.

"I realize this is one of the most difficult decisions you'll probably ever have to make, brother." My voice drips with sarcasm. "Do something right for once in your life."

"Let her sleep it off, Jesse."

"What part of animal house don't you understand, Jamie?"

"Christ," he groans, "you owe me, motherfucker."

"Me?"

Zoe

Standing in the center of my bedroom, I rest the heels of my hands on my eyelids and rub. Gently at first. Carefully rubbing away my thoughts, one at a time. But visions keep coming. Regardless of how hard I try, they can't be erased. My brain has been branded. My hands exert so much pressure my eyes hurt, but the horror is still here. There's no rubbing *this* away. I can't escape the nightmares since the attack, but last night's dream was different. Deeper. It felt so real, like I was back in that dark, musty room again, with his hands all over me. I tasted the foulness of his mouth that blocked the air from my lungs. Again and again I was hit with panic, and literally leaped from bed, gasping for air. Groping for my pulse, because my heart had pounded so hard, for a moment, I was sure it had burst.

These dreams. This reality. I can't do this. It's getting worse instead of better. Whoever said time heals all wounds is a liar. Evil is festering inside me. Growing in intensity. Spreading: causing nausea, tremors. I want to run, claw off my skin. My fists fly to my temples and I press so hard, squeeze my eyes so tightly shut, bright white orbs of light invade the darkness beneath my lids.

Mom enters my room so quietly, I start. My eyes refocus and I fix my stare at her. Instead of the face of a monster, which is still vivid in my mind.

Angling her head, she returns my stare. "Are you okay?" She sounds cautious, like one would when approaching the wounded animal they're attempting to rescue.

Quickly, I stop gritting my teeth. My poor teeth which I'm probably wearing down to stubs. "Yes. I'm fine. I was just thinking."

"Maybe you need to see the doctor, Zoe. It's not like you to miss school so often. Then when you do go, you won't let Dad drive you. What's up with that?" She's at my side, stroking my forehead. "What's this?" She runs her fingers under strands of hair concealing half of my face. "Your forehead's all blotched." Her fingers examine the area my hands have just punished, then her palm presses my cheek. "Your eyes are red too. Do you have a fever?" She draws back, drops her hand, and waits for my reply.

My mother has the strongest stare I've ever seen. She has a way of cutting through a skull with her piercing eyes. Normally, her eyes are soft. Tonight, she's stern. Firing questions at me. I feel like I'm on the witness stand. Being interrogated by a slick attorney.

I take the fifth, I say to myself, but to her I say, "I'd rather take the bus Mom."

"You hated the bus, which is why Dad agreed to drive fifteen minutes out of his way to drop you off at school." Shaking her head, her sigh is forlorn. So sad I could cry. "When you're home, you're locked in your room. We used to watch movies together. Share popcorn. I miss our mother-daughter time."

I draw my palms across my face. Hook my fingers in my hair and try to smooth it, so I don't look like a pathetic wreck. On the outside, anyway. "I haven't been sleeping well. I'm tired, that's all."

"Dee is on the land line. She said you're not picking up your cell phone." She crunches her brows, scrutinizing me.

I hate it when she looks at me this way. I think she can see right inside my head. Mom and I have no secrets. *Had*, I should add. When she was going through her crisis with Dad, she told me everything she felt. Confessed she considered divorce, mostly for my sake. She leaned on me. Why can't I do the same? Because it's not the same! She was sitting home waiting for her drunken husband to return. There's a big difference between alcoholism and rape.

How can I tell her? I'm frightened when I'm home. Frightened in school. I don't go anywhere alone. Make sure I'm in the center of a crowd when walking through the halls. Or in the bathroom. I'm waiting ... waiting for the hand to clasp over my mouth. To be dragged down the flight of stairs and into the boiler room again. My life is nothing but horror. Days in school, nights in bed. It's getting to the point, I don't want to go to bed anymore. Maybe I'll start sleeping in that chair over there. The one in the lighted corner my life size teddy bear occupies.

Together we stand. Almost facing off. "I'll call Dee back," I finally say, dismissing my overly inquisitive mother.

I don't want to talk to Dee! Not now. Please. Isn't struggling through school enough? Now Dee is nagging me about going to a party. I can't believe her. Hasn't my attitude told her I don't want to see anyone? Not even her! Do I have to spell it out for her? I hate everyone. Everything. Me. I hate me! Almost as much as I hate the man who did this to me.

After what feels like five minutes of silence, Mom says, "Well, I guess this conversation has ended. I'll be watching TV. Call me if you need me." Pausing in the doorway, she adds, "If Dee is still on the phone, I'll tell her you'll call her."

The moment Mom leaves my room, I grab my cell. Angrily. Resentfully.

Our house is small. Without much privacy. Mom calls it cozy. I call it invasive. My room is closest to the living room, where I don't have to strain to hear Mom and Dad's conversations. Normally I tune them out. But tonight, when I hear Mom's urgency, my attention is pulled from my developing headache, and I focus on her voice. When I hear what she says to Dad, my heart nearly stops.

"I don't know what's wrong with Zoe, but I'm worried, Grant."

"I've never seen you like this, Annie. What is it? Is Zoe sick?"

Mom's sigh could break a heart. "Not physically. I don't think."

Dad's voice pitches. "Emotionally?"

"She won't talk to me, but I know something is wrong. She's building a wall around herself and won't let me in. We've always been so close—"

Dad lets out a chuckle. "And you're feeling left out. I think you're overreacting, honey. It's her first year of high school. She's in a different world. Meeting new friends. Testing new waters."

"I have a bad feeling it's not simple growing pains."

Mom's tone holds a steady pitch of worry. Dad's drops with concern.

"You don't think she's getting bullied, do you?"

"I would hope she'd tell us if that were the case. She's acting so strange. Secretive."

"Maybe she's discovering boys?" Dad's voice is gruff. I hate the tone his voice is taking. Realizing just how overprotective my father is, my throat tightens. "I hope she hasn't gotten in with a bad crowd. And is isolating herself from her family."

They're tearing my brain apart, bit by bit, and are so far off course, it's pathetic. I should march out there and tell them I'm not mentally deranged. I don't have boy trouble. I wish it were that simple.

"Zoe would never do anything like that."

"We should talk to her. Together."

"I already tried." Mom sounds close to tears.

No! I quickly shut the inch of door I'm listening through and snap the lock. *Don't even think about coming in here to third degree me again.* This time *both* of them? My eyes fly to the window, which appears an appealing escape from my parents. Temporarily, anyway.

I clutch my phone so tightly, I feel the pulse of my heart. My palm begins to sweat: is it from holding the phone? Or from the sheer anxiety of it all? After a moment of staring through eyes blurred by tears, I take a deep breath and punch in Dee's number.

"The last thing I feel like doing is going to a party," I snap, the moment I hear her voice. "I thought I made it clear." Even though she can't see me, I grimace. I've never behaved so ugly in my life. I glance around my room, at the pumpkin colored walls, the ivory print bedspread Mom sewed for me because we couldn't find anything to match my orange decision. Now I realize orange is a terrible color for such a *cozy* room. Bad choice, Zoe. Will the rest of your life be a series of mistakes? I feel like a caged animal searching for a way out of captivity.

"Zoe," Dee violates my thoughts. "I've been trying to–"

Before giving her a chance to get a word out, I growl into the phone. "Reach me? I'll pass. The dead don't attend parties."

I imagine the look on Dee's face at this very moment. Disbelief in her best friend's behavior. I envision her actions, should she be standing beside me. "Now you sit right down and listen to me, Channing!" She'd shove me onto the bed. Hands on hips she'd tower over me. Just because she's got five inches over me, thirty pounds, and is a year older, she thinks she's intimidating.

And just as I expected, through the phone line, the sermon starts.

"Zoe, you need to get out. The worst thing for you to do is brood in your room. I know what happened to you was horrible–"

"Brooding?" I pace the room and glower at my mirror. "I can't believe you're treating this so lightly, Dee. How would you know how horrible it was?" My cheeks feel so hot, I want to douse them with ice water. "I hate when clueless people try to comfort someone with dumb things like ... like when someone dies, people say, Ohhh, he's in a better place. How the fuck do they know where a dead person goes? Or what a better place is!"

Dee responds with fear in her voice. "Who's talking about dying? You're not thinking of ... you would never ..." After a brief moment of silence, she says, Oh my God, Zoe. You need to do some deep breathing and calm down, girl. Better yet, I'm coming over there."

I choke out a moan, then grit my teeth. "No! You don't have to. I'm not thinking of killing myself." *If I told you the truth, you'd tell my parents and they'd have me locked up for my own safety.*

My protest falls on deaf ears, because Dee has terminated our connection. Before I can think of an excuse to tell Mom, so she doesn't invite Dee in, my best friend is walking into my room. This is the worst part about living two minutes away from someone you really don't care to see at this very moment.

Running her fingers through her hair, she sighs. Her face is pulled into a knot of compassion. Like that day in my kitchen when I shared my horror.

"It must have been a nightmare, but you can't dwell on it or you'll never be able to move on. Think of the bright side: you didn't get pregnant, didn't get any weird disease, be happy about that."

"Yeah, I'm real happy the creep didn't shoot me up with an STD." Thinking of diseases such as Syphilis sends a chill down my spine. Controlling a shudder, I swallow hard, considering her suggestions. Maybe I should get away. Away from here. Away from me. What better way than to get blasted to oblivion at one of Trent's parties? I've never been to one, but I hear they're amazing. Wild. Just what I need.

Dee grabs my hands, examining my fingers with the pads of hers.

I scrunch my face defensively. "Yeah, I'm chewing my nails. So what?"

"Stop it, Zoe. You have to stop it!" Dee's tone, and demeanor, are desperate. "I know it feels like your life is over. I know you'll never forget what that bastard did to you. But you have to try to climb out of the hole you're burying yourself in." A moment before her arms go around me, I watch a tear roll down her cheek. "It's been weeks. I miss my best friend. Please, Zoe–"

My face burrows into her shoulder. "I feel like shit, Dee. I'm sorry." A sob escapes, then a sniffle. "I'm blubbering all over your shirt."

"Don't be sorry." Her voice cracks. "For being you, or for the shower." Her chuckle sounds like a snort.

I pull away to stare into her eyes. "I shouldn't be taking this out on you." Reaching for a box of tissues, I pull out a handful for both of us.

"You always hurt the one you love," she teases with a wink while blowing her nose. "You need to spread some heavy duty cover up under those eyes, girlfriend. You're starting to look like an owl."

"Who Who." I'm so sarcastic, I can't stand myself.

She waggles her ample brows, and the caterpillar-like movement is enough to cause a smirk.

"You think that's funny? Watch this." Pulling her hair back, she proceeds to wiggle her ears.

"How do you do that?" I want to laugh. I just can't.

"Loose scalp."

My bottom lip won't stop quivering. "What would I do without you?"

Resting her hands on my shoulders, she takes a step back. Her eyes are wide and hopeful. "My parents will drive if yours will pick us up." She's like a little kid pleading for a ride to a toy store.

I bite the inside of my cheek and take in every inch of her face. My lips can't help but break into something of a grin. "Are you about to cry again?"

"What?"

"Your eyes are shiny."

"I'm naturally misty. What can I say? So?"

"So ... You got your way I guess."

The force of her body slam of joy nearly knocks me off my feet. Her bubblegum breath warms my cheek. "It's the right thing to do, Zoe. You'll see. You'll feel so much better. We'll hang together. I won't leave your side." With an impish grin she says, "Jesse Sinclair will be there."

"How do you know?"

"He's tight with Trent. Besides, everybody's going."

"So what?" The last thing I need is to face Jesse Sinclair.

"So, he likes you. That's what."

The shock overtaking every muscle in my face is a perfect representation of my emotions.

"He's wondering where you've been."

"Why?"

"Because you've been in hiding."

"He asked about me?"

"Listen, I only have one class with him, but I can tell he's interested."

"So he didn't ask about me." My stomach sinks. Why? Because a month ago, I would have loved to be having this conversation. Right now, it's breaking my heart.

"What's the diff? You have a king sized crush on him, no?" She tosses a balled up tissue at me.

"Had!" I slap my palms over my ears. "Don't start!"

She frees my ears and becomes dramatic. "I'm not blind. I watched you two sneak glances at rehearsals."

"Used to," I correct. "Everything has changed. And if he's into me, why didn't he ever talk to me in Art Appreciation class?"

"It's a big class. Maybe he never saw you. Maybe he's shy." Examining her red painted fingernails, she shrugs.

"Why are you even going there? What's the point of discussing any of this?"

"My point is, get out of the house and move on. Make the most of what you have left, Zoe. A full life ahead of you if you can just get past this."

"I'm miserable." A sob shortens my words. "What does it matter now? A Broadway agent could be at Trent's party waiting to sign me and I wouldn't give a damn. It's obvious you don't understand Dee. It's nothing I could explain to you. You'd have to have experienced it."

She ignores my tirade. "He thinks you're adorable."

"He said that?"

"Not with words, but I see how he looks at you on stage. He's all yours for the taking, girl."

"I've already been taken. I don't want to talk about it anymore. I feel like I'm going to throw up."

"I'm just trying to help. In any way I can."

I'm frowning. Mumbling. My mind is racing. "You're such a nag." My heart rate is picking up. Cocooned in despair isn't helping. If I don't break out soon I'll suffocate. Maybe Dee is right. Maybe being with Jesse will wash away the filth I feel inside. "I'll go, but I can't promise how long I'll stay."

"That's fine. One step at a time." Grinning, she shoves a

thick lock of hair behind each ear. "So you think your parents will bring us home? Because my father—"

"Yeah. I'm sure they will." I slide my fingers through my neglected hair, which feels limp, then study my fingernails, which I decide to file all down to one short length.

###

I stand in the shower, letting a curtain of water glide over me, wondering why I'm even going to a party that will, no doubt, turn into a circus before the night ends. I wasn't very social to begin with, but now I feel like a total outcast. Dirty and worthless. I wonder if anyone besides Dee knows what happened to me. *Did anyone see me fly out of the boiler room and through the school doors like there'd been a bomb threat?*

"Nothing like being prepared," I mumble, wearing bra and panties beneath a robe, rummaging through my closet for something neutral. Something morbid to match my mood. Basic black sounds good. Head to toe.

Mom enters the room quietly. I feel her before I see her. "Nothing like last minute," she says.

"Funny. I just said something similar to myself."

She laughs, joining me before the open closet. Separating a broad range of clothing, she pulls out a skirt I bought during an extravagant shopping trip to the city. I never intended to wear it; it was just something beautiful I wanted to own. Where would I ever wear a black long skirt with splashes of red roses? "How about this?" She arches her brows at me.

"Really?"

"Why not?"

"Too dressy."

"If you've got it, wear it," she giggles like a teen.

"I guess," I mumble. "I don't really have a top to match though." I plan on standing in the shadows, and wearing this skirt might not be the best choice. "Better keep looking. Maybe just jeans and a–"

She snaps her fingers. "I'll be right back."

While she's gone, I step into the skirt just to see what it would look like if I were to decide to wear it, which I'm not, so why bother, still I do anyway. Not only do I step into the softest fabric ever, but I have the nerve to tug it up to my waist and clasp it. When I slide my palms over my flat tummy, rounded hips, turn in the mirror to check it from behind, I don't look damaged. I just might consider this. I almost feel normal. Upbeat? I wouldn't go that far. How much attention would this attract? Too much? The wrong kind, maybe? Attempting to tone it down, I pull a bulky sweater over my still damp hair, and face the mirror. Even I have to laugh. Sarcastically of course. I look ridiculous. I'm just about to call Dee and tell her I have the flu, when Mom bounces back into my room.

I don't want her asking questions again, so I try to act normal. Happy, like any girl should be who is going to a party should be.

"Try this." She tosses a plain black stretch top into my hands. "That'll tone it down while still being stylish." She wrinkles her nose. "Yes, I'm a mind reader. I never liked to stand out in a crowd either. You don't always have to. Sometimes subtle is best. Let the boys come and find you." She winks. "You're too beautiful to have to advertise."

"That's yours Mom. I can't," I say while pulling the top over my head and smoothing it over my waist.

She lifts her brows. "Don't worry. Some things never change. Like tank tops. I can't believe my little girl looks better in my clothes than I do." Her eyes glisten.

Decision made. I'm wearing this outfit.

Before heading out the door, I pop into Mom's room. She's burrowed deep into her closet, rifling through clothing.

"Nothing like being last minute," I deadpan.

"That's what happens when you really don't want to go

someplace. What's your excuse?" She eyes me cautiously.

"I'm just feeling lazy tonight. I'd rather stay home and watch a movie with you." I tilt my head and grin.

Mom grabs me, holding me at arm's length, spinning me around a few times. With each revolution, I meet her sparkling eyes.

"You're glowing," I say, feeling far from new and shiny. I frown, because the look in her eyes is making me uncomfortable.

"You look absolutely stunning. I wish your grandmother could see you." The mention of Grandma dulls the light in her eyes: snagging me in a bear hug seems to bring a quick recovery.

Things might look good on the outside, but she should see her lovely daughter on the inside, I think wryly, practically cringing, hoping my grandma can't see us from the other side. Do the dead know what happens to the living? Can they see us? I shudder at the thought. Can they give us strength and otherworldly knowledge? That thought is encouraging.

"Let me help you." Mom takes the jacket I've tucked under an arm and holds it out so I can shove my arms through the sleeves. "You have goose bumps. Cover up. Best your father doesn't see this top." She chuckles. "I realize it's the *in* style, but I have a feeling he would prefer you go out in a zoot suit."

"Huh?"

"Or maybe covered from head to toe in a trench coat." She laughs. "You know how fathers are. Make sure you stay close to Dee," she cautions. "Tame as we've tried to make it, I don't want this outfit giving any ideas to the–"

"Guys? No worries. Unless you'd feel more comfortable if I wear that drape around me?" I say sourly, gesturing to the geometric patterned fabric concealing her bay window.

The honking of a horn makes my heart trip. I take a deep breath. As long as it doesn't completely stop, I should make it through the night. "There's Dee. I have to go." After a quick stop in my room to spray on perfume, I pick up my bag and am ready to bolt.

Dad stands by the kitchen doorway, arms crossed, ready to lecture me before I can exit. If he's trying to smile, it's not working. His tight lips tell me he's uneasy.

"Don't leave the party," he drops a kiss on my forehead.

My gaze shifts to Mom whose expression is saying: humor him. "I won't." He should know how glued I'll be to the interior of the house and Dee's side.

"Be careful. Boys your age are filled with testosterone and bad ideas."

My face heats. "Believe me. I'll keep my distance."

"Your mom and I will pick you up around midnight. Is that too late?"

Shaking my head, I mutter, "Uh uh."

"If you need us sooner," Mom chimes in, "just call or text me. I'm not into poker night like your dad is." She winks. "You can rescue me anytime."

Trent Holloway lives in a huge house in a classy area. I've never been there, but maps to his house get passed around school like candy so kids can find their way to his parties.

His father is a big-shot real estate investor. Most of the party will consist of seniors, but Dee knows a lot of people in school, so she'll be fine. She's been a social butterfly since the day we met. Which is how I met her. She rang my bell and handed me a candy bar, introduced herself, pushed past me, and started watching TV with my mom.

I settle into the back seat of Dee's family car and before closing the door wave to my parents. Dee hops in the back, too, leaving her father up front to chauffeur us to Trent's house. We each lean close to our windows. As we drive, my fingers long to grip the door handle. Pull it open, so I can tumble out of the car and be taken to the hospital. Which would be better than attending Trent's party. I look down at the blooming roses decorating my skirt and my stomach churns.

"Why did I ever wear this? I look like a jerk. I'm overdressed."

Dee moves to the center of the seat and whispers, "You look elegant."

Sitting close to Dee in the back seat while we're chauffeured, with her whispering into my ear, is the icing on the cake. "This could be extremely embarrassing if it were anyone else other than you," I return her whisper. "You can move over now."

"Stick close," she replies, sliding to her own side. Clandestine. On any other occasion, it would be comical. "Be my wingman and you'll be fine."

"Yeah, right. I hope so. Or it will be a short night."

In less than thirty minutes, we arrive. The house is lit up like an airport. And just as busy.

Now my trembling fingers *don't* want to reach for the door handle. "I'm having second thoughts, Dee."

"Don't. It'll be fine," she assures me as we make our way through the mass of strangers. Strangers to me. Not Dee. "You might even have fun." She looks at me and nods. "Think of this as therapy. Group therapy. By tomorrow you could be an entirely different girl with her life back on track. Trust me."

"So what am I supposed to do? Hang on your arm? I don't recognize a soul."

We enter the house and Dee is already ten steps ahead and scoping the place out. She doesn't reply to my "Hey. Wait up." Is this therapy too? Immersion as they call it? I'd call it shock.

I feel terribly awkward, and angry at myself for caving to Dee's coaxing. As it tries to console me, my mind draws its own conclusion: my entrance is like tripping over a trash can, or stepping in dog crap, in public. If no one you know is there to watch your clumsiness, there's no one to remind you of being an ass. And it can easily be forgotten. My analogy sounds ridiculous. I shake my head, attempting to conjure more comforting thoughts.

Maybe it's better this way, crosses my mind. *If no one knows me, how can they know my secret?*

I wander into Trent's rec room where most of the party is happening. Trent refers to this as the panty party room. I'm relieved Jamie has gotten Claudette out of here. In her vulnerable condition, she wouldn't be safe here. How safe is she with Jamie? Then again, he's probably going to dump Claudette off as fast as possible so he can get his ass back to Greshan. I laugh at the thought, and the few choice words he left me with while exiting the house with Claudette in his arms.

Not much of Trent's estate is off limits. Inside or out. The air in the rec room is heavy. Fully charged. With the amount of bodies in motion, even this enormous area feels overly warm and damp, like a stifling summer night brewing up a storm. Filled more with used breath than fresh oxygen. "Phew." I stifle a yawn, fluttering the collar of my shirt with the light grip of two fingers.

One of my hands is now at the small of my back. My other massages my aching neck. Arching my spine, I stretch. Lying beneath a customer's car for two relentless hours, dislodging and repairing rusted parts that refuse to cooperate, is hard on a body just beaten by the raucous game of basketball I finally found time to play.

Carefully, my fingers check my *pompadour* as Christian called it, forming something of a flowing wave at the top of my head. I let the stylist chick have her way with me. Simply suggesting, short on the sides, kinda long on top, I walked out with this. Don't get me wrong. I dig it. Even more after she told me girls fall over for this cut, then asked where I'd be later that night. Unbeknownst to me, I'd end up in her apartment. With her climbing onto my lap, a glass of wine in hand, ass rocking back and forth on my dick, complaining about her boyfriend who just didn't understand her. Isn't sensitive to her needs. Doesn't want to settle down."

"So, let me get this straight," I inquired with furrowing brows. "Besides not being good in the sack, he doesn't want to marry you? So you hook up with me? Should I be honored or insulted?"

She winked at me. "I'm getting even. You're getting lucky."

"Is that what girls call cheating these days?" I choked out a laugh.

"It's what girls call satisfaction. Shut up and kiss me."

Along with my lips, she took her aggression out on my head. My newly cropped hair. This chick was wild. The wine glass fell to the floor where we crashed. Where I screwed her till she rolled over, panting praises.

Just recalling one of the fastest lays of my life, I feel like I've run a marathon. Or played center in two exhausting games. I assure myself my haste was brought on by the fact that her boyfriend could have broken down the door at any minute.

I left her with the truth. "I never shy away from a fight, but don't want to be the cause of one, babe." Refusing to let her type her number into my phone, I convinced her she's permanently stored in my memory. What a pair of dumbasses we are: her for believing I'll call. Me for thinking about her now.

Then I examine my conscience with honesty. You're tired of one-nighters, fool. Looking for something more ... permanent maybe? You're such an ass, Sinclair. Like Christian says, grab what you can when you can. And that boy does. With surfer looks, and just don't give a fuck attitude, he's got ladies crawling all over him.

Why do so many girls gravitate to guys who treat them like shit? Rubbing my chin, I shake my head. I might never understand the opposite sex. However, visual appreciation is another matter.

An arm resting on the long granite island separating the chef's kitchen from great room, I tune out obnoxious voices, enjoy the music in the background, and let my mind wander. Wonder where the night will take me.

My eyes flick over the multitude of liquor bottles that have been lined up. Some full, some already drained. Turning to a keg in the corner, I grab a cup, press the tap, and hold tight until rich golden liquid overflows onto my hand. I down most of the brew, lick suds from my lips, then hold the cup under the spout for another round.

According to the dude standing beside me, who's in the middle of the process I've just completed, we've got less than twelve hours to drain this keg. To retain the quality of the beer. What is he, a distributor?

"I doubt that'll be a problem," I say with a chuckle, before showing him my back.

My eyes return to the liquor bottles. Will this be just another *wasted* night? Finding myself in one of the bedrooms with some chick's legs wrapped around me, lips teasing, exploring, mine not really tasting. Will the *someone special* I have in mind be here to make this night worthwhile? Or will this be just another Trent-like fiasco, meaningless, leaving trails of vomit rather than paths to an earth-shattering promise.

Glancing around the room, I see the same faces I see in school five days a week. Before I consider ditching the party, I force my thoughts to shift back to the main reason I have come here. I might be a senseless romantic, but I'm searching for something extraordinary. Something to capture my mind, my soul. Take me from this mundane nothingness to a place beyond any red-blooded guy's imagination, or dream. Her face springs into mind. Actually, it's been here all along. It's just more vivid now that the *right time* is near. And if she shows, I have no doubt, the timing *will* be perfect.

I agree with some guy's assessment of the Yankees, only half listening to what he's saying. While I slug more beer and analyze. Zoe is the kind of girl who adds something special to your life. Something you didn't know was missing, not until you sank into her soft blue, knee-buckling eyes. The power in her eyes could stop a heart: mine. Right now, my emotions are percolating.

I'm waiting. I'm tiring. I'll give her a few more minutes, then I'm mingling. At least find something to do so the entire night isn't a loss.

I pull my phone from a pocket and scroll through some messages, occasionally glancing at the doorway. One minute the space is empty. The next it's not. And I do a double-take. Because, as if by magic, Zoe is here. Or about to be. She stands at the doorway, a look of uncertainty shadowing her face. Unaware that I'm even breathing, frozen to the spot my numb body is occupying, I stare. At least my churning butterflies respond. Teaching me new sensations. They're standing at attention, dying off one at a time, while I come to life. Or maybe they've choked to death, because my stomach is beginning to seize.

I'm not sure how to approach this situation. Things don't look like they'll be going as planned: Zoe would walk through the door, all adorable and giggly. I'd be standing a few feet away. Her eyes would reach mine, giving me the perfect opportunity to walk right up to her. Laughing too. Asking, "What's so funny? I'm glad you came. Come on, I'll get us some drinks. Show you around."

Zoe doesn't step through the doorway, however, with her usual grace; she's shoved by the bodies pushing into the room behind her.

Immediately, I gauge her face. She doesn't look happy. But she looks breathtaking. Which I'm good with, for starters. She's here. That's all that matters. I'll have her busting her sides with laughter. After we kiss or before? Decisions.

Zoe is like a sudden storm that charges the air, leaving it sweet and fresh. Clean. Plain and simple, Zoe is pure energy. I've been attracted to girls before, but never like her. Never this intensely. Even if she doesn't know you're alive, Zoe is someone you watch out for. Enjoy watching. Look forward to sharing things with. Cars. Motorcycles. Movies. Conversation. Life, and so much more. My thoughts are enough to make my stomach fall ten floors, on the way down, filling me with too many butterflies to fit my internal space. Mostly, I'm garnering hope that she'll be more approachable in an atmosphere like this than in the halls of Jefferson.

Her wavy blonde hair is full and pinned up on the sides. Barrettes sparkle when she moves. Her jacket clings to her chest, wraps her narrow waist and hips that look to be the perfect size for the palms of my hands to rest on when I pull her against me. When I'm loosening her up enough to make her feel at ease with me. I don't care how she treats the rest of the world. I just want her to be comfortable with me.

I slide my phone into my pocket. Hands swiping through my hair, my eyes are pinned to her face. Christ, she looks so hesitant. Let down your guard, I want to send out a telepathic message. Give yourself a chance. Us. Don't disappear, girl. I'm on my way.

Before I am able to plow through the crowd, Zoe and Delorese blend with the others. There are too many heads in the way for my stare to track them.

I wonder if a couple of guys have swooped in on them. I couldn't blame them. I revisit the keg, draw another beer, and start trolling the room, in search of Zoe Channing, the girl I'm totally infatuated with. I'm about to be the guy who makes Zoe smile. Who *claims* Zoe.

They surface on the other side of the room. Zoe is definitely a knockout. I watch jaws drop as she glides through the sea of bodies, pressed to Delorese's side.

Stick to the plan. Wander over. Say hello. Don't blow a perfect opportunity.

My heart keeps beat with her movements. Dee marches ahead and Zoe pauses. Like radar, I hone in on her.

Moments before I am able to intercept my target, the two girls disappear into the crowd again. One hand stuffed in a pocket, the other holding my beer, I crane my neck to see over heads, around shoulders, through the space left by girls and guys already dancing on furniture. "Thank Christ this isn't my house," I mumble as I slowly cut a path, eyes raking over the room.

You're not making this easy, Zoe.

Zoe is eased into a corner. A girl like her can't be hiding. I think she's calculating her next move. She wears every emotion on her pretty face, and in her captivating eyes. Immediately, I know something is off.

I can't say she looks exactly frightened, maybe just not ready to mix with a bunch of shitfaced losers. What does this say for me? I set my cup down on the nearest table before proceeding.

The two girls stand close to one another, almost merging as one. Dee has an arm around Zoe's shoulder, a hand cupped to her ear. I'm trying to figure out what they're scheming. Convinced Dee is coaxing Zoe into talking to Zack Benefield, who's standing only a few feet away, openly staring at them. Gawking is more accurate. Zoe lights up the room. What guy wouldn't want to call her his own? The thought makes my legs move faster as I push through couples dancing front and center, injecting myself into her space.

I don't move right in on her, of course. The last thing I want to do is look like a stalker. Worse yet, desperate. The thought makes me nervous. Doubtful. Then, like a much needed shot of reinforcements, her eyes casually brush over me, and lock on mine before quickly flicking away. Delorese taps her shoulder, whispers in her ear again. Zoe's head jerks up, and they both stare across the room at Benefield. They smirk, as if sharing a private joke. He's a point guard and in a rock band. There it is. One of them is about to hit on him.

Before either girl can take a step, I make my move, angling my body, blocking their view.

"Hey, Delorese." Going for casual, I reach for her hand, slide my palm over hers. My eyes drift to Zoe and remain there. Burning. Devouring. Telling her things I hope. Things my voice cannot express at this very moment. She's pinned me. I couldn't drag my gaze away if I tried. And I'm not about to. I must be so obvious. Zoe's eyes widen, shooting sparks of curiosity. Along with something else I can't put my finger on. She's making me uneasy. Good uneasy. Rocky uneasy. I manage to shift my attention back to Dee. "Hey girl, good to catch you out of class."

I'm a dead giveaway, so bad that Dee rolls her eyes and releases a drawn out, "Ugh," while I hold in a groan.

I smile. Zoe half smiles. "Hey," I use my smoothest voice. The one that always gets me exactly what I want. "What are you pretty things up to." Pretty things? Holy shit, what's wrong with you, Sinclair? "Great night. Epic party, huh?" My hands slide through my hair, then fall back into the pockets of my jeans.

"Zoe," says Dee, "You remember stagehand Jesse, right?"

"That's me," I assure, shifting from leg to leg, "stagehand Jesse. Need a prop? I'm at your service."

"Sure," Zoe replies idly as her fingers gracefully check the position of her earrings.

"Where's Jamie tonight?" Dee shows such interest in her dark eyes, it irks me.

I shake my head and pull my mouth into a sarcastic frown, annoyed that just about every girl I encounter asks about my brother.

I shrug. "Slumming with one of his harem, no doubt."

Zoe lifts a brow and angles her head, while Dee laughs knowingly.

"You've probably never heard about my bro," my gaze is glued to Zoe's striking blue eyes, "being that you're a– that this is your first year at school." I shift my weight to one leg, bracing for a letdown, cocking a hip to preserve my alpha.

She scrunches the side of her mouth and her brow lifts higher. "Uh, yeah." The *yeah* is drawn out, telling me she's wondering what I'm up to.

"Jamie graduated a couple years ago."

"Oh." Her indifferent reply makes me feel inadequate.

"Yeah. My brother has a rep I take the blame for." I chuckle.

"You're not kidding," Dee chirps. "He's got a rep ... and he delivers." She flutters her brows. "So *where* is he again?" Her smile is devious.

"Sorry. I'm not in charge of his itinerary." I jerk my head to relocate a lock of hair that's fallen close to my eye. "And if I were, I'd spare you the sordid details." I wink.

"Ass." Dee smacks my arm and focuses on Zoe. "I'll get us some drinks. Back in a few." She turns to leave, then swings her head around. "You're in good company." She winks at Zoe and dances in Benefield's direction.

I jump right in with my heavy hitting, previously practiced, pickup line. "You're great on stage. A real natural."

She rolls her eyes. "Thanks."

"You look right at home out there. I couldn't remember all those lines, much less act in front of an audience. Takes courage."

She shifts her stance. Grips her forearm with her opposite hand. "I'm not sure it's courage. I just like it. I get carried away, I guess." She tosses long strands of her hair which have worked their way over her shoulder, behind her where she seems to want them. "Into another world. A place you can be what you want to be."

"I know just what you mean. It's an escape. You have an awesome voice."

She squints up at me. "Are you an understudy for someone?"

Doesn't she know I hang around rehearsals because of her? If I were an understudy, we'd be rehearsing together. Among other things. Standing this close motivates me. "I could be. Want to run some lines?"

She looks befuddled. Her lips part, but nothing comes out. Just a well-aimed breath that ruffles her bangs.

"Where's your guitar? You could play the party tonight." I offer my most disarming grin. The one that usually works like a charm. "Where'd you learn to play like that?"

"I just picked it up over the years."

"Picked it, huh?" I tease. "Over the years? What are you, thirty?" I chuckle.

She offers a small smile, turns her head as if to scan the room, then targets me again with her killer gaze. "I think we're in the same Art Appreciation class."

Grinning, I tug my earlobe. "I know. I sit a few rows behind you." My tongue somehow clucks without my approval. "I've been wondering if you'd ever turn around."

She pulls her jacket tight, her crossing arms securing it. With a tilt of her head, she nonchalantly states, "We never spoke in class. How come?"

I spread my arms out. "The moment the bell rings, you do a disappearing act. You don't give a guy a chance."

We both laugh. Stiff. But it's a start.

"Are you really into art?" I ask.

Lifting a brow, her mouth pulls to the side. "Why?"

"You don't show it. On the brag wall, I mean."

Her silence is unnerving.

"That was meant to be a joke."

When she still doesn't laugh, I'm about to walk, but freeze in step when she says, "You are. I've seen some of your work. You're very good."

I don't know why, but I bow, which is apparently a tension breaker, because she lets out a genuine laugh. I never noticed her dimpled cheeks before. Maybe she just never smiled this broadly. Score one for me.

"You'll be graduating soon, right?" she asks, gaze shifting.

Trying to track her intended target, my reply is distracted. "Yep. A couple of months and they'll let me back out into society."

Her gaze returns. She offers a smile, accompanied by a brief chuckle. Her full lips curve just the right amount to form a pout. Irresistible "You should laugh more often. You're beautiful."

Her shoulders twitch, as though a chill just shot through her, then stiffen.

"Sorry. I didn't mean to make you uncomfortable. I'm known for saying what's on my mind."

She studies me for a moment. "You don't have to apologize. Honesty is good, Jesse."

When she says my name, the chill runs down *my* spine. A sinking feeling hits my stomach, as if the floor just opened up and is about to swallow me ... like her steady blue gaze.

"Thank you for saying that," she says quietly. Her fingers inch over the buttons of her jacket, until she chooses one to twist.

"You don't have to thank me. It's true. Every guy in this place knows–" Stop right here, fool. Why not just offer to introduce her to every shithead here? "Why don't you give me your jacket. I can hang it up over there." I hitch my head toward the spacious entrance foyer, which is bigger than my bedroom. "It's hot enough in here to suffocate. I could use some air. How about you?"

After a moment of thought, she begins to shrug the jacket off, but gets no further than slipping it an inch or so from her shoulders. I'm dumbstruck by the top she's poured into. Actually, by what's inside the top she's wearing. Filling it out fabulously. Now I'm getting even hotter. I've got to do something quick, before perspiration starts trickling down my neck.

"You want to get out of here or what?"

Her eyes widen. "What?"

"Outside I mean. In the yard. It's cooler out there. Why don't you give me your jacket to hang, so you can get more comfortable?"

She shoots me a harsh stare, as if she's about to scratch my eyes out. Wraps the jacket tighter around herself. Her nostrils flare when she draws in a breath. "I'm fine," she says, chin lifted, eyes boiling.

If any other girl treated me this way, I'd turn around, walk away, and never look back. But I get the feeling, even though the icy surface has been cracked, Zoe is as reserved as a girl could be. Maybe this is why I want her more? Maybe not. For certain, it might take some doing to break through her shell, but I'm willing to hang around and be the guy who wins the game. Or at least, scores. Hopefully for more than just one night.

I figure if I get her away from the crowd, she'll relax and fall into irresistible me. Sliding my hands through my hair is my way of coping with stress. I do it often. Tonight is no exception. "Okay. Well, how about taking this *conversation* outside? It's cooler and a whole lot quieter. I'll show you around. Trent's backyard rocks like a resort."

Her eyes sweep the room again and she grimaces. "His entire house rocks like a resort."

"I guess Dee isn't going to make it back with those drinks. I'll grab us a couple cans of ... I'll get you a soda," I grin, "and we can–"

The look on her face slams me like a balled up fist. I'm not sure if I insulted her with offering a soda, instead of a beer? Or if I'm just coming on too strong. I could use a brew right now. But I'd almost settle for a soda if it makes her more comfortable. Almost.

Her eyes scroll over my face and touch my neck, then she gazes up and shrugs. "I guess," she says, her smile somewhat pasted. "I don't see Dee anywhere. Maybe I should find her before I leave. Tell her where I'll be."

"I'm sure Dee can take care of herself." I grin. "We'll catch her later."

When her brows lift and lower, I feel the concept seems to satisfy her. "So that's a yes?"

"Yes." While she nods, she eases out of her jacket and hands it to me, kind of like she's entrusting me with her safety. Her movements are smooth. Graceful. Watching the fabric slip down her arms, baring inch by inch of soft-skinned shoulders, I wonder if she realizes how seductive she looks.

My voice is firm. "Don't move. I'll be right back." I'm gone in a flash.

I slide her jacket between the tons of sweatshirts and other stuff cramming the closet, making space so hers isn't crushed. Cruising back to her side, I cup her elbow and guide her to the kitchen, where I grab another beer before we exit the house through a glass sliding door and walk out into the yard. Over two acres are landscaped with shrubs and flowers, which makes it inviting.

Intimate. The balance of the Holloway property is part of the thick forest surrounding us. In the most private part of this yard is where I plan on utilizing every ounce of the charm I've been blessed with.

"It's good to get out of there for a while," I say, expanding my lungs with clean air. "Fresh air makes me hungry. Maybe we can get a bite to eat."

"It's nice," she replies, distancing herself enough so that I can watch her from behind as she walks. Without her jacket, her curves are tempting. "I'm not hungry," she tosses over a shoulder. "I had a late dinner."

"Maybe later."

The darkness is seductive. The wheels in my head start spinning, which causes my stomach to do all sorts of crazy things. Can a stomach thud, or is it my heart? My chest is aching. Aching like my arms that hang at my sides. My arms that have one purpose tonight. To lead Zoe into a secluded corner, hold her lightly at first, then possessively as my lips crush hers. I want to do so many things with her. To her. Kissing her within the next five minutes is exactly how I plan on starting. If she warms up, that is.

I can wait. I say this with all honestly, because I admit to myself: this is what you've been looking for. The pint sized girl looking the other way. The feeling in my heart tells me this is what it's all about. The bells ringing in my head convince me it's so right. She's right. I'm filled with anticipation. These feelings are foreign to me, and have caught me off guard. Know it or not, this girl is throwing me for a loop. Making me realize, there is so much more to life than the very strong physical attraction I'm feeling.

"Let's check out the pool." My fingers lock around her slender arm, slide to her wrist, and her hand is suddenly captured by mine. I've wanted to hold her hand. Bring it to my lips. Romance her until she falls into my arms again. Willingly this time. I enjoy the feel of her hand in mine. Soft. Gentle. I want to feel more than her hand. I guide her around the patio, to a row of lounge chairs. "Leave it to the Holloway's to set the place up like a country club. Ever sunbathe in moonlight? How about a moon tan?"

Her hand withdraws from mine. Slowly, but deliberately.

"Impossible," she says, her voice stronger now. "It takes a certain amount of ultraviolet light to make your skin produce melanin."

I can't believe she's taking me seriously.

I'll be needing the freedom of both of my hands to show this girl what she's been missing, so I set my beer down on one of the boulders lining the path,

"Thanks for the science lesson." I slide an arm around her shoulders and am hit with wave after wave of her intoxicating perfume. Flowers and spices? I'm not sure, but the fragrance is amazing. Resting my head close to hers, I point up at the sky. "Check out the moon you've just dissed. You can't see all of it through the trees, but it sure as hell lights up the place." My hold on her tightens. "By the way, you smell delicious."

When she gazes up at me, my legs weaken. I argued for butterflies, but agreed rubber legs were reserved for girls. I'll have to tell Christian about this. Tonight, I'm learning more than I have in the last five of my seventeen years. Yeah, twelve year old boys are the worst. Testosterone overload and curiosity. A dangerous mix. Judging from the tightening of my crotch, I'm realizing I haven't evolved much over the last few years.

The message her eyes are conveying says she's fragile, struggling, desperately wanting to run across the highway, but afraid of getting hit by traffic. Trucks. No, it's stronger than that. She's afraid of standing out here with me. Being hit by an asteroid. That's the feeling I'm getting.

Gazing deeply, I'm convinced she's for real, and not just putting on an act of innocence. I'm not sure if this puts me at ease, or causes confusion. Do I want to go that route? Innocent, I mean. Am I physically able to go that route?

I'm thankful for the insect sounds that break the silence. My train of thought. This girl is beginning to make *me* nervous. And she doesn't want that. I'm sure I'd act on impulse. Or instinct. If I become mindless. Which I feel incredibly close to becoming.

"Okay. Sitting for a while would be okay," she says, plying herself from my grasp. "The gardens are pretty." Her hand circles in a series of pointing motions. "That one reminds me of mine. My mom and I plant every spring. The bushes are already budding. Summer is close."

"The roses you mean?" Reaching for her hand again, I pull her back but not quite against me. Not yet. I gaze down at her. "My mom was into gardening too." My arms go around her waist, and I urge her into a slow dance. Even though the music surrounding us is fast. Although she doesn't bolt, she holds her body a safe few inches from mine. So all that's really touching is our breath, and the electricity I hope we're creating. I know I'm feeling it. "Maybe the moon can't produce melanin, but it's sure as hell making your eyes sparkle. And you have the most beautiful eyes, Zoe."

Even in dim light, her blush is detectable. She escapes my embrace, does a side-step, and turns her back on me just as quickly. I watch her profile as she examines the water with her "Angel eyes." I take a deep breath. "Did I really just say that?" I feel like I'm in training. Without trying, she's molding me. My hairline is damp, yet the breeze is washing over us. "Are you cool with sharing a lounge chair?" I consider sliding onto one and patting my thigh for her to join me. Which is what the girls I go out with would normally do to me. Being with someone passive is new to me. Arousing.

Night couldn't shadow her face more than her expression when she says, "Maybe I should go inside." I'm not sure if she's annoyed with me, or herself. But she's no longer passive.

"No. Wait." I slide a single chair toward her. "Here sit. I'll grab another."

I can see that I won't be needing both hands for quite some time. After retrieving my beer, I drop into the chair I had planned on sharing, and balance the warming can on the armrest. I sprawl and I stretch. Emit a throaty, caveman-like groan. Low, but I'm certain, audible. And I watch her. Wondering if she's going to decide to join me, or leave.

Zoe does not use the additional chair I've offered. Instead she paces, now and then pausing to turn. And when she turns, my eyes follow the movement of one sleek leg peeking through the slit in her sexy skirt. Keep moving. Turning. Unlatch your arms from your chest. So I can admire every last mouthwatering inch of you. Tonight is going to be stored in my mind with the best of memories. Forever. I feel this way because I'm not sure about her. I'm not sure I'll ever be able to get any closer to her than I am at this moment. Me in my chair. Zoe in hers. Two feet away, if she ever sits down. And I'm sad.

To add insult to injury, before surrendering to the chair, she slides it an additional inch or two away from mine. My eyes bypass Zoe, aiming straight ahead at the light coming from the kitchen door. At the bodies molding together. Wishing it could be this way for us. The heat of her stare competes with the lovers on the back porch, the ones that move as one. So I turn to confront her.

The problem is, Zoe is the one who turns confrontational. She snaps the chair up from its reclining position and drops onto the seat, crossing her arms, and her legs.

"Don't you go out with Claudette?" Despite the fact that I'm suffering from the first rejection of my life, I let out a laugh. Sarcastic. But a laugh just the same. "That would be Jamie. Well, used to that is. Claudette and I are just friends. She nags me for advice–"

"She wants you to help her get your brother back." She's blunt. "Right?"

"Something like that."

The staring contest begins.

"Will he?"

"Never happen. He's got a few others at the moment. Jamie's a ... you'd have to know him to understand."

"Maybe she'd like you to replace him. Ever think of that?"

I snicker. "Yeah," my words turn well-defined, "but it's not gonna happen. Not in this lifetime."

Her arms unfold, and I watch her bring her Pepsi can to her mouth. She barely wets her gorgeous lips, and in a second she's lowering the can to the armrest of the chair.

Exquisite comes to mind. But not what I imagined.

"What's wrong? Are you cold? Want something else to drink?" I prod, although I'm gearing up to excuse myself if she doesn't stop treating me like an intruder.

I slug my beer, crush the can, and drop my hands onto my thighs.

"No thanks. I'm fine," her reply is delayed.

"If you want to talk, I'm a good listener."

Her legs are still crossed, and I notice the slit in the side of her skirt exposes more of one long, smooth leg and part of her thigh, which raises my pulse. My hands itch to take a walk right up that leg and under her skirt.

She must read my mind, because she shifts positions in the chair, so she's almost full facing me and is completely covered. Her eyes are unreadable. "Why are you talking to me?"

My neck muscles tug with an automatic recoil. "What?" My fingers clutch the crushed can of beer I'd drain right now, if I hadn't just done so. This girl is full of surprises, and she's definitely getting the better of me. I've never had problems coming on to girls before. Challenge, runs through my head. She's not a challenge. She's a once in a lifetime. Maybe. I wonder if she acts this way with all guys. I try to decide: is she a snob, a tease, or just inexperienced and treading water?

"You have girls falling all over you. Why aren't you inside?" she shrugs her head in the direction of pulsing bass, rowdy voices and coiling couples, "having fun, instead of sitting out here with me boring you?"

"Boring? Seriously?"

"I'm not exactly the life of the party." She frowns and her head snaps to the side.

"I like what I see. Good enough reason?"

Her eyes attack mine. "What do you see?"

I slide off the chair to stand before her. Take her hands in mine and bring her to her feet. She's slight and somewhat fragile. Featherlike. Stunning. I'm sinking deeper. So deep, I'm about to drown.

Resting my hands on her shoulders, I gently position her so her back faces me; surprised she permits me to manipulate her this way. Considering what's gone on between us ... not. Not yet.

She could nestle perfectly against me; *could* is the operative word. My chin rests just above her head. I feel the electricity from her hair; maybe simply from being so close to her. The fragrance of her hair reminds me of the beach. All ocean and freshness. I'm lost in her scent; want to wrap my hands with her beautiful, soft hair, bring it to my face, touch it with my lips.

"What shampoo do you use? It smells amazing."

One sculpted shoulder lifts dramatically, but only her head twists around, furious, and there they are again, those big blue eyes, digging into my soul. "What are you doing?" she gasps.

As though I've encountered a red hot iron, and my fingers have been burned, I release her shoulders in less than the second it takes for me to digest the shock on her face. But I manage a grin. "I'm looking for your wings. Sidetracked by the smell of your hair."

"Seriously?" Her entire body then spins, and I believe I hear her first groan of the night. Soft, barely detectable. "Give me a break."

"Come on. Turn around," I tease, "let me see your wings." As I try to spin her again, my fingers slip from her shoulder, accidently grazing her breast, and I think she's about to faint or slug me.

"I'm sorry. I didn't mean to do that," I say, trying to deal with hands that are on fire. The sensation shooting through me is disabling. I want her. Badly. Which isn't going to happen. So I joke my way out of it. "Blame it on my clumsiness. Your wings. Whichever makes you happy." My hands fly into the air.

Sucking in her bottom lip, she says wryly, "They're just part of my act. You should know that. You designed them, didn't you?"

My brow goes up. "Oh, really? What's the rest of your act?"

"More importantly. What's yours?" Her eyes bore right through me, as though she's searching for something she's not sure can be found.

"You know," I shift my weight from one leg to the other, because my hard-on is growing painful, and I tug on my ear, "I see you up there on the stage," I shake my head with disbelief, "in the play. You're excellent, Zoe. I thought it would be nice ... you know ... to talk." The tone of my voice turns husky. "To get to know you and those ... angel eyes." My fingers trace her cheek, landing near her ear, where they twirl a lock of her hair. I've just taken one of the biggest chances of my life. She'll either run or fall into my arms. Yeah, I'm sure I'm that charming.

"You watch the play from backstage?" I watch the rise and fall of her chest. "I thought you set up and cut out. I never see much of you."

"Sure, I stay. I even know some of your lines. I like that song you sing. Did you write it?"

"I did." When she nods, her earring twinkles from beneath the long strand of hair I've been twirling. "For the play. But I write other stuff. Rock. You know?" As though an afterthought, she adds, "not metal or anything. Soft rock."

Soft. Mmm. This I can see. Taste. Feel. My tone drops dangerously low. "I figured you for folk." My other hand works its way from my pocket, to the shadowed side of her face, where my fingers tiptoe across her cheek to trace the curve of her delicate neck. "Talented." I'm taking a risk. Dropping into my zone. "Girls like you don't come along very often. Beautiful. Talented. Different."

"You think I'm different?"

"I do."

"Different how?"

"From the girls inside."

"What's wrong with the girls inside?"

"They're not you."

"How do you know who I am?"

"I have a good idea. Which makes me want to find out more." My lips are aching to drop onto hers, which are plump, moist. Just inches away.

She must feel it too, because she switches gears. "What will you do after graduation? College?"

"Art school."

"Nice." She lowers her eyes. Twists a sparkling ring on her finger. "Going away?"

"It depends."

Slowly, her eyes lift to mine. I'm so caught up in the moment, I'm sure the look on my face is far too intense.

"Depends on what?" Her voice is a soft whisper.

"On things that might keep me rooted to the area. You never know what might develop. When one explores their options."

"I guess one never knows what the future holds. Like ..." she sighs, "sometimes you think there's nothing but darkness. Then the sun breaks through. Unexpectedly. If you're lucky, I guess."

I'm not sure what direction she's taking. She's staring through me, as if talking to herself. Dropping into a place far too deep for me. I clear my throat and gaze up at the sky. "I might have to help out in my dad's garage. He's kind of retired." I search for a grounding force. Sure. A constellation would be appreciated. Better yet, a shooting star. "It's nice that you listen."

She angles her head.

"It's nice to have someone to talk to. You seem to understand things. Most girls want to party. I'm not saying you're not fun."

"I think you *could* be a good listener. Sometime." Her expression goes from grim to grin. "I think I know what you're trying to say. And I think it's great that you're concerned about your dad's garage."

"I worry about his health. I might have to stick around to run the place if it doesn't improve, and I kind of resent it. Do you think that's selfish?"

"Not at all. It's your future."

Our eyes lock tight. "I might want to stick around. For other reasons."

Her smile is slight, but thoughtful. "I almost didn't come tonight."

Now my head angles. "Why not?"

Biting her bottom lip, she shrugs. "Personal stuff. I'm kind of glad I let Dee talk me into coming though."

"So am I."

Being here with Jesse, I almost forget who I am. He makes me feel safe. Confident. His compassion wraps me in a temporary state of amnesia. From a distance he gave me butterflies. But up close, he makes me tremble. In a good way.

I can't believe I'm standing out here, in the dark of night, with Jesse Sinclair. Not only is he willing to be seen with a freshman, he seems to be falling deeper and deeper into our conversation. Not in hooking up. He's actually left every other girl inside, to be out here with me.

Jesse acts like he doesn't know how popular he is. Maybe he doesn't care. He's serious and silly, too. He's fun to be with. And he's hot. Too hot for me. Still, I wonder what might have developed between us if ... if I was the girl I was a month ago ... before"

What's the use in what ifs? I'd date him. He'd leave for college. Break my heart. What would be the point? What's the point now? That's just the point. There is no point. I want to laugh at the irony of it all, but don't want Jesse to get offended, or think he's standing beside some rich kid's Olympic sized pool with a psycho. Even if it's true. So I bite back my sarcasm, and tears that threaten to flow, because he's so nice. I'm so messed up, but doing my best to act normal.

He seems to be interested. Realizing just how interested, my limbs go weak. My stomach twists. My heart skips beats. God help me. Do I go for the ride? Maybe being with someone like Jesse would ease the pain. Emptiness. Turn me into normal again? Maybe he'd want sex. Of course he'd want sex! Oh shit. I could never have sex now. Maybe never again. I'm definitely attracted to him, but all I would want is to be held in his arms. Comforted. Like he'd really be satisfied with that? I'm damaged. Who could ever want me?

"What's in *your* future, Zoe?" he asks.

He looks so cute. Approachable. Touchable.

Stop it right now, *Peanut*: sarcasm whips through my brain. Cruel. My life is ruled by cruelty. Irony. Agony. I'm so close, yet deep down inside I know I'm not ready. There are no such things as miracles or instant cures for what's wrong with me. Not even Jesse can help. And it wouldn't be fair to him to even try.

You can't start something you know you won't be able to finish. The struggle inside me is getting the better of me. I turn and pace the length of the concrete pool patio, listening to the click of my heels. Insects in the air. Contemplating. Controlling the beat of my heart, the rubbery feel of my legs: my impossible desire for this guy.

"This water looks inviting. I love to swim. Do you like to swim?" I'm breathless, not from my rapid pace around the pool, but from being near Jesse. Fighting urges I'd never be able to cope with.

Jesse is on his feet, pacing me. But I'm all over the place, mind and body, so he's mostly following behind. His questioning voice reaching out to me.

"I hope you're not thinking of jumping in," he teases. "Hold up. You're wearing the patio out. Shortening the life of the soles of your shoes." He chuckles. "And mine."

His statements bring me to a halt. Embarrassed, I don't look at him. He steps in front of me and with the tip of a single finger, he lifts my chin. Gazes deep into my eyes. I permit my eyes the luxury of focusing on his lips. Only for a moment. They're parted. Ready for mine. My heart is pounding. God help me. Please. Through the surging blood in my ears, and music blaring from the house, I can barely hear him. But I watch the movement of his lips. And the moment is pure magic. I'm not Zoe. I'm someone like Claudette. I have no past. There's just tonight. No party. No one else in the world. Just Jesse and me. Me and Jesse. And I'm about to be kissed like a woman. Treated like I'm something precious. He needn't say a word. It's all in his eyes.

He brushes a lock of hair off my forehead, his finger tracing the strands to my cheek, tucking it behind my ear. The tip of his finger trails my neck, ever so lightly.

"I've been wanting to talk to you in school, but there's never been time, or opportunity."

"Yeah. We're all pretty busy, I guess," I hedge, attempting to lower my eyes, but his intense gaze has me pinned. I watch his jaw work. One eye twitches. He blinks. The tip of his tongue moistens his lips. Mine follows.

For a moment, all we do is stare. Barely touching, we breathe and stare. Then Jesse takes the leap. "Would you want to hang out? Maybe go to a movie sometime? Maybe a drive-in?" He doesn't wait for my reply. He's so boyishly adorable, I can barely stand to be this close. I so want to give in. Fall into his arms. Sob on his shoulder. Let our lips touch. Could he ever understand the knots inside my stomach? The hole in my soul? The filthy secret I will carry with me for the rest of my life? The one I don't feel I could ever share with someone like him.

"There's an awesome zombie flick playing at the Overlook. Double feature, actually. Are you into horror?"

I've lived through horror, I want to scream, and toss my head from side to side, attempting to shake out memories, misery, reality. But I'm too frozen to move, to speak.

The pressure of his finger beneath my chin increases, so I'm unable to lower my face, but my eyes take a dive. I'm staring at his chest which seems to be moving up and down pretty rapidly. Not as rapidly as mine, though.

"I..." I address his molded pectorals. The top four buttons of his shirt are open. His neck is smooth, thick. So masculine. Kissable. "Maybe we could, sometime." I force a backward step, and I feel his finger brush my cheek once more before his hand drops to his side.

My reaction, or lack thereof, has disappointed him.

Zoe, you are so screwing things up. Don't mess with this guy. He's too sweet. Should I tell him what happened to me? Yeah, sure. He'd run like hell. What do I do? What *can* I do?

I shiver and instinctively run my hands up and down my bare arms.

His warm palms replace mine. "You're cold." He slides his palms up and down my arms, gently, slowly. His voice is soft. Persuasive. God help me. I would love to turn the clock back. Then he'd see the real Zoe Channing. Not this shell ... this boneless jellyfish. The friendly, maybe even sexy girl inside this body that won't stop trembling.

His head lowers, angles, and as his face grows nearer, I close my eyes and wait. But he doesn't kiss me. Just teases me with his nearness. Oh God, he's experienced. For a split second, I imagine the slide of his lips on mine, the moist tip of his tongue. Then he breaks the moment. "Wait here. I'll get your jacket." His breath is warm, beer scented.

He's too close. I can't breathe. I almost succumbed to his charm and it's scaring the hell out of me. I thought I could but realize: I can't do this. No. No. No.

Avoiding his eyes, his tempting lips, I jerk away. I've just shut him down and am now about to deliver the ultimate insult. "That's okay. I should go back inside. Look for Dee." I pull my cell phone from my bag and check the time. It's not even eleven yet, but it feels like I've been with Jesse for hours. Nice hours. Fun hours. Forgetful hours. So involving, for a few moments I almost forget who I am. Why I shied away from coming to this party. To any party.

His hands fall and clap against his thighs and he takes a step back. An uneven breath flows through his lips. He runs his hands through the sides of his gorgeous dark hair. My fingers would love to tangle in it. But that's impossible. Life is impossible.

"I hope I didn't give you the wrong impression," he says, his tone soft, pressing. I'm surprised he's not angry. Disgusted with me, like I am with myself.

"No. You're really a nice guy, Jesse. It's just that–"

"You have a boyfriend. Of course." His head jerks to the side. His jaw works hard.

I long to reach out and touch him, bring his face back to mine. Explain that I'm incredibly attracted to him, but I'm afraid if he came too close, I'd fall into a nightmare and scream. Frighten the hell out of him. Me. "No. It's just ... complicated."

"It's complicated." His head makes a series of deliberate and very slow nods. "Famous last words."

I can't take anymore. Of Jesse. Of me.

Like a frightened forest creature, I bolt. Without looking back, I rush toward the kitchen door, almost running out of one of my sandals as I take the steps two at a time. A guy on his way out the door steadies me when I almost fall into his arms. He takes advantage of the moment and pulls me against him. "Would you look what heaven just dropped on the porch?" His breath is foul with liquor and garlicy junk food that's heaped in bowls placed all around the house.

"Back off!" Guttural. I sound wounded. I sneak a quick survey of the area. Is Jesse watching? Following? My heart thuds. My hands shake. My thoughts spin out of control.

"Gladly, bitch," he growls. Abruptly released, I'm thrown into a group of others who laughingly push me off. "She's trashed," one slurs. "Out of her mind."

"Look who's talking." Controlling my voice, I manage my defense.

When I hear a deep voice proclaim, "Look who I'm about to carry upstairs," my heart almost stops. It's Trent, holding a quart bottle of Jack, and he's staring straight at me.

Trent doesn't move. He just watches and sneers as I am turned into a bean bag toy, tossed back and forth as a laughing voice warns, "Don't puke on me."

They don't realize how close I am to vomiting. But not from being tossed around.

My chest is throbbing, so my heart must not have stopped after all. My eyes strain for the sight of Dee.

After a jog around Trent's wooded backyard, I'm able to release some of the tension this thing with Zoe has built. I fucked up. Scared her off. I'm not exactly sure why, or how it went wrong. But it did, and the situation calls for a do-over. Tonight I'll leave her alone. Let her think about us. Me. Her perfect fit in my arms. The almost dance we shared. Almost kisses that would have fueled a rocket to outer space, had our lips had the chance to touch, while our bodies worked together. Zoe could never deny this. I saw the way she looked at me. Her eyes saying things her sealed lips would not. There was a draw between us. Something monumental, swift and promising. And I'm not about to let it go.

If not tonight, I'll approach her at school. On neutral ground. Backstage perhaps. But I'm not giving up. Now that I've made what I feel is a small crack in the wall she seems to have built around herself. Zoe is one complicated chick. One thing for sure, figuring her out will be anything *but* boring. I'm the guy to do it, if she'll just give me a chance.

Inside the house, the party is deafening. I have a few more beers. Faces blur, not from my alcohol intake, but from the smoke in the room. Clouds of it. Enough to taste, to choke on. The good thing is, none of us ever get behind the wheel when we're wasted. We all plan on crashing in the thoughtful tents outside. Possibly in every interior room. Nothing ... no one ... is off limits at Holloway's house. God help his house ... and the cleaning service when they arrive tomorrow.

My eyes water. My lungs burn. Obnoxious music, and my ringing ears between songs are wearing on my already raw nerves. I back into the same corner Zoe did, and I chill.

I leave my corner only to grab another beer, returning to find Christian standing beside a hot redhead. Wearing cutoffs and halter top, she's dressed for summer. I haven't had the pleasure of meeting her, which is surprising. She must have come with a friend. This must be the first party of Holloway's she's ever attended.

He's edging her into the refuge I claimed for my own. I look from face to face. Hers is set. His is dropping more and more with each shot he downs.

I realize he's fucking with her, and wasted out of his mind. I'm not sure if she picks up on this. He's telling her how seriously gorgeous she is. Asking if she models. Because he knows someone who could turn her into a superstar.

She tells him she's from Florida, visiting her grandparents, and a friend invited her here. She graduated high school last year, and yes, she gushes, telling him she's looking for an agent that will launch her modeling career. Something about her attitude tells me she's fucking with him too.

When I wedge myself deeper into the corner, resting a hip against the back of an easy chair, their conversation ends abruptly. Because Christian's eye catches mine.

"Hey," he says. Throwing an arm around me he hangs on my shoulder. "What's up, bro? Last time I saw you, you were carrying Claudette upstairs. What happened to her? Up there?" He flexes his brows. His grip on my shoulder slips and he begins to slide around me, as though I'm a pole on a street corner and he's the town drunk. "Shoulda called me for help. I'm good with inebriated females." His chuckle runs into a cough.

"You're sad, Jenkins. Who's your friend?" I feel like shit for the girl Christian is dissing, even if she's not the innocent she's pretending to be.

"Kirby."

"Hey, Kirby. How's it going?"

Her head jerks toward me and her green eyes widen. "Who's he talking about?"

"A friend," I reply and my gaze swings to Christian. "Christ. How much did you drink? Your breath is lethal, man." I steady myself on both legs, then I steady him, because he's swaying like a sapling in a storm. "Did you see me carry her back down, like about an hour ago?" I shake my head. "Of course not. Your head has been up your..."

Kirby is studying my lips, so I don't insert the word ass.

"No. I didn't see that part. What did you do? Dump her on the lawn?" he roars, "or in one of the tents. Maybe someone should go out there and check on her. Maybe I should."

I drag a hand down my face, then send eye signals to the furious redhead, telling her to move on. Don't waste her time. Christian is a douche when he drinks.

I cannot identify with him when he's like this. I don't ever want to be like Christian. Drunk and out of control. Using it as a morning after excuse for disorderly conduct charges, or waking up in another state, because someone played a joke on him and put him on a train.

I'm flippant. Expectant. Annoyed. Mostly, I'm scanning the room, looking for Zoe. I know I said I'd let things cool down, but knowing she's here, and I'm standing here without her, doesn't make things any easier on me.

"I handed her over to my brother. It's about time he takes care of his responsibilities."

Thoughtful, Christian nods. "True, man. So, Claudette's gone?"

With that, Kirby disappears. No good bye. Fuck you. She just splits.

"You're an asshole."

"What did I do?" His slackened jaws drops further.

"You're acting like a douche bag, Christian. That's a cool girl you just blew off for Claudette. Who's not even here. Who wouldn't give you the time of day if she was."

"Claudette's hot. I like her. What can I say?"

"Claudette's trouble. My advice is stay away."

"Look who's talking. You're hitting–"

A voice explodes in my ear. "Jesse James!"

I haven't heard that tag in a while. But I know what's coming. Groaning, I spin around to see my brother making his way through the party the way a boxer enters an arena. Shoulders squared. Head bobbing. Fists up and ready. Jamie is high fiving with everyone he comes in contact with. Hoisting girls up into the air. Kissing them on the way down.

I listen to a chorus of: Good to see you, man. Where've you been hiding? Got any weed?

Jamie has a girl under each arm. When he reaches my side, he releases them with a pat on their butts. Then he shoulder checks me. Sticks his face an inch from mine, and stares. "What's up little brother?"

All his breath smells from is tobacco. And since he's sworn off drugs since his last arrest, I believe he's operating in a normal state of mind. Normal for Jamie, that is.

"What are you doing back here?"

As if staring directly into his careless brown eyes isn't enough, his arm loops around and wraps me in a neck lock. "Your bidding, dude. Taking care of business for ya."

"I thought you were with Claudette." I personally set her onto the passenger seat of his pickup hours ago. Figuring he'd stay with her. Sober her up. Console her and deliver her home safely.

The fact that a vulnerable Claudette might be someplace alone, instantly snags Christian's attention. "Where'd you leave her off at?" he asks Jamie.

"Yeah. Where is she?" I cut in, inquiring for an entirely different reason.

"Don't worry. She's at the house. Resting comfortably." Releasing my neck, he slams his fist into my shoulder.

"You brought her to our house? She's sleeping there? What about Dad?" I shake my head. "I can't believe you."

His open palm slams my upper back hard enough to dislodge air from my lungs.

I rub the front of my neck. "Thanks for the makeshift Heimlich, dick."

His shoulder length hair clings to his forehead and neck. His cheeks are unusually red. With a room full of ladies, I'm not about to ask why.

"Like you said. She's my worry, not yours. Not Dad's." He runs his fingers through his clumping hair, loosening strands, which now hang in his eyes. Using his forearm, he brushes them from his face. "She's in my room. Sleeping it off. You can take her home in the morning."

"Me? Why can't you?"

He grins. "I'm heading back to Jersey."

"Greshan." I roll my eyes.

"Like that stuff, huh? Wanna join me?" His grin broadens. "I'm sure she could round up one of her stewardess chick friends to show you the town." He yawns. "If not, I know she'll accommodate your needs. She's a very accommodating girl."

"So I've heard," I reply sarcastically.

Christian's drooping eyes open so wide they bulge. You'd think Jamie was offering to split a winning lotto ticket. "I'm in." He jumps at the chance. "I'll go with you, Jamie."

Watching them walk away, my mind begins to taunt me. Nothing new. Right now it's telling me I'm a dumbass. I should be going to Jersey with them.

As the night wears on, the crowd thins. Bodies are strewn on the floor. Some make it to the backyard, some stumble to the tents. I search the remaining faces, but I don't see Zoe again until I hear a racket coming from one of the rooms off the hallway leading to Trent's father's library.

I make my way to the doorway, noticing the big oak desk has been shoved aside. The Persian rug remains, covered with bodies instead of oak clawed feet.

A tight circle of guys and girls sit on the floor where the desk had stood. They're laughing and joking. Leaning on one another. Sloppy runs through my head. Followed by fun.

Someone spins an empty wine bottle. Before the neck of the bottle hits their direction, couples are already sucking on each other's lips. Necks. Other body parts. If it were a movie, I guess it would be rated R. On second thought, when I see a girls top come off, then her pants, mark this room as X.

I stand and watch, not because I'm a creep, because I believe I should be in there, warming up for a hook up. If not with Zoe, then with the redhead from Florida. Who is nowhere around anyway. Which leaves me out on both counts.

The earlier rush of adrenaline has left me, along with any alcoholic effects, but my pumped up dick still hasn't recovered from its rejection on the patio with Zoe. When she shot it down. Shot me down. My dick wasn't even in question at that point.

The room is dim and chaotic. Dark and eerie is a better way

of putting it. Dark because the lights are out. Eerie because of the unnatural moans coming from corners I can't really see into. Ready to call it a night, my eyes take a final sweep of the faces I'll be seeing on Monday. At school. Where we'll rehash who did what with who. I hold back a laugh, realizing I won't have much to talk about. Other than my current experience as a peeping Tom. Christ is this night fucked up. Fucked over. Fucked in plain English. Fuck. Fuck. Fuck. Yes. Yes. Yes. I'd be happy to.

My eyes flash across a lineup of faces attached to bodies leaning against a far wall, where the hallway light paints them like ghosts. Is that Zoe? Unscathed by the party. Untouched by human hands. My mind spins. She's standing on the sidelines. Why? What the hell is she doing in here? With these animals? Zoe, get outta here. Let me take you home, baby. Let me bundle you into my car, hold you in my arms, let my roaming tongue do the things it's been longing to do, beginning with your luscious mouth.

Not far from where she stands, Trent sits, legs crisscrossed, eyes just about the same, and gazing in a stalker-like transfixed manner. This I can see because he's playing with a flashlight. Shooting the beam at the girls sitting across from him. Boobs and crotches are his targets.

When his head turns, it's easy to trace the path of his eyes. The bastard is flashing the light at Zoe, and his eyes are glued to each and every part of her. The beam runs up and down the length of her body. Flicking. Stalling. I wonder if she even realizes. This makes me nervous. Nauseous. Not from booze, but from worry. Worry about a girl who doesn't even want to give me the time of day. Not tonight, anyway. Tomorrow's another day. The butterflies fight the knots.

Fool, my mind says, and I want to leave, but I can't.

I don't think she notices me, but she must feel the heat of Trent's stare, maybe his flashlight beam, because her arms latch around her middle, attempting to cover what's beneath her clinging top.

I hate the discomfort on her face. I want her to smile. Not frown. *One jacket, coming right up, Zoe.* I want to shout to her, "Stay right there. Don't move a muscle. I'll be right back with your jacket and I'll take you home." But I hesitate to leave her. I lost her once tonight and don't want to lose sight of her again. Especially when she's in the company of wolves. And I don't like the look on Trent's face. Should I drag her with me? After what happened outside? What would Zoe do if I marched up to her and said, "Let's get out of here." What would Zoe say if I told her, "I'm the guy who's looking out for you."

These things and more, I mull over in my mind. As I stand here. Hands alternating between hair and pockets, pockets and hair. As I procrastinate.

Is she waiting for me? No such luck. More likely, she's waiting to get into the bathroom, where a line forms before the door. She'll be fine. I'll be right back with her jacket. Be her savior. Her friend. The one she confides in. The one to get her the hell out of here.

Okay, she's obviously been waiting to use the restroom, because the line is moving. She's taking small steps. Still hugging herself. Eyes front and center. Not speaking to anyone. The door opens and closes a few more times, now it's swallowing Zoe.

I make a mad dash to the closet.

Zoe

I wander through every downstairs room. Dee is nowhere in sight. Neither is Jesse. I want to go home, but I can't call my parents until I find Dee. On my way to the bathroom, I stumble over two sets of legs sticking out from behind a living room chair. A couple is making out hot and heavy. The guy's hands are under the girl's top. Their bodies are grinding. I can't tear my eyes from the way they're kissing. The passion they're creating is contagious. Their display isn't exactly what I have in mind. But all I know is I want to be with Jesse. Kiss him that way. I want to get over myself. Over the past. I can do this.

I notice a line building outside the bathroom door. I have to pee so bad, I squeeze my knees together. While I wait my turn, I consider searching for another bathroom, but find myself caught up in watching the tight circle of guys and girls playing spin the bottle in the middle of the floor. If they weren't slurring and pawing each other, they'd look like Kindergarteners.

Trent appears the most wasted. He's flashing a light around the room, at the girls and their body parts. I feel the light flick over me and my heart beats wildly. But it's my turn to use the bathroom, so I'm safe.

When I exit the bathroom, I instantly take inventory of the kids left in the library, wondering if Dee is one of them. This seems to be the area with the largest concentration of people. I don't see Dee, but my eyes freeze on something that causes my heart to turn over in my chest.

Trent is still at it. Teasing everyone. Being a fool. Only now he's worse. I watch in horror as he crawls into the middle of the circle, attempting to drag a girl with him. His muscular hands are under her armpits, and he's yanking her, his voice guttural as he says, "Heav ho. Somebody catch this on video. This is going on Youtube." He's disheveled, sweaty, a lock of hair falling over one eye. He loses his balance, and lands on the helpless girl who begins to moan. "Ouch!" she cries.

"Not yet." Trent emits a deliberate laugh that turns my stomach.

It's only been a matter of moments, still, I can't believe no one is even trying to help this poor girl.

Those in the circle fold over with laughter. I know the girl from school. I think her name is Elena. She's a junior. When she came to this place, I'm sure she never expected to be sprawled out on the floor, a limp bundle of arms and legs. Clothing soiled and abused. Eyes closed, she has no clue she's about to be exploited. Maybe violated. The thought of date rape sends a chill down my spine.

My stomach knots and my legs are like jelly. I'm dying to break them apart, pull her from his arms, save her from humiliation. Before I have a chance to consider the consequences, my body is in motion and I'm standing inches away, my knees in Trent's face. I can't fight the urge, so I knee him square in the nose. He's knocked off balance, a hand over his face, crying out. "Fuck!" Reaching down, I take the girl's hand, then an arm. Now I begin to pull.

"Come on. Stand up. Let's get you out of here." Is this my commanding voice? Is this me?

"Hey," Recovering his balance, Trent slurs, and we begin a tug of war. "Want to join us? Get the camera going. Zoe the ice cube is about to be melted down to my size." He laughs hysterically, eyes watering. He looks like a demon. His fingers lock around my wrist, and I feel myself being dragged down beside him.

"Let me go," I try to level my voice, to not create a scene. "You're drunk. Leave me alone. Leave her alone." I try to shove him away, shake free, but he's climbing to his feet. So now there's nothing to fight him off with other than words. I'm totally outweighed. Outsized. "Sleep it off, Trent!" My tone is urgent. "I'm not playing games with you."

He laughs. Hands innocently dropped to his hips, he looks as if he's about to help her off the floor. Slur some smart ass comment to me like fuck off, sweet thing. Instead, he turns frighteningly serious.

"Oh yes you are, baby." Before my mind can process, he pins me in a suffocating embrace. The next thing I know, I'm lifted off the floor, flung over his shoulder, and he's howling like a wolf.

"Let me go!" I scream, but no one seems to hear me, or care that I'm being tossed around like a sack of flour. Why should they care about me? They didn't even care about one of their own.

Laughter is louder than music now. I kick, beat his hard back with my fists, but I'm no match for his strength, even his pumped up strength. So I sink my teeth into his meaty shoulder.

"Bitch!" he howls. At the same time I hear a thud, I feel the impact of our bodies slamming into the wall. I'm upside down. My head is hanging, my pinned up hair dangling almost to the floor. As if the position I am in isn't compromising enough, I gasp with horror as, staring at his bare feet, I watch him open a closet door. Darkness. Isolation. We're inside. The door slams. A bolt clicks. The darkness is as suffocating as the lock of his arms. I am able to slide from his shoulder, onto my feet. But not from his grasp. The slide down his body has lifted my top, twisted my skirt around my hips. I believe I heard fabric tear. From hanging upside down, my head still spins. His hands are everywhere. His breath is so foul, I can't concentrate. Can't plan my next move. I don't have a chance to catch my bearings. For the blood that's pooled in my brain to right itself, flow back into a normal course. He's squeezing me so tight, I struggle for air.

"Please!" My gasp fills my ears, along with my pounding pulse. "Let me out. Someone let me out of here!" I sob. "Trent. Don't do this, Trent. Please."

I'm in the boiler room again. Imprisoned by the weight of a maniac as he slumps against the wall, with me beneath him. My attacker's alcohol breath is on my neck. His lips search for mine, then his slimy tongue slides down my neck as his body grinds against mine.

"Oh God. No. No. NO!"

Something pounds on the door. Angry fists. A demanding voice shouting, "What the fuck is going on?" This slackens the hold of the arms that are locked around me. The lips are lifted and slide across my cheek. Wet. Beer. Disgusting.

The fists on the other side of the door are so desperate, I'm sure the wood will split and whoever is out there will come tumbling into the closet. So I do my best to press into the wall and out of the way. But his arms keep finding me.

"Trent! Let her the fuck out of there! I'm gonna break your fucking neck." My spinning mind tells me it's Jesse's voice. Jesse's fists. It could be the swat team and it wouldn't calm me. I'm frightened, furious, kicking, punching. My moves are totally intentional. Going for his face, I try to scratch his eyes out. He's protected by his size. Filled with rage, I land a well-aimed foot in a soft place. Much closer to my reach. Trent's crotch, and he folds in half and grunts. Calls me bitch a few more times before I hear a click and the slide of the bolt.

The door flies open and Jesse is standing before me, wild-eyed, red faced, my jacket tucked under one of his arms. I don't stop to thank him or to snatch my jacket. I don't even turn when Jesse cries out my name. I run and run and don't stop until I'm out of that hell house and far enough down the street where I feel halfway safe. If safe is such a thing.

It's scary out here, and I keep reeling. Although Trent's house fades into the distance, I still fear he'll be coming after me. I'm holding something, relieved when I realize I had the presence of mind to grab my bag before taking off like a lunatic. Not my jacket though. And it's cold. Sliding my palms up and down my bare arms, I keep looking behind me. Around me. In circles I spin until I'm so dizzy I could collapse to the pavement.

Noises in woodlands are common, right? Small animals? Deer? Not maniacs. Please not him. My eyes play tricks on me. Forming undulating shapes, dissolving phantoms. When I close my eyes, I see splotches of red. Slashes of white.

Get control of yourself, my mind screams. You're on a dead end road, sure, isolated, unprotected, but you have left the danger behind. I don't see anyone chasing me, still, I can't control the beat of my heart which is about to pound out of my chest. My feet are moving again. I have no idea where they're taking me, but I have to stop running. Need to catch my breath.

Palms on thighs, I fold at the waist drawing rapid gulps of air. Damp and fresh, night air cools my sweating body and I begin to relax and focus on the situation I've found myself in – let myself become involved in. I'm not frightened anymore. I'm filled with anger. I hate the janitor. I hate Trent. I want revenge. I've had it with men. All men. I refuse to be a victim. Not ever again.

Once my heart rate slows and my breathing is normal, I pluck my cell phone from my bag which is crushed against my chest, and text my mother. PICK ME UP ASAP. I check the time. It's almost midnight. The witching hour. The time Dad said they'd come for me. Before I turn into a pumpkin. Or a witch. Or something gruesome. Like a corpse lying beside the road.

As I slip my phone back in its compartment, I notice the outline behind me. Wavering in the center of the road. Lightning fast. And I freeze. My heart picks up speed again. The figure is definitely running, in my direction. Toward me. For me.

A slumber party horror story comes to mind about a girl named Mary who is listening to the stairs leading to her room creak with each step of a knife-wielding madman. Haunted by the situation I've gotten myself into, I can't help but put myself in her shoes. My panic escalates, and the countdown begins:

Zoe I'm on the last step. Zoe I've got you! fires through my head like a jolt of electricity. The fear I feel is enough to make the hairs on the back of my neck stand up. That's when I begin to scream. Not only in my mind, but horrifying sounds rise from my throat, replacing the stillness in the air. Attacking my ears. Something tells me to run, and I do. In circles. Getting nowhere. So I dart across the road and huddle beside a tree. In my mind I am a tree. Part of the posted forest. Protected.

It is there that I crouch among branches, like a small part of the earth, waiting for Trent's flashlight. If I'm a tree he won't find me among thousands of others. Wait right here. And you will be safe.

My mind is in high gear, trying to figure out what to do. Grow into a mighty oak? Grab a rock? Stab him with a branch? Sink into darkness and remain a sapling?

When I gain the courage to sneak another look, I decide the loping phantom coming down the road is nothing more than a black thing lost in the night. Alone. Like me. I don't see a flashlight, so it can't be Trent. Could it be Dee? Of course! Dee's come to find me. Thank God, it's you, Dee. Thank God I didn't flee into the woodlands. You would never have found me.

A familiar voice shouts my name, breaking the silence. The tension in my limbs eases enough for me to unwind from my shelter. The male voice sounds urgent and breathless. As filled with fear as I am.

I no longer think with my brain, my adrenaline controls me. The jellyfish has grown some bones. The figure heading straight for me looks like something out of Animal Planet, with graceful but determined strides. I can't quite make it out! If it's an opponent, I'm so ready for a fight. I feel I could kick my way out of more than a closet right now. Bring it on! I say, my lips no longer numb.

As the figure approaches it takes shape. A beautiful shape. A welcome shape. Catapulting toward me with strides long enough to cause the body to tilt and roll head over heels, the sight strikes me as comical. But I don't laugh. I can't laugh. I'm too stunned. This has been one insane night. And it's far from over, because Jesse is suddenly standing beside me, folding almost in half, panting, head angled, staring at me as though I'm about to break.

Doesn't he realize I've already been broken?

"Zoe." My name is as subtle as the breeze stirring the leaves at my feet.

I can't reply: I'm stuck in a world of my own. A place where my mind is protected. I believe it's called de-realization. I'm desperately trying to snap out of it. To normalize. But I'm vaporizing. So the real *me* is no longer in danger. No longer able to function.

"Zoe, it's okay. It's only me, honey," Jesse wheezes, struggling to catch his breath.

Honey? He's trying to calm me. Doesn't he realize I've already calmed myself?

He's jabbering. Gaping. Hopping from foot to foot, like

someone does in the dead of winter when they're not appropriately dressed. But Jesse is dressed so nice. Perspiring, still desirable. Blue shirt, perfect fitting jeans. I notice this more now than in Trent's backyard. My mind is clearer, or has my brain jumped into a tranquilizing state of meditation? The air is his cologne. Surrounding me. Waking me. Grounding me.

Jesse appears desperate as he helps me to my feet. "Zoe," he whispers, then his voice pitches, and my head rocks as my body jerks. Jesse's hands are on my shoulders and he's shaking me, crying out, "Zoe! Answer me! Are you okay?"

"Jesse?" I reply, trying to get my bearings, because I'm too overwhelmed with emotion to comprehend what's happened tonight, or that Jesse is standing beside me.

"Holloway's an asshole. Did he hurt you?" His jaw tightens. I can tell he's restraining anger.

"No he didn't hurt me, and yeah, he's an asshole," I reply through chattering teeth, because I'm still trembling.

I feel my jacket touch my shoulders, then he helps me slip one arm in, then the next.

"This isn't how I envisioned tonight," he says softly.

"What are you talking about?" I say coldly.

"I wanted to. I wanted us to. I thought maybe–"

I feel he's about to reach out to me, but he doesn't.

Instead of holding me, or trying to kiss me, or explaining why he's stammering, he does the oddest thing. Odd, not creepy. Jesse could never be creepy. Jesse is handsome. Jesse is wonderful. Jesse is my understudy. He must be, because he is now singing my song from Fae.

My head is spinning and I feel absolutely drunk. What does a drunk do in the middle of the road in the dead of night?

Sing.

So I start singing. Between laughing and crying, I sing the lines of Fae.

Fear not darkness
the Fae will light your way
sprinkling stardust cross her skies
brightening every day

I sing along with Jesse, and we're suddenly nothing more than two people singing their hearts out. In the middle of a dark road. On the brink of hysteria. But only for a moment.

Jesse is the first to regain composure. He stops singing and watches me intently. I must be frightening him. This girl is not angelic Zoe Channing. The girl who fled the arms of a nice boy, only to become locked in the arms of a creep.

In that one moment of sanity. The one I experience between breaths as I choke out my lyrics, my mind will not let me rest. Exactly why did Jesse follow me out here? Certainly not to hurt me. This makes me happy. If not truly happy, at least relieved. He's my friend. Not boyfriend. Just friend.

And this I begin to sing. Replacing the Fae, I sing:

Jesse is my friend. We're just two people struggling to see through darkness. But your eyes are the sun. Even if mine are the moon and shadowed. I'd see you through midnight.

I have a notebook filled with lyrics at home in my desk, ready to be put to music. My mind is like a filing cabinet when it comes to music.

why can't I be
why can't I belong
so many things I wanna be
but it's impossible
just being me
is unbelievable
irretrievable

Watching me, Jesse is a blend of confusion and relief. Then he joins in, and we're both standing in the middle of the road, like two idiots, singing again. A variety of songs. Anything that comes to mind.

"Do you know this one?" he asks.

you're an empty sample
in a pressure sealed jar
examined by what you resist
feeling no need to exist

"I could have written it," I reply, joining in.

you can't close the book
or turn yesterday's pages
you can't catch a break
yet you can't fade away

Our shuffling feet drag along the pavement in a silly dance. Stiff. Like zombies. I figure he thinks I'm happy. I'm not happy. I've gone off the deep end and I feel like a raving lunatic ready for a final breakdown.

I belt out my songs with the small piece of heart that's left inside my aching chest, even play air guitar while I shout the chorus. Then I fall into Jesse's arms.

I pound the door with my fists. I'll kick it in if I have to. "Zoe! You okay? Trent, open this fucking door! I swear to God, you're a dead man."

After what feels like an eternity, the door flies open. Zoe is wild-eyed. Her skirt is twisted around her hips, the soft fabric of her top is stretched and hanging loose around her slender waistline. The neckline bares one creamy white shoulder, imprinted with red blotches from where she was restrained. This I notice, because with each beat of my heart I am taking in every inch of Zoe. Examining her for damage. Before I can stop her, she bolts past me, sobbing. For a moment, I'm speechless, because a girl half my size has almost knocked me off my feet.

My first instinct is to chase after her, make sure she's okay, but when I visualize what he might have done to her, I'm filled with adrenaline I need to work out of my system. Trent is on his knees in the closet, laughing like an idiot. "I was only fucking with her. I wasn't gonna hurt her. Christ, that girl is one unfriendly bitch." He stares up at me with one eye open, the other shut. "Hey, man. At least I got her to show some emotion."

I don't take the time to think. I react. I grab the collar of his shirt, yank his face up and level with mine, draw back and pound his jaw with my fist. His eyes roll up into his head and he sinks to the floor.

My boot finds his side. "You're not worth my time, douche bag. Zoe better be okay, or I'm coming back and finish this." Through gritted teeth I add, "You're lucky I'm in a hurry."

Clutching Zoe's jacket as though it's her, I ram my way through the front door, unsure of the direction she's taken. Surrounded by forest, it's pitch black outside. I jog down the driveway, out into the road. Left leads to the circling woodlands. So I take a right, and I run. I run like my life depends on it. Zoe's might. This makes me run even faster.

I think I see her up ahead. Exerting every ounce of energy my legs can withstand, I shift into full speed, my feet skimming the air more than the pavement, chugging until my lungs feel they'll burst. I'm making incredible headway, but when my target doesn't move, I realize I'm closing in on a street sign. Dead End Ahead

And so I run. I jog. I sprint until my knees are about to give out. But it's the blood curdling scream that takes me to her. My legs can't keep up with my mind. Zoe's in trouble. Zoe's being attacked. Zoe is freaking out. As I grow closer the screams stop. A figure runs in circles then darts across the road.

By the time I slide to a stop at her side, my head is pounding, my stomach is in knots. I'm mentally cursing Trent, absolutely positive I'll settle the score tomorrow. When he's sober.

"Zoe. It's me. Jesse," I call out a warning before reaching out to touch her.

"Jesse?"

"Yeah. It's me."

She stops crying, but is still trembling. Her eyes are glazed, barren.

"Here," I extend my hand. "Your jacket."

When I try to drape it over her shoulders, she backs away, eyeing me suspiciously, then finally lets me help her slip it on. "What do you want?" she says in a flat voice. This causes a fist to tighten inside my chest.

"Hey," I say, trying to calm my own voice. "Are you okay?" All the while my heart's drumming. I control my breathing as best as I can. "That guy's an asshole. Don't let him get to you." Pausing for a breath, I take in the heaving of her chest. "He didn't hurt you, did he?" Thinking of his hands on her, the finger marks on her shoulder, my stomach tightens along with my jaw.

"No he didn't hurt me, and yeah, he's an asshole," she replies through gritted teeth. She's pissed as hell. Who can blame her? But she's more than that. She's different. I don't care to wonder how or why, I just want to be with her.

After finally getting to know her tonight, darkness should bring us closer. I should have the right to reach out to her, pull her into my arms, touch her lips with mine. Finish our conversation. Begin a relationship. My mind whirls with things to say to this girl who's stealing the breath I've just recovered. I need to reach her: wants and words are just not working. She's slipping further away.

I have no clue why, but I start reciting the words of her song lyrics. Maybe I feel this is something Zoe can identify with. Something she loves. Something that will bring her back to being Zoe. Instead of a brittle statue standing before me. Cold as ice. Trembling hard enough to break.

trees not shed
the world needs your splendor
birds sing sweet and far
so the lost can find shelter

Her eyes widen. She must think I've lost my mind. Correction: we've both lost our minds. She slowly starts dancing around me, singing:

If you see a Fae you're forever blessed
She holds the lamp of kindness
An intriguing bit of magic
with a drop of human tears
Once your eyes have brushed her wings
you'll fall in love for years

"Now I know what your future holds, Nightingale." I chuckle. "Broadway."

"Nightingale? I like it!" She flaps her arms, singing out, "If I don't fly away, I'll be studying law."

"Ah. Nice to know."

"And why is that?" Dancing around me, she's breathless.

"If I ever need a lawyer, I'll know who to call."

"Oh yeah?" She comes to a halt before me. We're almost nose to nose, because she's standing on tip toes, attempting to stare me straight in the eye. "If I need an artist, I'll do the same."

Does she know she's doing things to me she might be sorry for? My breath comes faster, because I feel like I'm reaching out to touch an angel. Can a guy get this lucky?

She tumbles right into my arms, which naturally fold around her. She's soft, warm, and smells of honey and flowers. I'm balancing on a ledge, feeling lightheaded, ready for a risk.

I graze a finger along her throat. "Hmm," I hum to the side of her neck.

"What?" she says, somewhat defensive, drawing back, so I guess I should explain myself.

Taking her hand, one at a time I roll her fingers. They're cold. I'll warm your fingers and toes and every other part of your beautiful body, and your mind. Cannot forget your beautiful mind. "No wonder you're so talented. Besides your throat," I press the same spot again with a light touch, "even your fingers are musical. Long, delicate, a reflection of your charm."

She smiles up at me. Dubious, but still a smile.

"Would you want to go to Prom with me?" I whisper directly into her ear.

Her face tips up to mine. She's exhausted from dancing. Hoarse from singing her heart out. Her eyes are sparkling. She snuggles deeper into my embrace. My chest feels the vibration of her words. Then once more her eyes are mine. "You're asking me to go to senior prom with you?"

"Yup," I grin. "You're angel eyes again," I whisper, brushing my cheek against hers. "I really like you, Zoe," my lips work around her ear, "so much." With a finger, I lift her chin for another glimpse into her eyes which are filled with passion, elevating mine. I want to kiss her, but don't think I can tear my gaze from hers. Watching her intently, I let my lips lower gently to hers, softly sliding my mouth across her cheek as I zero in on the base of her neck, which I begin to suck.

She jerks her head and yells, "What the hell are you doing?" Then bursts into tears. The next thing I know, we're in the middle of the road, me holding her up, her struggling to escape. Blinding headlights are aiming straight at us. I hear the screech of brakes, a car door slam. A man literally leaps out from behind the wheel and starts shouting, "Zoe! What's wrong, Peanut? Is this clown bothering you?"

When she says, "No Daddy," her voice shakes.

Daddy? From his behavior, I figured he is some kind of psycho.

"Get in the goddamned car, Zoe," he bellows.

In the glow of the headlights, I watch his face. It's red, his features distorted. I've never seen such anger over nothing in my life. If I didn't know I could handle myself, the man I'm facing would be frightening. I think he's about to take a swing at me. Throwing my hands up before me, I take a few steps back. He advances. If it wasn't for the fact that this is Zoe's father, he'd be laid out on the pavement by now. But for her, I suck in my pride and restrain rising anger.

Zoe is yelling, crying. "Daddy. Stop! Nothing happened. I'm okay."

She's throwing her hands around in desperation. He's growling. I'm about to shrink into the pavement I want to disappear into. Why did I even follow her out here? She's just a kid. No wonder he's going psycho. I should stick with girls my own age. Like Claudette? No freaking way do I want a girl like Claudette bending over for me every chance she gets.

The passenger door is flung open by a woman who jumps out as if the car is about to explode. She stomps into the middle of the road and grabs Zoe's arm, attempting to shove her into the back seat. Zoe's stare shoots from the two irrational people to me. She wraps her fists around handfuls of her hair and twists. She's in a wide-eyed state of panic. Holy shit. I want to bolt, but something holds me firmly in place. The look on Zoe's face. That's it. If she needs me, I'm right here. Not running for cover.

The scene is surreal. My mind spins, searching for reason. All I can think of is to repeat, "I'm sorry. Nothing happened. We're just friends."

"Mom," Zoe continues her tearful protest. "Make Dad stop. Make everything stop. Please make it stop." Cradling her head, she rocks at the waist, up and down, as though she's about to self-destruct.

I watch her cover her ears as if her mother's voice is breaking her eardrums. But it's quiet now. Zoe's sobs have glued their mouths shut, frozen everyone to the spot.

I continue to back away, and am now in the shadow of the

trees. "No sir." My voice sounds pathetically weak. "I didn't touch her. I swear."

I've blown any chance I might have had to date this girl. Her father hates me. "I know Zoe from school. We were just ..." I'm unable to finish explaining, because he sweeps her into the car as if she's a little girl, and I'm the big bad wolf that came out of the woods to eat her. The car doors slam, and the vehicle does a one eighty, then it disappears around the corner.

Holy fucking shit. I stand at the side of the road, shaking like the leaves on the trees in the breeze that's turned into gusting wind. I look up at the sky. The stars Zoe and I stood under only moments ago are hidden behind clouds. It's getting ready to storm. With an aching heart, I walk back to my car. I'm sobered by the night I've had. By Zoe. By my over-stimulated imagination.

Zoe

"**W**hat were you doing in the middle of the road?" Dad asks, his voice shakes. "Is that guy a friend of yours?"

"Was," I reply through gritted teeth. "My life is destroyed thanks to men. What the hell does it matter if Jesse Sinclair thinks ... knows ..." *He thinks I'm a whore. That's why he came after me. Tried to kiss me. But he asked me to Prom ... so he must really like me. Why? Why? Why did this have to happen to me?* I press my palms to my temples, wishing I could crush the misery from my skull.

"What men?" Dad is gruff. "I hope you're not including me in whatever is going on with you."

Mom cuts in. She's trying to control her tone, but it's not working. Her voice hits an unnatural pitch. Does she even believe what she's saying? "I'm sure your friend will understand your father's concern. He'll have more respect for you if he knows your parents–"

"I'm sorry, Peanut," Dad's voice overcomes Mom's. "It was a lousy night. I lost at cards to Carl. I hate losing to Carl. Then to top it off, I saw that guy's hands on you. And when you pushed him away. I just thought. Oh hell. I don't know what I thought. I saw red. That's what happened. No one messes with my girls." He chuckles.

How could he be chuckling? Why does he call me Peanut?

"Why are you so goddamned overprotective of me?" My voice doesn't sound like my own.

Mom gasps. Dad growls with shock. He almost sounds like he did when he was yelling at Jesse. "What did you say?"

"Jesse is a nice guy. Why did you act that way?" I'm me again, but with more determination.

"I know how guys his age operate." Dad's laugh is sardonic. Who is he tonight?

"Leave her alone, Grant. You've already upset her."

He's pissed me off so bad, I want to hurt him as much as he hurt me tonight. As much as that demon did. "Is that how you operated, Dad?"

"I just want to protect you. That's all." Dad's voice is edged with annoyance. "And no. That's not how I *operated*. What's gotten into you?" After a brief pause, he grudgingly adds, "I said I was sorry."

"Sorry? Is that what you said when you found out Mom was pregnant with me and that you had to marry her?" Once the dam breaks, I can't stop. "Is that why you became an alcoholic?"

The car accelerates and Mom starts to panic. "Grant," she begs, "slow down."

Mom slides around in her seat to face me. "Why are you doing this, Zoe?"

"Me? Do you think I'm stupid? I know I was born seven months after your wedding. I wasn't premature, was I?"

"Jesus Christ!" Dad yells. "What the hell happened to my daughter?"

"Zoe, what is it. You haven't acted right for days now." Mom turns around to settle back into her seat. "And to set the record straight, your dad proposed to me before I became pregnant with you." Her voice is firm but shaky.

"Does that settle it, Peanut?" Dad chimes in. "Can we go back to normal now?"

Normal? I need to get out of here. I can't take anymore. Run. I just want to run and keep running until this is over. Until I forget. Until I'm dead. Please let me be dead. The bridge is ahead. The span of lights glisten on either side of the car. Snaking. The lights. The road. Or is it my eyes? My head is swimming. Brain swirling. Every sick thought fights to cram inside my pounding head at once. My palms cover my ears, cradle my head. I beat my fists on the window. I can't stand it anymore. Anything. Nothing. Life. Sucks. Agony. The agony of being me is overwhelming.

"Peanut?" I scream at the top of my lungs. "I'm almost sixteen! I'm not your Peanut! I'll never be your Peanut again."

"You'll always be my Peanut." Dad sounds confused, close to tears as he tries to smooth things over. "But, I'll stop if you want me to. I'm sorry I upset you, Zoe. Embarrassed you. I'll speak to the boy. It's the Irish in me. Overprotective–" He forces a laugh. "You're my little girl, Zoe. I'd never let anyone hurt you."

"Hurt Me? Are you drinking again? Is that why you acted so weird back there? So possessive? Do you think I'm a slut you need to lock in a room?"

"Zoe!" Mom's head flies around. Normally the peacemaker, she's choosing sides. Even in dimness, the glow of anger in her eyes is evident. "Why are you acting this way? You owe your father an apology!"

From the back seat, I watch Dad's head shake from side to side. I can imagine what he's thinking. His voice levels with hurt. "I'll never drink again, Zoe. I thought we were past all that. I'm sorry for what I put you and your mother through. I don't know what else to say. Or why you're so upset."

The car falls silent. I imagine my parents are trying to figure out why I'm acting insane. I *feel* insane. Out with it! My mind screams. Now. You can't live this way anymore. Get the evil off your chest, the worms out of your brain.

"It's not you, Dad. It's not Jesse. It's me!" My head pounds with the beat of my heart as the pressure inside me builds. I'm not in the back seat of my parents' car. I'm in the boiler room. The disgusting man is hovering over me. His mouth is coming down on mine. I can barely breathe. Vomit rises to my mouth. I reach for the window control, feel the rush of cool air hit my face. Shout through the wind burning my eyes. Slapping me senseless.

"I'm not your Peanut anymore Dad! I was raped!" My ears echo with the cruel sound of my words. I'm shocked at what I just said. I planned on telling them. But not like this. *Oh my God.* I begin to shake.

I feel the car swerve as Dad's head spins around and his arm flies over the seat. "What? Who the? Tell me who, Zoe! Where did it happen? When?" His voice is ragged. "Was it that boy?"

He must be so shocked, he doesn't realize he's driving. Erratically! He'll kill us! The look in his eyes reminds me of something. Has he been drinking? Shoots through my head. Is that why he screamed at Jesse? His eyes are drowsy, watery. He jams a foot on the brake, then the car lurches forward. Several times this happens, causing the car to rock. It feels as if we're caught in a hurricane. Maybe a tornado?

I watch his hand close the space between us as he reaches out for me, staring into my eyes as though I've just shot a bullet through his skull.

Mom's gasp breaks what's left of my heart. The one that just burst and is rising up my throat.

"Grant!" Mom screams as she lunges for the steering wheel.

My mind struggles with confusion. I'm lightheaded. Brain

detached from body. Mom screeches, but the chilling sound is distant. Dad fights with the wheel: I catch a glimpse of his panicked face as he turns to Mom ... for help to stop the careening car? Helpless. We're all helpless. I brace for the impact. Pray for the car to make it across the bridge without wrapping around one of the iron girders; Colliding and scraping, it sounds like something tearing away the metal covering the outside of my door.

A flash of light breaks my trance. A horn blares long and loud, or are my ears ringing? *What's happening? My family is about to die. I'm about to die.* At the same instant jumbled images jar my shell shocked brain, I'm thrown back against the seat. I hear an explosion. My body is beaten, wedged between the seats, thrown. Gasping for breath, I try to grab onto something, but the only thing surrounding me is night. I'm freefalling through the air, in a tailspin, then there's nothing.

I drive. I think. My lungs work hard, inhaling as much fresh air as possible flowing through the open windows. After the night I've had, the wind hitting my face is almost as refreshing as a shower. I'm trying to clear my head. To figure out what just happened. What *did* just happen? Poor Zoe. I feel so bad for her. I hope things have calmed down with her parents.

The street I live on is silent, homes barely visible in darkness. When I pull into my driveway, a dog yaps in the distance. A halo of light trims the living room window, flooding my chest with a fondness only father and son could understand. Dad must have crashed in his favorite chair. He doesn't consider this waiting up for me. He calls it habit.

Entering quietly, I pass through the spotless kitchen and into the living room, following the cacophony of erratic snoring. There he is. Asleep in his recliner. I'm happy he's home from the hospital and feeling better. Is he feeling better, I wonder? He looks peaceful, but pale. His headful of dark hair is normally neat, but looks so damn bedhead right now, a sense of dread washes over me. With the bottle of pills on the table beside him, the scene is far too reminiscent of ICU. *Hang in there, Dad. Let your heart heal: from overwork, from losing Mom. I don't want to lose you.* Everything will be fine in the morning, I convince myself.

Sometimes I help him to bed, but tonight I decide not to wake him, so I just lay a blanket over his sweatpants and shirt, drop a kiss on his cool forehead, and snap off the table lamp.

Before showering I check Jamie's room. Claudette is sprawled across the king sized bed on her back, one leg bent at the knee, the other angling to the side. Dressed only in a t-shirt, she's wearing high heeled shoes, which has to be Jesse's doing. I shake my head. The last thing I want to do is disturb her, which could mean the difference between a decent night's sleep and enduring an interrogation: Why doesn't Jamie love me anymore? Is he hooking up with that other girl? Move on already! I want to shake some sense into her.

I kick off my boots, creep into the room and gently remove her shoes. Her breathing is deep, rhythmic. Carefully, I reposition her body so that her head rests on a pillow, then pull the covers over her. This is the second time in one night I've tucked you in, Claudette, I think while sighing. I also think it would be nice if Claudette was the kind of girl I could talk to. It's kind of nice having her around when she's not being a total pain in the ass. When she's not drinking or whining about Jamie. I'd like to have a girl's interpretation of what went down tonight with Zoe. My mind is all over the place. Claudette, Zoe, Jamie. Christ, my head's ready to explode.

I almost make it to the door when Claudette stirs, mumbling, "Jamie, come back to bed."

Ignoring her is my intention, however, when she throws her legs over the side of the bed, I don't believe she's sleepwalking. She's apparently on her way to find Jamie.

Before her feet hit the floor, I'm back at her side. "Claudette," I whisper, pressing her back into bed. "Go back to sleep. It's the middle of the night."

"Come with me," she says, her words raspy, sleepy. Her eyes are closed, but she lifts her arms in the direction of my voice. "Back to bed, baby."

"Go to sleep," my tone deepens with annoyance. "Jamie is not here. It's me, Jesse."

Rolling onto her side, she mumbles into the pillow, "Jesse, stay with me, please ... Jess ..."

I stand beside the bed for several minutes before creeping back to the door. I feel like I'm leaving an infant in a crib, waiting for it to wake for another bottle. "Damn, girl," I groan when I'm safe in the hallway. "You are high maintenance. No wonder Jamie split." Then logic tells me Jamie split for other reasons.

I shower, and wrapped in a bath towel, slug down a glass of juice in the kitchen. It's gonna take more than juice to combat the darkness inside me. So I snatch a bottle of Jack from the cabinet and head to my room at the end of the hall. I've never set out to deliberately get trashed, but if tonight doesn't call for a blackout, I don't know what will. When I pass Jamie's room, Claudette is mumbling something in her sleep. When I don't hear my name, I let out a breath and hold in a chuckle.

My desire to chuckle is short lived.

I'll settle this score with my brother, next time I see him.

I'm too amped to sleep. I've got an ear out for Claudette. Concerned she might stumble through the living room and wake Dad.

Tossing and turning causes more anxiety. I pace to the window, stick my nose through the blinds to stare at the night. Pacing again, I reach into a drawer for my jar of buds and pipe, but my fingers just swipe, then I slam the drawer shut. Instead of getting high, I grab the bottle of Jack and slam it on the makeshift plywood and sawhorse table containing my painting supplies. I'm about to release every ounce of frustration that's gnawing at my gut. Moonlight drizzling through the windows gives just enough light to find my way around the room. A long time ago, I learned dimness equals inspiration. And with the mood I'm in, this should be one hell of a night for the creation of something bizarre.

I dip a brush and let the bath towel slide from my hips to the floor. I don't consider the memorable sunset I had planned on earlier. Without pause, I get to work.

I'm not thinking about what to paint, my objective is just to paint. The brush in my hand is my conduit. Vibrations from my soul flow through my fingers, causing the brush to cut its own path across the canvas. I dip and my brush moves, striking, swirling, sliding at will.

When I take a step back, I see that I've painted midnight: the place Zoe and I stood together not long ago. Moonlight filters through woodlands like strands of tinsel dancing on a Christmas tree, but mostly there is darkness. At the center, a tree stands out from the rest. I cock my head, bite the inside of my cheek, and I study my masterpiece. This is one of your best, Sinclair. Not only is the night fucking moody, but that tree rocks. Half oak, half woman. If it had a face, it would be Zoe's.

Moist lips caressing my cheek are attempting to wake me. Unsuccessful. I'm not about to leave Zoe's side. Her mouth is warm and I want it just where it is. On every part of me. The sensations she arouses are amazing. My muscles tighten, especially the central one, as my body responds to her touch.

The lips work harder, moving down my neck. A hand creeps beneath the sheet, grazing the inside of my thigh. The moan that partially awakens me is real. Mine. Distant. I can't wake up. Not yet. I need more time with Zoe.

In some recess of my brain lies a sense of reality. Urgency. When fingers skim my dick, my morning wood is about to explode. Zoe's all over me, lowering herself onto my shaft. She's grinding slowly, and I'm slipping into ecstasy. It feels so fantastic, I believe I'm ready to come. Out of nowhere, my hips stop moving and my brain shouts: Holy shit, I don't remember slipping a condom on! Mid-thrust I freeze, thinking; fuck, that was some realistic dream; am I having a dream within a dream? My eyes crack open. A brilliant slice of sunlight causes my lids to snap shut. In another part of my mind it's midnight and the moon is on fire. I refuse to let the smell of bacon, the pungent aroma of coffee, destroy these moments with Zoe. But Zoe would never let me screw her on our first date. I need to kiss her before she runs off into darkness.

A fingertip lifts my eyelid; ignoring the next brash burst of sunlight, the featherlike touch, I swat a hand away, as if I'm chasing a fly from my face. My brother. "Get the fuck outta here, Jamie. You're such an asshole. I don't want to eat now. I'll eat later." Much later. And I let myself sink. Deeper and deeper.

I'm in Holloway's backyard, sprawled in one of the lounge chairs, and Zoe is snuggled beside me. Her arms are wound tightly around my neck. Between kisses, she whispers, "I'm glad I let Dee talk me into coming tonight."

"So am I." My groggy voice fills my ears. This is cool. I'm straddling two planes. Controlling sound, smell, touch. I'm lowering Zoe onto my dick, and the feeling is enough to stop my heart.

The coffee is magically perfume, flooding my senses. The fingers I feel are Zoe's. I want her so badly, my body throbs. Something has pulled me from the depths. Abruptly. I don't think it's my voice. Or coffee. It's the pressure of the fingers that are digging between my thighs, the clasp of tight, wet flesh running up and down my morning wood.

My eyes fly open. "What the fuck?"

I throw off the sheets and along with them, Claudette. She hits the floor with a thud. "Holy fuck. Claudette! What are you doing in here?! Were you? You didn't just?" I leap from the bed. My movements are so brisk, for a dizzying moment my head feels like it never left the pillow. Disoriented, I stare into drowsy eyes. Cloudy gray and catlike.

"Claudette ... what the fuck?" I palm my forehead. "Did we just fuck?"

"Mmm." She giggles. "I confess."

My already sick stomach drops. "You confess what?" Holding my breath, I wait for her answer.

She gives me a lopsided grin. "Just a little."

"There's no such thing as just a little fucking. Did you just sit on my dick?"

Cross-legged, she gazes up innocently. "Don't be such a puritan, Jesse."

I have my answer and I want to vomit. "I just fucked my brother's girlfriend."

In one sleek motion, her body lifts and she stands beside me, waving the bottle of Jack I emptied last night in front of my face. "Ex. And maybe if you didn't drink so much you wouldn't wake up drunk."

"Look who's talking," I snort. "No condom. You're lucky I didn't come." *Actually, I'm lucky I didn't come.* I sink onto the edge of the bed and hold my head in my hands trying to bring everything into focus. My mind, my body, my eyes. My peaceful sleep has been torn apart and I'm slammed by everything that's gone down. "Christ. What a night. What are you doing here?"

"You brought me here, doof." She drops down onto the bed beside me. Her hands close the gap between her legs and private space which I haven't seen but apparently entered.

It takes a few seconds for her words to register. Lifting my head, I stare into her eyes. "Jamie did."

"I slept with Jamie last night?" If Claudette was capable of blushing, the look on her face tells me her cheeks would be rosy red. A satisfied smile creeps across her lips.

"I have no idea what you two did last night. All I know is you crashed at the party, and he brought you here. As to why, I'm clueless."

"I have a pretty good idea," she says ruffling my hair. Her giggle brushes my face. "Speaking of eating, I made breakfast," she draws back to give me a pert smile, "your dad is in the kitchen, waiting for you."

In avoidance of her hand which is sliding up and down my back, I lean to the side, then stand on wobbly legs. "I'm fucking beat. I feel like I ran a marathon." As more of last night comes into focus, I remember I did everything but jump hurdles.

Gazing down at Claudette, I follow her eyes as they slide from my face to my hips, realizing I'm naked and dick-level with her stare. One hand flies to my balls while the other covers my swollen manhood, which is in dire need of complete satisfaction. For a split second I consider finishing, then realize I'm not that desperate. If I were facing Zoe on the other hand, like in my fantasy world ... well ... we'd be rolling in the sheets by now and I'd be in heaven.

Claudette giggles. "I can still help you with that. I can always reheat breakfast if you'd like."

"I have no intention of *consciously* screwing my brother's ex in my bed," I give her a disgusted look, "or in any other location for that matter." *Or eating a cozy breakfast with her and my dad.* I turn my back grab my jeans and pull them on. "I'll take you home."

My returning gaze slides over Claudette. A t-shirt, which I recognize as Jamie's, covers her top, but her lean legs are smooth and bare. I'm aware of exactly how high the bareness rises.

"I trust you wore a robe in the kitchen while cooking?" My gaze narrows, delivering a warning. "My dad's heart is bad. You know that, right?"

Laughing, she leads me from my bedroom as if she owns the place. In a way she is part of the family. Having dated Jamie off and on for four years, she's spent a lot of time here. Spends time here is more accurate.

Wiggling her butt, Claudette laughs and pads down the hallway to Jamie's room, while I meet Dad at the kitchen table. He's sitting near the window. Sunlight emphasizes the laugh lines which are now grooves that make their way around his mouth. Around his dark eyes. He hasn't shaved yet, but his hair is combed and he even has a bit of color in his cheeks.

"Did Claudette wake you?" Coming up beside him, I ask, worrying his answer might be "yes."

He smiles. Tired. "I should be so lucky," he teases, lifting a mug of coffee to his lips.

"Yeah. Right. That kind of luck you and I don't need."

He laughs. "Leave it to your brother."

"To dump her on us you mean?"

"I could think of worse things. Pour yourself some coffee, Jess. Sit down. We need to talk."

"This sounds serious." My stomach knots. I've had enough serious for one weekend. "Is it your–"

He waves my words away. "It's nothing to do with my health. I feel good enough to pick up and continue on with business as usual. But the doctors feel differently. They tell me if I don't change my lifestyle, I could be facing another heart attack." He taps the white t-shirt covering his chest. Frustrated. Sad. "Or open heart surgery."

"We're not about to let that happen. What do you want us to do, Dad? Anything you need. You know you can count on me."

"Your brother, now that's a horse of a different breed." His laugh isn't sarcastic. It's filled with disappointment, but also with love. I've always felt Jamie was my father's double. The stories Mom told me over the years confirmed it.

"What's the plan? Hire someone to run the station?"

"No sense in repeating myself. I was able to reach your brother this morning. He'll be here soon. I'd like to speak to both of you, together."

Without another word about Dad's health or future plans, we finish breakfast. Claudette's nowhere to be found inside the house, so I figure she's in the yard smoking a joint or whatever. I find her on the back of my bike, wearing my extra helmet and baggy sweatshirt and jeans she had to have found in Jamie's closet.

"Make yourself at home," I say wryly, slipping onto the seat in front of her.

"Always do," she chirps, snuggling against me. "Let's hit the road and keep riding," her voice fills the air as I hit the throttle, "straight out of town."

I figure she wants to extend the ride not only to enjoy the spring day that's just beginning, but because of her parents, who could be waiting for her at the door, ready to read her the riot act for all I know. But giving Claudette a mood altering tour of the town is not part of my plan. What Dad said is bugging the hell out of me. I need to get back to the house and find out what he wants to discuss with Jamie and me. My next order of business is to make contact with Zoe. One way or another, I need to reach that girl. Tell her how I feel. Age difference, her uncooperative father, nothing is going to keep me away. Not after last night. Being with her confirmed she's the girl of my dreams.

Cruising down Claudette's street, I snap out of Zoe and ease off the throttle. Immediately, her arms tighten around me, and the helmet she's wearing hits me between the shoulder blades. Rolling to a stop before her house, I let the bike idle. Claudette's still wrapped around me. Swinging around, I peel free. My eyes dig deep into hers. "You called your parents last night, right?"

Brows gathering, she chews her full bottom lip.

"I take that as a no. Should I get ready to run?" My voice is as flat as my mood.

Claudette smirks, but I'm dead serious. I've had enough parental altercation to last a lifetime.

"Yeah, I called them. I guess. Maybe." Grudgingly, she slides off the bike and shoves the helmet at me.

"You need to tone down the drinking, Claudette. You don't want to lose yourself."

Shaking her hair loose, she shoots me an indifferent stare that turns thoughtful, then serious. Analyzing me, her head tilts from side to side. "I wish you were Jamie," she says, then abruptly turns and runs to her front door.

For a moment she pauses, then swings the door open. Before entering, she briefly turns, and with a look of despair, enters. Thinking of what might be awaiting her, my gut tightens. So, I wait at the curb, just in case she needs me. The windows are open, with a drape pulled to the side. I watch figures that look too large for the living room cross the floor and disappear. After a few minutes of hearing nothing more than the sounds of passing cars, I assume things are cool. I hit the throttle and cruise home.

Jamie's truck is parked in the driveway. An unusual sight these days. I'm relieved. He's a dick, but at least when he's around there's another pair of hands, another brain. Or half of one.

I enter the kitchen to find Jamie slumped over the table, massaging his head. I don't believe his hangover is as bad as mine. Maybe he's coming down with one of his migraines. The ones that put him out of commission for a day. Or two. Or three. When he goes to the cabinet next to the sink and grabs the bottle of plain old aspirin, I figure it's just a normal headache. Like mine. No, it can't be as bad as mine. I have some kind of crazy hangover, like a band around my head. Not only from booze. From stress. From life.

Two partially filled glasses of orange juice sit on the table. I grab a mug from the cabinet, pour the juice from the bottom of the container, and pull out a chair.

"What's up?" After chugging down two aspirins I snatch from Jamie's palm, I ask.

"I was just telling your brother what a great cook Claudette is. And that he's a knucklehead for kicking her out the door the way he did. Good women are hard to find."

"Yeah, well, that's Jamie's business. What else did I miss?" I flop onto a chair across from Dad. Elbows on table, I cradle my chin.

Dad swaps juice glass for coffee mug and wraps his large hands around it. "Nothing. I told you I wanted both of you here, so I waited."

Jamie, who has returned to the table, abruptly lifts his head. After delivering a text message, he slides his phone to the side. "I'm getting a sick feeling, Dad," he says, frowning, "didn't they fix you up in the hospital? You're okay, aren't you?"

I watch my brother's face, which has been wiped clean of arrogance.

"Things are going to change, Jamie. Like Dad's lifestyle. And yours." I bring the mug to my lips, open my throat, and let the orange juice flow.

"We hiring a helper?" Jamie asks. He looks relieved. I would have preferred he suffered a while longer.

"We're going one better," Dad says. Spinning his mug methodically before him, his eyes avoid ours. "We're selling the garage."

"Dad." I'm certain my shock is not concealed, because Dad's head shoots up and he stares. "You built that place up to what it is today, single handedly. Why sell? We're doing okay—"

He stops me with his raised hand. "With your mother's help."

"I don't mind helping out. And Jamie's here." I stare daggers at my brother. "To work full time. Right?"

Jamie scrubs his stubbly cheeks with both hands. "Sure. I'll jump in too. When I can."

"This is what I'm talking about. I love you both, too much to dump all of the responsibility on you, Jesse." Dad's talking to me but staring at Jamie.

"But, if Jamie takes over for you. And I help out after school. Why can't we keep the garage?" Rubbing my temples, I try to release building tension. "At least keep the pumps open?"

Again and again my fingertips circle my forehead as I wait for my world to completely explode. I'm sickeningly reminded of the days following Mom's death, when, gathered around the kitchen table, the three of us had conversations like this. Deciding what we'd do. How we'd make it without her. Those conversations are still too vivid in my mind to have any more. Especially regarding Dad. He's the root of the family. Our very small family. My stomach sinks. My eyes dart from Dad to Jamie. Jamie to Dad. And my heart is so heavy, I'm not sure how I'm going to handle this.

"I've decided it's best to sell the place. Best for all of us. With medical expenses," he falters, "and the place has been closed more than it's open lately, so we've lost customers."

Guilt washes over me. "I'm trying, Dad."

"I know *you* are." Frowning, he looks at Jamie, whose face is buried in his hands. "I'm tired, Jess. And to be honest, I'm looking forward to a change of scene."

Jamie's head snaps up and we both fire in unison, "You're moving?"

Dad stands and steps to the kitchen window. "I might be."

"So, wait," I jump at him, "we're not only selling the garage, but the house too?"

When he turns, his eyes crawl over my face, around the room, landing on Jamie, whose jaw is loose. "I won't sell the house out from under you boys. You can stay here as long as you like," he smiles, "or join me in Dallas."

"Dallas?" Again, Jamie's voice and mine simultaneously hit the same pitch.

On his way to the refrigerator, Dad chuckles. "I've been thinking about a ranch. Horses. Maybe some other livestock." He pulls out a carton of milk and adds, "I'm thinking of moseying out there and take me a look around."

"Holy shit. Dallas is a far cry from Pleasantville," Jamie laughs, rocking his head. "Dad's gonna be a cowboy," he slaps the table, "sonofabitch, Sinclair Ranch. I like the sound of that." He cocks his head and nods. "Hmm. Cowgirls. Now there's a pleasing thought."

Dad's facial muscles tighten. He looks almost like he did when Mom was diagnosed with cancer. His eyes hold a warning, and leave mine to focus on Jamie. "I don't want to uproot you boys because of my selfish dreams."

"You? Selfish?" My palm slams the table so hard, the glasses rock. I glower at Jamie then focus on Dad. "It's about time you thought of yourself. Your future."

With a grin Dad approaches. "If you decide to stay here, the money from the sale of the station will be enough to run the house and pay for school until you both have jobs. But," the container of milk hits the table hard, "this house won't be turned into a brothel, James. Consider the neighbors ... and your mother's memory." The harshness in his voice breaks when he faces me with a nod. "There are art schools in Texas, Jess." He winks. "You might want to look into coming on down. Be nice to have my boys with me."

"Miss Texas here I come." Jamie smirks and grabs his crotch.

"Dude ..." I shake my head and roll my eyes. "Have some respect."

Dad shakes his head, too, laughing more with resignation than humor. "You can pluck a grape off the vine, but no matter how you crush it, it's still a grape." His smile clears. "I did more than just think. I researched." He levels his gaze at me and winks. "Checked out real estate and contacted agents. If you boys can handle the sale of the garage with me on the other end of a telephone—"

My head pops up, followed by Jamie's. "You're leaving right away?" At the thought, my stomach dips.

"I'd like to. My retirement will get me there, and the garage and house will keep you both here until you make your decisions."

The living room TV Jaime left on captures my attention. I strain to hear the announcer's mechanical voice: Channel Six breaking news. The occupants of the vehicle that somehow lost control during the early hours of this morning have been recovered. Authorities are still investigating and trying to piece together how the vehicle could have broken through the barriers of the bridge which has been under repair since March of this year. Our team is on the scene, filming. I have to warn you, the footage you are viewing is live. We're not sure what the divers will be pulling up. You might want to remove children from the room." After clearing his throat, he continues, "A witness tells police he watched the car suddenly careen back and forth as it sped across the bridge, narrowly missing the front end of his truck before becoming airborne after slamming into a steel abutment."

I'm the first to jump from the chair and sprint into the living room. Jamie's a close second, followed by my dad. We don't sit: we stand before the screen, speechless, staring as cameras roll. The scene is gruesome. I'm filled with horror as I watch the car hoisted up by a crane, water gushing from missing windows and open doors. To think there were people inside blows my mind.

"Hudson's Bridge," Dad's voice hitches, "I cross almost every day. They must have hit a section of loose guardrail," he swipes his head with a hand, "is all I can figure."

"Maybe jumped it? As said, speed kills." Jamie's scratching

fingers move from his head to his chin. "That's near Holloway's place," he adds with disbelief. The scene is even affecting my heartless brother. "You were there last night, Jess. Could it have been one of the kids from the party? Holy fuck. Did some trashed dickhead get behind the wheel? I thought it was gonna be an all-nighter."

"Can't be. I didn't see anyone leave. In fact, when I left, the party was shutting down. Kids were crashed inside the house. Out in the tents we pitched. They were going strong all day, so— I don't think ..."

My head begins to pound again. The only car I remember, which sped off like a bat out of hell, was the dark vehicle Zoe was practically thrown into. My heart all but stops beating.

Zoe

Rising from the depths of darkness is not easy. The sensation of choking, followed by a desperate struggle for air, fills me with terror. Awakening with a gasp, I find myself in a bed. The sheets are crisp. Arms press my body to the mattress. "Mom?" My first thought is, *where the heck am I?* The next is, *am I dead?* Because fleeting flashes of reality, like slivers of shattering glass, pierce my brain. My head throbs with pulsing blood. My entire body aches. A dull voice inside my mind tells me I'm in a hospital, not home in my bed where I long to be. And the restraining arms are not my mom's.

I hear screams. Moans. Wails of desperation. When my head finally clears, I realize the blood curdling sounds I hear are mine. "Mom! Dad!" Again and again, I scream.

I am ethereal, floating in haze, incapable of movement. My head tries to roll from side to side, but something stops it. I can't feel my neck. But I do feel a tightness, as though my neck is being hugged.

"Shush. Everything is okay. You're fine," says an older woman dressed in a top dotted with yellow daisies. She's sympathetic, hovering over me with kind pale eyes, which I squint at. The pressure of her hands on my shoulders increases. I believe I'm trying to lift myself out of bed and she's trying to restrain me, as gently as possible.

"Try to calm down, dear. I don't want to give you any more medication. You've got a lot in your system. But ... try to control yourself." Her tone deepens, switching from soothing to authoritative.

What I notice most is her drawn mouth, though, and the deathly silence surrounding me, now that I've stopped screaming. My vision is blurred. The room is filled with muted light and quivering shadows. My eyes dart through empty air, landing on a window. Slatted blinds are partially open. I believe there is night on the other side of the glass. My ears feel stuffed with cotton, then something other than the woman's stern voice penetrates: Mechanical beeping. Click, soles of shoes. I sense she's walking around my bed, with a brisk touch, checking and tucking my gown, the sheets.

"My parents?" I manage. Then I sob, because memories come crashing down in one explosive moment, splitting my head that already hurts like hell. "Oh my God!" I gasp. "Are they here?" Swallowing is difficult. My throat is raw. My bulging eyes tug at the dry lids attempting to shield them. If I had a mind, I'd be losing it. "Where are they? What happened? Where am I?"

"Don't try to talk," she whispers through tight lips tinted peach. Through the haze before my now watering stare, I watch the tip of a hypodermic needle pierce a tube that's attached to my arm. I don't believe I've ever felt so drowsy. Peaceful. Senseless.

When I awaken, the sun is shining through the open slats of the window blinds. I have no idea how long I've been out. My unconsciousness wasn't black, or dreamy. It was kind of gray and lifeless. Similar to the way I feel at this moment when thoughts begin to circulate. I rub my temples, then my head. That's when I feel the large bump on the back of my skull.

A different woman appears at my side. She's young and humming the melody of a Norah Jones song. I know who Norah Jones is. My mother plays her CDs all the time when she's working around the house, planting flowers in the garden, driving the car. She sings along, stopping to make comments like, "I love the way Norah Jones sings." One day, her voice turned serious. "The way you sing reminds me of her, Zoe. You can really croon the blues, baby. Almost like Norah." Then she chuckled and asked me to sing for her. "Sing the Fae, Zoe. Come on, please? Give me a little preview of the play. I'm so excited. Can't wait to see you up on that stage. What I wouldn't give to have a rock star in the family." Then she started rocking out behind the wheel. We laughed so hard, we ended up with hiccups.

"Hi, Zoe. I'm Nancy. I'll take good care of you. Don't you worry about a thing, honey."

Biting my lip doesn't stop another sob that rips from my lungs to hang in the air.

"It's okay, honey," she coos, "everything will be fine. Has the doctor been in yet?"

"Doctor?" I know I sound clueless.

I'm drained of energy. On the verge of blacking out again. I fight the darkness. I don't like the sensation of passing out. It's scary. I think my heart will stop beating and never start up again. Although, losing consciousness is easier than this. No thoughts. No images cramming my brain.

"Your hair is so pretty," she says, leaning over my bed to straighten my pillow. I feel her stroking fingers on my head. "Are those natural streaks?"

She doesn't look much older than some of the seniors in school. Doesn't act it, either. "Are you a nurse?"

She smiles, apparently reading my thoughts. "Sure am. I don't look thirty-one with two kids, do I?"

"Uh uh." I try to shake my head but my neck is still stiff.

"That bothering you?" She reaches for the apparatus which is restraining my movements. "I asked for a soft collar for you when I came on duty this morning. The doctor approved it."

"It doesn't feel soft." I grimace.

"It's all about attitude."

"Huh?"

"Staying young. You need to feel it to look it."

I slide a finger beneath the edge of foam gripping my neck and tug. "Ah huh."

Rather than feel, I hear her loosen the Velcro straps that are flattening my Adam's apple.

"Self-image is a must. Especially for us girls." She winks. "There, I loosened the collar. That should feel better."

My neck might not feel like it's crushed in a vice anymore, but my self-image is that of an overloaded garbage can. So, no, I don't feel better. Nothing feels better. I'm floating through some sadistic nightmare. On the verge of a panic attack.

"Is my neck broken?" At the thought of being paralyzed, my stomach seizes.

"No, hon. It's just a precaution," she says, fidgeting with the bags hanging on the IV stand beside my bed. "You were actually pretty lucky. Mild concussion. Bruises, but nothing that won't heal."

"You call this lucky?" Palms up, my hands find their way into the air. "That's why I have this bump?" I prod the back of my head and let out an, "Ouch! And my parents? Were my parents admitted too?" I wrack my brain to remember the last time I saw them. Spoke to them. Was it before or after the accident? Oh God. Why didn't I wait to tell them about the rape until we were home! I made Dad lose control of the car. This is all my fault.

The look on her face tells me something is very wrong. A sense of dread washes over me, a feeling they're badly hurt. And this woman doesn't want to admit anything until they're out of the woods. *Please let them be out of the woods.*

Her eyes shade, and her lips draw into a tight line. "I'll ask the doctor to come in and speak with you. He can tell you more about your injuries, but," she winks, "I think you'll be out of here in a few days. Oh and good news, you've had some visitors. They were here last night, but you were out like a light. They said they'd come back today."

My first thought is Dee. My second is Jesse? I don't want to see Jesse! Rather, I don't want Jesse to see me here, like this.

But Dee and Jesse would have no way of knowing I'm here. Would they? My chest tightens. "Who was here?" I croak, my swallowing easier now. I lift a hand to my face, testing for bandages. There are none. My skin is smooth. No blood? Not even a scratch? "I'm fine. Why am I here? Who's coming? My parents?" When I try to sit up, my body feels stiff and my chest and sides are gripped with pain, cutting my words short.

"I can't breathe," I whisper with panic.

"That's because your ribs are bruised. And your head hurts because you have a mild concussion. Your body took a beating, hon, but the water saved you. The water and the man on the bridge who was there to pull you out right after the impact. He saved your life."

I feel the bulge of my eyes. "Water? Who pulled me out?"

"You don't remember?"

"I remember lights. A crash. And yes, I remember flying in the air?" I sob.

"Don't dwell on it now. It will get easier. You'll be fine. Just don't get out of bed." She shoots me what I consider a forced smile. "I believe your aunt was here. And a girl named Nina?"

"My cousin? My aunt? Why?" My heart rate picks up. My mind races. I rarely see my father's sister, who lives at least fifty miles away. Close to New York City. The last time I saw my cousin Nina, we were little kids. Playing with dolls on her back porch.

When I got back home and opened my doll box, I noticed some doll clothes and shoes were missing. Nina had ripped them off. That's the last time we played together, or visited, for that matter. So why would they show up here?

Hospital sheets are cool and crisp. So crisp they scratch against the bare skin of my arms and legs when I move. "Too much bleach," I mumble. "Maybe starch. Why the fuck do they bleach the sheets so much they smell? Bleach and antiseptic mixed with disgusting smelling food. Steamed vegetables? Black tea. Meatloaf with sticky gravy. Ugh."

"I'll bring you a tray, hon. And lunch is not meat loaf," she chuckles, "you've got to be hungry though, to conjure up that meal."

"Why?"

"Because you haven't eaten in over twenty-four hours."

With the soft collar, I'm able to swing my head to the side to face Nancy. "That's how long I've been here? A whole day?"

Movement at the corner of my eye interrupts my calculation of time: Aunt Molly stands in the doorway. Beside her, Nina doesn't stifle her wide-mouth yawn. My eyes rake over them.

Holy shit, my mind spins. If it isn't dysfunctional Molly and klepto cuz. I feel my lips pin together. Wondering why they're here, blood drains from my body.

Molly is still blonde. If I remember correctly, most of her over-bleached hair broke off, so she started wearing hair pieces and wigs years ago. Today she's wearing a bunch of platinum curls. They're peeking over the crown of her head. When she turns and whispers into Nina's ear, I notice the fake hair cascades down the back of her head, lodging at the nape of her neck. Matching tendrils partially cover silver chandelier earrings.

"What are they doing here?" I demand of the nurse who's on her way to usher them into the room, without my permission. She greets them with a smile. "Perfect timing. She just woke up." Her tone tenses. Easily, I hear her concerned whisper. "She's asking questions."

Molly strolls to the side of my bed. Nina schleps behind, wearing Converse. The long strap of a satchel drapes one shoulder. She's holding an iPhone and texting as she drags her feet.

Molly married a decent looking Italian guy named Nino Romano, at least I remember he was kind of pleasant looking. They had twins: Nina and Nino. Nina took his dark personality, and color, but not his features. Sections of her cropped black hair are dyed purple, some red. Half is chopped. Pierced with studs in ears, nose and bottom lip, she doesn't wear makeup. Molly wears too much. Her plump face is painted like a clown. No. She looks more like a leftover Halloween decoration.

"What day is this?" Ignoring them, I ask Nancy.

Before Nancy can respond, Molly chirps, "It's Monday."

"I should be in school."

"How are you, Zoe?" Molly asks, setting down her oversized handbag on the foot of my bed. She adjusts her shirt which is tucked into baggie pants.

"Why are you here?" I don't care if I'm rude.

Molly looks stunned. Nina just looks.

"Didn't they tell you?"

"I've been here over twenty-four hours and no one has told me anything," I snap. "Do you know where my mother and father are?"

Molly's face creases. "My brother died in the accident." She reaches for the tissues on my nightstand and blows her nose hard.

"What? What the fuck are you talking about?" I scream so loud, Nancy flies to my side.

Nina, whose shoulder is tucked against the wall, stops texting. She stares at me with fear in her eyes but remains silent. Molly stops sobbing long enough to say, "Your parents are gone, Zoe. You're coming home with us as soon as you're well."

I'm in the midst of trying to digest her words, their actions, refusing to believe. I shake my head. "No way. You're just trying to scare me."

I cannot accept the fact that I'm confronted by these near strangers. And that the wide eyes and red mouth of this blonde woman are insisting she's being truthful. I'll never see my parents again is infiltrating my brain but refusing to actually penetrate my thick painful skull.

I want to leap from the bed. Run from the room. I want to call home, because I'm that certain this is a cruel joke, or more realistically, a nightmare. For a moment, I emerge from shock and the immensity of Molly's words jars my bruised brain. A pain hits my chest. It feels like she's plunged a knife into my heart. With each revolution of the spinning room, I become more nauseated.

If I squeeze my eyes shut, maybe they'll be gone when I open them. Shit! They're still here. My ears are ringing so loud they'll burst. But nothing matches my rupturing heart. This is too much for me to comprehend. I must fall back into shock, because my eyes are dry, and I hear myself objecting to Molly's offer.

"It's not an offer, Zoe. Or an option. It's the way it has to be. Your parents named me guardian."

I'm laughing. I'm crying. Is this the meaning of hysteria? "No way," I sob. "I don't believe it. They'd never leave me with you. I can take care of myself."

My gaze darts to Nina. Why? I have no clue. Standing behind her mother, she rolls her eyes and shrugs. From what I recall, they never got along. Apparently, nothing has changed.

"You're not of age yet. You have no choice," Molly explains, her tone cold.

If this is true, I'll run away. I recall their small apartment and screech out, "What?"

"You can bunk with Nina."

"Sure, and be molested by your perverted son, *little* Nino? I don't think so, Molly." My voice hits a pitch that makes my ears ring even louder. I watch an invasion of small black dots cloud my vision as my eyes pulse with the beat of my heart.

"Get them out of here before I!–"

"You'd better leave," Nancy bristles. "Zoe's obviously not ready to be discharged."

"We'll see you tomorrow, Zoe. I'll explain everything that will happen when you come to live with us. And I'll speak to your doctor. With luck, you'll be released in time for the funeral." Molly throws the callous comment over her shoulder on her way out the door. I'm not sure if her cavalier attitude is put on for my benefit, or if she's just plain cold and doesn't give a shit.

Nina grimaces at me, holding up a peace sign on her way out the door.

I glare at Nancy. "If my parents are dead, what else is there to explain to me?"

Can a detached person fall into shock? I think I'm a freak because I know I'm dead, yet I'm drowning in a flood of emotions. I leap from the bed, dragging my IV stand with me, and head straight for the closet. The pain is enough to cause my gasp, but I don't care.

"What are you doing?" Nancy snaps.

"Going home." My voice is flat. "Don't try to stop me. No way am I going to live with Molly and her twins. I'd rather join a circus."

Nancy catches my arm before I can reach for ... my clothes? The closet is empty. "I have no clothes?" I'm dumbfounded. "Did I come in naked?" I cringe at the thought.

"You're clothing is in a ... in a bag. Along with your parents'. I'm so sorry, honey, that this is happening to you. I would have told you in a gentler way," she controls an eye-roll by blinking rapidly, "but your aunt said she wanted to." Her voice falters. "In her own way. Which I thought was best. But now I'm not so sure."

I don't speak. Don't listen. Just stare. My nurse might be explaining something, but my mind is doing its own thing. Painting dark pictures of the night of the accident. I have no concept of time or reason. I just know I was raped, my parents are dead, I'm an orphan.

"Being an orphan is a shock to the nervous system," I hear myself saying. "It's the weirdest alone I've ever felt. It's not like being alone in the shower, or in thought, or while you're sneaking a private shit at a friend's house. It's an endless cave with no top, no bottom, no nothing. Not even air. This must be hell."

My voice is lifeless. Of course it is. I'm dead.

"You're not alone. One of our social workers is waiting to talk to you. There's help right here."

"This *alone* is like falling through a black hole. No ceiling. No floor. Black and endless," my lifeless voice drones on. "It's like being sealed inside a wall. Hearing life go on around you. Never able to be a part of anything because you've bled out." I stare at her paling face. "My blood is gone."

Her cupped hand is skimming my mouth as she leads me back to my bed. "Here, hon. Take this. You'll feel better." The pill she's holding scrapes my nose as she reaches for a glass of water on the nightstand.

"I'll never feel better."

I'm pinned to the screen, waiting for the baritone newscaster to bring the microphone back to his trained lips to inform me the vehicle's occupants were taken to the hospital, and that they're all okay. But when the scene dissolves into regular programming, without another word on the condition of the occupants, I turn my back, cover my face with my palm, and groan. "Holy shit." Pacing, I run my hands through my hair. Shake my head, repeating, "I can't believe this shit," over and over.

"What's up with you?" Jamie grabs the remote, flops into a chair and crunches his brows. "You look like you did when Mom dropped you off the first day of school." He shifts the lever and the chair reclines. His long body jerks with the thunk, then settles in a sprawling position. "Freaked out. Ready to bolt or piss your pants," he chuckles with sarcasm, "or cry."

I can't deal with Jamie right now, so I ignore him. Otherwise, we might end up rolling around the floor, breaking another one of Mom's lamps.

"What's wrong, son?" Dad's hand on my shoulder brings me to an abrupt halt.

"I think I might know the family ... in the car ... on the bridge." My stomach knots at the thought. Tears sting my eyes.

"Oh no," says Dad. "I'm sorry."

"Maybe I'm jumping the gun." I'm hit with the memory of being with Zoe only hours earlier, possibly moments before the crash. If it was her car, which I pray it wasn't. If I'd been able to grab her number, I'd be texting her right now. My mind races, trying to think of who might have her info.

Dad shakes his head sympathetically. "Hopefully they all survived."

"Yeah. Hopefully," I reply, mostly to myself. "See you later," I say, breaking free of Dad's grip. I tap his shoulder. "Let Jamie do some stuff around the house today. Like taking the garbage out," I fire off with gritted teeth, swinging my head in my brother's direction.

"Where are you going?" Dad looks alarmed. "Not to the bridge I hope. From the looks of things, they've got that entire area blocked off."

I shake my head. "Someone has to open the garage." Grabbing my shirt from a chair, I pull it over my head and across my chest, glaring in Jamie's direction.

I have to get out of here. Find out if Zoe is okay. The possibility she was involved in the accident is freaking me out. I don't have her number, so the next best thing is ... drive by her house, idiot. I google her name for an address, but can't find a Channing in this area. "Fuck."

Jamie stretches his tattooed arms over his head, then his hands drop to lace around the back of his neck. "Why bother opening the garage? We're selling the place anyway."

Jamie looks freshly showered and wears only jeans. What appears to be new artwork, scrolls over one pec and around a shoulder. A leopard's tail? I guess the ass is sitting on top of his.

My brother's indifference elevates my rising distaste for him.

I turn at the door to shoot him another glare. "*We're* selling? Since when is anything around here *we*?"

"Wait," Dad shuffles toward me wearing stretched out slippers. "I'll go with you."

"It's okay, Dad. Sunday's aren't busy. I can handle things. You stay here and take care of yourself."

"I'll take care of the homestead," Jamie says glibly. "And Luke." He seems to think being on a first name basis with Dad is humorous, but I find it annoying, especially when he calls Dad Luke in public. "We'll have dinner ready when you get home." He smirks, flipping me off.

Ignoring his obnoxious attitude, I'm out the door and throttling my bike before Dad can voice another objection or attempt to join me.

I don't stop till I reach the corner, where I pause at the curb and balance the bike. I pull out my phone and start searching the Net for hospitals.

"Was a family named Channing brought into Emergency last night?" heart throbbing in my throat, I manage to ask the first medical facility I reach.

"No one by that name," an operator replies.

One down, two to go. Too early to heave a sigh. My chest is filled with butterflies.

The next hospital I reach is a bit further away, but who knows where they'd be taken? Would it depend upon their injuries? And which hospital was best equipped?

This time, I can barely breathe when I ask. "Was a family named Channing brought into Emergency last night?"

When the steady voice on the other end says, "No," my heart pounds as I disconnect.

"One more shot," I whisper to the dead air surrounding me. "Please don't let them be there." After a deep breath, I tap the number. "Was a family named Channing brought into Emergency last night?" I ask before the operator even finishes her "Good morning," spiel.

"Are you a family member?"

"No. Why?"

"Information is only available to family. Sorry. Is there anything else I can do for you?"

"Please. Just tell me if Zoe Channing is there. And if she's okay."

"I'm sorry. We can only give out information to immediate family."

When I disconnect, my hands are trembling. I could use a shot to relax me. Or one of Dad's oxys. No, then I'd be like Jamie was after Mom died. That's how he got started.

"Immediate family, huh?" I grunt. "So, I'm a long lost cousin."

This is the approach I plan on taking as I casually walk through the hospital doors. "Shit," I mumble when I run headfirst into an information station. They've got guards standing behind the desk. My eyes shift around the lobby. "Fuck."

"May I help you?" a woman wearing a smock asks. Her smile is annoyingly bright.

"What room is Zoe Channing in?" It takes all the strength inside of me to level my voice. Relax the muscles of my face.

Through glasses her dull eyes appear too big for her fragile cheekbones. She searches her computer, then my face. "Are you immediate family?" Fuck. Did she just lift a brow?

"She's my cousin. I ... I need to see her."

Her lips tighten. "I'm sorry. Immediate family only." She shakes her head and dismisses me.

"Well, can you at least tell me what her condition is?" I'm visualizing Zoe lying in ICU hooked up to life support. I feel like I'm about to vomit. I hate that my voice is shaking, "Is she conscious? Will she be okay? Are her parents"?"

"Son," the lips of woman whose name tag reads, "Rita," form a soft frown. Her eyes close for a long moment. "Only the immediate—"

Fuck me. This must be some bad shit. "Answer me!" I cut her off with a voice too loud and slam of my fist on the counter. "Are they gonna make it? Is Zoe?" When the guard shoots me a warning look, I take a deep breath. "Listen. I just—"

"Buy a newspaper," he calls out to me. "You're not getting any information here."

When I shoot him a glare, he advances a step. But I'm staring him down, so he crosses his arms and holds his ground, giving me a *you don't wanna take me on* look.

Fuck knows how bad I want to take this joker on. If we weren't in a hospital, I would. Then I think of Dad, and my sinking heart calms my rising temper. But before turning to leave I shoot him a smug, "You have yourself a good day, Boss. And maybe you want to check out Help Wanted for a real job." Then I laugh. I laugh because I'm so pissed I could explode. I laugh because I'm worried sick about Zoe. About Dad. I want to go home and beat the crap out of my brother. I have to unload on something. So, with arms in the air, the next best thing to do is to laugh in the guard's face before sauntering out the door.

Riding relaxes me. Ride! My brain screams. So I ride hard and long. Up and down side roads before hitting the highway.

The neighborhood is quiet and the bike sails with ease, but the area surrounding our garage is busy. Other garages are operational. I'm glad I decided to open ours, but I still can't get Zoe off my mind.

After a profitable day of selling gas, even a couple of oil changes, I begin shutting down for the night. Working has tired me out. Being tired has calmed me. I stand in the office, nursing a bottle of water while closing the register, when the screech of brakes grabs my attention. What happens next holds it. I feel like

I'm viewing an action flick, maybe a comedy. A black Honda bucks across the parking lot and rolls to a stop in front of one of the closed garage doors. Steam seeps from the under the hood.

A tatted arm flings the driver's door open. Bare legs slide out, shoes hitting the pavement so hard, I expect one of the spike heels to snap off. There stands a girl. Mouth moving a mile a minute. Hands on hips. Bending at the waist, she dips back into the car and pulls out a huge tote bag.

I'm mesmerized. Not only by her fine ass, but by her bizarre behavior. Reading her lips through the glass storefront isn't difficult. Despite my agitation over Zoe's accident, I can't help but laugh. The scene before me is a pleasant distraction. Before clutching my chin with two fingers, I wipe my palms on my jeans. "I know this chick," I say to myself, and my memory search begins.

Not only does she slam the door with brute force, but her foot leaves a dent in the fender she's just kicked like a goddamn placekicker. This is when the heel of one of her shoes does snap off.

"Holy fuck..." I brace for the shit storm that's about to hit because she catches me gawking. My amusement grows as she hobbles along the pavement and pokes her head in the door.

"Are you open?" she grunts with a voice that doesn't fit her appearance at all. Her curly hair wraps a shoulder, flowing over a small but perky breast that pokes through her white shirt. When she slides her enormous sunglasses up onto her head, I realize she's the chick Christian tried to hook up with last night.

"Just caught me." I quickly throw my hands up in surrender. "But if you're looking for a punching bag, I'm not your guy." I grin.

"I'm assuming you witnessed my little temper tantrum," she says wryly. Rolling her eyes, she clomps into the office leaving the door wide open. "I hope you enjoyed yourself. You'd throw a shit fit too if you had a piece of crap car and a deadline."

Arms crossed, I curl a shoulder against the wall. "What makes you think I don't?"

She shoots me an arrogant look and shrugs. "If that's your Suzuki parked out front, you can't possibly have any idea of what I'm talking about," she draws a breath, "or the day I had."

She's holding onto the edge of the desk for support, so I motion to a chair. "Why don't you sit down. Tell me what the car's doing and I'll see what I can do to help you out."

"It started acting up the minute I left my sister's house. Overheating. Making screeching noises." Beginning with my worn out boots, she checks me out until her gaze openly lingers on my face. "Hey," she says, "you were at that party last night." Settling behind the desk and swiveling the chair, she crosses her legs and tugs down her jean skirt, attempting to cover her thighs. A far cry from Claudette enters my mind.

"I remember. You were with Christian." I nod a few times and grin.

Continuing to study me shrewdly, she lifts a brow. "If Christian is the jerk who tried to feed me that played out modeling line, yeah I was with him. For all of ten minutes." She pins her lips.

Speaking of jerks, I wonder if Christian is still in Jersey with Greshan. If I don't hold in a laugh, I might be the next thing this chick takes her frustration out on.

"So, not a model I assume, or looking to be?"

She rolls her eyes again, and I notice this girl has great eyes. Very expressive. Copper. Big. The kind you avoid staring into because you could lose yourself in them. The only pair of eyes I want to lose myself in are ocean blue. So I shift my gaze.

She holds up a leg, neither long nor sleek, but interesting just the same. "Do I look like a model?"

"Maybe." I shrug. "Visiting?"

"Yup."

"Been here before?"

"Nope."

"Don't let Christian leave you with a bad impression of Pleasantville." I wink. "Or the guys ... the people."

She sighs. "It's been one thing after another since I got here. Then the *epic bash* I was dragged to last night turned into a circus." She tilts her head, lifts a brow, and cracks a smile. "Any chance you can fix my wheels so I can get out of here?"

"I was just about to–" I shut the door and point to the hanging closed sign. "Any chance this can wait until tomorrow? I don't want to tear it apart and not be able to put it back together." I adopt her brusque tone. "No parts stores open today. I can offer you a ride home though."

She smirks. "Florida's a long way." Reaching into her bag, she pulls out an elastic band, gathers her hair and fastens it on top of her head, her ponytail fanning out like a palm tree. "Part stores closed. Figures."

"Florida? Is that where you're heading?"

"Was. Got an extra helmet?"

Zoe

"Oh my God, Zoe." Dee makes a theatrical entrance and flings her body onto my bed, attempting to wrap me in her arms. "I'm so so so so sorry." Her rolled down bottom lip juts out. She's head to toe annoying today. My eyes lock on one of her oversized hoop earrings that brushes a shoulder as she tilts her head. "You okay? Talk to me. What the hell happened that night?"

My stare shoots daggers at her. "You've decided to make an appearance. I have to thank you for your thoughtfulness." My voice is cold, and I must look like a piece of stone.

Her reaction is to draw back and carefully inspect me. Her narrowing eyes dig into mine. Much deeper than I'm comfortable with. I know mine are blank. Hers are filled with fear, pain, anguish. Everything I should be feeling, but am not. Not while staring into the eyes of my best friend who deserted me.

Part of this is her fault, I convince myself. Had she stayed with me at the party, the thing with Trent would never have happened. I wouldn't have run from the house like a psycho. Jesse wouldn't have had to chase after me. Dad wouldn't have freaked out like a lunatic. I wouldn't have been so miserable, so angry, that I blurted the horrible news to them in the car while we drove over a bridge! Yup, Delorese started off the awful chain of events that killed my parents. Brought me here. No, the janitor did. It's his fault. He forced me onto this path of self-destruction. He took what I should have willingly given to the man I loved. Love will never be mine.

"As soon as I found out where you were, I came." Dee's face flushes. Her eyes are wide. "I heard Jesse was here, but they wouldn't let him in. He almost caused a riot because they told him family only."

I tuck strands of hair that's tickling my nose behind my ear. "How'd *you* get in?"

When she grins, her lips quiver. "I'm your sister. Didn't you know that?" She holds up a fake ID. Beneath her selfie is the name: Dee Channing.

"Clever you." I prune my face. "Jesse was here? He knows?" The small amount of food I was able to ingest shifts inside my gut.

"Yeah. Want me to get him in ... tonight maybe?"

"No!" I shout so loud my ribs hurt. "I don't want to see Jesse. Or anyone." My lungs suck in air, distorting my voice. "Don't tell anyone anything about me, or what happened," I threaten with my narrowed eyes. "It's no one's business but mine."

"I won't."

"Promise!"

"I promise." With her finger, Dee crosses her heart. "But just so you know, the accident is all over school. No one knows any details though. They're just guessing. I'm about to kick some ass, too, because of the rumors floating around. What happened that night, Zoe?"

I feel my cheeks redden. "Rumors? What rumors?"

Dee pales. "Nothing. It's nothing. I shouldn't have even said the word."

"So why did you?"

"Kids are wondering, that's all. Out loud, ya know? They're not saying anything hurtful. I promise. Cos if anyone did," she rolls her hand into a fist, "they meet with this." Her attempt at a reassuring smile is to appease me, I'm sure. Then she prods, "Tell me, Zoe. What made the car..."

When I close my eyes, the scene flashes before me. My lids instantly pop open so wide, my eyeballs feel like they're about to pop out of their sockets. "The car went over the bridge and hit the water, without me in it. I must have been thrown. I don't remember anything. I was unconscious. Some guy dragged me to shore before I drank the river." I feel my gaze soften, but my voice holds venom. "Where did you disappear to that night?"

"I should have been there for you," her dark lashes brush her cheeks, "considering what happened to you and all. Don't hate me," she pleads, wringing her hands, twisting a silver ring she's wearing on her index finger.

"I don't hate you." Can I be this bitchy? "I asked you where you disappeared to? Were you fucking Zack Benefield while I was locked in the closet with psycho Trent?"

"Oh my God. I heard about that. What a jackass." Her eyes avoid mine. "You know how long I've been stalking Zack." Her giggle is strained. "I never knew he was crushing back on me till we got together at the party. He even gave me this ring." She presents her hand, quickly dropping it to her side, as if hiding it is an afterthought.

"My parents are dead, and all you can think about is Zack Benefield and the ring he gave you?"

"No Zoe." She pulls her face into such a tight grimace, her eyes are slits. "It's not like that at all. I feel terrible about what happened to them. To you. I wish it never happened!"

"And I wish you and Zack Benefield all the luck in the world. Now leave me alone." Rolling onto my side I give her my back and bury half of my face in the pillow.

The shift of my body must knock her off the bed, because I hear a thud. In moments she's at my side, her face close to mine. Her hand carefully drops onto my shoulder. "I can't leave you like this! Please, don't be mad. I didn't cause the accident!"

Propelling my upper body to a sitting position too quickly sends a rush of blood to my head. I swat her hand away and confront her. "So, what *did* cause the accident? What rumors are really going around school?" I glower. "You let it slip, so it must be true." I stab a finger at her face. "Tell me! Are they blaming a drunken driver?" My jaw clenches. They better not! My dad hasn't had a drink in–"

Crossing her arms, she stammers, "I don't know, Zoe. Kids in school are just guessing. The cops are still investigating, but there weren't any other cars involved. Just yours and the truck that was coming the other way before the crash. Thank Christ the guy in that truck was there. He called 9-1-1 and that's all I know." Her voice is weak, filled with fear I'm sure. "You must have gone airborne. That's probably why you're–"

"Why I'm alive and they're not." I turn my face to the window. "How do you know the gruesome details, anyway?"

"It was all over the news, Zoe. Some dude pulled *you* from the river, but the car ... it sank ... your parents didn't get out."

"Stop! I don't want to hear any more. I can't bear the thought of them suffocating. Drowning. Oh my God. It's too unthinkable!"

Dee must think I'm about to launch myself right out of bed. She lays a heavy hand on my leg which is tucked under the sheet. "I don't think they suffered, Zoe. They had to have been unconscious before the car even went over." She doesn't come to close to my face again. Maybe she thinks I'll hit her.

My bulging eyes cause the pain in my head to intensify. "How do *you* know they didn't suffer? How could *anyone* know ... but them?" I sob.

"The coroner–" Her hand flies to her mouth.

Biting the inside of my cheek, I nod. My neck feels so sore, but the collar is gone, so I guess my neck isn't broken.

"They think your dad lost control. The car hit the guard rail so hard it flipped over and crashed into the Hudson." She cocks her head. "But what I don't understand is why? What happened that night, Zoe? Why did your dad lose control of the car?"

Reliving the jerking motion as Dad hit the gas and brake, again and again, while throwing his arm over the seat to reach for me, I shudder. The room spins and I feel like I'm about to black out. I gasp for air.

"Breathe," Dee shrieks. "Zoe. You're just having a panic attack. Breathe!"

My body feels so stiff, yet it's twitching. I think I'm convulsing. The back of my head digs deep into my pillow again and again, pressure building inside.

"I feel like my brain is coming out my ears, Dee." I know I sound crazy. But my brain is swelling inside my head, pushing on my skull.

"I hate you! I hate me! I hate him!!"

I ram the back of my head deep into my pillow again and again until the throbbing pain causes my vision to blur.

Dee grips my shoulders. "Stop it! You're gonna hurt yourself!"

"I should be dead too. It's my fault." I squeeze my eyes shut. Pound my head with my fists. "All my fault."

"No it's not." Dee uses her most convincing voice. My eyes snap open. Her twisting fingers bring my attention to the silver ring again, and I'm angry. Angry because while I was getting fucked out of parents, she was getting fucked for pleasure.

"I told them I was raped. Dad went ballistic. Mom was screaming. She grabbed the wheel, but ..." My heart is breaking. "It's my fault. Not yours. If I didn't tell them, they'd be alive. I'll never forgive myself."

Dee thinks she's comforting me, but I don't care if I never see her again. I don't want her anywhere near me. I don't ever want to see anyone from school again " even Jesse Sinclair " especially Jesse Sinclair. *Life brought a brutal end to a nothing start.*

"I'll let you rest," Dee whispers, using a coward's excuse. "I'll call you."

For a moment, I turn from Dee to face the window where the sun dives behind clouds. "Good luck with that. My cell is somewhere at the bottom of the river." I choke on a sob.

She edges toward the door. I've never seen her look so miserable. "When you get a new phone, call me, okay?"

Jesse

The news hits school like a nuclear explosion and spreads like wildfire. The place is buzzing, all ears tuning in to what kids consider excitement. And it doesn't seem like it's going to end anytime soon. The gossip of what forced the car Zoe was riding in off the bridge keeps haunting the hallways. Haunting me.

I keep replaying those last moments I spent with her over and over in my head. Like watching a disturbing video, I continue to torture myself. Should I be blaming myself? Was it my fault that her father lost it when he saw us and went berserk? Zoe was upset about something, but why was he? The entire night remains a mystery to me. Zoe hangs with Dee, who's nowhere to be found, so I can't pump her for info.

Nothing this horrendous has hit the headlines since Paul Houston crashed his Harley one night on a rain-slick highway when he skidded into the path of an eighteen wheeler. The bike slid right under the trailer and ignited. Paul was killed instantly. The girl who was riding on the back finished school in a wheelchair. Those stories hung around long after she graduated.

Some kids are genuinely saddened by the news of Zoe's

accident. A rainbow of ribbons are tied around trees and poles. I guess no one knows which particular color to use, because they don't know the reason, or the cause, or the outcome of one girl's tragedy. Still, they're grieving for her. Because that's what everyone is supposed to do. Show support for a classmate.

Some dickheads start a rumor that Zoe was the one driving. If the losers don't stop cracking jokes about her sitting on her dad's lap, I'll start cracking heads.

The remarks about Zoe and her family infuriate me, which in turn, makes me stalk from class to class with balled fists and wearing a mug on my face.

"Dude," in the hallway, Christian surprises me from behind and slings an arm around my shoulder. "You look ready for war. What's up?"

"Nothing. Busy, that's all." I gauge him from the corner of my eye.

He cocks his head and stops walking, so naturally, I stop walking and full face him. "Does your mood have anything to do with the blonde chick you were with at Trent's party?" When he sweeps away a handful of hair, I watch his forehead crease.

I don't want to share my thoughts with anyone, not even a good friend. My gaze drops to study the floor, while my fingers run from my chin to my cheek. "I don't know, man. So much is happening right now. I just don't know."

"I heard she's in the hospital. But her parents didn't make it." He shakes his head. "Such a shame. She's hot. I hope she didn't get too messed up in the crash."

"You're an asshole."

"You know what I mean. Like broken bones, scars on her face." He shrugs. "She's so little. That's all I mean. It's not like you or me taking that kind of impact."

The thought of Zoe being pinned inside a car, or thrown clear, breaks my heart. "You're digging yourself deeper, dude. You can quit right here."

"I wonder if she's coming back to school."

"I don't know. No one seems to know much other than–"

"Listen," he slaps my back, "I gotta run." I watch his eyes follow the ass end of a brunette swaggering by. I'm not sure if he's about to stalk her, or maybe our discussion is too intense for him and he's using the chick's rear end as a diversion. "If you need someone to talk to, I'm here, okay, bud?" His words sound meaningless.

"Yeah." I turn to him and smirk. "I'll definitely keep that in mind." I have the sudden urge to bust his balls. Before he can leave, I grab his arm. "How'd you make out in Jersey?"

He rolls his eyes. "Man, you shoulda been there. If you think Jefferson chicks are hot," he flicks his wrist while his puckering lips whistle softly, "you shoulda seen those babes. They were women, you know? Not girls. Holy fuck is all I can say, besides, your brother can really find them."

"Yeah," I scowl, "my brother is a real hero."

"I'd like to pick up some of his leftovers," he grins, "like Claudette. She's something else."

I cock my head and just stare. His attitude and his words make me realize something: I'm protective when it comes to Claudette. I'm trying to decide if this is a good or a bad thing, when the bell rings.

"But then I guess the only guys Claudette wants to screw around with are the Sinclairs." Christian chuckles, but I've never seen his eyes so calculating. "Better keep an eye on your old man."

"Don't even go there, jack-off." I poke his shoulder with my index finger. "You are seriously demented, not to mention disgusting."

Exchanging, "Later, dudes," Christian goes his way and I go mine. I stroll into class, flop into a chair, and begin listening more to the whispers surrounding me than the lecture my history teacher is giving as she struts around the room.

I sprawl in the chair, stretching my legs, pulling them in, trying to find a comfortable position while I run my hands down my face, then through my hair. Restlessness is something that's been cursing me for days.

I hope this shit gossip dies down soon. I just want to forget. I can't take these constant reminders of how it felt to open up to Zoe and to finally come face to face with the girl of my dreams. Even if it was only for a short time, it was enough to hook me for a long time. I feel like I'm not making sense anymore. To myself or anyone else for that matter. Fuck Jamie's opinion, but what my dad thinks of me is important. And right now he's worried about me. I really need to get my shit together.

Class is finally over and I'm the first one out the door, cramming stuff into my locker, ready to leave for the day. The heavy fragrance of musk hits me first, followed by Claudette as she hip-checks me.

"What's up, babes," she says, hooking her arm through mine. "Leaving?"

"Yep. It's that time."

"Gimme a ride?"

I bang my locker door shut. "Where's your car?"

She tilts her head and scrunches her mouth to one side, then her bottom lip rolls down.

Shoulder braced on the locker, I study her. "Your face is like rubber. Anybody ever tell you that?"

She sucks in her cheeks, makes a fish mouth, and says, "My wheels are squealing. I'm afraid they'll fall off."

I can't help but break into a grin. "They squeak when you make a turn you mean?"

"Yup. That's it. When I turn the steering wheel." She pretends to steer.

I shake my head. "Your wheels aren't falling off. Sounds

like the brake tab. Bring it over to the garage and I'll take a look at it."

She clutches her backpack to her chest and in a quiet voice asks, "Did you hear about the accident after Trent's party?" She grimaces.

"Of course I did. Who didn't?"

"I heard you were with that Zoe girl." Her brows lift.

"So?"

She runs a purple polished fingernail across her bottom lip. "I heard her dad was blitzed and lost control of the car."

"Oh yeah?" I'm not sure which clenches tighter, my jaw or my gut. "You heard wrong. He wasn't."

"Geesh. Don't shoot the messenger." Her head jerks up and one fine brow arches. "How do *you* know?"

I slam a fist into the locker door, then rub my red knuckles. "I just do." My fingers slice through my hair. "Anger might have impaired his driving, but definitely not booze. I stood close enough to smell his breath when he shouted. He had garlic breath, not booze."

She scrunches her mouth. "When he shouted? What are you talking about, Jesse?" Her hand goes to her mouth long enough to stifle a gasp. "You were fighting with him before he crashed through the bridge?"

Zoe

Every day I spend in this hospital is agony. I can't wait to get out of this bed. Get home. I miss my parents so bad, I just want to go to sleep and never wake up. I want to see them. Say I love you. Say good bye. No, not good bye. This is a nightmare. Our brains are supposed to have the ability to control our dreams, but hard as I try, I can't control mine.

My head still hurts and my ribs are sore, so I'm unable to be released from the hospital in time to say good bye to my parents at the funeral home. What does it matter? I've said good bye a million times already. In my head, my heart. They wouldn't know if I sobbed over their caskets or in my hospital bed. What's the difference?

Molly says the wake was lovely. Closed caskets, pictures of my mother in her wedding gown, Dad in his tux, resting on the lids, along with loads of beautiful flowers covering the polished mahogany.

"The Wake was mobbed." Molly sounds like she's describing a movie premier. "People really cared for your parents."

"This should make me happy?" I snap, fighting the urge to rip her hairpiece off her head and stuff it down her throat.

The horror of her description breaks through my grief long enough to give me a near death experience, before pissing me off enough to hop out of bed and slam her big red mouth shut. In my head, anyway.

"There is nothing beautiful about drowning, or being sealed in a box, Molly." Thinking about their bodies rotting in the ground, my shaking legs threaten to cave so I let myself drop back onto the mattress.

"I didn't say that." Hands on hips, she stands at my bedside, staring indignantly.

"Jesus Christ, Molly. Have you no compassion for the daughter of the dead people you're making a carnival sideshow out of?"

I'm positive Molly will need Rent A Mourner at her funeral. I bet her kids won't even show. The only emotion I am truly capable of these days is sarcasm, and Molly brings out the worst in me.

I've turned off. My brain knows there's no way I can cope with the trauma of what's happened. The only other emotion I feel, and much stronger as time passes, is anger. Anger with Molly for being a heartless witch. Anger at myself for causing the accident. For killing the people I loved. For being cursed with living. I don't have any physical scars, just the scars no one else can see.

I want to slash my face, carve "Killer" across my forehead, so each time I look in the mirror, I'll be visibly punished for what I've done.

As if taunted by fate, by the time the memorial mass ends, a sunny morning has turned into a dreary, drizzly day. Our car leads the living procession from the church to the cemetery. Actually, the hearses lead our way. First Dad's. Then Mom's.

It takes ten minutes to drive to their final resting place: ten minutes of my eyes riveted to the scenery as I stare out the side window. I'm trying to shake the urge to leap from the car. Yes, it's that bad. I can't face the ass end of my mother's ride. Accidentally, I catch a fleeting glance of her casket peeking through the small glass portal in the rear of one of most depressing vehicles Detroit could have ever designed. That's when I brace my neck, my heart, my empty stomach. Now I need to regain control of my mind, as well as my body.

Good bye Mom. Dad, it wasn't your fault. It was mine. I love you both so much. Your fucked up daughter is so sorry. She will spend the rest of her hopefully short life paying for her sins. *What will I do without you? See how selfish you are Zoe? Thinking about your misery. What about theirs?*

The almost endless ride is over. We're here. The procession of mourners proceeds on foot, following the rolling caskets. My chest throbs. Every bone in my body aches. My heart aches the most. God, how will I live without them! This is too cruel! Why didn't you take me too?

Moisture from the already soggy grass seeps through my sandals, which are barely visible beneath the legs of black jeans. I can see my toes: that's where my eyes focus. On each and every wiggle of my toes as I proceed, ever so slowly in my death march.

The mourners hunch in a circle. I step away from the shelter of umbrellas. Lift my face to the sky. Are those hawks or eagles? I'm trying to figure this out by wingspan, colors, markings, shapes. Who the hell knows. I love birds. They're comforting. They can fly away.

A hand attempts to pull me beneath the canopy, which was quickly set up above rows of chairs. The caskets rest in drizzle. Keeping the living dry seems to be most urgent. I jerk away. No shelter for me, thank you. I find peace in the emotionless rain.

As the minister turns pages of a book, reciting compassionate words, I find that distinguishing between raindrops and teardrops running down my face is most difficult. Impossible, actually. My eyes are closed as much as possible. I want to remember my mother and father smiling and breathing, not pickled and boxed and lowered into the muddy ground, which is now pooling around my naked, frozen toes.

I opted for cremation, but once again, the Will overruled. The Will and Molly. Face still pitched skyward, I become disoriented by dizziness, so I have no choice but to level my head, open my eyes, or I think I'll puke up every ounce of bile in my gurgling gut.

I decide to watch Molly, who plays the role well. She sobs so loud, the minister has to stop praying so he can personally comfort her while the congregation stands around looking at her sympathetically.

I'm pondering my future. Trying to figure out what time the last bus for Texas pulls out of the station. I love horses, which is why Texas is my first choice. I'm also pondering my newfound family, and exactly why I'm leaving first chance I get. How life can change so drastically in the blink of an eye is astonishing. My stomach sinks: I was part of a relatively normal family of three. Happy and secure. Now I'm a fifth wheel, thrown into a defective family of four. God help me. This is all revolving through my brain when I experience the surprise of my life.

From somewhere in the background, a husky voice whispers, "Hey, you okay?" The arm that comes around me, the body that presses close to my side, belongs to Nina. This is the start of our friendship. Right. We're not relatives. We're friends. I like it better that way.

"My legs are weak, but yeah, I guess I'll live through it. Like they say, suffering makes you stronger. And I've got a shit storm here, so I'm about to be a superhero."

"I know you're bitter." Her words puff strands of hair from my ear, so there's no buffer for the depth of her voice. "But you shouldn't blame yourself, Zoe. In no way do you own this."

"Here we go again. What are you, another grief counselor?"

"No. Really. I have an in with the state police."

"Sure you do." I force a harsh laugh. "When you were arrested for shoplifting?"

She ignores my sarcasm. I'm surprised I'm letting her lead me into a private conversation at my parents' funeral while the minister is speaking.

"I can fix it so investigators say your dad hit the gas instead of the brake 'cos he was swerving to miss an animal."

When I reply, my lips barely move because my teeth are so tightly clenched. "Animals don't cross that bridge."

"Well, this one did. And the tire hit a rut in the road, causing the car to fly into air and down into the river. So you can sue the state."

Her words are graphically shocking. Cringing, I shake my head. "You guys are all about money."

"I'm doing this for you. So you can get out of this shithole."

"Thank you not. I'll get myself out. Before I left the hospital, my father's attorney stopped by to console me." I roll my eyes. "I'll get a support check of twelve hundred dollars a month. And when I'm eighteen, I'll receive the full insurance benefit my parents left me, and sole ownership of the house, which is paid off. So I'll be fine. I can kick the renters out and move back in, if that's what I decide to do. Maybe I'll sell the place. Start fresh. Maybe I'll never go back."

Annoyed stares terminate our moment of bonding.

The minute we step through the door of the red brick multifamily house, Aunt Molly starts the tour. The floor the Romanos live on is cramped, and now they have to squeeze me into the already limited space.

Molly's Hollywood style bedroom reeks of perfume. The first

thing my eyes land on is the overbearing tufted headboard occupying one entire wall. The mattress is draped by satin. I follow her to a dressing table where she shows off some of her costume jewelry.

Holding up a pair of dangling chandeliers, her eyes widen with ... love or satisfaction? "Look at these earrings." Her fingertips pin one to my ear. "What do you think? Maybe I'll let you borrow them sometime." She wears a crooked smile, so much like a clown.

Nina watches from the doorway, a hand braced on either side of the jam. When she catches my gaze she rolls her eyes. Blows bubbles with her gum. Makes *get a move on* gesture with her hands.

"They're nice," I mumble, but something other than earrings catches my eye. "What's that?" I point to a familiar looking pearl necklace and get ready for a meltdown.

Molly lifts the necklace with two fingers and dangles it under my nose. Her face is close to mine. I can almost taste the peach colored powder that's caking her face. Or is it still the heavy scent of perfume that hangs in the air? I inhale the flavor of the lipstick she's smeared around her mouth. The combination is nauseating. "Nina gave it to me one Christmas a long time ago. Isn't it pretty?" she coos.

Inspecting it carefully, but only with my eyes, I swear it's the pearl necklace that disappeared from my bedroom gift stash one year, just after Thanksgiving, when the Romanos came to dinner. Or maybe I should say, the McCabes, as Molly dumped her first husband for her current loser, Rye McCabe.

I wasn't sure if Molly was intentionally neglectful. Now I know she's just plain selfish. Continuing our tour, I'm shoved toward the closet where she flings open a door. She tugs on the arms of several fur coats. The woman is so materialistic, so shallow, more emotionless than I am even after losing my parents.

I grieve for the animals that gave their lives to dress and please Molly Romano McCabe.

Molly kicks off her heels and as she slips her stocking feet into fluffy slippers, she sighs. "I'm spent. It's been an exhausting week."

I'm learning to ignore her careless comments, but inside, things are piling up. I test the waters to see if there is an ounce of humanity inside this woman I'm supposed to be calling aunt. "I'm tired too. But I'm still feeling dreamy. Like I'm not really here. Like I'm sleeping." If I'm sleeping, I can do whatever I want, right? Say whatever I feel? "You dressed up pretty fancy for a funeral. How come?"

Her head spins in my direction, her fingers drop the satin robe she's about to pull off a hanger. "Half the town came out for their funeral. Do you think I want to look like a slob?" Her eyes rake over me, taking in my sweat shirt, jeans, and bare feet.

"I don't see the need to put on a show, even if it's for half the town." My lips twist.

She's thoughtful. "There had to be a hundred people at that service. And as they say, a man's success is judged by the size of his funeral." She squints up at the ceiling. "Wait." Her tongue curls a problem-solving click. "Or is it the size of his penis? Whatever. It doesn't matter. Your parents were precious people who were loved by many. Including me."

Yeah, right. That's why you're so crude. "How are you related to my father again?" I can't believe they came from the same womb.

"We're not blood relatives."

"What?"

"Didn't they tell you? Your dad was adopted by my parents when he was a newborn."

"So my grandparents – my dad's parents – weren't killed in a train crash in Ireland before he was born?" My legs are about to let me down.

Her laugh is as brash as her hair. "Hell no. His daddy died in a mining accident – maybe that's where the train crash came in – but his mother came to this country with him inside her. After she gave birth, she left him on the steps of the church where your granddaddy Channing worked as a butler for the priests. He couldn't bear to see your dad sent off to a foster home, so he took him home to us. I helped take care of him. Didn't he ever talk about me? The childhood we shared?"

"Actually, no." What else didn't I know about my parents? "Was I adopted too?"

"No worries on that one, honey. You're a spitting image of your mom." She pinches my cheek so hard it stings. "Maybe a bit of your dad mixed in. You're an authentic Channing."

The night of the school play approaches and my guilt multiplies. Another girl has stepped into the starring role. Sandy Belmont is nothing like Zoe. She doesn't have the sweet sounding voice, angelic movements, or the talent. Most of all, she isn't Zoe.

I'm not sure if I'll be able to withstand watching the curtain go up. Knowing Zoe is in another place, and I might never see her again, is eating me alive. She'll always be a picture perfect memory. But you can't touch a memory.

I long for a do-over. Could I have made a difference? I remember some of the lyrics she sang that night:

you can't close the book
or turn yesterday's pages
you can't catch a break
yet you can't fade away

Zoe was definitely tuned into pain.

I decide the only way to pull this night off is to do what I have to do to get things rolling and then cut out. Enduring dress rehearsals was bad enough. I could never ride out the play; hear the applause that should belong to Zoe. She deserves credit for the Fae lyrics and music. Costume design, too. Poor Zoe. How she must be suffering. I have no idea where she is. If I did ... what would you do, Jesse? Show up on her doorstep announcing, "Remember me?"

People are gathering in the lobby with their tickets: adults are blocking the doorways, kids running up and down the halls. Even with monitors, the school is in a state of chaos. Nice I guess for those who are really into the occasion. Hell for those who aren't.

In a corner booth near the main office, the school is selling t-shirts and other paraphernalia commemorating the *Flight of the Fae*. The cash they're raking in is phenomenal, and for a good cause. Donations go to safe houses and victims of abuse. The entire cast and crew joined the administration, helping to decide which charity to donate to. Abuse won by a landslide.

Bypassing greetings emanating from the crowd, I snake my way down the hallway, heading for the auditorium. In a blind rush, I break into a jog, literally bumping into Delorese when I blow through the back door marked "Cast Members."

I'm hoping for a miracle; to hear the strumming chords that would light up my heart, the voice that will make the room spin. But all I hear is the buzz of chaotic voices. Unfamiliar faces, because Zoe was ... is ... my only focal point. But as with most miracles, the hand that's digging for gold comes up empty. Zoe isn't here.

The backstage area is large enough for me to avoid conversing with the cast. In various stages of flushing, kids are either scrambling around or ducking in and out from behind dressing screens at the far end of the room. The entire length of windows is shaded. I left the calming moon outside, and the stark lighting of this room is killing my sensitive eyes. I slip on my sunglasses, and trip over a box of fairy wings, followed by a brutal shoulder block into Dee. She throws her hands out for balance and yells, "What the fuck?"

Deciding squinting is better than collisions, I slip my shades back into my jacket pocket.

"Whoa cowboy. Where's the fire?" Dee says, regaining her balance. She adjusts the backwards cap on her head which the concussion of my body unseated.

My eyes dart around the room, unsure of what I'm looking for. What I might find. "Sorry Dee," I grumble, heading for the table holding my equipment.

"Jess—" Shocks my eardrums.

Halting mid-stride, I turn to watch Dee drop to her knees. A sewing needle dangles on a long piece of thread in one of her hands, her cell phone in her other. Shifting her gaze, she fusses over the fairy she's spinning and tacking, while quickly tapping a text, then her eyes reach up to mine.

"What's the hurry?" She slips her phone into a pocket and gives the fairy a shove-off. "You're snorting around like a bull." Climbing to her feet, she sticks the needle into pin cushion and drops it in a bag.

Ms. Jordan breezes by, checking her wristwatch. "Jesse. Glad you could make it."

I watch Dee's eyes roll. "What's up with her?"

"Opening night jitters, I guess," Dee snickers. "She'll probably be waiting up for reviews."

"Is the news covering this?"

"Not." Dee laughs. "Hillary thinks she's still on Broadway."

"Sorry I ran into you. Did I hurt you?" I slide a hand down my stubbly cheek, still feeling the rake of Dee's fingernails when we collided.

"The only thing that hurts is running out of data." Grimacing, she taps her pocketed phone.

My movements follow Dee's as she makes her way over to help the lead with her costume.

"I want to get some of this stuff out of the way before–" I blow out a breath.

"Yeah," she cuts in, "I can't wait to get out of here myself." She doesn't have to tell me this. The discomfort in her eyes is obvious. I can feel it in my own.

This is the first chance I'll have to speak to her privately. So I plan on taking advantage of the opportunity of crawling inside her head before we both disappear.

"Hey, Jesse." Her eyes flick from the meticulous fluffing of the replacement fairy, to me, who's not doing much of anything. I've wedged myself into a corner, trying to look involved, feeling totally out of place and inadequate.

My gaze drifts around the room. My mind starts playing games. Switching faces. It feels so weird to see another girl wearing the costume Zoe designed. Helped sew. Zoe loved it. I know this by the way her delicate fingers held the fabric. The look on her face when she walked on stage, adjusting the straps, smoothing the skirt. Zoe should be wearing the silky pastel outfit, not this ordinary chick who's not only wearing Zoe's costume, but her face. I shake my head, trying to blink it all away. Stop wishing, idiot! She's not Zoe, the girl you will more than likely never set eyes on again.

One of the downsides of life: love comes and goes, people enter and they leave. There's nothing you can do to change things. To make them want to stay, or keep them alive. Fate has you by the balls.

I shuffle through a box for the glittering wand I made for Zoe. When I grudgingly slap it into Sandy's waiting palm, the long streamers flutter. Eyes pinned to the wand, Sandy flashes a smile and breathes out, "Thank you, Jesse," which means nothing to me. I barely know her. But I do know, from the corner of my eye, I've caught her staring at me during her understudy rehearsals. I'm unaffected. Feeling nothing like I did when catching Zoe's gaze. I'd get all warm inside, and a grin would sprout on its own. Comparing the butterflies I felt during those moments, to the tightening in my gut right now, I sink back into the shadows with a lump in my throat.

I'm not sure if it's curiosity that causes me to take an occasional glance at this other girl, or some sadistic force I can't control. Something that's punishing me for not acting on my emotions when I had the chance. Fuck me. If I could kick my own ass I would. The next best thing is to turn my back and pound my forehead with my palms, because I lost the chance to latch onto the elements of life that for me were missing. Like belonging. Wanting. Caring to care.

Sandy dances around the floor, practicing her moves. Now and then the ceiling-high curtain she touches ruffles, and I imagine her busting through it, because she's what some call flighty. I call it clumsy. Imagine that, I muse. If Sandy went tumbling through the curtain and out onto the stage. She doesn't possess Zoe's grace. Nor does she look anything like her. Her voice doesn't even come close. Drowning in a world of Zoe, I'm heartsick.

"Hey, Jesse." Dee's voice grates on my nerves. *Stop interrupting. Can't you see I'm in another place, another time?*

"Hey." My eyes pull an auto-narrow when I respond. I'm not pissed off at Dee. I'm simply pissed off at the world.

The expression on Dee's face tells me she understands and is experiencing the same grief. Grief? Maybe. The same? Doubtful.

Yeah. I admit I'm filled with sadness. I know what a fucked up life feels like. With my mother gone, my dad about to play Texas cowboy, and my asshole brother blowing in and out of town faster than the wind, to say things are depressing is an understatement.

"Can you believe it?" Dee finishes with last minute adjustments to Sandy's skirt and aims her center stage, whispering hoarsely as she moves to my side. "She's such a nerd."

Sandy hasn't stopped smiling, obviously thrilled for the big break she's been given by Zoe's misfortune. "I'm so excited," she's saying as she spins for our reaction. "Do I look okay? Wish me luck!"

"Yeah. Cheers to you," I deadpan.

"As they say in Hillary Dillary's world," Dee shares my wry look, "break a leg."

"You really mean that, don't you." I grin. "You're bad."

She shoots me a wink with one of her caramel-colored eyes. It doesn't take much guesswork to figure out why Zoe was so close to Delorese. She's the kind of person who is able to take hard knocks and bounce back with her dukes up. Admirable. Inspirational.

"This is shit. I still can't believe what's happened." I shake my head, struggling with unresolved conflict. "I wasn't even going to show tonight. I knew it would be bad, but this is fucking bizarre." Am I really confessing to Dee?

"I thought about being a no-show too. It's so hard, Jesse." Dee works her jaw like she's in pain, then squints at me. "In a way, I came for Zoe. This was her thing. If I let the play down, I'm letting her down. Stupid, huh?" She slides her hands into her pockets and stares across the room, which is, except for us, empty of life. "You were the last one with Zoe that night." The strange look on her face is ... questioning? Accusing?

Naturally, I'm defensive. Every muscle in my body tightens as I brace for an argument. Or to explain myself. To tell Delorese things she has no right to know. I could use a good fight. If she were a guy, the shit would be on. "So what if I was with her?"

Dee appears far from intimidated. She looks more thoughtful than anything. "What was she acting like? I mean like, what were you two talking about?"

"Just ... nothing really. Not that it's any of your business." I cross my arms over my chest and stare her down with eyes as cold as my heart has become.

Dee wears overalls, the bib top hanging loose over her stomach. Lifting the straps that dangle to her thighs, she fastens them around her shoulders. When she's finished, she directs her attention to me. "What *nothing really* were you doing then?"

My hand goes to my hip, while the other works through my hair. "If you want to know if I screwed her on the side of the road and fucked up her life, the answer is no."

"That's *not* what I mean. How was she acting? Did she tell you anything?"

"Tell me anything?" I tilt my head, staring so deep into her inquisitive eyes, mine burn. "Like what?"

"Was she behaving ... normal?"

"Normal? After the shit fucktard Trent pulled on her?" My sarcastic laugh is more of a grunt. I relive the feeling of satisfaction as I recall the Monday after the party when I pinned him to his locker. Stuck my finger in his face. Drew back my fist. If a friend hadn't stopped my knuckles from connecting with Trent's jaw, I'd have ended up expelled a month before graduation. "Would have been worth it," I mumble, cracking my knuckles.

"What?" Dee snaps. "You're not even listening to me. Are you?"

"No. I was thinking about how it felt to have my hands around Trent Holloway's neck."

"I know." Dee chuckles then goes serious. "When I heard about it I wanted to kill him, too." She shoves her hands back into her pockets. "Stupid ass."

"Kill him? I don't think so. Kick his ass down the hall and out the door, sure. Why are you so worried about what happened between Zoe and me?"

She chews the side of her mouth. "Never mind."

"No. Now you've got me going. You're not trying to lay blame on me–"

"Shit. No, Jesse. Never. I'm upset. I let her down." She lowers her eyes. Fumbles with a button on her overalls. "I can't live with myself."

"How did you let her down?" The thought of someone else suffering with guilt, in a sick way, eases mine. Piques my curiosity. "Why didn't Zoe come back to school? At least to finish the year before disappearing?" If my chest gets any tighter, I won't be able to breathe.

"Too many memories, I guess. She's all alone now." A sob catches in her throat.

I feel like pinning Dee to the wall. "Where is she?"

Dee takes a step back. "No one knows, Jesse. It's a mystery."

"Did you ever try to contact her?"

"I saw her in the hospital, right before she was discharged. She never told me anything other than ... basically to leave. She was so bitter." Dee's face scrunches with a pained expression. "So unforgiving."

"Do you fucking blame her?"

"I can't talk about it anymore. Or listen to that applause. I'm outta here." Dee grabs her bag from a chair and slings it over her shoulder.

Ms. Jordan's body whips around the side of the curtain. She whisks by, saying, "Are you guys staying for the after party? I brought donuts," but doesn't wait for an answer.

"Screw donuts. Wanna grab a beer?" My voice swings Dee around, before my hand reaches her arm.

With furrowed brows, her hard eyes narrow. "Why. So you can pick my brain some more?"

I press the heels of my palms to my forehead; my attempt at smoothing away tension fails.

Dee must think I'm losing it, or maybe she's taking pity on me. I must look pathetic. Her hand comes down on my arm and squeezes. "You okay?" Her voice is soft.

"Listen, let's just get the fuck out of here."

"Sure. Why not." She shrugs and flips her cap sideways.

"There's a fridge full of Sam's at the station, compliments of bro."

"He's working again?"

"Working is a matter of opinion."

"Will he be at the station tonight?" Her eyes are wide.

I shoot her a smirk. "Doubtful." Lifting a brow, I add, "Hell, not you too. Shit. Look at your cheeks. You're turning pink." I laugh.

I feel the tip of her boot graze my shin. "Stop being a jerk."

"You're into my brother, and I'm the jerk."

"Every girl I know is into your brother." She grins.

I shake my head. "I've got my bike. I'll drive over there, but you get a ride home."

"What about you?"

"I plan on cleaning out the fridge. I'll sleep in the back room." With Dad in Dallas, the thought of going home to an empty house is even more depressing than standing behind this curtain, not caring what's on the other side. "When there's nothing to go home to, well, why bother?"

She shrugs. "Must be hell for you. Your dad leaving, and Zoe and all–"

"Sure. I feel sorry for Zoe and her family. At the same time, I feel sorry for me. Christ, I was just getting to know her and she's gone."

She runs a consoling hand up and down my arm. That's all it takes.

"I want to tell her I'm sorry about what happened. I want to support her. Help her through what has to be a nightmare. I know what it's like to lose a parent. She lost two. I want to help her heal. Fill something inside me at the same time." I feel tears that gather but won't let them fall. "I want to ask her what the fuck got her so upset that night." I shake my head. "The girl's a question mark. Was it something I did? Was there more to it than Holloway?"

The muscles in Dee's face are rigid. I watch the movement of her jaw as she grinds her teeth. "Not gonna happen." Her words could rip my heart out. "Like I said, Zoe's gone. No forwarding address. I checked in the school office. Admin's lips are sealed. No one knows, or maybe they just don't care."

Zoe

PHASE 2 ... A BROKEN LIFE

Exciting day! Not. Molly, Nina, and I stroll up and down the aisles of the supermarket. We pluck candy bars off shelves, rip the wrappers and stuff our mouths.

"Shouldn't we be paying for these?" Eyes skimming the area, I ask.

Molly walks ahead of us, munching. Her yellow dress hugs her hips and butt, the brocade fabric cutting grooves into her midsection. With each wobbling step she takes, I hold my breath, waiting for her feet to fall off her backless spike heels. I imagine her turning an ankle and sprawling across the aisle, screaming for the manager so she can blame the store's slippery floor and start a lawsuit.

An elbow hits my side, and I turn to watch the scrunching movement of Nina's mouth. "You think those fat bitches pay for the cookies they snatch out of the bins over there?" Her head hitches in the direction of two women sneaking cookies while stuffing bakery bags full.

"That doesn't make it right." I frown, eyeing a Baby Ruth. My eyes travel back to the women: two cookies in the bag, one in the mouth. I shake my head. "Don't they believe in using the wax paper wraps?"

Nina's stare is blank, then she laughs. "If you're a germaphobe, you better get over it, chickie. You see what my house looks like."

I roll my eyes and moan. Will I ever get used to this?

Molly stops sauntering ahead long enough to eavesdrop. Licking chocolate from her berry lips, she chirps in, "If you want to go stand on one of those long lines just to pay for a freaking candy bar, be my guest."

I shrug and discretely grab the Baby Ruth. "Since you put it that way."

"I hate food shopping," Nina whines. Her foot connects with the wheel of the cart, sending it across the aisle.

"Push." Molly's heavy hand collides with Nina's back, propelling her toward the cart. "Hate food shopping, but like to eat," she says sarcastically as she pulls cans of soup and baked beans down from shelves and drops them into the basket she's forcing Nina to push.

"I like to eat ... out," Nina snaps. "Where there's decent food."

When we do eat at home, it's usually microwave or canned meals. Which is fine with me. Molly isn't the greatest cook. Her nose is usually buried in romance books and fashion magazines. Husband Rye McCabe is a stranger who ignores me, thank goodness. The thing I do notice is, he spends less and less time at home, not only at the dinner table, but in general. I don't hear moans coming from their bedroom anymore. Just angry words. I can't help but wonder if it's due to my presence.

Molly's temper flares a lot, so I keep my distance. I have no place else to go, and although I find hiding my feelings difficult, I don't want to be thrown out on the street, or land in foster care. *Imagine what Moody's house is like? Does he have a family? Where does he live? Is he still doing horrible things to other girls?*

To his own kids? The scenarios make me want to vomit.

Instead of healing, my PTSD is increasing. At night, I submerge myself chin deep in hot baths, trying to relax, but my head plays horrific scenes. Dunking my head underwater doesn't help, or stop the trembling.

The twins have lives. Dates. I mope around in Nina's room and write the story of my life in poetry and lyrics.

Tonight, Nina is standing before the dresser mirror, sectioning her hair with clips. Exposed by sleep shorts and tank top, her arms and legs are lean and long. Her light tan skin is sleek and admirable. She's not yapping as usual about school or guys, but rather concentrating on coloring the top of her hair which she's just spiked.

"You could be a hair stylist," I remark, combing my fingers through my hair to fluff it. Pulling it up and into a bun, I wonder what I'd look with short hair. Maybe I should cut and color it too. Nina remains silent, so I mumble to myself.

"Changing the outside isn't going to change the inside, so why bother?" Tiptoeing around the bed, I whisper. My secret is something I always carry with me, no matter who I'm with or what I'm doing. When I'm alone, I discuss it with myself, so why am I doing it now, with Nina standing three feet away? Because you're dying to confide in someone, idiot. If you don't start venting, the memories will eat you alive. This is what the person on the other end of the crisis line told me one night when I phoned ... the one and only time I called but disconnected without spilling my guts, which I believe I'm about to do right now.

Releasing my hair to fall over my shoulders, I stand before the bedroom window, watching the night. Seeing nothing. Thinking of everything. "Maybe I should go to the police." I begin by mumbling, then my voice pitches as I turn. "My parents are dead, and he doesn't know where I live now, so how can he hurt me anymore than he has already?"

"What are you talking about?" Nina drops a handful of clips and deserts the mirror to whirl and face me. "Who's he? Hurt you? What are you talking about?" Her wide eyes light with interest.

I open my mouth, but nothing comes out. My eyes find hers then shift. I focus on the bottles of dye and pile of foils that sit on the dresser, ready to streak Nina's hair a variety of colors.

"Oh God." I fall onto the bed and cover my face with my hands.

Nina flops down beside me and peels my hands from my face. Her breath is so close I can almost taste the chili we had for dinner lingering on her breath.

Her brow is high. "I had a feeling you've been hiding something." She yanks up the slackened strap of her top.

I edge away from the side of Nina's body, which is plastered against me. Space. If I'm going to do this, I need space. I hug my pajama-clad midsection. "I'm not hiding. I'm just not facing."

Nina's hand comes down on my shoulder, forcing me to face her. "Come on, Zoe. Give it up." She's demanding, yet there's something compassionate about the way she's looking at me.

Pulling my legs up onto the mattress, I hug my knees and choke out a sigh. One that's been boiling inside my throat for weeks, aching to surface. I guess this is going to be the time I bare my soul. To Nina? Who would ever have thought I'd be leaning on my long lost cousin. And that's exactly what I do. I lean against her, permitting my head to slowly fall on her shoulder, and I spill my guts to the girl beside me who is too stunned to even ask me a question. When I'm finished, my face burns. My eyes have been cried dry.

After nerve-wracking silence, Nina finally speaks. I watch her face. Her tanned glow has paled. Her dark eyes are glistening.

"Oh my God, you could've gotten pregnant with a rapist's

baby," Nina laments as she stalks back and forth across the room.

"No," I manage to choke out, "the clinic doctor gave me pills to take."

Standing before me, her eyes pierce mine. They're wide with something I've never before seen in them. Fear? "You took them?"

"Of course … well, I couldn't have gotten pregnant anyway. I mean," I stammer, "I know my cycle."

"But still," Nina shivers, "say the pills didn't work. Say you got pregnant. What would you do?"

My chin drops to my chest. "I don't know. And it's something I don't want to think about. And why are we even talking hypothetical bull?" I flare.

Nina struts to the dresser where she stands sideways, gazing into the mirror. She pats her stomach with her palm. "I'd never get pregnant." She scrunches her face. "The only stretchmarks I'll ever have are from burgers."

She laughs and I roll my eyes at her stupid joke. But deep down inside I'm still crying.

"I cannot believe you didn't report that piece of shit when it happened," Nina laments as we wait for the bus that will take us to the nearest police station. "No one else knows?"

"No," I snap, squinting the morning sun away, "and no one else better find out." Although she towers over me, I shoot her a threatening look before pulling my sunglasses from my bag. "Well," gazing up at a flawless blue sky, rather than Nina's accusatory stare, I reconsider, "just one other person."

Nina removes her stare long enough to dig into her bag for loose change. Then she hawks me again. "Your mom?"

"I have bus money," I say as she shoves a dollar bill at me. "No, not my mom. Someone I thought was my best friend."

Nina shakes her head. "I learned long ago, rely on number one." She pokes her chest with a thumb.

"This I am learning," I mumble as we mount the bus steps, drop our fare into the box, and find rear seats where we can talk privately.

The bus ride is brief. Too brief. My knotted stomach hasn't had time to adjust to the fact that I'm turning the man of my nightmares in. I'm about to tell the world about Moody. The realization that I'm about to bare my soul, disclose the secret that's been tearing my guts apart, brings a bout of nausea, accompanied by a shudder, and consider turning around and running away as fast as I can. Nina's lock on my arm would never let me. My heart pounds.

"I feel sick," I mumble as Nina and I walk into a local precinct.

"Not on me," she says, yanking my arm.

"I think I'm gonna run. I'm not sure this is such a good idea."

Pulling me to a stop, her hard eyes narrow. "Romanos don't run. We fight."

I must look desperate, because her voice softens. "I'm with you. You've got this." At the moment, everything about her is pure determination. The way she holds her head, stomps toward the glass enclosed office, dragging me by the hand.

Without an appointment, it's anyone's guess who will greet us. Fortunately, a soft spoken desk sergeant asks why we're here, then takes us into a room, where we all sit around a table and stare at each other. Nina watches as he prods and I talk. It's not me. Someone else, someone who has crawled from deep in my belly up and out my throat is doing the talking. This stranger tells him the story, but not all the details. She can't. I can't either. She would gag. I would freak and flee from this small coffin of a room. But when I've gained the courage to speak, the stranger in me disappears, and what I tell him is enough to file a complaint.

"I don't have to go back there, do I?" Lifting my eyes to his, I ask.

"No, dear." With a soothing voice he relieves my fears.

I refuse to let him involve Molly and Rye. Even Nino, because Nino would take a trip to Pleasantville with his boys and more than likely end up in jail. Because of me. I've caused enough problems for others. For myself. I'm not about to own anymore blame.

A detective enters the room after the officer leaves. "The sergeant filled me in, so we don't have to go through it again," he lowers his gaze to shuffle through papers on the desk before sitting down. "We need evidence, Zoe. Did you by any chance save your garments? Anything that could have his DNA on it?" With the tips of his fingers, he flicks the papers in a folder. Is that me inside that folder? I feel like specimen.

Remembering the afternoon in my shower, when I considered wrapping up my soiled underwear, I hang my head. "I can't go there, detective. I'm sorry. Everything involved with that day went into the trash and is long gone." Everything but my memories.

"I'm not sure what we can do then, Zoe. It's your word against his. Without evidence or witnesses..."

"What about the Women's Clinic? Can't you get my records?" I think of Maggie and the business card she slipped into my hand, which is still tucked into my wallet. I fish it out and slide it across the table until it stops at his fingertips. "Here's the name and address of the doctor who examined me, after ..."

"They won't speak to me without your consent." There's something about the detective's eyes. They're sharp, stern. I believe he's been down this road before and he's seasoned by dead ends. *Now that I'm here, please don't let this be a dead end.*

"You've got it." My knee bounces beneath the desk. "You can have my records ... anything."

He rummages though a drawer, then slides a consent form and pen across the desktop. I sign and slide it right back. The form reaches his fingers, but the pen skids across the desk and rolls onto the floor. "Anything else you need?"

"No. That's all for now." He takes Maggie's card, flips it between two fingers, then says, "I'll do what I can. Where can I reach you?"

"I wrote my cell phone number on the form the officer gave me."

"Okay." He nods. "We'll be in touch."

"You can't talk to anyone but me," I caution. I can feel the size of my eyes. I must look like Popeye.

Detectives are supposed to be seasoned. Especially those in the intercity. But compassion spills from this one's eyes. The lined skin on his face is taut, but his lips try to reassure me. I want to ask if he has a daughter, but of course, his private life is not my business.

When we leave, I ask Nina, "So, what do you think?"

"He was nicer than I expected. But considering you were there for reasons other than ..." she laughs.

"Getting arrested for theft or drugs?" I shake my head. There's something comforting about my cousin. I can't believe I feel this way, but I do. Maybe it's because she's so real and nonjudgmental. But with her history, how could she judge anyone else?

"So, do you feel better?" she asks as we wait for the bus to take us back home.

I take a deep breath, slowly releasing anxiety and fear. While digesting the past hour with the detective, I begin to pant.

"What are you doing?" Nina asks.

"Breathing. What do you think I'm doing?"

"You look like a thirsty dog."

"I'm trying to release negative energy."

"Good. You've taken the first step. We'll get you through this."

"I hope they can find him. I hope I didn't wait too long. I want him to pay for what he's done."

"I'd like to get my hands around his neck." Hatred fills Nina's voice.

It doesn't take long for the detective to report back to me. The first words out of his mouth are that Maggie can't offer anything I haven't already told him, as I never went into specifics during my visit. She can only attest to my injuries. To make matters worse, she told the investigators I mentioned my boyfriend got rough with me, so this doesn't go over big with the NYPD office handling my case. They figure I'm angry with my boyfriend and decide to cry rape to punish him.

"That's not true," I cry into the phone. "I don't have a boyfriend."

"Calm down, miss. We plan on investigating further. I'll check back with you after we visit the school."

"The suspense is killing me," I complain to Nina after a week has gone by.

"I don't blame you. Suppose you have to go to court? Do you think you could handle it?"

"I'd be nervous, but I want him in prison, suffering, where he can't do this to anyone else."

###

Days pass and August threatens to fade into September way too early. A week before Labor Day, Molly talks about enrolling me in school, and I get nauseous. I don't want to go to any school, especially Nina's school. We live in a rough neighborhood. I'm not up for this crap. I'm stressed enough without having to watch my back.

I'm sitting on the bed one evening, strumming my guitar, when my cell chimes. The caller ID alerts me.

"Nina! Get in here! Quick!" My whisper is harsh as I tap on the door of the bathroom where Nina's just turned the shower off.

"Huh?" Nino says through paper thin walls from his room. "What?"

"Nothing Nino. I need to use the bathroom. That's all."

"Don't tie up the bathroom," Rye yells from the living room. "I need to shower."

"We're about to have dinner," Molly screeches.

"I'm eating out," Rye fires back, "I have business tonight."

"Hold on," I say to the detective, trying to cover my phone so he can't tune into the zoo-like atmosphere that is now my life.

"Family issues?" he says, authority but kindness in his voice.

I pull my cheek tight and groan. "You don't know the half of it."

"Yes I do. I went through your school records. I know about the accident. Your parents. If there's anything we can do."

"Did you find him?" I say, running into the bedroom with Nina, wrapped in a towel, on my heels. My heart is thudding so hard, I can feel it in my temples.

"I'm sorry to say ... no. We didn't. The alleged attacker must have been a temporary employee and left without notice or a forwarding address."

"Alleged?" I gasp my protest.

"That's the law. Until he's found guilty."

"Are you going to catch him so you can put him in prison?"

He gulps, and I believe he's just taken a sip of his coffee, no doubt. I'm waiting for him to start chewing a donut. "I have a stack of files, much like yours, knee deep in my office. We're working on all of them."

"What about the address he gave when they hired him?"

"It wasn't a residence. It was a deserted shack somewhere upstate."

"Why didn't the school check him out before they hired him?"

"Why doesn't the school do a lot of things." His voice deepens. "I know how you feel."

"No you don't."

His sigh into the phone sounds forlorn. "Zoe. Things go

unnoticed. People slip through the cracks. Administrators don't always check out their bus drivers, either."

I should thank him for trying, but instead, disconnect him without another word.

"A lot of good that did," I complain to Nina, who stands beside me dripping water from her wet head that's shaking with annoyance.

She prunes her lips. "Trust me. If it was me or Nino, they'd damn well find us."

Covering my face with my hands, I sob.

"You need a change, girlfriend," Nina says, prying my hands away. She brushes away strands of hair too long to call bangs from my forehead.

The look in Nina's eyes, and the way she waggles her eyebrows, reminds me of Dee. I'm not sure if I miss Dee or still hate her. This makes me sob harder.

"Come on. Into the kitchen with you. You're about to have a makeover."

I follow blindly. At this point, could anything in my life get worse?

"With the changes I'm about to make for you you'll rock the school. So that'll be one less worry."

"What?" I object. "What changes and what worry?"

"I'm starting to know you, dude. I know you're scared shitless about the first day of school." Her lips pull tight.

"Ugh. I don't want to know. Just do it. And don't talk about school, please."

I sit in a chair, back to the table, and feel Nina's expert touch as she sections my hair. I hear the crunch of foils, feel the cold mixture hit my scalp as she brushes dye onto long pieces of my hair. While I develop, as she calls it, we drink grape juice and eat Oreos.

The next thing I know, I'm on my feet, pushed across the

room, and my head is shoved into the sink. Nina removes the foils, shampoos and towel dries my hair.

"Close your eyes," she says, before positioning me in front of her dresser mirror. "Okay. Open up. What do you think?"

Tossing my head from side to side, I watch blonde strands cover jet black streaks.

"Holy shit, Nina," is all I can say.

I watch her in the mirror as she stands behind me. This is the first look of concern I've ever witnessed. "Bad shit or no you don't like it shit?"

"It's ... stark." I giggle. "I mean. Wow. Black streaks on blonde hair. What a contrast." I swing my head again, watching my hair lift and fall with the help of a blow dryer.

"What?" I say, because her gaze is burning into mine. "What's wrong?"

"Look at your eyes," she sounds amazed. "The color, they're like, man they pop, they're like crystal blue." She makes a sour puss. "I'm jealous."

"I love it!" I throw my arms around her. "Thanks."

She pushes me away. "Don't thank me yet. I'm not finished with you yet."

"Huh?"

Nina turns and tugs her shirt up and partially over her head. Beneath her bra strap her tattoos begin and run across her shoulders and straight up to the nape of her neck. I trace a finger around a dark blue star then focus on the rest of the art.

"Holy crap, Nina. You're a cross between a forest and animal kingdom."

She turns and cracks up laughing. "You like?"

"Yeah ... they're pretty."

"Tomorrow, we're taking a train downtown. Where you'll get your first tatt."

"Me?"

"**W**hy the hell not?" Throwing my hands up, I shout to my bedroom wall. Jamie's off on one of his sexcapades. Why am I the only one holding up my end of the bargain? I have to laugh; he might have the right idea. Not that I'm so moralistic, but I could never live the way he does.

Breaking my internalization of the way my scumbag brother lives, is the ringtone of my cell.

"Hey Christian. What's up, bro?"

"Nada. What's doing at the Sinclair's?"

"Not much. I'm thinking about taking off for a couple of days."

"No shit. Not like you, bro. What's going on?"

"Dad's in Texas, checking out a ranch. My asshole brother is on his own planet. Why the hell not close the station for a long weekend?"

"Your Dad's buying a ranch?"

I chuckle with affection. "That's the old man. He hasn't been the same since Mom died. Lost interest in just about everything, the station included." My sigh comes straight from the gut.

Christian gasps, "Selling the station? That's like losing an arm, dude. We go way back. That old place holds a lot of memories."

"Been kicking it around, but actually." I inhale deeply. I've finally reached a decision. "Not if I have anything to say about it."

"Cool."

"On a brighter note. I've I got a wallet full of cash, a fully fueled bike. Atlantic City sounds like a plan."

"Sweet. Room for one more?"

I stride to the living room window, crack open the blinds and check the setting sun. "Pack light. I'll pick you up in an hour."

"Hold a sec, bud." Christian clicks off to answer another call. When he clicks back on he's lost his sense of adventure. "Change of plans. Sorry, bro. Can't make the big AC."

I chuckle. "Who is she?"

Silence.

"Keeping the goodness all to yourself, huh?"

Throaty chuckle. "Kinda."

"You worry me, dude."

"Worry about yourself, Jess. I'll be in good hands tonight."

"Oh-kay then." I clear my throat. "Sounds serious."

Evil chuckle. "Could be, bro."

After stowing enough supplies to last three days in my saddle bag, I hit the open road. I'm not sure exactly where I'll end up, but I'm enjoying the night as a free spirit. Tonight is mine. No problems. No women. Just me and the open road. The moon's shedding just the right amount of light. It's a perfect night for riding; refreshing wind keeps my head clear, the roar of the bike keeps me grounded.

It's quiet for a Friday evening. With no taillights in sight, my eyes catch the trail of a shooting star. Yeah, this should be a good night. Bringing my focus back to the road, I notice something strange up ahead. With a light fog settling over the hillside, the shape is barely distinguishable, but it seems like the outline of a car, off the side of the road. My headlight hits the spot, and the Beamer shows itself. I throttle down and pull onto the shoulder, aiming my headlight down the incline.

What the shit? It doesn't look like an accident scene. Just this one car sitting in a ditch. *Drunk* comes to mind. I'm not sure what I'm about to encounter, so I kick into defense mode.

I hop off my bike, grab a flashlight from my bag, and let my boots slide down the slope, heading for the silver BMW that's still idling. I approach with caution, hoping I don't find a corpse inside, or be forced into an altercation with a six-five drunk outside. My eyes quickly scan the dimness around me. I snap the light on, following the beam. Nothing but trees in the distance. My mind clicks back to the night of Holloway's party. Standing in the road with Zoe, surrounded by darkness and trees. Only now, my boots are sinking into soggy grass, not cold pavement. I shake free of the memory and swing my attention back to the car.

I'm ready for anything, but what I definitely don't expect to find is a dazed brunette half slumped over the wheel.

Careful not to spook her, I tap lightly on her window. When she lifts her head, I'm met with blue sleepy eyes. She's a knockout. She's also half knocked out.

"Are you okay in there?" I call through the few inches of open window. Her response is a guttural groan before her head dips back down. "Open the door," I say firmly. "Are you sick? Car trouble?"

I have no idea of this chick's circumstances. Is she injured? Trying to commit suicide? So much for a quiet night.

Her head bounces from side to side, and with it her hair, which drags across her bare shoulders. "Who ... who are you?" She squints up at me. "Turn the light off. I just want to sleep."

This chick is gorgeous but she's out there. Definitely not running on all cylinders.

"My name is Jesse. I was riding by, saw your car so stopped to help. You alone out here?" I say before walking around the car, checking for damage. There doesn't seem to be any. "Maybe if you tell me what happened, I can help you out."

When the light flashes over the windshield, I watch her rummage through her Louis Vuitton bag.

"Don't worry. I'm safe." Offering a weak grin I try to assure her through the glass. "If you've got a gun in there," I hold up a hand, "don't shoot."

"No one can help." She lowers her head, drops her handbag and her grip on the wheel tightens. "I'm not gonna shoot you. Him maybe, not you."

"I told you my name. So what's yours?" I try my best to sound consoling, although I'm freaked out, wondering what this chick's story is. I'm waiting for someone to come running out of the forest bordering the road. Some guy, maybe taking a leak, thinking I'm hitting on his girl.

"Who's the *him* you want to shoot?"

She faces me, pulls strands of her hair from the side of her face, and widens her eyes, as if trying to decide whether or not I'm safe to be around.

You might not know it, babe, but I'm wondering the same about you, shoots through my head.

She should know how safe I can be, I chuckle to myself. Especially in weird situations like this. Now, if Jamie had come to this chick's rescue, he'd be behind the wheel by now and she'd be in the passenger's seat, leaning over his open fly, giving him head.

She pulls a pack of cigarettes from her handbag. "Smoke?" She sticks the filter end of one through the window.

"Uh uh," I shake my head.

"Clean living." She smirks.

My hip's resting on the door, my arm on the roof. "My mother died of lung cancer."

She grimaces. "Sorry."

"She didn't smoke."

"What did you say your name is?" Her clouded eyes half close again. She angles her head, resting a cheek on the steering wheel.

"Tired of bending over to communicate through your window." My knuckles tap the glass. "With your window," I mutter, shaking my head.

"Sorry," she says, straightening in the seat to light up.

My face is inches from the glass. Close enough for me to get a good look at more than her full pink lips as they pucker to clutch the filter. "Besides sorry, you are?"

"You're not a psycho killer or anything, right?" Exhaling a plume of smoke, she scrunches her mouth and shrugs. "And I'm not apologizing again for being smart." A long dark lash brushes her cheekbone in a lazy wink.

I blow out a breath, because hot or not, this chick is becoming a pain in the ass.

"Neither killer nor stalker nor psycho, I can assure you. Just a boy on his way to Atlantic City." My hand comes down on the roof.

"And I'm holding you up." I hear the click of the locks just before she rams the door into my side. "Sorry."

I step aside and the door opens wide. Out shoots a pair of long, bare legs leading to a pair of black high heels. The straps fastened to her slender ankles add to the sexy. She lifts herself off the seat, tugs down the hem of her clinging red dress and when she tries to take a step, she stumbles.

"Oops," she says and giggles when I catch her. "Damn grass. Stick to comfortable shoes my mother said." She's in my arms, staring up at me, eyes still sleepy. "Thanks. What did you say your name is again?"

"Jesse." I set her on her feet but don't release her. "Too much wine?"

"How'd you guess?" Her grin is silly.

"Your very pungent breath." My arm slides around her waist. "Come on, sweetheart." I lead her around the car. "Up you go." I lift her onto the fender and place my body between hers – and a possible fall to the ground. "Get some fresh air. Clear your head. You'll feel better."

"I don't think so." She pouts and runs her fingertips over the zipper of my jacket.

"What's your story, anyway?" I push her hair behind an ear. "Didn't anyone ever tell you it's not safe to drink and drive? You're lucky you only landed in this ditch, and not head-on into a tree."

"Did anyone ever tell you you have beautiful brown eyes?" Her fingers leave my jacket to slip across my cheek. "Deep. Sensitive. Soulful." When she traces my jaw line, I start sensing vibes. "Are you sensitive and soulful, Jesse?"

From the vacant look in her eyes, I get the feeling she's not flirting. She's comparing me to someone else. So much for the vibes.

"Where are you headed?" I ask.

"Nowhere. That's why I'm here." Sighing, she looks left to right. "In the middle of woods. In the middle of the night. Is it the middle of the night? What time is it, anyway?"

"Time for you to take a nap. How about we lock your car and I give you a ride."

"Where?"

"Home? Coffee shop to sober up?"

"Are you asking me out?" She slides off the fender and her very warm body skims mine before her feet land beside my boots.

"No," I say, although my body feels the aftermath of her

curves.

Her palms drop on my chest. "Good Samaritan."

I'm wondering what I'm gonna do with this chick? "Look. Do you want a ride or not, 'cos I'm not in the mood for games." I blow out a breath. "And I really don't want to take off and leave you out here alone."

She salutes me. "Yes sir. Whatever you say." Then her bottom lip folds down and like someone flipped a switch, tears pour down her cheeks.

"Just what I need. A sloppy drunk," I mumble as I steady her against the car, lock it up and throw her keys into her handbag. I also hurl an almost drained wine bottle I find on the back seat out into the forest.

I have one arm around her, half carrying her up the incline, and her handbag is slung over my other shoulder. Must be a cute scene. Christian should see what he missed. When I grunt a low, "Fuck me," she cries harder.

"Christ," I mutter. "What's wrong?" I'm becoming concerned about being with this ... by now I realize she's not a kid. She's got to be in her thirties.

"He left me," she sobs. "Right here, in the middle of the highway."

"Who did? Why?" From dragging both of us up the hill, I'm winded.

"We were driving back from Woodstock. Fighting ... as usual. His cell phone rang. There were headlights. We pull off the road. He gets out and into a car ... with ... with some girl."

"What a dick," I say as I stow her bag. "You don't do that to a dog. He's a fuckbag. You're better off without him, so stop crying and move on."

"You're not kidding. You wouldn't do that to a girl, would you, Jesse? Who would do that to a girl?" She plasters her body against mine.

244

I unwind her arms from around my neck and fit my helmet on her head. "Do you think you can ride without falling off?"

"I think so." She nods and with my help, settles onto the seat behind me. "I used to ride when I was in college. Those were the good old days, Jesse. Growing up sucks."

"Sure does."

"How would you know? You're a kid."

"Why are you yelling?"

"Because we're riding."

"Holy shit," I mumble and flip my head around to face her. "Are you sure you're up to this?"

Pulling the strap of her helmet tight, she nods.

Before lighting up the bike, I check her shoes on the pegs. "Hold on tight," I say, locking her arms firmly around my waist. "You can rest your head on my back. If you feel sick, poke me, yell, whatever, just don't throw up on me, please."

Without incident, we take a slow ride to the nearest exit where I stop at the first place with a lighted *open* sign. Sleepy Lane Diner. Appropriate.

By the time we're seated, she's becoming coherent. We sit across the table, falling into normal conversation.

"I was a pain in the ass back there, huh?" She shoots me a toothy grin.

"I've seen worse, don't worry." I grin back. "We should call a tow for your car."

She shakes her head. "Na ah. Where to have it towed is to be determined." Her plush lips gather to one side. "This coffee is doing its job." She's leaning an elbow on the table, her palm supporting her chin. "You're really nice."

I lift a brow, acting all kinds of serious. "And you know this because?"

"You could have done anything to me back there."

"Now you tell me," I joke.

"I'm serious. You're special, as some lucky girl must already know."

"Tell her father that," slips out of my mouth and then I'm sorry, because Zoe's father isn't around for me to apologize to. For what I don't know.

"So, you *do* have a girlfriend." Her grin is sly.

"Not A, some."

She laughs then narrows her eyes. "Some bitch got Peter hooked on coke," she says to me, but she's staring off at the counter where a couple truckers eat what looks like meatloaf and mashed potatoes.

"That sucks. Who's Peter? The creep who left you out in the field?"

"Yup." Elbows on the table, her palms support her head. Her eyes are brighter and curious, very curious. "Tell me about your girl."

My gaze takes in every inch of her face. The woman shooting me the interesting blue stare is cool, but her eyes lack the intensity of the eyes I'd love to be staring into right now. I shake my head and avoid her question. "Your ex is an asshole." I sip my coffee and slide the cup in circles. "You never told me your name."

"Alana. My name is Alana." She smiles. "What's in Atlantic City, besides casinos and beaches? Do you have friends there? Family?"

I laugh. "You know, I have no idea why I'm even going, other to just get the hell away from life."

"Life can sure suck." She nods and chews her lip. "Atlantic City sounds good to me. Want some company?"

I slap a five on the table and shrug. "Why not?" Strange company might be better than no company at all. This chick's managing to take my mind off things. It might be a good weekend after all.

We hit the road and arrive at our destination before sunrise.

Just in time to get a hotel room overlooking the beach. After testing out one of the softest beds I've ever had the pleasure of crashing in, Alana decides the hotel is as good a delivery address as any and calls a towing garage. We sleep side by side, and I'm not sure who starts snoring first.

The sun streaming through the open drapes wakes me. I hop out of bed and she stirs.

Throwing an arm over her eyes, she groans, "Can you say hangover?" Rolling onto her side, she props up on an elbow and looks around the perfectly untouched room. "Geeze, Jesse. We didn't close the drapes last night?"

I'm pulling up my jeans, hopping on one foot in front of the dresser mirror, examining my face, which is in dire need of a shave. "We didn't need to. We're twelve stories high and besides, we didn't do anything."

"Just slept together," she yawns, throws her legs over the bed, and pads across the room in her bra and panties. "Peter is a hedge fund manager. Did I tell you he bought me that car? That was in better days." She sighs and examines her face in the decorative mirror hanging over the equally decorative dresser.

"Must be nice," I nod, while my eyes can't help but take in the scenery. Not the beach outside the window, either.

"What must be nice, the car?"

"How the other half lives."

"He's a dick. If that's what it takes to be wealthy, I'll remain a poor girl from DC." She's posed in the bathroom doorway, a palm on each side. "It's nice to be with a gentleman. A handsome one at that." Her fingers slide seductively down the door frame. As she reaches behind her back to unhook her bra, in another seductive move, she lifts a brow. "You don't smoke, but you *have* to shower." Her tongue running over her full bottom lip seals the deal.

What is it about sex that clears your head? Makes you feel

like a million bucks and begging for more ... until your rush of endorphins finally dissipates. When my body calms, and I begin to think again, I feel guilty for fucking every girl I meet. Why? Zoe and I never even hooked up.

Alana lies on the bed beside me, running her fingers through my damp hair. After releasing a series of "mmmm's" she whispers, "Lucky me."

"Why's that?" I ask as she tucks herself under my arm.

"Cos I have you all to myself."

"Aren't you gonna answer that?" I'm referring to the cell phone in her bag that has been non-stop ringing.

She straddles me and lowers her face to mine. "Nope."

"Cancel it, silence it, throw it out the fucking window. I don't give a shit, just stop it from ringing," I grunt, "it's distracting." I nibble her ear before my lips suck on her neck.

She cradles my face. "*You* are." Her words are muffled as her mouth comes down on mine.

After this round of endorphins subsides, I'm ready for "the talk".

"When I picked you up ... I wasn't looking for a one night stand."

"Me either."

"I'm not looking for a relationship with you, Alana."

"Me either, Jesse."

"This room must cost a buck. You paid."

"And?" She rolls on her side, throws a leg over my hips and her fingers roam my bare chest, pausing to pinch one of my nipples.

"What do you do anyway?" I watch the rise and fall of her chest, circle her nipples with a fingertip, then take one between my teeth.

"Administrative assistant."

"Nice," I mumble.

"My job or my tits?" she says, growing breathless.

I emptied my pockets last night, and it just so happens a few condom packs are within arm's reach on the bedside table. Alana's face is buried in my crotch. Her tongue is lighting my shaft on fire.

"Come up here, baby," I whisper.

She does a slow crawl up my body, takes control of the condom, and rides me.

We spend the day alternating between the bed and the shower, screwing each other's brains out. By late afternoon we're starved. So we dress in clean clothes; well I do. Alana wears the same red dress we arrived in. So we tour AC, where we eat and we shop, return to our room, share a bottle of wine on the balcony. We watch the sunset over the ocean, hop back into bed and fuck, then fall asleep in each other's arms watching TV.

"I feel like we're an item," Alana says, yawning, stretching. "I haven't had this much fun in forever." She burrows against me. "Peter would never–"

My eyes are barely cracked open. "Spare me. I don't give a shit about Peter."

"You're right. Past is past."

"Is it? Are you over him? Suppose he calls you? Wants you back." I lean on an elbow, my fingers combing through her hair.

"It's kind of a difficult situation since I kind of work with him … for him."

"Kind of?" I roll on my side. "Christ. Well, I hope you two work it out." I pat my gut, which is growling. "As you probably hear, it's time for breakfast."

Alana chuckles. "Sometimes the unplanned is the best," she announces, prancing around the room in a t-shirt she bought at a boardwalk shop. "I'll have room service bring something up."

Fingers laced behind my neck, I stretch out with satisfaction on the mattress, watching her gather her spending spree items, paid for with her platinum card. "True that."

Sprawled out on the bed, sinking deeper and deeper into relaxation, I watch her do her girl thing.

She's standing before the dresser mirror, applying mascara. Now and then I catch her watching me through the glass.

"Girls," I chuckle. "You and your makeup. Doesn't look very comfortable." I check the tableside clock. "Plus, it's time consuming. Why do you think you need that stuff? You looked great to me in the shower without it." I flutter my brows.

"Are you implying you want to wash this stuff off my face again?" She looks seriously seductive. "In the shower?"

I feel the rise of another hard-on, then Zoe sails across my mind. I never saw Zoe plastered with makeup and she was beautiful. Thoughts of a shower with Alana fall to the back of my mind.

I punch my pillow and adjust my head. "Anymore shower and my skin will peel."

"One more walk on the beach then?" She shoots me a cutesy smile while tugging on cutoff shorts.

"Yeah, I guess. Then we better head back." My other guilt is a vision of the closed sign that's been hanging on the station door for three days.

"Will you call me?" she asks as she stands at the foot of the bed, nudging my leg with her knee.

Like a chick who doesn't know what to say when she's put on the spot, I bite the inside of my lip. I unlace my arms from behind my head and pull my body up to lean against the headboard.

Alana runs a finger over my semi-hard shaft growing beneath the sheet. "I'll take that as a maybe?"

Hopping off the bed, I pull on my jeans and slide my feet into my boots. "We better pass on the beach. I've got a business to run."

Zoe

The moment the train pulls into the station, we're herded through the open door and immediately hit a sidewalk cafe where my cousins and I pig out on pastries and mocha frappes. My head revolves in every direction, my brain struggling to keep up with my eyes that are traveling like the speed of light over the variety of passersby. The urban area is inspiring, to say the least, aiding me with envisioning my first tattoo. Do I want something hardcore or docile?

"This is a major decision." Reaching up, I tighten the elastic band securing my thick pony tail. "Since I'll be living with this for the rest of my life, it should match my nature ... me ... right?" I cock my head at Nina.

Nina belts out a laugh. In sunlight, her dark hair glistens as do her berry colored lips, which are dotted with powdered sugar. "No cute little mice with pink ears."

I shoot her a wry look. "Not funny."

"Just kidding. Couldn't help myself. Get something you can add to." Nina's dark, variegated eyes widen, as though the wheels in her head are spinning. "Cos you're gonna want a sleeve."

Nodding, she lays her partially inked arm out on the table. "Which is what I'm working on. Go basic black. Then you can add some muted color if you want. That would be sweet."

I run a finger over the swirling designs tracking down her forearm, focusing on the tangerine tentacles. "What is this?" Lifting my sunglasses, I squint.

"The ass end of the hero on my shoulder. You seen him, right? Sam, my octopus." She pulls down the neckline of her shirt, trying to expose a shoulder and Sam. "Doesn't hurt to have an extra pair of arms around you." She winks.

"Whatever." My mouth peels to one side. "You're covered with so many tattoos, I actually never picked out Sam. He kinda blends."

"My point," she replies, pulling her shirt back into place.

"Let's rock." Hopping to his feet, Nino dumps his empty cup into a trash receptacle and casually brushes his hands off. He hasn't joined our conversation. He's been eyeballing every girl who's passed by.

Nina stuffs her mouth with a last bite of chocolate croissant, and linking arms we dodge traffic as we cross the street. We hop the curb just before a bus skims by, bellowing exhaust.

When we stop before the glass storefront, I drain the last drop of frap from my cup as I take in the scenery. My stomach is filled with butterflies. I almost feel like hailing a cab back to Pleasantville. Maybe running after that smelly bus. After struggling through a wave of my old life nostalgia, I drop my cup in a trash can, take a deep breath, and square my shoulders.

"Ready?" I ask Nina.

"Are you?" Her dark eyes bore into mine.

"It shows, huh?" I scrunch my mouth.

"Don't freak out in there is all I ask. I have to come back here, and I don't want to be known as the girl who hangs with crazies."

"Dude, I'm down for it," I snap and jerk her arm. "Let's go."

Destiny's Tattoos and Piercings is located on a side street. Seeing the motorcycles parked out front, watching guys and girls ride by, I set a goal; if I can save enough cash and get my license, I'll have a Yamaha by this time next year.

I might even buy one for Nino. He's becoming like a big brother. No one will dare lay a hand on me in school, or so he promises. This remains to be seen. I get stomach cramps just thinking about school and what I'll be facing in this rough neighborhood, but I'm going to learn to fight like guy. Oh yeah, I'll be able to hold my own.

"You comin' with?" Nina asks Nino, who's decked out uncharacteristically neat for the occasion in clean jeans and wrinkle-free button down. His coal black hair curls around his ears, and his dark shades give him a mysterious Latin look. Standing tall with crossed arms, he attracts tons of female attention.

"Nah. I'll pass," he replies, shooting a nod to two dudes passing by. "I got plans." He slings an arm around my shoulders. "Good luck, Zoe. Check you later." For a moment, he eyes me, then lifts a brow. "Don't overdo it in there."

"Ha. You should talk," I counter, my brow lifting higher.

Nino's arms are covered with dragons, arrows, and sword tattoos. I glimpsed him exiting the bathroom once when he was wrapped in a bath towel. My eyes were glued to the Tasmanian Devil sprawled across his chest. When he turned, it got even better. His back is fully inked with what he calls his Enfield creature: a combination of fox head, greyhound, lion, wolf, eagle talons. It's pretty impressive. He's even got a spray of bullet casings cascading from his shoulder.

"I think you want to be some kind of war machine." Shaking my head, I grin up at him. "You sure you don't want to add a tank or a drone or something more destructive to your collection?"

"I doubt I could fit another drop of ink on my body," he laughs, "except maybe here." He smacks his blue jean ass cheek. "I think I'll check out some sound systems." He gestures to an electronics shop across the street. "Catch you ladies later. Text me when you're done."

Nina gets up in his face, shaking a finger. "No jackin', ya hear? Remember what the judge said. No more juvie or plea bargains. You're pushing eighteen. Next time it's jail or the army." She's seriously scary. At the moment, she's more maternal than Molly.

Nino grins with an innocent face. "Me? Steal? Come on, sis. The only things I lift are weights." He winks at me, but before he can stride away, Nina whips out her cell phone.

"Hold it!" Nina shrieks. "This day is monumental. This event we must document."

Nina and I pose for selfies. Nino does a couple of pose downs, but mostly flips the bird over our heads before wandering away.

"No more stalling." Nina reaches for the door handle. "The time has come."

I grab her hand. "No. Not yet."

She clicks her tongue and rolls her eyes, but shadows me as I stroll up and down past the painted windows, gawking at drawings. In the window's reflection, I also see myself. Nina trimmed my hair, but it still flows past my shoulders, and my ponytail twirls halfway down my back. I tweak one of my hoop earrings, peering closer to check my coal black eyeliner and mascara. After a quick glance of the rest of me, I feel secure I'll pass for eighteen, even without the need of the fake ID Nino bought for me. With my money, of course.

My concentration returns to the ink I'm about to have etched into my skin. "That one's cool," I say, pointing to colorful plumes.

"Which one?"

"That one. The bird."

"Sweet peacock. But out of all these cool pieces, only one?"

"I wish I'd lose these butterflies," I mumble, unleashing my pony tail, fluffing my hair so it falls softly around my shoulders and down my back.

Feeling detached from reality, I tuck my hair behind an ear and follow Nina, who's sauntering in like a pro. We're dressed all in black. That's the basic color we wear now. My blonde hair rocks against the contrast of my ebony streaks. Nina's hair is now jet black, no more red, and she's letting it grow. She paints her nails black. Mine are bare, but I stopped chewing them. My long tapered nails are natural, like my pale, scrubbed cheeks, which now feel like cherry peppers.

A couple of artists rush around us as we stand in the waiting room. I gaze through the doorway, mesmerized by another artist who is tattooing a girl lying on her stomach on a massage bench across the room. She stops him to take a water break.

"He's doing a full back image on her, which will prolly take all day," Nina whispers.

A receptionist stands behind the counter, juggling books of photos, trying to accommodate a few customers all at once. I check out the wall graphics, and flip through a book, but I already know what I want.

"A nightingale," I tell Nina in a low voice.

"I thought a peacock?" Her voice penetrates the air all around us, and my nerves. "Like in the window."

"Someone called me a nightingale once." My heart trips. "I liked it." I sound pathetically wistful as I shrug submissively.

"Let me guess," Nina lifts a brow. "Your Jesse."

I deflect her gaze. "He's not mine."

"Maybe if you would sing in his ear, he would be." She chuckles

Thinking of the night we stood in the darkened road, singing to each other, my head snaps back to face her. "Stop it, Nina." *If only ...*

I glance around, taking in the scene. Trying not to appear too impressed. I've never been in a tattoo shop before. It's awesome. The walls are plastered with excellent artwork and samples of tattoos and rock stars.

As my gaze drifts, I spot him. This retro artist with dark hair and lively brown eyes. He's deliciously muscular. If he wasn't wearing glasses, he could pass for Jesse. He's the artist I want. For more than one reason. Getting a tattoo is personal. Intimate. I'll close my eyes and pretend he's Jesse. I have to know how I'll feel when he touches me. Will I scream? I have to know if I'll ever be able to let another boy into my life again. This could be a starting point – or a catastrophe. At the thought of his fingers brushing my skin, my heart begins to pound.

He rushes in and out of an office, carrying on-the-spot drawings he creates for waiting clients. Then he tatts them.

"He's quick," I whisper to Nina, who is studying an image of a heart, wrapped by a snake.

"I think he takes the walk-ins. You usually have to make an appointment, but if you just want something simple, like you," she pauses to smirk, "then he'll take care of you."

Watching him, my racing heart skips beats. My stare is glued to his every movement, lingering on his thick neck, his form fitting jeans. I so want him to be Jesse. I want Jesse to be him. I finally admit, I miss Jesse Sinclair. My mind opens with a flood of memories. I block the tragedy, focusing only on Jesse and the few stolen moments we shared – and everything leading up to that night – during what feels like an eternity ago. I long for more. Filling my mind with Jesse is comforting.

"Geesh," Nina elbows me. "Can you make it any more obvious?"

"Huh?"

"You're eating that dude alive." She laughs. "Joking, cuz.

Coming back to life is good." She pats my shoulder. "Gawking is good. How about some piercings while we're at it? It's your day."

"Piercings? Hmm," I say quietly as I consider parts of my body other than my shoulder for my first tattoo.

"I'm trying not to act like a novice, but I'm nervous. Do I look nervous?"

A big smile breaks across Nina's face. "Go sign in at the desk. This place is a madhouse."

After I sign in, we search through notebooks and catalogs. Snapshots and drawings.

I toss my head around. "I'm more confused now."

"What do you have in mind?" Retro guy is suddenly standing beside me.

I must look startled when my head jerks up.

"Hey. I'm Mike." He sticks out a hand. "You're next, hon."

"I'm Zoe. I'm ... I was ..."

His entire face breaks with humor, and his smile is captivating. Contagious. My lips stretch as much as his.

"I was thinking of getting a bird. Right here." Stretching the scoop neck of my knit top, I peel it low enough to expose my left shoulder. With the pad of my finger, I rub a circle to point out the exact spot, beside my bra strap. I don't feel shy flashing a bra strap because I tell myself, getting a tattoo is sort of medical, like visiting the doctor's office. It's purely physical. Physical? I stop the gulp that's forming in my throat.

While Mike's eyes follow the movement of my fingers, his head rocks. "Hmm. Nice. I think I have just the right one for you. I'll be right back."

"Would you look at that ass," Nina says too loudly, making my cheeks burn till the skin feels about to peel.

"He's cute. He reminds me of someone."

"Cuz got lucky." She grins. "Do tell."

"Some other time."

Mike returns with a sketch. "How about this?" The paper he hands me contains a blue bird with a sweeping tail. Its face is tilted skyward, and its beak is parted in song.

"A nightingale?" As I ask, my heart begins to pound. I feel like I'm about to stamp Jesse on my back.

"So?" Mike's piercing stare dig into mine. "Watcha think?"

"Yes. Yes. That's it!" When my babbling hits my ears, I want to shrink into the floor.

"Come on." He chuckles, leading me to a chair.

He sweeps my hair to the side. "We could add a branch, running up your neck. Whatcha think?"

"Whatever you think would look good. You're the expert."

His smile is warm. His touch warmer. But he's all business, which stops a threatening tremble. When he touches me, I don't have the urge to scream. I'm lost in a world of calm, then my imagination kicks in. What would it feel like to have him as a boyfriend. Now I feel unfaithful to Jesse. Dumb, huh? I watch him in the mirror. In the background, I see Nina horsing around with a couple of dudes. They're drinking sodas and laughing. Now and then one of the dudes takes her arm, admiring her ink. I have a feeling she'll leave with his number. Or vice versa.

When Mike finishes, he gives me a hand mirror and motions to the mirror.

"Check it out. Let me know what you think." He steps back to watch me. His lively eyes deepen with intensity that could make my knees buckle, if I let them.

"Wow," I breathe, then whisper, "my nightingale is kick ass."

"Yes you are," he says with a wink before he strides away to take care of another customer. Of course, I'm nothing earthshaking: just another customer to him. I sigh.

After a day of excitement, during which I experienced a refreshing reprieve from stress and grief, Nina and I return to the apartment

... and Molly. Major bummer. Rye is out. Molly is on the warpath. Need I say more?

We enter Nina's room to find it torn apart. Like a tornado just touched down, crosses my mind. Her dresser drawers are open, with clothing hanging over the sides. My stuff is scattered around, too.

"What the fuck?" Nina screams, charging into the kitchen.

Molly, who is digging into the back of the refrigerator, reels and screams back.

"Who the hell has been into my Xanax?" She whirls, manicured fingers clutching a bottle of red wine.

"I have my own drugs," Nina snarls, slamming her handbag onto the table. "I don't need yours." She throws her arms into the air. "Here. Search me."

"What else are you hiding in that room is what I'm trying to find out," Molly hisses.

"What the fuck?" Nina bursts out laughing. "My arsenal of firearms, cocaine, and half the football team."

"Don't fuck with me." Molly pours half a glass of wine and downs it, which seems to satisfy her. "Where's your brother?"

Hands on hips, Nina taunts, "Out doing his thing. You know, like screwing around. Like your husband."

Molly's eyes slit. "Shut your mouth."

"You're insane." Nina's hoarse voice cracks. "No wonder Rye and Nino never want to come home. I don't either!" She stalks into her bedroom where she slams drawers and doors. "Want a condom?" she hangs on the doorframe and yells. "Oh, that's right, you don't need them since your husband's lost interest in you."

With a sinking stomach I watch them, my panicky expression turning sheepish.

I can't hide anything from Nina.

"You took them?" she snaps, scrutinizing my tightly

sealed lips.

My head refuses to stop nodding. "I'm sorry I got you in trouble."

"You shoulda just asked me."

"I didn't know you had any."

She shrugs. "Don't worry about it. I'm always in trouble. Besides, I like it when someone else besides me pisses Molly off so bad the veins in her eyeballs pop."

Unlike Nina, I don't find humor in Molly's distress. I feel I should explain. "My mind races so badly sometimes, I can't control it naturally. So at night, when everyone's asleep, I've been sneaking into the foyer where Molly leaves her handbag."

Nina bites the inside of her cheek and nods. "I hear you. Listen, I've got stuff that's even better. If you need, let me know."

"I guess your mother won't be leaving her pill bottles out anymore." I cover my spreading smile with my palm so my laugh doesn't leave Nina's room.

###

After showers and snacks, Nina and I head back to her room to reorganize our things. I fold mine. She rolls her stuff in balls. Within minutes she's snoring. The one thing Nina can do that I can't, which I envy, is sleep.

Lying on my side, so I don't disturb my nightingale tattoo, I do what I do most nights; relive the rape, which I've decided to refer to as attack. Attack sounds more external than internal, and not as ugly or invasive. Thinking these things makes me shake. With the rape comes the accident, and I'm on the bridge screaming for my parents. Then my mind shifts to the sanctuary of Jesse. Focusing on Jesse is the only thing that keeps me going. He's my unattainable dream, therefore, with Jesse, anything is possible.

For some reason, thinking of Jesse cleanses my mind. He's the only good thing I've been able to concentrate on since I moved here. Jesse melts the ice that's engulfing my heart. Thinking about him is like a fairytale. Which makes me think of the play, and I wonder which of the understudies stepped into my part. Was it Laura or Sandy? How did my costume fit her? Did she remember her ... strike that ... my lines? And the spritely way to sing The Fae song? Did Dee fuss over her? How about Jesse? Did his eyes warm her as they once did me? My heart sinks.

I bury my face in my pillow, trying to cry softly so Nina won't hear me. I try to recall Retro Mike and how cute he was. But he doesn't have a calming effect. I wonder what Mike would do if I started screaming and singing in the middle of the road? Would he take me in his arms like Jesse did? Or would her call me a freak and run? Other thoughts take over. Disturbing thoughts. My mind is like a river, and I start dredging up the old horror. I think about my visit to the police, and how they were unable to find Moody: and the fact that he's going to get away with killing me is so distressing, I believe I'll burst. Literally. Burst wide open and let all the pent up bullshit ooze from my body, flood the sheets with thick black blood. Mine.

Tossing and turning without damaging my nightingale isn't easy. Relax, I tell myself. Chill. But I can't.

I'm fuming and amped up because now that I've confessed to Nina and the authorities, I feel worse. I want to punish Moody now more than ever.

So, as time goes on I plot my revenge. Exactly what that revenge will be, I'm not certain. But when I lie in bed at night and close my eyes, the tables are turned. He's strapped to a cot, and I'm holding a butcher knife.

Zoe

I'm tied to a table. Flat on my back. Dressed only in a cotton robe. It's sheer, and half buttoned. The air around me is so cold, I want to cover myself, hug myself, but my arms won't budge. Maybe they're tied too. I think my feet are in stirrups, maybe that's why I can't move, get up and run. Run! That's what I want to do. Scream! But I'm choking. I have no vocal chords. He's standing over me – a faceless figure I know I should be afraid of. I'm not afraid, I'm terrified.

The room is dark, yet a spotlight looms overhead.

Help me, I scream. Someone help me. But no one does. Not even the rows of heads bobbing over the seats before me. Because I make no sound, other than gurgling. The pleas are only in my head. Even though I'm on the stage – and the figure is engulfing me, I'm alone. I'm helpless.

Mysterious green eyes stare down at me. The most vibrant green this side of Ireland. No – Brown! Warm and caring. Jesse? Jesse! What are you doing here!

Zoe? What's wrong? What are you talking about?

Get me off this table. Out of here!

We're in school, Zoe. Stop it! Everyone's waiting for you. Your mom. Your dad. Look, he points with my wand, they're in the front row. He turns my head to the darkness beyond. I see nothing.

Here, take your wand. It's time to sing. Don't let them down. Everyone's depending upon you. You're the star. You make the room light up, Zoe. How about a movie tonight? Maybe dinner after the play. How about going to bed with me? Let me fuck you. I mean, make love to you. I love you.

Suffocation awakens me, along with cold sweat dripping down my neck, between my cleavage. Sticky gross. I hear a gagging sound. Mine. It's not loud enough to wake Nina, but I believe she stirred. I'm standing. Embracing myself. My heart is pounding. I want to wake her. Tell her about my nightmare. I want her to call an ambulance, because my chest hurts so bad, I must be having a heart attack. I welcome death. Scream! Wake the world! You can't live this way.

The room is dim. So silent, I can hear the sound of my own breathing. Or is it the muffled air and scratchy sounds escaping Nina's open mouth? Her head, turned on its side, is tucked deep beneath the pillow and sheets. A river of drool trickles from her lips. Is she dead too? Is she so miserable, she wants to be dead too? We're both the same. Helpless. Hopeless. Stuck in this tiny room. With no way out. Is this what death is like? Purgatory? Hell? Which place is this good Christian girl in?

I crawl back into bed, burrow against my pillow, which is flattened against the headboard and damp. And I try to relax. But I can't. So I think. My mind spins. Not the room. The room is quiet, motionless. My stomach is bouncing around inside me. No, wait, it's my heart. Stop it Zoe! You're not dying. What do you do when you're home – correction " what did you do when you were home and couldn't sleep? Hold your guitar. Write music. Lyrics.

I tiptoe across the room, but my guitar is not where I left it. If Nino took it to sell it for drug money, I'll kill him.

No paper or pencil around here either. I'll remember the words twirling around my head. I'll remember because this is the way I feel. This is my life:

I'm the fucked up reject
you scammed off the street
I bent and you pushed
I fell and you laughed

it could hurt
it could hurt so bad
it could hurt so bad but I'm numb

too painful

me it's always me
I feel selfish it's always me
but things I intend
never come through

it's too painful

there's a big sky for everyone
but mine's getting smaller

eagles soar cos they're peaceful
I can't it's too painful

The ringtone of my cell startles me. I snatch it from my bag and click it on.

"Zoe?" The voice is warm and rich.

Confusion causes hesitation. Turning my head, I check the alarm clock on the table. Midnight?

"Yes? It's Zoe. Who's this?" *Is there an emergency? Did someone else die? Silly. There IS no one else.*

"It's Mike. From Destiny's. Did I wake you?"

"Wake me?" I parrot.

His laugh is soft. "Yeah, I woke you. Are you snuggled in bed? I was hoping you'd be dressed and ready to party. But then, snuggling in bed could work."

"No. You didn't wake me. I was up actually. Writing lyrics."

"Songwriter, huh?"

"Kinda."

"So my choice of birds was right on. You sing." His voice oozes through the phone and my heart begins to race.

"I did."

My mind is spinning, trying to figure out what he wants.

"Where are you?"

"Downtown, at a club."

"Manhattan really is the city that never sleeps," I mumble.

"What?" he says. The background noise causes his voice to grow louder.

"What do you want?" I'm rude, but who gives a shit.

"I've been thinking about you."

He doesn't sound wasted. Is he for real? I'm at a loss for words.

"Zoe. Are you there?"

"I'm here."

"I thought you fell asleep on me." He's playful. "How's your nightingale?"

"Fine," I reply all too quickly.

"I was thinking " maybe you'd like to come down here " meet me." Now he's stammering. "The club rocks... If you don't have wheels, I can come by and pick you up." I hear the breath he sucks in. "Unless you're involved with someone?"

"I can't get into a club." My voice is flat. "I can't drink, I mean. I'm not twenty-one."

"Not twenty-one?" His tone immediately changes and there's a nervous edge to his voice. "How old are you?"

"Sixteen." I'm blunt.

"Wow." He blows out a whistling breath. "I thought you were older."

My fingers run over my face, searching for frown lines and crow's feet.

PHASE 2 OF A FUCKED-UP LIFE

I have a problem letting go. I still miss my mom, but I know there's nothing I can do about it. She's gone for good, and I accept it. I'm a believer in the afterlife. I hope I'm right, and that I'll see her again someday. I have another problem though, one here on earth. Zoe Channing. I examine the past year; the first time I set eyes on her. Brief encounters in school that whet my appetite. I only knew her casually. What the fuck is wrong with me? Then I think of that night, the one that keeps fucking with me; when I held her in my arms it felt so real, so right. I swear to God we connected. This can't be all in my head. She gazed up at me with those big blue eyes and the elevator I was floating on fell fifty floors. There was definitely something passing between us that night. Something I can't let go of. I cannot accept the mystery surrounding her disappearance. I cannot accept that I'll never see Zoe again.

Thanks to Dee, I now have her address. I do a few drive-bys before idling at the curb before her " strike that " before the house she once lived in. A middle-aged guy wearing a Yankees t-shirt is in the driveway, washing his SUV. I kill the engine, stow my helmet and for a moment, stand on the sidewalk watching him.

As I make my approach, he stops the flow of water but aims the nozzle in my direction. "Something I can do for you?" he calls out in an authoritative voice.

I give him a friendly wave and stop halfway up the driveway. "Hey. I was wondering if you know anything about the family who used to live here."

He shoots me a suspicious look and takes a few steps toward me. "Who are you?"

"I'm a friend."

"Of who?"

"The people who used to live here. I was wondering if you have any idea where Zoe is," my voice pitches, so I take a deep breath and swallow my hope.

My hands stuff deeper into the pockets of my jeans as I shrug. I must look desperate or defeated, because he drops his guard and frowns. "I know little about what happened, son. We dealt with an agent. Sorry I can't help."

He turns and starts hosing down his car. Just like that, I'm dismissed.

"Thanks for nothing," I mumble as I head back to my bike.

All day as I work, I can't shake the feeling of loss. Zoe and I were onto something. I sure as hell felt it and unless I'm more of a jerk than I feel like right now, she felt it too. This is what I'm struggling with when someone creeps up behind me, shocking me back to reality.

My natural instincts kick in and I spin. "You shouldn't sneak up on a guy with a wrench in his hand."

Huffing out an exaggerated, "Whatever," through plump red lips, the girl rolls her eyes. "I came for my car?"

"What's your name?" I give the redhead standing beside the lift in the Sinclair garage the onceover. I remember her. Who wouldn't? She dumped her car off and never returned. I drop the wrench, wipe my hands on a towel, and cell phone in hand I prepare to store her information, so if she goes missing again, I'll be able to reach her.

"Kirby." She sighs.

I shoot her a blank stare. "Kirby what?"

"Hayward."

"I'm Jesse."

"I didn't ask for your name. How's my car?"

My whistle is more air than tune. "Needs a water pump."

"Didn't you order it?" Her tongue clicks.

"No." I deadpan.

"What?" Hands on hips, her cute face turns sour. "That means you have one?"

"We don't stock all parts." I scratch my stubbly chin, enjoying her annoyance. "And you never came back after dumping that load of crap in my yard. You're lucky I didn't have it towed."

"So are you," she snaps, adjusting the strap of a large satchel hanging from her shoulder.

I grin. "Where've you been? I was about to advertise your piece of shit on Craigslist."

She stares at the ceiling, lowers her chin and scowls. "I had business, not that it's any of yours. When will my *car* be fixed?"

"Not sure. And you're the one who called it a piece of crap the day you left it here – what? Two months ago?" My arms cross my chest and I stare deep into her eyes. I like pushing her buttons. She'd be fun to play with. In more ways than one.

"I have a job I'd like to keep. I had to take a flight back home to work," she shoots back. "And now I want my car. Is that okay with you? I guess the parts stores don't stock water pumps either?" Her eyes flash, dying sunlight turning them forest green with lighter flecks.

I check the clock on the wall, then point out the window toward the sky.

"What am I looking at?" she squints.

"See those clouds?"

"Yeah."

"See what's under them?"

"Half of the sun?"

I nod a few times. "Very good. Which means it's closing time. Come on. I'll show you some Pleasantville hospitality. We'll deal with your crappy wheels tomorrow."

Her penciled brows arch. "What kind of hospitality?"

"I'll take you to the diner," I joke, offering my arm.

"What choice do I have?"

My brows shrug. "You could walk home and eat alone."

"No bike ride?" She tilts her head, cute again. "Like last time I was here?"

"Nope."

"You're forcing me to go out with you." Her brow lifts.

"Hell no." I chuckle.

"Oh for God's sake. You're confusing the hell out of me. Okay, fine. I'll take you up on your diner offer. Then you can take me home. How long will it take to fix my car?"

I shrug.

"You better be a great tour guide because it looks like I'll be hanging around for what, a few days?"

"Yep. Come on." Ushering her out the door, I lock it behind us, then lead her to the rear of the garage. "Hop on the bike."

"I thought you said no bike?"

"I said no bike ride *home*." I grin.

"You're unbelievable." She shakes her head. Throwing her leg over the seat, she hangs onto my arm for balance.

"So I've been told." I shove an extra helmet at her. "Put this on."

We ride for about a half hour – her arms locked in a death grip around me – then I pull down a side road and stop beside a field.

"I thought we were going to the diner?" she says, sliding off the back of the bike, adjusting her Yoga pants.

I grab the strap hanging from her helmet. "I told you to snap it."

"What are we doing here?" She looks around, spreading her arms out, shaking her wavy hair free and into place.

After stowing the helmets, I run a hand over my hair to smooth it. I take a deep breath and let it out slow. "This is your tour. Ah, smell that air."

Aiming her head skyward, she inhales. "Yeah. Nice, I guess."

"More than nice. Peaceful. This is where I do a lot of thinking. Hopefully it'll have a calming effect on you."

"Okay. So there's a lake over there," she points, "and a waterfall. Now what?" She squints up at me. "I'm already calm."

"If you were wearing boots, like me, I'd take you out in the woods."

She bursts out laughing. "And do what? Shoot me?"

I can tell this chick beats to her own drum. Shaking my head, I laugh. "You're something else."

"So are you. What can we do in the woods that we can't do here, beside the lake?" Her eyelashes flitter.

"Hike." I drop onto the grass and pat the ground beside me. "Come down here. You'll never see a sunset like this." I gesture to the horizon.

"It's beautiful. Is that your career? Working at the gas station?"

"It's my dad's place. What brought that on?"

"Just wondering."

"We're thinking about selling it." Why I tell her this, I have no clue. Maybe it's the burning curiosity in her eyes. Or my need to get things off my chest. Why is talking to strangers so easy?

"Oh. What then?" Sitting cross-legged, she hugs her satchel on her lap.

I watch pink and purple brilliance envelope the fiery sun. "Graduation and off to art school, I hope."

"What do you mean you hope? No set plans?" she asks, twisting blades of grass in her fingers.

"It depends on what happens next."

"That makes a lot of non – sense." Gracefully, she lifts herself to her feet and extends a hand. "Let's take a walk."

Taking her arm, I lead her toward the tree line. As we walk, I feel her eyes on me.

"You paint?"

"Paint, sketch, sculpt. A little bit of everything."

She jerks my hand and runs her fingers over the coiling tribal art on my forearm, exposed by my rolled up shirt sleeve. "You design this?"

"I did."

"Did you ink it?"

I chuckle. "No. A friend did. You said you have deadlines. Pretty young to be a reporter, but you sure as hell act like one."

"I work for a local magazine, which by the way, has an opening in the advertising department."

Pulling me to a halt, she stares up at me, intentionally batting her long mascaraed lashes. This starts the wheels turning in my head. With just about everything I've known my entire life gone, what's left to hang around for?

"An opening, huh?" I scruff my chin. "Swim?" Playfully, I push Kirby toward the lake.

She slams me with her satchel, then lets it fall to the grass. Then she unbuttons her shirt.

"Whoa," with popping eyes, I chuckle. "I was joking."

"I'm not," she says, unhooking her bra.

Not many things shock me. This chick just did. It's not that I don't want to have sex with her, but, "That water is freezing," I say, fearing a cold and uncooperative member. "Are you sure?"

"Sure of that fact that from the look on your drooling face you're about to keep me warm?"

She giggles. "Yeah, I'm sure."

Zoe

I'm running down an alley. A wolf leaps from a window ledge not far from my head. I suddenly have a gun in my hand. Before I can take aim, I'm swarmed by a mob of hairy people. I have no idea who the hell they are. I'm carried off and jammed into the center of the crowd. I don't want to go with them, but I have no legs, so I have to float with them. Whereever they go, I have to go.

I wake up shaking. No, my heart is pounding, and perspiration gathers at my hairline, but I'm not shaking. Nina is shaking me awake. Her lips are so close to my ear, her hair is tickling the side of my face.

I bolt from bed and we clunk heads. "What's wrong?" I pant.

"Ouch," she whispers, rubbing her temple. "Be quiet!" She shoves me back onto the bed. "I'm going out."

I check the clock then crawl back under the covers. It's after midnight.

"Where are you going?"

"With one of the guys from the tattoo shop."

"What are you, crazy?"

Grinning, she nods.

"The one who kept playing with your arm?" yawning, I ask.

Her grin broadens. In dimness, her eyes sparkle with a dreamy look I've never seen her wear before. "Yeah. Sam's jealous that he had his arms around me, but he'll have to deal."

I know she's talking about Sam, her tattoo. "You and your imaginary friends," I grunt, stretching out a kink in my leg as I let my foot dangle off the side of the bed.

"Well, this one's for real. His name is Scott." She plops on the edge of her bed, slipping her feet into sneakers. "I should be back before Molly gets up, but just in case I'm not, tell her I woke up and went out early."

"For what?" The thought of trying to lie straight into Molly's x-ray eyes makes my stomach quiver.

"Job hunting. That should make her happy. Whatever. Just cover for me so I don't have to listen to her shit or be locked in my room."

"I'll do my best," I whisper as she stands in the doorway, zipping her hoodie. "Be careful!" I hiss.

I hear the apartment door creak closed and hop out of bed to pad to the window. Scott is sliding off his bike, so I can't see much other than the outline of his body-in-motion, which is impressive.

Odd. From up here he doesn't look like a Scott. More like a Rocky or Hulk. Do I look like a Zoe? I have to laugh at myself. Right now I probably look like shit.

Craning my neck through the half open bedroom window, I watch Nina as she flies down the front steps and onto the sidewalk. Only half a moon lights the night. The streetlights on this side of the road are broken, so I don't get a good look at his face, but he's standing beside his Harley, arms crossed. He's removed his helmet, and I can't tell if his head is shaved, or maybe his hair is slicked back. Is that a pony tail at the nape of his neck? My face is pressed against the glass. My breath fogging the window. What I can tell is he's a big guy. Scary looking. But when Nina reaches his side, he unfolds his arms and lifts her into the air. As he lowers her, they kiss. He gives her a bear hug, nuzzles her neck, hands her a helmet and helps her onto the bike. Although he looks rough, he seems to be handling her with care. If this is what she wants, I'm happy for her.

I think of the arms that once held me that way, fall into bed face down, and bury myself between the mattress and blanket.

Days drag yet time passes quickly. Strange. Time, I mean. It never stops, yet I'm in the same place today as I was yesterday. Like the hands on the clock never moved, but the trees are dropping leaves, and the air is cooling. I enroll in the same school as Nina and Nino. They're juniors, I'm a sophomore. My grades were perfect in my first year of high school, so there was never a question of me repeating ninth grade, even though I never finished the year or took finals. I never failed anything in my life. Until now.

School in the city is way different from the suburbs. There aren't woodlands, no animal life other than alley cats and annoying dogs that constantly disturb my attempted full nights of sleep. Life is wall to wall people and buildings. Broken windows, graffiti facades, lots of motorcycles and bus fumes.

Traffic lights flash. The blinking one on the corner I'm approaching matches the beat of my heart. Mothers push strollers on the narrow sidewalk, so the twins and I step into the gutter to politely move around them, although Nina mumbles some smart ass comments like: "If I knew wheels were allowed on the sidewalk, I'd have ridden my Harley here."

Little kids, who look like pre-school or first graders, attached to their mothers' hands, joyfully skip. Memories of my first day of school are torturous. I remember Mom dropping me off at kindergarten. She didn't realize I could see her stalling in the hall, peeking into the classroom. I wanted to run out the door and go home with her. By day three, I had friends and wouldn't have noticed my mom if she'd been flagging me from the doorway.

Choking exhaust from a city bus brings me back to the present. The city is teeming with the first day of school. I watch a taxi pull to the curb to let out some passengers, and I fight the urge to hop onto the back seat two well-dressed women have vacated. "Take me uptown," I'll tell the driver. "Take me anyplace, as long as it's away from this bedlam." I'm not adjusting well to living in chaos. To being an orphan; I hate the word that has formed a permanent attachment to Zoe Channing.

The women, enrapt in conversation, have colorful scarves tied around their necks. They carry leather-like satchels and head for the wide cement steps my cousins and I are approaching. I assume they are teachers, maybe part of the administration.

"Welcome to my nightmare." Nina squares her shoulders and points her flat nose in the air, the same way she does when facing adversity, like the day she kicked a girl's butt for line cutting at a Coney Island ride. I'm not sure if her attitude is intentional. Is she as uncomfortable as I am? "Summer come back," she groans. "I can't take another winter in this rat dump." She doesn't turn to see if I'm listening, and continues her rant. "I told you I think I have SAD, right? I'm moving to LA first chance I get."

"You might have seasonal depression," I chew the inside of one of my cheeks, "mine is year round."

I feel like I've been sentenced to prison without a chance of parole. With a tug of her arm, I slow Nina's pace. Dragging my feet toward the steps, I feel a sickly imploring look gain control of my face, which she must find comical, because she breaks into a throaty laugh and shoulder checks me, propelling me up the flight of cement steps leading to the overpowering, very institutional-looking, brick building.

"Oh shit," I mumble, my eyes studying the way my straight-legged jeans barely reach the top of my black Converse. My fingers run over my form-fitting shirt. Am I wearing an acceptable outfit? Was I right to take Nina's 'basic black' advice? I've never dressed all in black before. My head is spinning. My jeans feel a bit tight in the crotch. My sweater suddenly feels too clingy. Like me.

"Come on, chicken shit. Make the best. Just think, for the next seven hours you'll be able to observe a zoo full of animals without even paying for an admission ticket. Where else would you get to see a bunch of elephants and hyenas for free? Bet your old school wasn't this packed full of wild game." She seems to be entertaining herself. Her head bobs to what I assume is a song that's playing through her ear buds. From what I've come to learn, not much else plays in her head.

Nino shuffles ahead of us, baggy pants dragging at the back of his sneakers. He fist bumps with a lineup of scraggly haired guys. One adjusts his ear buds and starts head-rocking to a rap song which I can hear through the short space between us.

As I slide through a turnstile, and pass some uniformed security guards, a shudder zips through me. The crowd is converging into a vestibule. The room is shrinking. It's a shoulder to shoulder nightmare.

I've thought about this day for weeks, but thoughts can be captured, erased. This is the real deal, and my stomach knots. I'm suddenly encapsulated. The noise in the hallways must reach at least a hundred decibels of shouts, screeches and laughter, but I'm emotionally locked in a cell with no windows or doors. So no one can reach me, thank goodness.

Okay. Calm down heart. You're safe. No you're not. You're an outcast. Well, you're with your two idiot cousins, remember? So you're not exactly alone. You should be used to unique individuals by now. Although I promised myself not to, I can't help but compare this place to my suburban high school.

I force my tightening neck muscles to unlock, and my head

circles like a lighthouse beacon. A guy stands before a locker and bangs the door against the one next to his. Even though his locker is open, he keeps banging the door rhythmically. He doesn't look angry. What the hell? Between swings of the crashing metal, he studies the contents, but doesn't remove books or anything else. He lowers the waistband of his jeans, adjusts his shirt and crotch, slams the battered door shut, and swaggers away. I'm staring at his entire underwear clad butt. My eyes fall in another direction. Clones. Many more clones.

In my old school there were basically three groups of kids: the ones like myself, approachable, normal, well, the way I used to be. Those who didn't know you were alive, and you'd never share a lunch table with, and the intellects. It was easy enough to know who you could befriend, who to steer clear of.

My old school had a name: Jefferson.

My new school has a number: PS 243

I don't have a chance to react as I'm body-slammed by something that feels like a Mack truck; a guy is plowing through the crowd, running up the flight of steps I'm heading to which will bring me to the second floor. Knocked off balance, my shoulder swipes Nina's, but it's the arms of another boy that stop me from crashing headfirst into a row of lockers.

After a moment, I'm able to catch my breath, organize my thoughts. Careless. Thoughtless. Asshole! I want to scream. But all I can say is, "Sorry," because my body has rammed an innocent bystander forcefully enough to knock a hole in any wall. Still he doesn't budge. He's tall. Muscular. He's lifting one brow.

He gazes down at me with the greenest eyes this side of Ireland. Stunning against his cocoa complexion. I'm at a loss for words. Simply because he's beautiful. His lips glide to one side, forming the sexiest grin imaginable. He's unaffected. My heart pounds. Although my eyes are blurred by anxiety, I can see this guy is incredible. I'm not looking for a heartthrob, but who can ignore beauty when it's standing right beside you, staring you right in the face?

"No worries. It's cool," he says with a soothing voice that makes me want to know him. Only as a friend. Because at this time, my raw emotions could use soothing. But in a series of long strides, he's heading up the iron staircase and disappearing from my throbbing eyes, but not before casting an interested look over his shoulder. Or was it calculating? Either way, not interested, gorgeous.

With the increasing noise level, the bell is faintly detectable. When the bell rang at Jefferson, the halls fell quiet. Here they get noisier. My first instinct is to bolt; the last thing I want to do is be late and have to slink into class when everyone else is already seated.

"I'll walk you to homeroom," Nina says. She's heavily made up, her dark lips barely separating as she offers, "I'll show you where to hang, and where ... and who ... to avoid."

"The bell rang," I reply, her words jarring my brain. Avoid who? What, will I be jumped? Maybe worse? A chill shoots through me.

"I don't give a shit if I'm late," she says, adjusting her backpack which dangles from one shoulder. Its folds make it appear almost empty.

I shake my head. "Uh uh. I don't need to be walked to class." My chin lifts higher than hers, my mouth pink, but every bit as inflexible.

"Suit yourself." She snatches the paper schedule from my open backpack, which I've also slung over one shoulder. Only mine contains school supplies, not makeup and hairbrushes. "Fifth period lunch." She looks impressed. "Me too. See you there." Before a deliberate turn, she advises, "Save me a seat near the rear exit doors. Not the gym. And don't buy hot lunch." She pulls her mouth down and stresses her jaw. "Unless it's pizza. It's delivered. Won't give you salmonella."

I don't speak to anyone and no one speaks to me. In homeroom, I sit in a middle row, near the back of the musty room, dump my bag under my seat and cross one leg over the other. After ignoring a few "Hey baby, wanna sit on my lap," comments, a teacher enters, takes attendance, and first period bell sounds.

As I expected, day one and the shit hits the fan. Nina never warned me not to enter the girls' room alone when classes are in session. I feel like I'm battling IBS, so I have no choice but to raise my hand during third period pre-calculus.

"May I be excused?" I ask loud enough for the teacher to hear, quietly enough to keep a low profile, but I cringe when all heads turn.

"You'll find the door over there," he says wryly, "the same one you entered though," eliciting a round of laughter, followed by chatter. "Grab a pass off the rack on your way out."

Apparently you just get up and walk out of class when you feel you have to. I seem to be learning everything the hard way, especially integrals, because I can't concentrate at all.

A guy sitting across the aisle, the one who's been staring at me for a full fifteen minutes, instead of the teacher, whispers, "Want some company, sweetheart? You're looking good. Like the way your pants fit." He winks.

Sick! Ignoring him, I lift my bag off the floor, dust off the bottom, and slide from my seat. Unable to make it to the door fast enough, I trip over my feet, which causes another round of laughter.

The halls are silent. Dim. Deserted. The entire scenario scares the hell out of me. I can't help but remember another school, another dim hallway. And I begin to shake. If I wasn't afraid of soiling my underwear, I'd hightail it right back to class. I'd rather be laughed at in there than be raped out here.

My stomach gurgles, and I have no choice but to maintain

my current course; I pass a few open doors, one of which is the main office where I notice one of the women who stepped from the cab I wanted to escape in. Pausing, I stare in her direction, deciding whether or not to show her my pass. Emotionless, she returns my stare then drops her eyes to whatever is on the counter she's standing behind.

"Need a pass?" she says after I scoot past the door. "They're on the rack by the door."

Holy shit. This place has no regulations or much security. Back-stepping, I pop my head around the door frame, "Just going to the girls' room."

She's not listening. Maybe she'd pay more attention if I peed on the floor.

I push through the door of the girls' room. When I enter a stall, I unzip and pull down my jeans, careful not to let the cold china touch my bare skin. This proves difficult when my stomach is cramping. Well, it's not IBS. It's my period. Early. No pads in my handbag. Great. I stuff my panties with toilet tissue. Before I'm able to flush, I hear the entry door creak open.

This sets off the race of my heart against my hands. Zip your jeans, quick! Grab bag, slide keys between fingers, get ready to strike before you're tackled.

Ready for anything, I exit the stall, do a quick scan of the bathroom, which is empty. Cautious, I tiptoe down the row of stalls, noticing a pair of boots with legs attached. When I hear the musical tinkle, I'm relieved it's another girl.

After dropping my keys back into my bag, I dig for a handful of change and wander to the tampon machine. I stand and stare, disturbed. It's either broken or empty. Filled with frustration, I'm ready to throw in the towel on my first day here. Should I leave for the day or check with the nurse's office? They must have feminine pads there.

I stand before the sink, scrubbing my hands, when I hear the air assist flush from the stall where the boots stood. Intentionally minding my own business, I don't lift my head to view the flusher, but feel the presence directly behind me. Way too close for comfort.

Instinctively, my eyes dart from my soapy hands, up to the water speckled mirror before me. My focus falls upon a girl who is practically pressed to my back. I feel her hot breath on the back of my neck. Smell the odor of morning mouth. She's taller than me, maybe five eight, and built broader. Nino would call her a brick shithouse. Nino would call her a bruiser he'd love to bang. I'd call her intimidating and someone to avoid.

"Move," she says in a flat voice.

Taken by surprise, I stare harder, my puzzled look turning to alarm, my mind beginning to race as I determine what the hell her problem is. When I don't move, mostly due to shock, she brushes her body around mine and delivers a violent hip check to my side. "I said move, bitch."

"There are two other sinks," I say evenly, desperate to sound menacing, although my pulse is picking up speed.

"I want to use *this* one," she informs in a throaty voice that sounds like she has laryngitis.

I stare into her cold dark eyes, deciding it's best to let it go. But I have to somehow defend my honor, so I weakly protest, "It's just a sink. But here, it's all yours."

Because she doesn't move, I'm boxed in and forced to slide against her body.

"Have at it," I mumble, grossed out because I believe what I'm smelling is B.O. I crank the faucet on the sink beside me, but before I can run my hands under the water, she's hip-checking me again, emitting a guttural, "Move it, hoe."

Hoe? *Look in the mirror* ... Now I'm getting pissed. Not only due to monthly hormonal issues, but because this bitch is getting on my nerves. Turning, and unfortunately, looking up at her, I use a warning voice. "Okay. So we're playing games? I didn't realize this was kindergarten."

"Yeah, and I'm a teacha," she snarls and shoves me into a wall. From the impact, my shoulder pains. My heart pounds, but I quickly recover, reacting with a drawn back fist aimed at her cheek. She catches my wrist before I connect, and twists it. Caught in a painful arm lock, I bring my leg up to deliver a kick I know will be painful for her, when I hear the door creak open again. Friend or another enemy, shoots through my head. It would be amazing if the person entering was Nina, but I know my luck ran out months ago. This all electrifies my brain, while I'm pondering my fate. Both my head and my aggressor's turn to watch two more girls pile in, none of which appear friendly. Talk about luck. I believe they're here for a reason. Me.

The three exchange smiles, a few words in something that sounds like gibberish, and the next thing I know, I'm lying on the filthy tile floor, taking excruciating kicks to my back, then my ribs, which knocks the wind from my lungs.

I refuse to scream. Instinct tells me to remain silent, but my hand reaches out, captures an ankle, which I dig my fingernails into. The leg tries to shake free, but I cling like a crab. This probably isn't the wisest move, because hands are suddenly on me, attempting to rip me apart.

"Get the fuck away from me, bitches!" Is that my voice? "I'll fucking kill you!" I'm growling now, like a cornered animal.

"Nothing personal, girlfriend. Initiation," one says and the others laugh.

In avoidance of a black eye, or broken nose, the best thing I can do is to cover my face and head with my arms and hands until their game has ended.

Do I go home? Never. In the nurse's office, I demand a pad, refuse to explain why I look the way I do, use her restroom to wash blood from my lips and nose, straighten my hair, and march back to class. Head held high. I've survived my first encounter. I'm a survivor.

After a very late dinner, I drop Kirby off at her aunt's house, making sure I leave with her phone number. I turn into my driveway and roll to a stop. Claudette is sitting on the front steps.

"Everything okay?" I hop off the bike and sit beside her, wondering why her bottom lip turns down, figuring it's got something to do with Jamie.

When she leans her head on my shoulder, a deep sigh rushes through her lips. "My grandma died."

My arm goes around her. I know the feeling of loss all too well. "Oh no. I'm sorry." After a compassionate squeeze, the muscles in my arm decide it's safer to go limp.

She peeks up at me and purses her lips. Her eyes are so big and pleading. "Can I stay tonight?"

Not this roommate shit again, runs through my head. Where the hell is Jamie when you need him? How the fuck can I say no to this tear-stained Bambi face? Claudette really knows how to play me. "Come on inside. We'll talk about it."

"Hungry?" I ask when we enter the house. It's eerie without Dad here. In an odd way, I'm grateful for the company. Even if the company happens to be persistent Claudette.

"I guess. I haven't eaten all day. Where the hell were you? You should have closed the garage hours ago." A tigress replaces Bambi. She yanks the collar of my shirt. "Hey. You're damp?" When she tilts her head, long shafts of coal black hair cover the strap of her bust-popping tank top.

"I had a dirty evening." Recalling Kirby and the lake, a chill runs down my spine, triggering a reaction in my groin. "Showered before I left the garage."

"Ah ha," she says, nodding dubiously.

I heat the oven, and in a fifteen minutes we're sitting at the kitchen table eating leftover pizza, drinking Cokes.

"What is it about my house that you're so drawn to, Claudette?" I ask before biting into a bubble of crust half covered with saucy mozzarella cheese.

Her cheeks grow pinker. She dabs sauce from her mouth with a paper napkin. "Your house is warm. Fun."

I almost choke. "That's news to me."

She sips her Coke and dabs her lips again. Then she laughs. "See. I'm grieving the loss of my grandma and you have me laughing. What does that tell you?"

"That I'm funny looking?"

A balled up napkin skims my head. "Want to see her picture?"

"Who?"

"My grandma, dummy."

"Sure."

She pulls her shoulder bag off the back of the chair and digs around until she finds her wallet. She flips through a few plastic sleeves, then stops abruptly and slides the fanning wallet over to me. I watch a single tear work its way through her lashes and bury itself in the crease beside her nose.

I quickly check out the nice looking woman with silver-streaked black hair. "She's pretty, Claudette." I hold the photo beside her head then pass the wallet back to her. "I see a strong resemblance. I thought your family was in France. Other than your parents."

"My grandmamma, as she liked to be called, came to live with us about ten years ago."

"Hmm. I never knew that."

"Why would you? I told Jamie all my secrets. Not you."

I tip my head. "Secrets?"

"She wasn't legal." She wrinkles her nose.

"Your secret's safe with me. Too late to turn her in anyway." I give her a shrugging grin.

With a tilt of her head, Claudette shifts the direction of our conversation. "Have you ever been in love, Jess?"

"I never said I'd tell *you* my secrets." When another tear follows the same path as the first, I soften. "What's wrong, Claudette? Besides your grandma?"

"I feel like everything is coming to an end."

I angle my head and bite into my pizza, because I have an idea of where she's going and there's nothing I can say to comfort her.

"Here, wipe your nose." I slide her a napkin.

She pushes her plate aside, dabs her face dry, then rests her elbows on the tabletop and clasps her hands, forming a perfect perch to rest her chin. "Aren't you going to ask what I'm talking about?"

"What are you talking about?" My mouth is covered by a napkin, hiding my discomfort.

"I've known your family forever." Her lashes form a series of long blinks, covering her misty gray eyes.

Reaching across the table, I touch her arm. "I've never seen you this way."

"You're so different from Jamie." She folds her bottom lip down.

"I appreciate that." I wink. "More than you can imagine."

She giggles. "You have so much more going for you. You're hot," she grins, "you're charming. You're hot."

I burst out laughing, push the chair back, and proceed to clear the table. Whatever possesses me to stand behind Claudette's chair and massage her shoulders, I'll never know, but I find myself doing just that.

"Mmm. That feels good." She takes one of my hands and brings it to her lips. In a single heartbeat, she's on her feet and in my arms. Her lips seeking mine. For a moment, I indulge. I know it's wrong to lead her on, but thanks to Claudette, I'm feeling very human tonight.

Her arms wind around my neck, mine go around her waist, and we stand in the middle of the kitchen, lips massaging, our bodies pressing close. I'm not sure if it's attraction bringing us together as much as mutual loss. Loneliness, perhaps. We sway. We grind. Our mouths work hard. But when she reaches for my fly, my senses snap into high gear: she's my brother's Ex, she's my brother's Ex! I take her hand and bring it to my lips.

"When you asked me if I've ever been in love..."

She gazes up at me, eyes warm with passion.

I take her face in my hands, my thumbs stroking her cheeks. "You're beautiful, Claudette. You're sweet."

Her eyes narrow. "I can see a *but* coming."

My hands drop to her shoulders. "Tell me about you and Jamie."

It's not that I'm interested in my brother's sex life. I'm more interested in a girl's perspective of love. If that's what they shared. Claudette's half of the pseudo relationship, anyway.

"Jamie is what my grandma would call un voleur dans la nuit."

I chuckle, and tuck a lock of hair behind her ear. "You French girls are something else." I remember Christian calling Claudette something else, and my hold on her tightens. "Are you going to tell me what it means, or should I use my imagination?"

"Get that look out of your sexy brown eyes, Sinclair. Grandmama would never talk sex with me." She giggles. "It means a thief in the night. My grandma called Jamie that. She said he stole my heart when I wasn't looking."

My finger traces the curve of her neck, circling her collarbone. "Were you looking?"

She arches a brow. "Wasn't every girl?"

My arms drop to my sides and I take a step back. "What is it about my brother?"

She throws her hands up. "What is it about you? That you don't see how girls look at you. How I look at you."

I find her ribcage and dig my fingers into her toned muscles until she's laughing hysterically.

"You don't want to hear it," she manages to say, then begins to hiccup. "But it's true. I find you very attractive." Abruptly, she stops laughing. "As I said, I feel like things are coming to an end. And I'm afraid."

"Of what?" I sling an arm around her and draw her to my side.

"Having to give up on Jamie. There's only so much I can take ... so long I can wait."

My bottom lip finds its way into my mouth and I bite down hard. "He's so not worth your time. And speaking of tools, watch out for Christian."

Her face crunches with confusion, then she smirks. "He asked me out."

Before I can react, she giggles. "It was just for fun. I told him nothing serious. Someone else has my heart."

The look in her eyes tells me I better set ground rules. "I should tell you. I'm not Jamie and never will be. In more ways than one."

"You don't like me." Pulling away, she pouts.

I bob my head a few times, thinking of how to explain. All I can come up with is, "Not in that way."

She trickles a finger down my neck, pressing firmer when she reaches my chest. "Why?"

For this, I turn my head. Stare out the window at the street lights. "I never felt much for any girl until I met..."

Urging my face to hers, she presses her index finger over my lips. "Come on. Take me upstairs and tuck me in. We'll both feel better. If you can't have what you want, take what you can get."

I squeeze her shoulders, then tap the tip of her nose. Playfully, but I'm dead serious. "I'll tuck you in, but I'm sleeping in my own bed."

Claudette frowns, but follows me up the stairs, going on and on about how things used to be and what a prick Jamie is now.

After giving Claudette a t-shirt to wear, I blow a kiss across the room and close the door, leaving her to the solace of my brother's room. Then I do what I always do on complicated nights like this. I paint. This time the lamp in my room is on; with Claudette in the next room, so are my jeans. I pick up the brush and begin dipping into jars. Tonight, my imagination runs free.

Stepping back, I let my eyes focus at will on the once blank canvas, which is now covered with clouds and stars. A moon and the bust of a woman are set to one side. Feathery wings extend from behind her shoulders and up into the sky which is edged with pink and purple ribbons. When I study the painting closer, I realize the face doesn't resemble the girl I've been with tonight, or the bare flesh I've touched. I've painted a stunning blonde with sparkling blue eyes. The pastel rainbow crossing the midnight sky is her wand, and in the distance is a muted red rose.

I lie in bed thinking about Zoe and what might have been between us had things not gone south. I can still feel the magnetism that drew us together. I wonder where Zoe is, and if she ever thinks about me.

I finally drift off to sleep, only to be rudely awakened by slamming car doors. I hop out of bed and stand at the window. Jamie's truck is in the driveway, and he's on his way up the walk with not one, but two girls. Holy Fuck. Claudette is in his room. I jog down the hall, and by the time I'm able to wake her, Jamie is blocking the doorway, smirking, flanked by the sweet things wearing shorts and tank tops. Cheerleaders, runs through my mind. Just his speed.

Claudette rubs her sleepy eyes and stares first at me, then at him.

"Jamie?" she rasps. "What are you doing here?" She swings her legs over the side of the bed and hops to her feet.

"I live here, and you're in my room," he says so coldly, I fight the urge to plant a fist in his face. "And unless you plan on joining us," he propels the girls into the room with swats on the asses, "you should leave, Claudette."

Claudette falls back onto the bed, stunned. She looks like she's been slapped in the face by a bully. And right now, my brother is a fucking bully.

How he can be so cruel is beyond me.

Claudette bursts into tears and flies into my arms.

"There you go little bro. Enjoy." Jamie grins. "You don't need to thank me."

His eyes roll over me, and his grin stretches when he sees I'm wearing only boxers.

"You're a fucking dick," I snarl, pulling Claudette out the door with me.

With Claudette plastered against me, we walk down the hall and into my room.

Gripping her shoulders, I guide her. "You can have my bed. I'll sleep on the couch."

"No. I don't want to sleep alone, especially with them in the next room. I can't believe he brought them here. Not one, but two." Her voice chokes. "Stay with me Jesse."

"Christ," I groan, "this is against my better judgment. Only till you're asleep." I let out a sigh. "Only because you're upset."

I tuck her in and climb on top of the blankets, keeping a safe distance between us. Immediately, I turn my back. Within seconds, Claudette is wrapped around me. She buries her face at the nape of my neck, hugging me like I'm her pillow.

I feel her body curl around mine. Christ, my brother is in the next room, humping two chicks, and I'm in here spooning with his ex. How much more fucked up can it get?

I don't try to untangle myself until the steady puffs of air warming my neck tell me she's asleep.

If I had earplugs, I'd use them so I didn't have to hear the animal sounds coming from my brother's bedroom. This makes me rethink Dad's suggestion of selling the house and moving to Texas before Jamie turns the place into the roach motel.

Claudette's arm drapes my shoulder, one of her legs are slung over my hip. Each time I edge away, she clings tighter. Her soft breasts slide across my back. By now, my dick is half hard.

"This isn't working," I mumble, trying to avoid a painful erection. "I'll never sleep like this."

"You're used to sleeping alone," she states groggily.

"I guess," I whisper, rolling to my side so I can flip her over and distance myself. Wrong move. In moments, her butt is pressed against me, which is even warmer than her tummy, and it's heating my crotch almost to the point of no return. Her hair tickles my nose. I inhale her scent – no it's mine; my shampoo and body wash are rising from her skin.

Reminding my dick she's like my little sister, I smile into her hair and let my arms wrap around her. Right now, I feel like I'm five and sleeping with my teddy bear.

Zoe

The blend of steamed/boiled/fried food odors engulfing the cafeteria is not very appetizing. Nauseating actually when you're also inhaling perfume, aftershave and perspiration of the students filing in. Boiler room comes to mind. For a moment I panic, then fight the urge to scream and flee. I want to fall back into amnesia, at least hold my breath. Maybe I can pass out and this nightmare will end.

Now I understand why Nina warned me about hot lunch. I tuck my torn shirt into the waistband of my jeans as best as I can, but I have a feeling my girls' room encounter will not go undetected.

Nina barges through a group of feet-dragging kids. "What the hell happened to you?" Eyes bulging, she almost dives across the table I'm coiling behind. "Look at you. You're wrecked. Was your first morning that fucked?" Her eyes cover as much of me as possible in the few breaths she takes before continuing her interrogation. "And your pants are stained with ... white shit? Ew. What is that crap, cum?"

"You're disgusting." I give her a loud click of my tongue.

"Okay. You look like you've been working in the kitchen making Molly's shitty biscuits." She chuckles and flops onto a chair beside me. "Is that more appropriate for your virginal ears?"

Attempting to act unaffected, I stare straight ahead, avoiding her intimidating dark eyes. I'm focusing on a cackling guy climbing over a lunch table, thinking for sure I've landed in the zoo Nina warned me about. "There was something sticky in the bathroom, all over the floor," trying for nonchalant, I give her my cool reply. The last thing I want to do is admit to my streetwise cousin that I'm a nerd who had her ass kicked.

"Why don't you ask the janitor?" I snap. Did I just say that?

She picks at some loose strings hanging from the collar of my shirt.

I'm wrapping myself with my arms, trying to conceal the scratches that are starting to bruise. Nina grabs one of my wrists and yanks my arm straight. When her head tilts, her eyes narrow.

"Floor?" The tone of her voice forces me to face her. Bug-eyed, she slides her stare from mine long enough to rub the skin of an apple with a napkin before digging her teeth into it. "And your shirt is ripped." She lifts a pencil-darkened brow. "Truth, Zoe."

My voice is as flat as the buttered roll my fingers are squeezing. "I made the mistake of using the unmonitored bathroom during class."

She swipes her lips with the napkin then rolls the half eaten apple in it. "You were jumped?" Her face tightens, and shock leaks from her voice. Her brows settle, telling me she expected as much, but didn't want to warn me ahead of time for fear of me leaving town without a forwarding address.

"Great timing," I mumble as Nino bops toward us. "I didn't think he'd find us in this chaos." Then my fingers run across the initials carved into the underside of the table, telling me Nina, Nino, and a bunch of other kids, have claimed this section as their own.

Nino, fingers and wrists cuffed and covered with chunky silver jewelry, balances fries and a soda in one hand. His other hand is waving "come on over" signals to a perky blonde sitting two tables away.

"Zoe got jumped this morning." I'm almost stomped to death and Nina is now casual. I shake my head.

"Who did this?" Outraged Nino, who had plopped onto a seat, jumps to his feet and pounds the table with a fist. "Bitches or dudes?" His attention is divided between me and the blonde, who is grinning at him but not moving from her seat. So I'm not sure if Nino is really outraged about my ass-kicking or putting on a show for the flirty girl who repositions herself, hiking her skirt up to show off more than I want to see.

"Do guys beat up on girls in this school?" I'm sickened at the thought.

Nina shakes her head. I'm not sure if she's replying to my question or just confirming I'm pathetic.

"This calls for revenge. Details," Nino prods. His fists are balled. I haven't seen his face this flushed since Nina hijacked his cell phone to make prank calls to a girl he had his eye on. "No one fucks with the Romanos." He retakes his seat and flips a fry into the air, catching it in his teeth.

I look from one face to the other, happy they're familiar, not so happy to be stuck here with them, no less related to them. "So now I'm a Romano ?"

"Yeah. You're one of us," they say in time, nodding.

I swear, they might not look identical, but they're attitudes and habits are spot on. It's as though one thinks and the other verbalizes. Amazing.

"I'm a Romano. Great. Just don't ever tell me Molly is my mother." I try to laugh, but fight off a stomach churning sensation of loss and desperation. I want my old life back. I want a lot of things, but since I can't have what I want…

They laugh. "Only if you don't remind us that Molly is *our* mother."

"Kidding aside. Just let it slide. I don't want any more trouble," I say, picking at my roll. From the corner of my eye, I watch a guy and girl sitting close together. The guy is cute and looks nice. He's gentle with her. Does he love her? He reminds me of Jesse, and how he acted the night of the party. This makes me even more homesick. Lost. Pissed off that my life has been forever changed.

"If you don't retaliate, they'll be back for more, believe me." Nina's warning sends a chill down my tightening spine, which I'm in the process of soothing the spasms from with the palm of my reaching hand.

"This has happened to you?" Unable to visualize anyone bullying Nina, I feel my eyes will fall out of my head.

She cracks her knuckles and frowns, then pulls out a lipstick from her bag and applies a red coating to her mouth as she replies, "Once. When my back was turned." Lip-smack. "They'd never come to my face. Now I have eyes in back of my head. Trust me. They didn't walk naturally for a week." Her laugh is caustic.

The way Nina talks is disturbing. She's calmly serious and scaring the crap out of me. What kind of place did my parents will me to? I know our family is small, and my grandparents are gone, but couldn't they have found a safer place for their only daughter?

"Describe to me, who did this to you," Nino is relentless ... and restless. He's up on his feet and pacing, one pumping fist slapping his palm. One would think he's on uppers. Come to think of it, maybe he is.

Painfully, and with embarrassment, I disregard Nino, describing the trio to Nina, and she instantly knows who they are. As I speak, her facial muscles shrink more and more until I think her cheeks will implode.

Nino, still pacing, repeats, "Hoot-de-van. Sounds like a little after school detention."

"Hoot-de-van?" I squint at Nina.

Shrugging, she tosses her head. "Imbecile jargon him and his idiotic boys dreamed up so they can talk shit and no one else will know what they're saying."

Unlike me, they seem to be enjoying the thought of confrontation.

Breaking the tension, Nina spins half around and sucks in a breath. "Oh my God."

I freak, thinking she's just spotted my attackers. "What? They're here?" I fight the urge to cover my eyes and peek through my fingers.

"Yeah," her chuckle is long and devilish, "right over there."

Pulse picking up, I dare to follow Nina's hitching head. "What am I looking at? Those guys?"

"They're not just guys, dude. They're Chasing Dinero."

Filled with confusion, my head snaps back. A tiny bone in my neck clicks. "Huh? I thought it was those girls—" I emit a deep sigh of relief and the band around my chest releases, so now I can breathe again.

"You're into them?" Chin in palms, I study the trio. Idly, because they're involved in conversation and I feel confident they're only tuned into themselves. I doubt they'll feel our investigating eyes examining every visible part of them.

"Duh. Who doesn't? They're a local band, but someday they're gonna be big." She nods with reverence as she speaks. "We can say we knew them when."

"When what?" Considering my appearance, I fluff my hair and clip my lips together to feel if they're bare or somewhat glossy.

"When they were just hot guys playing cool music." Elbows on table, chin in palms, her stare is also pinned to their table.

"Mmm," she moans. "Delectable."

"You don't have to convince me." Immediately, the wheels in my head begin to turn. Anything, anyone, related to music piques my interest. "I'd like to hear them sometime. Where do they play?"

"Richie's garage sometimes," Nino says, stuffing his mouth with fries, oblivious to the fact that Nina and I are acting like stalkers.

"Richie?" I tilt my head, trying to guess on my own which one he is. Has to be the one with the curling dark hair, I assume.

Finally tearing her eyes from them, Nina looks at me as if I should know. "Yeah, it's Richie Santana's band."

"Which one's Richie?" I could kick myself for asking, because Nina points a finger at their table, making me want to hide under ours. Pulling lip gloss from my bag, I ask, "Do they ever play in public?"

Crushing his soda can, Nino belches. "Sometimes down at Deluge. It's a French place where the kids hang out."

"It's not French, idiot," Nina snaps, throwing her apple core at him.

Mental note. French or not, find out where Deluge is. Gather the courage to walk through the door, well, maybe gawk through the windows first.

"Zoe, you play guitar," Nino says, deep in thought, as his eyes refocus on the blonde, whose actions say she's begging Nino to join her. "Maybe you can hook up with them sometime."

"Yeah. Sure. Like they'd hang with a nobody." I drop my head to the table, inadvertently clunking my forehead.

"Yeah, they're somebody," Nina's eye roll tells me she thinks I'm more of an ass than a nobody. She stabs one of my sore ribs with her elbow and chuckles. "Don't make yourself right, but do right. Get me?"

"Yeah, sure," massaging my forehead, I agree, with no idea

of what the hell she's talking about.

"Hey, maybe I could slip Richie some of your music sometime," Nino's eyes glow. Demonic.

"My stuff?" I shake my head so furiously, I jar my brain. "No one's heard my stuff. No. I couldn't."

"But I could," Nina says in a devious way.

"You just want a reason to hit on Santana." Nino cackles. "Fat chance of nailing him. There aren't enough months in this year for you to get your claws into Santana."

Nina shoots Nino a scowl. "Fuck you, dick. Bet you can't make that blonde."

"Watch me," he says slyly. "Let her idle her sweet little engine a while longer."

Ignoring my cousins, I make my second mental note. Find out where their lockers are. I can easily slip some of my music inside when no one's around. Maybe with a polite note, on second thought not. As I connive, I become more conscious of watching them, now concerned my magnetized eyes might draw their attention. Still, this doesn't stop me. Being in the same room with a popular rock band is mesmerizing. Uplifting. My one joy left in this world is my music. Although, I haven't written anything great since … since all the shit went down. Pounding words onto paper used to be as easy as breathing. Not now. Now I'm locked inside myself. Straining for every word that refuses to be turned into a song.

Richie looks dangerous. Sleek black hair drapes one of his equally dark eyes, coiling down his neck. He wears leather straps on his wrists, and he has that mean look girls like me want to steer clear of but are so damn drawn to, regardless of the consequences. Tattoos creep up his arms and around the neck of his t-shirt, and Lord knows where else.

"Who's the guy bathing his bun with ketchup?" I giggle. Though my eyes are cautiously focusing on Richie, my peripheral is working overtime. Taking in the cleaner-cut-looking guy with brown hair covering his ears. He wears a five-o'clock-shadow mysteriously well. He doesn't look dangerous. Very impressive.

"That's keyboard," Nino blurts, hopping off his seat to perch on the end of the table and pump his legs like a child on a playground swing.

"Denny Brisk," Nina cuts in. "He plays keyboard and guitar."

"How do you know everything about them?" I ask. "Are they in any of your classes?"

"Hell no. They're out of here this year." Nino stops pumping long enough to spin his head in my direction, so he must have one ear on our conversation and both eyes on the blonde chick.

"Everybody knows them. Even nerds like you. See, that's what popular does for you." Right now Nina appears as nasty as Richie, so I shift my attention back to the guy called Denny.

Denny has the look of a band member but doesn't wear a "touch at your own risk" sign, like Richie does. I begin to imagine. This takes my mind off my ass-kicking bathroom incident and ensuing confrontation with three of the meanest girls I've ever met. Come to think of it, half this school is mean and nasty, so the twins fit right in. Nina more so. Maybe this will happen to me some day too. The thought makes me shudder, so I daydream about sitting in the audience at Deluge, watching this band, hearing them put my words to music.

"I wonder how they sound? Who sings lead?" My eyes sweep over their bulging, tattooed biceps. Richie is snapping his fingers to what must be his own imaginary beat. Denny starts drumming the table. Maybe they're working on a song? Their heads lean in and inch away, as though sharing secrets, then Denny whisks a shaft of sunlit brown hair off his cheek and starts throwing his arms around. At first I believe he's rocking out to the hit they've just created. But Richie leaps to his feet and pumps a fist. His neck flushes and he stalks toward the exit doors.

"Uh oh," Nina's eyes follow Richie, "trouble in paradise."

I take in a sharp breath. "They're fighting?" Great. My only possible chance of getting my lyrics into the hands of a local band and they're breaking up. So goes my luck.

Nina throws up a dismissive wave. "They always argue. Richie and Denny both sing. Out of this planet fucking awesome, might I add. But they don't always agree on stuff." She shrugs a shoulder. "You know, kind of like us, but not really 'cos I'm cool and you're …"

"A nerd," I twist my lips, "I know I know." I blow out my cheeks. "You don't have to keep rubbing it in."

Ignoring me, Nina continues her commentary. "The rest of the band is awesome too. They're not all in school. Jonny Champion is so hot. He works as a mechanic. He's their drummer." She blows out a whistle. "Did I mention Jonny is hot?" Dropping her face directly in front of mine, she wiggles her eyebrows.

Thanks to Nina, I'm thoroughly indoctrinated on Chasing Dinero. "Tony Swan kind of manages them. He plays keyboard once in a while, but mostly gets them gigs." She pulls on her hair so it spikes. "The other guy over there, he's Corky Bastian, he plays bass." And she goes on and while I half listen, because I'm focusing on Denny, who is now scribbling in a notebook. In a way, he reminds me of myself. Hunched over a book, writing furiously, pushing his hair back each time it falls in his eyes.

By the time Nina finishes her breathless babble, I feel I know each guy personally.

Stomach filled with dread, I check the wall clock. Almost time for the bell to ring, bringing me back to my misery. Nope. I pin my lips. Screw the bell. I'll stay right here, at this table, watching the remaining two guys. Time to focus on Corky, who appears unaffected by Richie's outburst, and rhythmically flips a plastic fork around his fingers. My eyes flick back to Denny, only to watch in horror as his eyes reach across the room. He elbows

Corky and they both start grinning. In this direction. Holy shit. Holy shit. Holy shit.

"Oh my God," I consider diving under the table, "Nina, look," I whisper, trying for inconspicuous, "they're looking this way. Did they snag us stalking them?"

"I hope so." Nina wags her fingers in their direction, and my face overheats.

Nino, still oblivious, bounces off the edge of the table. "Later." He swaggers toward the blonde.

I drag myself through the rest of the day alternating between daydreaming about the band and dreading dismissal. Dreading dismissal wins out. I'm petrified of the retribution Nino is craving.

After school, we congregate outside on the wide steps surrounded by kids lighting up cigarettes. There aren't many buses. Most kids walk home, or to the nearest pizza shop. The three of us mosey around the building and across the courtyard where kids are shooting hoops, some shooting up. Jaw dropping, I stop dead in my tracks to gape, then realize it's none of my business, and I don't want any more trouble, so I quickly pull my eyes away and break into a trot. We stop at the back door of the cafeteria, where Nina and I wait while Nino takes care of business, or so he says. Next thing I know, he's back and leading us toward an alley off school grounds. That's when my fear of IBS kicks in again, so as I follow, I begin the deep breathing relaxation exercises I watched on Youtube.

"Where'd you go?" breathlessly, I ask, trying to keep up with his long strides. His hair bounces as he walks, and in what's left of sunlight, it's so black it's almost blue.

"To the bathroom." He turns his head to grin, and shoves a long lock of hair behind his ear.

Suddenly, we're surrounded by graffiti brick walls, and my stress level is so high I feel faint.

"What's going on?" Backed against the wall, I dare ask Nino.

He grins again, only this time, sardonically showing his teeth. "Eh. I poured on the charm." He winks. "You up for this show, right?"

"What show?" My stomach tightens as I my brain scrambles to figure out what the heck he's talking about. I'm almost too afraid to ask, "Ready for what?" I croak.

Nina laughs and slaps my shoulder. "You'll learn more valuable lessons out here with us than in that shit hole they call a school. See what happens in there?" She slides her black painted fingernails over the bruises on my arm.

Nino's meaningful nod captures my attention, then his stare takes mine to the mouth of the sunless alley, which is at least twenty feet away. That's when I really look around and notice I'm sandwiched inside a far off road leading to nothing but a dead end. Holy shit. I have nowhere to run. My knees are buckling. I think I'm about to vomit as I watch my three attackers appear. Linking arms, they swagger toward us like the plow of a wide sweeping bulldozer. Nasty comes to mind, replaced by evil.

One has close cropped bleached blonde hair and is bopping to a beat pounding through her earbuds. The heads of the other two swing from side to side, as though they're in some kind of verbal exchange. But they're laughing. The tallest one is the instigator. Her knotty hair was all over her face and sweeping her shoulders in the girls' room, but now it's tied up in a high, bushy ponytail. As they near, their eyes brush over Nina, then me, before falling on Nino who's slouching a shoulder against the wall, hands in the pockets of his jeans. He's totally relaxed. I'm freaking out. Oddly enough, I don't appear to be their focal point. It appears I'm invisible, I'm about to heave a sigh of relief. Maybe he's brought us together to make friends? My heart rate slows.

"So ... is this the spot?" The tall instigator gets up in Nino's face.

He shoots her a stony look.

"We burnin' or what?" Her chin juts out then her eyes narrow.

I'm thrilled to be ignored, but something tells me I won't remain invisible for long.

Nino whips his hands from his pockets like a gunslinger, then aims his forefingers at me.

"What's she doing here?" This brings her boiling eyes straight to me. Her hands drop to her hips. No one says a word. I guess we're all in our zones, just waiting.

The death-stare contest begins. I'm the center of attention, and under the scrutiny of so many pairs of eyes the hair on the back of my neck starts bristling. Oh heavens, I am so not up to this, but if this is my new fate, I guess it's time to woman up and grow a dick. Hell, I'm even beginning to think the way the Romanos talk.

I'm feeling lightheaded. All of the anger, frustration, agony I've felt over the past months has built and is about to escape. I know why I'm here, and I'm going to vent all over these bitches.

"As they say, payback is a bitch." Nino smirks and shoots a warning look in my direction. I see something in his eyes. Concern or pride. Not sure. Don't care. Let's get on with it, my mind screams.

"What's goin' on, yo? You holding out on us ? Or setting us up?" The cropped blonde demands. She pulls a hand from the pocket of her sweats and shakes a finger at Nino. "Me and my girls don't like fakes ... or bullshitters."

"Hoe. I don't bullshit," Nino grunts, "especially when family's involved." He shucks his head in my direction.

By the blonde's altered expression, she obviously knows we're here for retaliation. "She's your relation?" She rolls her eyes and bobs her head. "Pfft. My condolences."

She turns to me. "Sup sista?" Her tone is light. "Ready for notha ass-kickin?" Crazy. Her voice is low but the pitch of her laugh is deceivingly shrill. Maybe she's not so tough after all. One on one, I mean.

I hold out my arm, displaying some of the bruises she and her friends inflicted.

Her burning eyes narrow. Her square jaw is intimidating, yet inviting.

It's a hell of a target, rushes through my mind, and I consider a sucker punch.

Her eyes dart to her two friends, who are sizing up Nino and Nina, now blocking the mouth of the alley, arms crossed, like two bouncers. I have to admit, they do look intimidating. No wonder they walk the halls of the school without fear.

"Go on," Nino nods at me, "one at a time," gruffly, he says to the girls. "Even playing field this time." Unlocking his arms, he reaches into a pocket for a cigarette. "Take your pick, Zoe. Who on first?"

Take my pick? Is he really talking to five foot two me? Holy crap. And so it starts. Two blinks later, the shortest girl, who still towers over me, beats me to the punch with some expert moves. Before I can think, sh e's bitch-slapping me.

Although I know why I'm here and definitely amped, she has caught me off guard. My limbs are stiff yet jelly-like. Is my chest heaving? It feels tight as hell. I take a wild swing, but she intercepts my intended blow and twists my arm. "Ouch," I scream.

"You ain't seen nothin' yet, hoe," she snickers, a sick pleasure filling her eyes.

While I protect my face with my forearms, she sticks a foot behind mine and we hit the ground. Then we roll. Her hair is too short to pull, so I grab at her clothes, but she's on top and her body weight says she plans on staying there.

After getting my ass kicked yet again, for longer than I think I can take, fear turns to fury. I feel like the Hulk. This is the beginning of unloading every ounce of festering pain.

I'm learning the meaning of self-defense, developing my own aggressive moves I had no idea I was capable of. Freeing hatred feels good. Hurting someone else feels even better. Kicking into high gear " bringing a knee to her crotch " I'm up and on my feet, hoisting her with me. Is this me going psycho? Screaming so loud my throat burns? Fists are flying. Mine. She's holding her hands up for protection. Gotcha, bitch.

"No one will intimidate me again." Jaw clenched, I vow.

In Pleasantville, the only girl fights I'd witnessed consisted of yelling, hair pulling and scratching. But these girls throw punches like guys. Thank you for the lessons, bitches. But I'm not overly confident. They're strong, and they are a trio. The concern of being carried away with a broken nose, maybe even bones, fuels me, and I want to end this. So I throw a couple of surprisingly powerful rights that all but break my knuckles, nailing the bitch in the face and her nose explodes. Without stopping, I tear into the second one who immediately tries to use *my* face as a punching bag. We're bopping and dancing, our hate-filled stares attacking before our fists.

When you have to fight for your life, you catch on quick. By the time I lay the second bitch out, I'm in a full blown, growling like an animal, rage.

Catching the instigator by surprise, I grab her by her horse tail and yank her head down with a snap, while my other hand wraps around her throat .When she tries to pry my fingers away, they tighten so hard they tremble. She's flushed and sweaty. From the look in her face, which by the way, I'm staring *up* at, she's shocked. I use this to my advantage and spewing obscenities, fling her against the wall. They say insane people are crazy powerful. I'm both.

Satisfaction flows through me when I see the disbelief in her eyes.

I pin her to the bricks and curse through gritted teeth, "You ever fucking come near me again, I'll kill you," as I land more shots than she can block. She doesn't stand a chance against the hatred pouring out of me.

In some distant part of my mind I hear Nino and Nina cheering. I feel something I've never felt before. Ashamed of myself for feeling good about hurting another person. I'm the girl who rescued flies before my father could swat them. Is this really me?

This girl, the one who started the feud by shoving me from the sink, freaks me out by holding her hands up in front of her, mumbling in defeat, "It's done. We're good."

"Let it be," her friends say as they circle us.

The instigator is dripping sweat, her clothing in worse shape than mine. With the exception of the twins, we're all bleeding from one place or another. I haven't felt this drained since this morning. My body pains. I don't think I'll ever be able to use my hands again. They feel broken. But I'm high with satisfaction.

"It's how we get to know each other, ya know?" Through blood pumping in my ears, I hear her say as she pulls her shirt, which is now missing buttons, closed.

"So now we're best friends forever, huh? Not. Don't ever even look at me again. Understand?" With my words, a rain of bloody spit fills the space between us.

I feel the arms of the twins wrap me, lead me from the alley. Then Nino lifts me up and over his head, chanting, "Cuz is killer. Welcome to the clan."

Then he sets me down and calls over his shoulder, "Don't mess with a Romano, bitches."

Nina leans into me with amusement in her voice, "I can't figure how you came out on top, being you're a small shit. And a nerd." She shakes her head. "But I guess size doesn't matter. It's what's inside that counts." She pokes my already sore shoulder. "I'm proud of you, Zoe."

"They're fighting for fun," my reply is smug, "I'm fighting for vengeance." I don't have to close my eyes to see my rapist's face. The entire time I was kicking his ass, not the girl's.

"You're a fucking wreck," Nina dabs a tissue over my lips which long to tremble but refuse to. "Guess we should clean you up before Molly sees you or she'll be threatening to pick us up from school for the rest of the year."

We laugh until tears roll down our cheeks.

Jesse

The garage is a mess. Cursing under my breath, I kick empty cans into a corner, then proceed to dump thick, used oil into a waste drum, grumbling. "For fuck's sake, Jamie. God forbid you clean up after an oil change—on your own damn car no less." That's how it's always been; Jamie's the slob and I'm the slave. He cruised by earlier with his current hotrod and hotter chick. This one wasn't too bad, the girl I mean; we hung out in the office while he got the rod ready for inspection, and had an intelligent conversation about colleges. I could tell right off the bat, this girl wouldn't be around long. She seemed to have more than half a brain.

The amount of engines and transmissions Jamie's blown, almost equals the number of blow jobs he's gotten from girls. Of course, I'm exaggerating. Truth be told, he dumps the wrecks on Dad and I when he's done with them. Okay, that's stretching it. He dumps the wrecked vehicles on us, and bums rides with the girls, until he picks up another set of wheels, and tits, then he dumps the human wrecks back to wherever he found them.

I'm stacking tires at the rear of the garage, when I feel

something brush up against my leg. A paw digs under my jeans, digging into my ankle. "What's doing, Shoo?" Crouching, I run a hand over the matted back of the stray cat I adopted, or he adopted me. Whichever, he's an orange striped fur-ball and he's cuddly. Mangy but cuddly. "Come on, buddy. Ready for dinner?" Weaving through my legs, he follows me into the office where I lift a can of food from a shelf, zip it open, and set it down on the floor. "One of these days you're gonna get a good brushing." Hand on hip, I smile down as he goes to town on the shredded fish. "Soon as I get you a brush."

I hear the front door fly open, so I leave Shoo slobbering over the can, and crash into the office. I haven't cashed the register out yet. So my feet and brain hitch into high gear.

"Hey Dee. What's up?" I'm not at all surprised to see her.

Delorese has started hanging out at the garage, showing up near closing time a few days a week, usually carrying a green bag containing a six of beer.

"Closing time?" She stands before me, curly hair swept off her round face, mostly hidden under the hood of her fully zipped sweatshirt. I have a feeling she's here for reasons other than to help me clean up the place. Still, she asks, "Need any help cleaning up?"

"I could've used you an hour ago," I joke. "Done and ready to shut down."

"Have you decided whether or not to list with the real estate agent your dad sent? I thought you said you were keeping it. Then I saw the car with the agent sign on it out front–" She breaks for a breath and squints.

"I'm still not sure about dumping this place," I confess, dragging my hands through my hair. "Part of me does …" My eyes shift from Dee's sympathetic frown to the dusky scene outside the garage windows which have accumulated far too much grime since I'm the only one caring for the place. "It would be like selling a part of me. So, unless an epic opportunity rocks my world—"

"Then don't, Jesse. When the time is right, you'll know. You don't want to make a mistake. Once it's gone, it's gone." There is an expression in her eyes I can't pin down, but whatever it is, hits home.

"Like other things." My stare hardens. I wipe my greasy hands on my even greasier work jeans.

She plops a six of beer onto the desk, unzips her sweatshirt, and her black painted fingertips brush the hood from her head. She sweeps loose strays of hair into place. Dee is an attractive girl. Our work together during the school play brought us pretty close together. Two things we had in common. Stage work and Zoe Channing. I say "had" because both are over.

Dee slaps a compassionate pat on my back.

"It's nice being with a girl – friend, for a change. I can be myself." I'm vulnerable tonight, and being a guy, don't want to let on to Dee. Must keep up the macho. Sidestepping her, I flip the closed sign on the door and clasp the lock. Realizing the floods are still gleaming on the gas pumps, I flip another switch, throwing them into a blackout, which should definitely discourage anyone from pulling into the yard. Even though the office lights emit a low glow, I've had people try to pound the door down, with the closed sign hanging in their faces. In the old days, I'd actually open the pumps for them. These days, I'd rather throw them out on their asses, and keep everything closed, twenty-four-seven.

Dee's voice cuts through my broodiness. "I know you've been through a lot. Time will heal, Jesse. Take it from me." I hear a pop and she hands me a beer.

Studying her, I wonder why she's so wise for her age. What has she been through that she can offer so much comfort to others?

I don't know if it's because I enjoy Dee's company, or because she was the closest link I had to Zoe " which makes me close by association – but I don't mind Dee hanging around. She helps break the tension that's woven through my life.

"Where's your sidekick tonight?" I slug and the ice cold beer hits the spot.

Another pop and Dee's can is level with her lips. "Ah, that's good," she says, licking foam off her mouth. "My sidekick?"

After another slug, I set the can down on the desk. "Claudette. Come to think of it, she's been pretty scarce the past few days."

Dee slides my can out of the way, replacing the space with her butt. "Dunno. Maybe she's got a date." She eyes me closely. I believe watching for my reaction. Does she think I'm into Claudette?

"Hmm." Scrubbing my jaw with my fingertips, I fall into thought. Visions of Claudette hanging over some guy irritates me. Not that I want her hanging all over me; she's like family. Scratch that; you don't check out female family assets. Sure, I look, but Claudette is off limits. For more than one reason. My concern stems from not wanting to see her taken advantage of, which she's proven can be easy.

Shoo is scratching at the back door, so I leave Dee talking to her beer, and let him out to do his thing. "If you want a warm place to sleep tonight, better make your mind up fast, buddy. It's almost closing time," I warn affectionately. "I might just get you a litter box, Shoo, so you decide to stay inside more nights, you dirty old alley cat. Maybe I'll start calling you Jamie." I chuckle with sarcasm.

When I return to the office, Delorese has just finished weaving her hair into a braid.

"Got a rubber band?" she asks, her fingertips pinching the end.

"Help yourself. They're in the top desk drawer." I don't give many people access to my desk, but I trust Dee.

While I cash out the register, Dee fastens her hair. She turns the radio on and starts singing along, doing some kind of slide across the floor. This reminds me of other nights. All we're missing tonight is Claudette. The fact that I'm even thinking about Claudette annoys me.

Pushing a broom, I sweep around Dee's feet. "You and Claudette have really bonded. You two are gradually turning this place into hair salon slash saloon." I muse.

"She's my drinking buddy." Dee sounds grim. "Now that my talking buddy is gone." She bites her lip. "Sorry, Jess. I didn't mean to bring up Zoe."

"I didn't catch that." My jaw tightens. I lean on the broom handle. "I thought we were talking about Claudette," I snap.

"Hmm you're interested?" Shooting me a sly grin, she dances around me, poking my chest.

"Hmm I'm surprised." I grab her hand and guide her back to the desk. "Sit. You're making me nervous." I swing a chair around, drop onto it; my chest hits the slatted wood back, and I think aloud. "Jamie's back in Jersey or on his way to Dallas. Who the hell knows or cares? Has Claudette been seeing someone?"

Not that I'm envious, but I guess I feel dissed because Claudette hasn't confided much in me lately. Come to think of it, she hasn't been showing up at the house much, either.

"Who's the lucky guy?" I rest my chin on the chair-back and wait.

Dee shrugs a shoulder and pins her lips. "Beats me." She shoves a beer at me. "I figured you'd know." Slipping off the desk, she heads for the restroom, leaving me in thought. Beer in hand I pace, stopping only to peer out the window. The street is well lit, and traffic is light. Quiet. Too quiet.

Shoo breaks the silence by scratching on the front door this time. "Hey Shoo. So you think you're a customer now?" Bending down, I pet him. "No more back door for you, huh? Coming up in the world?" From the fridge, I grab a carton of milk I keep especially for Shoo, pour some into a bowl and set it down. Then I return to my chair to ponder Claudette's whereabouts. Shoo laps up some milk, then hops onto my lap where he burrows into my chest for his nightly pet-fest. The more I stroke his dusty fur, the louder he purrs. This reminds me of Claudette and I laugh. My cell chimes. Lowering Shoo is a challenge, he keeps climbing back up my leg. By stretching my arm I grab my phone from the desk and in seconds Shoo is on my thigh, my cell resting on his back.

"Hey bad boy." Her voice is low and tempting. Too tempting to be so many miles away. Kirby is the last person I figured would be calling. I guess because she's the last person I think about.

Shoo is taking full advantage of my good nature, kneading my chest, while Kirby is purring into my ear.

"Bad good?" I chuckle, smoothing Shoo's fur.

"Thinking about the lake." Giggling wickedly, she asks, "What are you up to?"

Remembering our drenched, sliding bodies drifting together in the cool lake water, lifts Shoo a few inches higher on my lap, giving him a harder seat, if you get my drift.

"Now I'm thinking about the lake, thanks to you. And playing with my kitty." I have to slip that in for effect.

"Kitty?" Her giggle deepens devilishly. "I never knew guys had kitties."

I burst out laughing, knocking Shoo off my lap in the process. I need to stand, walk off my wood before Dee comes out of the john. "Change of subject. I'm at a disadvantage here."

"How so?" Kirby teases. "Are you thinking about my kitty? How you got me all wet in the lake, and I'm not talking water wet." She moans into my ear. "Now you got me all horny. How about some phone sex?" Her deep breath blows through the phone and into my ear. "I'm lying naked on the sofa, Jesse. Running my fingers up and down."

I groan. "Some guys are fine with it, but I find tossing off cold a bit too clinical. Even with you on the other end of the phone talking dirty."

"Clinical?" she purrs.

"Desperate. Okay?" I huff.

"Poor baby. If I was in town, I'd be doing the relieving. Not your fist."

I object, although if Dee wasn't in the next room... "What makes you think I'm jacking off?"

"You're breathing very heavy." She giggles. "When are you coming down, Jesse? There's an opening waiting just for you." Her coo grows softer. "Not only in the advertising department."

My mind shifts gears, putting my body on idle. "Really? In the art department?"

Her wicked giggle morphs into a hoarse whisper, "In me first."

I groan and run my palm over my fly. "You are a bad girl, Kirby. But you've managed to get my attention. I'm thinking here." Liar. You're not thinking. You're walking, and walking is painful.

"Are you okay?" Her whisper is sexy as hell. I can feel her hands again, touching all the right places. At this rate, I'll never deflate. For a moment, I think of Dee … Nah. She'd probably hit me.

"I'm coming down." I chuckle.

"You came?"

"I'm coming down from work." I laugh and lean a shoulder against the wall, seriously considering a quick trip to Miami. "And our interesting conversation."

The toilet flushes, the water in the sink runs and the faucet shuts off with a metallic screech.

"I'd love to keep this up … and I do mean up, babe, but I've got to run," I whisper, "a customer just walked in."

"Consider my offer, Jesse." Her purr rivals Shoo's.

"I'll keep in touch." A tap of my finger cuts our connection and I toss my phone onto the desk, then rub my burning ear.

I turn to see Dee push through the door of the restroom. "What's up? You sick?"

Her eyes are red and swollen. Her arms wrap her sweatshirt tighter than when she first walked in.

"Are you crying?" I toss her a pack of tissues. "Why are you crying?" My masculine side gets ready to cock a fist, bury the guy who's inflicted enough pain during a bathroom phone break to cause her to look like she hasn't slept in a week.

She lifts a beer then slams it back onto the desk so hard it hisses and explodes. I rescue the other three, then mop up the foamy mess with a greasy towel. "This isn't how I expected my summer to be." She takes a quick glance around the office. "Where do you think Claudette is? She hasn't been returning my messages."

"Never around when you need her I guess." Guiding Dee to the desk, I press her down onto the chair and rest my hand on her shoulder. I bring my face close so my lips touch her ear. "I guess I'll have to do. Talk to me," I whisper, then draw back.

She looks up at me with eyes almost as sad as Zoe's were that night in the dark. In the road. In my arms. "I'm a horrible friend, Jesse." Dee chokes out a sob, but her eyes must have emptied all of their tears in the restroom. They're red but dry.

I balance my butt on the desk and lean toward her. "How can you say that? You girls were so tight, at one point, I wondered about you two." I tease and tug the long braid hanging over her shoulder. "Hell, she dodged me long enough. When a girl can resist my charm, it can mean only one thing."

The fluttering of my lashes squeezes a tiny laugh out of Dee. "Come on girlfriend," giving a grin, I coax, "close your eyes. I'll raise my voice a few octaves, and you can pretend you're talking to Claudette. Okay?"

Dee bursts out laughing. "No wonder Zoe loved you."

I feel like she just hit me in the chest with a brick, and my jaw immediately drops. "She told you she loved me?"

Dee nods and nods and tears start falling. "You're sweet. No wonder she—"

I don't want to hear it. I can't take anymore. Hearing once that Zoe loved me is enough. The past tense of it is killing me. "When you walk in here at least four times a week with beer, how can I be anything but sweet?" My fingers work over her braid. "You have a great head of hair. Your braid is as thick as a rope."

"Thanks. So do you." She sniffs. She coughs. Her voice chokes. "I know you're trying to make me feel better. But it's not working. You have no idea, Jesse."

"Don't be so hard on yourself. Nothing can be bad enough to make you cry your eyes out, babe." Turning, I check my reflection in the window, wondering where I went wrong.

"You don't know the half of it. You'd hate me too, and my life if you had to live it."

"Doubtful. But try me." Dee's always been emotional, but seeing her this way reminds me of the depression my dad sank into after Mom died. I blow out a breath. "I don't know what to say. Words are useless." Now I'm talking to myself. "All we can do is try to plow through, and *be*." Not liking my reflection, I turn abruptly and face her. "Be strong for each other." I shake my head. "At least you know what you did wrong. Even if you don't want to talk about it." My hands jam into my pockets. "I on the other hand, have no fucking idea—"

She bites her lip. "I lied," her stare is chilling, "I lied to Zoe when she was in the hospital. Her last thoughts of me were fucked up."

The mere mention of Zoe in the hospital raises my antenna and I cock my head, watching tears pour from Dee's eyes. I let the waterworks continue; I don't want to stop the dam now that

Dee's about to open up.

"She thinks I took Zack Benefield over her. It's not true! I lied about the ring. I didn't want her to think I left her alone to be with him. I wasn't with Zack. I told her he gave me his ring. He did " but just to hold while he dove into the pool. I forgot to give it back to him."

Disappointed the confession hasn't brought me any closer to my answer, I frown. "Forgot, huh?" I slide a hand over my sprouting beard which I haven't shaved in days, then grab a clean napkin from the cabinet to dab her eyes. "Intentionally forgot?" Pulling up a chair, we sit shoulder to shoulder, mine pressing into hers. "I've had girls do that with my t-shirts," I tease, hoping to hear her laugh. "I'm constantly running out of t-shirts. People think this office is a confessional, you know that?"

Trying to smile, she grunts, then her bottom lip quivers. "I wanted to wear his ring for a while. Just to see what it felt like – you know – to have a guy like him crush on me. Like me enough to give me his ring."

"Girls." My cheeks swell and blow out a harsh breath. "I swear to Christ, I'll never understand women. Which brings me back to Zoe. Not to piss on your parade, Dee. But she was so hot and cold. I've been wracking my brain – going over everything that happened that night. She treated me cool at first, you know, I figured she was shy, but she warmed up and I thought for sure she was into me. Then my lips brush her neck and she goes psycho." Shaking my head, I throw my hands into the air. Then let them fall to my thighs.

Every muscle in Dee's face tightens.

"What is it? What do you know that I don't?" I jump down her throat.

"Geesh. Calm down, Jesse." Her head swings away from mine much too quickly. I know she's hiding something I'm not supposed to know.

I tug her braid. "I'm sorry. Listen, we're friends, right?"

Her face swings to mine but her eyes watch the wall. "I can't tell. I promised."

"Come on, dude. You can't do this to me. It's bugging the shit out of me. I can't help but feel I'm part of what happened to her that night." A chill races down my spine recalling the look on Zoe's face. Her father's. The accident. "Dee. You can't leave me this way!"

"It's Zoe's secret. She'd have to be the one to tell you. I've done enough. The least I can do is–"

I want to shake the answers out of her, but her narrowed eyes tell me even water boarding wouldn't force the truth through her pinned lips. "Whatever." My jaw tightens, but my mind spins freely. "Secret? Like was she abused or something? Her father was really protective. Holy shit, he didn't–"

"Oh my God, no," she fires at me, "Mr. Channing would never do what you're thinking."

"How do you know what I'm thinking?"

"By the look on your face."

"So what the fuck is the big secret?" I scrub a hand over my face. "She told you she loved me. Why did she leave?"

Dee rolls her full lips into a firm line and shakes her head. "You just need to forget her, Jesse. We both do."

"Forget her? Doubtful. Live with the bullshit questions you refuse to help me answer ... friend? No choice."

Dee's fingers play with the zipper of her sweatshirt. "We don't always have a choice."

"I don't know about that, Dee." I toss my empty can across the room into a metal drum. It makes a hollow thud. "Sometimes the way you feel about someone leaves you no choice but to make a choice. If that makes any sense." I blow out another breath, this one full of exasperation. "She was too young for me anyway. I felt like a stalker that night." My gut twists as I talk more to myself than the bug-eyed girl sitting before me, dark stare suddenly glued to mine. "Her father seemed the type who'd whip out a thirty-eight and threaten any guy who came near her." My attempt at a laugh fails.

Dee breaks the intensity between us and grabs a beer. She slugs like a thirsty guy. "Let's end this conversation."

I shrug halfheartedly, hiding my frown. "Yeah, what's the point?" I hop to my feet and pace around the desk.

"There is none. Got any weed?" She tilts her face and grins.

"No." I reach across the desk and shove another beer at her.

Being with Delorese is a gratifying reminder of Zoe, but it also hurts.

"I need a change of scene," I say, running a hand through my hair, which has grown out of the pompadour stage and hangs in my eyes, annoying me. Thinking of annoying brings my mind back to Claudette. I restrain a laugh. Claudette is like my long hair, hanging in my eyes, my house, my bed, annoying the hell out of me. But now I'm dying to know where the hell she's been? And who she's been with?

Dee moves to the edge of her seat to slam her empty beer can on the desk, then she stares with astonishment. "What are you talking about?"

"A move to Florida." My words are stronger than my inclination to pick up and leave everything behind, but starting fresh in a new place is something to be considered. Something pretty damn alluring. Kind of like Kirby. The thought of Kirby taking my mind off Zoe offers a glimmer of hope.

Dee stalks to my side and digs her fingers into my shoulder. "What?"

"I met a girl," I say, pushing her off so I can stomp to the vending machine and kick a bag of potato chips out without inserting cash.

Dee is on my heels. Before she catches my shoulder again, I

feel her breath on the back of my neck. Putting her face in front of mine, she stares at me as if I've stuck a knife in her chest. "You're serious with someone? Like moving in with serious?"

"Christ, Dee. Don't act so wounded."

"I'm shocked, that's all."

"If you're going to try to lay a guilt trip on me about leaving all this," I say sarcastically, fanning an arm around the room, "don't bother. In this matter, I do have a choice."

Her hand drops to her side. She looks defeated. "No, I'm not laying guilt. I'm just surprised you met someone and you're thinking about leaving."

"It's nothing like a relationship, or whatever it is you're thinking. So you can close your drooping jaw." I tap her chin with my index finger. "It's a job opportunity. The place Kirby works at needs a graphic designer. It could be a big break for me." I can't admit to myself that my potential move might land me more than a job. Am I ready for an involvement with Kirby? Fuck no. But it's a way out of the hole I'm falling into. Sometimes stumbling across something unplanned works out better than tearing your hair out searching for the right answers.

"Kirby? Who is Kirby?"

"The girl you're making me talk about."

"What about college?"

"Ever hear of on the job training? Plus you know I can do any kind of art–"

"Yeah, I know, but this could be a risk. Plus I'd miss you, Jesse. You're the only one left I can really talk to now that Zoe's gone." She hangs on my shoulder, eyes pleading. "Other than Claudette, but all she does is whine about Jamie. Who is this Kirby girl? Do I know her? Where does she live?"

"Miami." Half of my mouth springs into a smile.

"So this is a long distance romance?" Dee sputters, looking slightly satisfied.

"Who said anything about romance?" The thought of becoming serious with Kirby makes my mouth twitch.

"Well, you're leaving everyone here to go down there with her." Dee crosses her arms, and the room, to lean against the door and sulk.

A final kick lands me a bag of chips, which I tear open. "Everyone who here?"

"Your friends. Your family. Me."

Offering the bag to Dee, I frown. "My family?"

Dee is quiet for a moment, thoughtful. "Yeah. Jamie. You don't need to explain. And your father moved. To where again?"

"Dallas."

"Did you always know you wanted to be an artist, Jess?"

"Yeah," I nod, wondering where this line of questioning is leading.

Dee covers her face with her hands, then clasps them at her waistline. "I never really wanted to be anything, Jesse. Is that weird? To have no aspirations other than to party?"

"Maybe you haven't found yourself yet." I grab the keys from the pegboard and start shutting off the interior lights.

"Who has?" Dee shrugs.

"Christian." I laugh dryly. "He's in Pittsburgh, working on his career. I always figured after graduation I'd be in some school like Pratt." I shake my head. "Where am I? Dragging my feet in Pleasantville and thinking about relocating to Miami because of someone I barely know."

Dee's hands fly to her hips. "So you *are* going to hook up with this chick?"

Zoe

The stack of lyrics scrawled across loose leaf papers tucked into a drawer tells my story. It's easy to vent, to come clean with the world when the words are on paper. I believe this is my way of coming to terms with what's happened, where I'm heading. Where I eventually want to be. So I write. But tonight I want to put some of these lyrics to music. I search Nina's and my room from corner to corner, and no, Nina hasn't stashed any of my stuff in a haphazard frenzy to "clean your friggin' room" as broom in hand, Molly demanded earlier.

"My guitar ..." I mumble. "Where they heck are you, guitar?"

Could Molly have swiped my guitar during one of her cruel fits of rage? I nose around the apartment, and when I realize Molly isn't anywhere in sight, I rummage through her *wannabe* princess room, almost gagging on fumes because she has tons of open bottles of cheap perfumes sitting on her dresser. I check closets, drawers, under the bed, behind the drapes. I even check the fire escape outside her bedroom window. "Nothing!" I shout. "Where the hell is my guitar?"

"What's up?" Nino bellows from across the hall.

I thought I was alone in the apartment, and the fact that Nino has startled the hell out of me doesn't stop me from barging into his room. I fling the door open so hard, the doorknob carves a notch into the wall. Nino is sitting at the edge of his bed, plucking strings on my acoustic. Mouth agape, I freeze.

"What the?" A scream builds in my throat until the look on his face calms me. "So this is where it disappeared to." I shake my head and shoot him a chastising grin. "You're blushing," I laugh, "I've never seen you embarrassed Cuz."

Avoiding my gaze, he clears his throat. Clumsy fingers trying to caress, he plucks a few more times. "Always wanted to play one of these." Half of his dark bangs hang over one of his chocolate brown eyes. Between his long hair, and muscular, tattooed arms, he looks like he'd easily fit in with a rock band. If he could play, that is.

"I was afraid you might have pawned it for drug money. Then I'd have to kick your ass," I say wryly, plopping down beside him. "Look. Hold it like this." Positioning his hands, I guide his fingers while attempting to teach him chords.

After a few frustrating minutes, Nino shoves the guitar at me, "Here. You play. I like the sound you pull outta that piece of wood." He nods and winks. "You're okay Zoe. I have to admit, I wasn't happy about you coming here, but you're one of us."

I shoot him a side glance, unsure whether or not I should feel gratitude for being chosen as "one of them." Have I come this far? I want to laugh. Am I just like them? What would my parents say if they knew I'd transitioned into a Romano or a McCabe? Stupid thoughts cram my head, so I sit up straight and concentrate.

I permit a small smile to creep over my lips, and take a hard swallow before daring to share myself with Nino. "Here's something that just popped into my head the other night," I say, strumming a tune that played with my brain while I was writing.

Nino's expression looks childlike. "Music just pops into your head?"

"Yeah. Like random thoughts, images. They flow and I play."

"Let me hear what you've been working on."

A subtle wave of confidence washes over me, and without trepidation, I oblige. My fingers move while my voice follows.

why
why can't I be
why can't I belong
so many things I wanna be
but it's impossible

just being me
is unbelievable
unlivable

I'm sinking
like a ship in a tidal wave

why
why is life just for some?

I think they're looking down on me
I feel so small
so insignificant

why?
why can't I be?
why can't I belong?

"That's sad, Zoe." Nino cocks his head. "Really cool, but sad. Do you really feel that way?"

"I guess. Sometimes." I draw the guitar close to my chest, cheeks warming because I let Nino breach some of my inner emotions.

Staring straight ahead, he lectures. "You need to move on. Fuck anybody who doesn't like it."

He has no clue how difficult it is to even begin to try to move on.

"Like what?" My heart trips, concerned Nina has blurted out my confession to her brother. "What do you mean by that remark?"

Facing me, his mouth tightens. "I don't know. You never talk to me like you talk to Nina. I'm the outsider, but I know you've been fucked over. Fucked up, I guess." He falls into thought. "Hey, you really need to give this stuff to Richie or Denny."

My smile is coy. "I slipped some stuff in Denny's locker. He looks safer than Richie."

His side glance is shrewd. "Did you tell Nina?"

Twisting my lips, I nod. "She never told you, huh?"

"We're twins but, well, Nina does her own thing, ya know? She's secretive."

Secretive. Just what I want to hear. I wasn't sure if I could trust her with my secrets, now I know I can.

"You made my day." I take a swat at the back of Nino's head. I'm sure he has no idea of why I'm dancing around the room, singing his praise.

He belts out a laugh. "You're pretty cool for a loser … just kidding."

"From one loser to another," I grin, "I never meant to make you feel like an outsider. If I did, I'm sorry." I bump his shoulder with mine, then lean into him. "Yeah, Cuz, you're okay, in your own idiotic way." Cradling my guitar, on my way out the door I wink.

The front door slams, and Nina walks in. Disheveled but smiling.

"Where've you been? Or shouldn't I bother to ask?" I roll my eyes and pluck the collar of her rumpled shirt. "Hanging with scumbag Buddy Rice?"

Her lips form a snarl, and I believe she wants to haul off and slam me. "Mind your own shit." She smooths her shirt and pulls the two bottom buttons through their holes. "He's a senior. And a football star."

"Hah." I snort. "Football star until his grades dropped drastically after he got a girl pregnant."

"She's a slut. There's no proof it's his."

Hands on hips, I chuckle. "That makes it all okay?" I shake my head. "He's got some legal issues going on. Child support, maybe."

Brushing past me, she clicks her tongue. "Know it all."

I follow her into her room. "He doesn't give a shit, Nina. I don't know why you're into him. Plus he's in a cesspool of shit. Don't let him drown you in it."

"Take your own advice," she snaps. "Can I borrow your underwear?" She pulls my dresser drawers open and rummages.

Guys, babies, and cesspools quickly forgotten, I stare as though she's asking for my blood. "Eww that's gross."

"I don't have anything decent."

"That's because you aren't decent," I snicker.

"Not funny, bitch." She holds out a hand, trying to hip-check me away as I block my dresser from her invasion. "Hand 'em over. I saw the goodies you stuffed into your drawers," she whines, "I need something sexy. You've got a shit load of stuff." Hands on hips her eyes drill mine. "It's not like you'll be needing them anytime soon." She smirks, then frowns, realizing she's hit a nerve. "Come on, Zoe. Please."

"Geesh. You and your brother. Is nothing private around here?"

"What did Nino do?"

I huff out an irritated breath. "Swiped my guitar."

Her lips pull tight, displaying the chords in her neck. "Sinful. I'll have to kick his ass."

"Don't play me," I reply. Her pathetic appearance softens my mood. "I have a better idea. I got my check yesterday. Let's take the bus to the city mall. They have a Victoria's Secret there." I shoot her a cheek stretching grin.

She grips my shoulders and shakes me. "How did I live without you?" Then she hugs me till I almost choke.

"I still don't think you should be messing with Buddy, Nina. He's got a horrible reputation. He's got a record."

"Hey, don't worry. I can handle me and Buddy. You just worry about you and Richie."

"I'm not with Richie." I'm indignant, but my tummy flutters at the thought of something other than an imaginary relationship. "He's into my lyrics, not me. We've never even spoken."

Nina scrunches her face into a question mark. I feel a flush begin to rise.

"He wouldn't know me from ...."

She gawks at me.

"From ..." I stutter, "from a microphone stand. Okay?"

"If you say so." Clicking her tongue, she smirks, then lifts a brow. "So why do you hang at the Deluge all the time if you're not with him?"

"Music, Nina. I love to play and I'm part of it there. I'm actually part of a band – even if I'm not really on stage with them. They like me through my lyrics. They've been playing my songs. I can't believe it, Nina. The audience likes my stuff, which must mean, they like *me*. I'm somebody now. Somebody other than Zoe Channing. I'm part of Chasing Dinero."

"Chasing Dinero, chasing daydreams. Maybe nightmares. Watch your step youngster. Play with fire and..."

My eye roll stops her rant and we burst into laughter. "Okay so I'm acting like a mom." Her eyes widen. "Just don't ever let me get like Molly!"

"This world can hold only one Molly. Lucky you." As I

swagger past her, I flick the tip of her nose with my forefinger. "Ready to shop, bitch?"

Nino insists on driving us. He hangs at the gaming shop racking up a three digit tab I end up paying, because he can't decide which games to buy and which to return to the clerk. His puppy dog eyes seal my fate.

"Maybe you manage to get laid with that look, Nino, but from me, all you'll get is a few bucks and a kick in the butt." I laugh. "Is that the look you give the dumbass girls who fall for you?"

"I got style, babe. Hang around me. You'll learn how to catch your dream man."

"I don't have any dream man. Guys are nightmares."

"Best left in the dark recesses of your mind. Am I right?" Nina chirps in with a meaningful wink. "Oh Jesse. Where are you my Jesse?"

"Stop it!" I scream, oblivious to the people around us.

"Who's Jesse?" Nino bellows.

I shoot Nina a deadly look of warning. She crosses her lips with the tip of a finger.

"You two are like the CIA with your secrets." Nino shrugs. "Whoever he is, go for it. You have to come out of that cave sometime, Zoe. You're gonna shrivel up and die. And who'd buy us all this great shit then?"

I laughingly elbow him. "Why ... Molly, of course."

"Or we'd five it," Nina chirps, clutching a big bag of new clothes close to her chest.

We all crack up then pile into Nino's old Dodge which he considers a race car.

###

"I don't feel like going home yet," Nina complains.

I'm in the back seat, rearranging shopping bags, groaning as I think about missing the long hot bath I've been waiting to take.

"I don't suppose my vote counts?" I grumble, gazing out my side window as the sleek buildings of the mall disintegrate into an overgrown park, followed by low income housing.

"Not a chance." Nina taps her knuckles on her side window. "Coming out was your idea, remember?" Her imitation of my voice is spot on when she says, "Let's hit up Victoria's Secret."

"See if I offer to buy you anything again." I scrunch around in my seat, trying to adjust my black yoga pants which are hugging my crotch too tight.

"I was all set to dye my hair." Nina's voice is distracted.

"No. You were trying to rip off my underwear, remember?" I snap, finally reaching a comfortable compromise between my pants and body.

"All this talk about underwear is giving me a boner," Nino says.

"I can't believe I'm stuck with the two of you," I groan, pulling from a bag an adorable pink stretchy top I just bought.

Nina laughs. "You love us. You know it. And we are going out tonight."

"Where to then?" Nino asks, breaking near an exit. "Tell me now before I take the turn."

Nina dials up the radio and starts rocking out, bopping up and down in her seat. "The Dive," she sings out. "I wanna see if someone's there tonight. I haven't heard from him all day."

"Someone?" I set aside thoughts of slipping into the pink top, and my antenna goes up instead. "What happened to Buddy?"

Nina blows a "Fuck him," through her lips hard enough to dot the window with a breath-fog, and loud enough to reach the back seat. "I haven't heard from him all day." There's a whine in her tone.

"Him who?" I press. Hunched over in the seat and hopefully

out of view, I peel off my old top and slip the new pink one over my head. "Not Buddy?" When I surface, I check to make sure Nino's eyes are not focused on the rear view mirror.

"All day," Nino mimics Nina's whine. "How will I ever make it another night without getting laid? Who is the jerk, anyway?"

"None of your business. And fuck you too, bro. You wish you had my luck."

Nina's fist meets his shoulder and the car swerves. "You wish you didn't have to wait a month to find a girl stupid enough to lay down for you."

"Hey you two. I'd like to land wherever we're going in once piece. And do we have to keep talking about sex?" I shift in the seat, pulling my top up high enough to cover my entire cleavage, then tugging it down so it covers my entire belly. It's a losing battle. Both parts are exposed. "Why did I buy this top?" I mumble under my breath.

"Sorry, Zoe," Nina chuckles. "I forgot the entire male population is on your shit-list." She half turns in her seat. "What the hell are you doing back there?"

"Changing."

Nino laughs. "It's about time. Your current personality sucks."

"Not funny, idiot." I apply a layer of lip gloss and smack my lips.

Putting a damper on the mood, we cruise past an old cemetery with tall monuments scattered among more affordable headstones, illustrating the contrast in life but not in death; in the end, we all share the same ground. Moments later, Nino parks the Dodge in the dimly lit lot, and the three of us pile out.

The Dive is a creepy building that should have been demolished instead of refurbished. Lodged between a service station and all night deli, it's lit up like a construction site, which makes it look creepier. The narrow alley behind the building makes me nervous. Our shoes crunch on a crumbling sidewalk as we make our way toward the entrance.

Slowing his gait, Nino whispers, "Check it out," and breathes out a chuckling wolf whistle.

A guy has a girl backed up against the brick side of the building. They're making out like crazy. His arm is elbow deep beneath her skirt. Her hand is on his crotch. They're both writhing in rhythm. As we pass, my eyes dart in another direction; across the street at an Italian restaurant with a blinking sign. *Pizza Delivery till 11 PM.* I have no idea where we are, but why would I? All I know is whoever zoned this part of town needs to lose their license.

It's kinda early to party, so the Dive isn't at full capacity yet. While asking the guy at the door what gym he works out in, Nino flashes his fake license so fast, the bouncer shoos him right in. Nina and I are wearing pounds of makeup, and with our fake ID's, we easily pass for twenty-one. Before walking away, I watch the bouncer's eyes rake up and down the back of Nina's skin tight jeans.

We pick a table near the dance floor, and each scope the place for our own reasons. Mine being, is Richie Santana around? I'd love to hear him sing some more of my songs.

Nino's eyes are glued to the waitress wearing butt-baring shorts and tank top. "I'll have whatever you got on top, babe." He smiles at her cleavage. Her face springs into a sarcastic expression, and he corrects, "I mean on tap. I'll take whatever you have on tap."

Nina rolls her eyes at me, orders a Tequila Sunrise, then starts bopping to the music blaring from overhead loudspeakers.

When the waitress's eyes meet mine, I order the same as Nina, a Tequila Sunrise.

"What time is the band playing?" Nina yells up at her.

The girl's head swings toward the huge clock hanging on the wall behind the long bar, which is filling up fast. "Eh. About an hour or whenever they decide to drag their sweet asses in." With a wink, she wiggles away, carrying Nino's eyeballs with her.

By the time our third round of drinks arrives, I can barely hear the music, because the place is over capacity and noisy as hell. At this point, we don't bother talking anymore, because unless we're lips to ears, we can't hear one another, and our voices have become hoarse from yelling back and forth. My head feels the pressure, so I drink down two aspirins I pull from my bag.

That's when the crowd parts, the dance floor clears, and I get a perfect view of the stage. The band is already positioned. A drumroll, a few chords, and Chasing Dinero is breaking into their first song.

Instantly the dance floor is overflowing with fans, cheering and throwing their arms around.

"Come on," Nina grabs my arm, "get your little booty out there. Life is waiting."

After sucking down the last bit of my third Tequila Sunrise, my too small top and yoga pants are the furthest things from my mind. Nina and I push our way to the front of the crowd, and I find myself sandwiched between a raging mob dancing directly in front of the stage. Music fills my soul and my body begins to sway with the others as I sing along with Richie Santana.

Richie is front stage. A few feet to the side is Denny Brisk, working out on the keyboard. I know them both from school. Seeing them on stage is amazing.

They're a typical raggy-haired band, wearing worn jeans and a variety of concert t-shirts. The drummer is the exception. His bleached hair is cropped short and spiky. Beneath the heat of the overhead stage lights, he's already breaking a sweat which stains the neckline of his plain blue shirt.

The song ends, and Denny deserts the keyboard, moves to the back of the stage, and returns with his guitar. It's an acoustic. I'm thrilled. They're so in tune, musically and mentally.

Impressive. Mesmerizing.

The drummer blasts out a short intro then stops dead. Denny is front and center. He strums a few chords, drops his face close to the mic, and his deep voice is like velvet.

forever searching for a place to feel

what exists for others yet for some unreal

have I been nurtured in a house so full of lies?

for there's no peace inside a restless mind

They're playing my song, and Denny is singing for me. Only me. His passion drains the blood from my limbs.

He wails the chorus: *erase me misplace me forsake me come take me I want you to make me make me into something fine.*

When he delivers a guttural finish with: *where is the lust I miss the most? my skin is stained with me*, the place erupts. My heart can't beat any faster. Denny's deep brown eyes say he's dedicating these words to me. Does he remember I'm the girl who left the songs she wrote pinned to his locker in school? If not for the circle of bodies crushing against me, I'd be lying flat on the floor.

I almost collapse with total heart failure, because Denny stops strumming, gets even closer to the mic, groaning out lyrics without music, staring directly at me. Our eyes are locked, and the only thing that breaks us apart is Richie, who leaps out of the background and with his guitar shatters the moment. He forms a riff by breaking up some simple chords, and the girls scream even louder. I'm afraid I'll walk out of here deaf. My stomach sinks when Richie grabs the mic and starts dancing around the stage, guitar slung over his shoulder, wailing out his new song:

remember me and what you set free when you're thinkin about somethin' else besides yourself.

My moment has ended. Denny's gone back to his place and surrendered his guitar to the keyboard.

334

I cash out a customer who decides to hang around while he waits for his wife to get her hair done in an upscale salon down the street. "She gets her hair colored," he tells me with an affectionate laugh, "and I get my oil changed." His frown is half-hearted. He's playing the role of the dutiful husband. The guy is obviously a talker. He wants to unload, but I have my own problems, and a shit ton of work to do. There's a car on the lift, waiting for brakes and tire rotation. Can't he see I'm busy? Go get a haircut, I want to lash out at him. This is a busy garage, not a fucking barber shop where you sit around and bullshit.

"So my daughter is dating this bozo with no job." He follows me from the office, out into the shop, yakking his head off as I sort through tool chests.

Daughter dating a bozo? Sounds like she's had the misfortune of meeting Jamie, I don't say, I just shake my head when I'm facing him and smirk when I turn my back.

"I hear you." Nodding my agreement, I take extra time digging through an assortment of sockets, wondering if he'll give up on his one-sided conversation and disappear, as all I'm giving him is my back. "The world has its share of tools, but never where you can find them," I mumble. Claudette is the exception, though. She can find all kinds of tools. Anytime, anyplace. While I chuckle at the brilliance of my jovial nature, my head bounces another nod or two as I keep rummaging through metal drawers, hoping this guy will get the hint and that I won't have to ask him to leave.

"He's a real tool," the guy complains. As I move, he moves.

"Yeah, I know a few," I acknowledge with a grunt. "You'd think a girl with half a brain would be able to spot them though. Run the other way." I grab an impact wrench and start removing lug nuts from a suspended tire. Neither the shrill of the power tool, or my rudeness, affects him. Leaning in, he continues to chew my ear off.

"Now you're a hard worker. I can see that," he says, folding a magazine he then clasps under his arm, "for a young guy. Don't see that much these days. Do you go to high school?"

I can see I'm getting nowhere, so I unhook my trigger finger to cut the power and try ducking under the car I'm trying to work on.

"Graduated."

"College?"

"Soon."

"What will you major in?"

"Art ... Graphic design," I grunt, sticking my head out from under the lift.

"I don't know of any art schools in this town." His brows furrow and he scrubs his chin, as if he's trying to solve a problem for me.

Listen Buddy, I'm tired of your Q&A ... I look him square in the eye. "I'd like to stand around and bullshit but I've got work to do." Trying for diplomatic, I'm afraid I'm coming off as a shithead. Not the nice young guy he thought he had me figured for. Maybe he wants me to meet his daughter? Maybe he's just trying to be social. Nah. He's just killing time. One thing for sure, I want to keep his business, so I slip him half a grin. "I don't mean to come off as a dick, but I'd like to get out of here sometime tonight." Realizing my choice of words doesn't exactly deliver the apology I'd planned, my grin fades. I can't win today, so I just shrug.

"Sure. Sorry I'm holding you up. A young guy like you must have plans. Hot date, huh?" His smile is brief, like a quick but necessary curtsey before leaving the stage. Why does everything I say or do land right back on Zoe?

"You're a nice kid. Good luck with your art career. You'll do well, I can tell." Winking, he lifts a hand in mock salute. "I'll be back in six thousand miles, maybe sooner if the wife decides she doesn't like her hair color," he chuckles before moseying out the door.

After installing a water pump in Kirby's car, I even go as far as washing it for her. I'm a nice guy, the man said. Maybe it's true. I laugh.

"Hey there. How's my car?" Kirby makes her entrance wearing a sexy short skirt and emerald green top. She's carrying two Starbucks cups.

A couple guys from school have been hanging in the office, playing blackjack, drinking Gatorade. They nod to Kirby, who offers a casual, "Hey."

"They were just leaving," I say, giving them the evil eye, because I know, guys being guys, they're about to start wisecracking. They're eyes are all over her, so I'm ready to get physical with them. When I shoot them a glare, they shrug and retreat. Kirby rolls her eyes and chews her lip, giving them her back. On their way out the door, they flip me off, shoot peace signs and A-Oks, mouthing, "Hot."

I pull Kirby in for a quick hug. "Ready to go, babe? Come take a look." I hitch my head toward the doorway the goons just vacated. While I'm hitching, my eyes are dipping into her cleavage. She gives me a 'you're a bad boy' grin, but appears thrilled I've noticed. After giving me sufficient time to drink in her breasts, she makes a weak attempt at closing the space between her boobs and the knit using a two-finger pullup. My stare shifts to the color of her eyes that mimic her shirt. Changeable eyes. Changeable girl.

While taking turns sharing events of our unremarkable day, we stroll outside, sipping caramel iced lattes. "Awesome!" Kirby squeals when she spots her lump of shit car. Sucking in a breath, she brings a hand to her mouth. "Oh my gosh, Jesse. You washed my car," she coos to me, like she's talking to a baby. "It's so shiny. It looks new. Well ... almost." She giggles, gets up on her toes, and plants a caramel kiss on my cheek. Then the Kirby I know returns. "A lot of miles on this baby." She slaps a fender and kicks the front tire, then cocks a hip.

"Yeah, you should try washing it once in a while." My grin is sarcastic, but I'm happy she appreciates the time and effort I put in.

She slugs my arm. "Hey. I'm a busy writer, trying to make a living." She pouts and slides a soft hand over the scratched fender she just slapped. "I guess you're right." Giving me an energetic smile, she tosses her head. "Hey, how about lunch?" She gives her cup a shake, then nibbles the end of the straw. The movement of her lips is appealing. Either I'm weakening, or she's coming on stronger, because I'm seriously considering her offer. Maybe more.

I shake my head, adding a tongue-click to indicate how disappointed I am to let her down. "Can't." I force a frown. "I'm alone." I squint at the sun that's sliding behind the irregular rooflines of the business center across the street. "Besides, it's kinda late for lunch, don't you think?"

"Supper then." She puts her body square in front of mine

and, hands on hips, stares up at me with a stubborn gleam in her eyes.

"Supper?" I laugh. "Who are you, grandma?"

"Very funny. Supper is an early dinner. We can do both." Her lashes flutter. "If you can't leave, then supper shall be delivered," she wrinkles her nose, "and it's on me."

Her energy is exhausting. Her persistence perpetual. "Since you put it that way, how can I refuse supper?" I shrug a shoulder and suck the last of my drink, giving her a bite-the-straw smile for effect.

Kirby is a fun girl. Fun to play with. Someone to spar with. Someone I'm sure I won't have to deal with seriously. If it makes her happy, I'll play along. Christ, is she growing on me?

She hops into her car and rolls down the window. "I'll be right back." Smiling, she pulls away. In sunlight, her curly hair is glistening strawberry blonde. With great features, she'd make an interesting model. Watching her taillights flash, I have the urge to paint her. In the car, just as she looks at this very moment. Maybe at the lake, with forest green woodlands as a fabulous backdrop. Problem is, knowing Kirby, we'd probably end up painting each other with our tongues.

I go back to work, finishing up odds and ends, and when Kirby returns, she's lugging a Wendy's shopping bag.

"That's some supper," I call through the door I'm holding open.

"Hope you like everything on your burgers. Onions. Pickles. Ketchup. Mustard. Cheese. Because that's what I got us." She plops the bag on the desk and digs purposefully inside.

"We'll be keeping our distance then," I joke as I reach for a pack of fries. But for more reasons than one, I'm serious. Each time I try to take a bite, the door opens and closes, so I alternate between bites and cashing out customers.

"It's impossible to catch a ten minute break, the pumps are

hopping today." Pushing aside my half eaten lunch, I grunt as another customer approaches.

"Figures," she says. "But that's good. You're bringing in the bucks. Speaking of which, what do I owe you?"

"Eh. Just the parts. We'll settle up later."

"Ooh. That sounds fun." She runs a fry across her lips and lowers her lids.

"Loving the show, but sorry." I mug. "Supper was thoughtful of you though." I tap the tip of her nose with the pad of my finger. "And considering the fact that you fed me, no charge on the pump."

"So what time do you get off?" she asks, stuffing an extra bite of burger into my mouth.

Covering my bulging lips with a napkin, I munch a reply. "I close around seven. I'm good, you can stop feeding me now. I'm a big boy." I flash a dramatic smirk.

"Don't I know it." She makes a swoony face, then taps the corners of my mouth with a napkin and her expression turns wistful. "How about a farewell drink? Someplace nice, and definitely where we won't be disturbed by customers." She runs a finger around my ear and down my throat.

"Farewell?" I give her my brow and toss my empty soda cup into the trash. "Am I going someplace?"

Her pout morphs into a kissy-face that droops into a frown. "I am. I have to get back home. Hey I spoke to my boss about you." She brightens, and the variegation of her irises draws me in.

"I like the color of your eyes. I'd like to paint you." I pop the last bite of burger into my mouth and crumble the paper. "Too bad you're leaving."

One brow arches. "My portrait?"

"Maybe. So what's this about your boss?"

"The graphic design job ... it's still open." She gives a convincing nod. "I could put in a really good word for you."

Does this girl think I need a career counselor? Is she just being friendly? Or does she have ulterior motives? It doesn't take a rocket scientist, just a deeper look into her glimmering eyes.

"And why would you do that?" I tease, ruffling a lock of her soft hair.

She shoots me a brow and eye roll.

I run a finger over her reddening cheek. "What's the paper you work for?"

"Miami Choice. Print and Internet fashion, news, weather and sports." She rocks on her heels.

"Never heard of it." My voice is flat. With a fading smile, her head snaps beyond the reach of my twirling finger. *She's doing you a favor and you insult her. You could have gone along with her, jerk.*

"We're small." I believe she's trying to preserve her dignity by lifting her chin, and her soda cup which she sucks the hell out of. Once more, her puckering lips are intriguingly malleable and plump. "But we're growing." With a toss of her head her spunk rebounds.

"So am I," I tap my gut, "if you keep feeding me like this my pants won't fit."

She smirks, disregarding my comment, but her cheeks grow rosy. "It's a cool place to work, friendly, compassionate bosses, plus I get to hang out in some awesome clubs " on the paper's tab."

I gather the food wrappers, crumble and pitch it all into the trash can. "They pay for you to party?"

She wrinkles her nose. "They pay for my sodas, but still, the entertainment's like adrenaline overload. That makes up for everything." Her hazel eyes light with a multicolor brilliance.

I find myself nodding a lot, drawn deeper into her life, and thoughts of Miami, not to mention, her eyes which are sinking deep into mine, making me uneasy.

She keeps talking, but my mind isn't really concentrating on what she's saying. It's on Miami. What would it be like to ditch these winters? Hang at the beach. Paint at the beach. Screw on the beach.

"I get to hang out in some of the sweetest places and rub elbows with bands and all," she explains, dancing around me as I push a broom around the shop floor.

"Really?" My brows shoot up. "Rub up against anyone I might know?"

"Literally?" She giggles. "It's kinda hard to get an in with the big groups, even with a press pass, but the struggling bands," she winks, "they know my name."

"Is that all?" I wink, sling my arm around her shoulders and lead her to her car.

"The old piece of crap looks good, Jesse." Slapping the hood, she grins up at me with rapidly blinking lids.

I open the door for her and close it after she settles in. She tilts her head and lifts a brow. "I could use some exercise." Her narrowing eyes study mine. "A few more laps around the lake?" She reaches out to tap my shoulder. "Before I leave?"

I'm resting my arm on the roof, my face near the window. The look in her eyes is enticing. Hey, I'm only human.

"Give me a few to clean up and close the place down." After a quick lock up, I shower, hop into clean jeans and t-shirt, jog back to the car and poke my head through Kirby's open window. She's texting. "Was I long?"

Head down. Furious fingers. Silence.

I intentionally clear my throat. "Miss me?"

"Huh?" she mumbles without a glance at the guy who's practically hanging over her lap. Her fingers are flying over the keypad. When she's finally finished, she lifts her head and our cheeks smack. "Sorry," she says with a big smile as she brushes her fingertips across my lips.

"Boyfriend?" I don't know why I ask this. I could give a shit if she's cheating on some Floridian dude. I guess I'm just wondering what the urgency is that totally blanked her out.

After stuffing her phone into her bag, she clicks her tongue and looks up at me with a scrunched face. "Work stuff." She shakes her head. "They don't pay me enough for all this crap. I can't even take a break without being hassled." Her chuckle is fake. "Mmm. You smell yummy."

My lips brush hers, and before pulling myself from the car, my nose touches her neck. "You do too."

I jog around the front end and fall into the passenger seat with a sigh. After pulling the seat lever, I stretch my legs under the dash. My arm slips around the top of Kirby's seat. Not lovingly. Not protectively. Just robotically. "Remember how to get there?"

"I remember everything." She shoots me a coy grin.

My hand slips from her seat to her thighs. I swear I have nothing to do with it; my hand has a mind of its own. "Remember this?" My fingers casually slip between her legs. Warm. Soft. Difficult to concentrate.

She grips my hand and urges it higher, working my fingers so I'm kneading the crotch of her panties. The entire time she's gazing deep into my eyes, like she's trying to rip my brains out. She wants to know what's in my head, what makes me tick. *If only I knew...*

"Kind of," she purrs then a sly grin glides over her lips, followed by the tip of her tongue. "I wouldn't mind a refresher course." The longing in her eyes snaps me to my senses, and I pull my hand back to my own crotch, which has doubled in size. But she's not looking at my crotch. Those devilish eyes are still probing mine.

My chuckle is tight. I want to do her right here. Relieve the swell in my jeans, quell the desire in her eyes. The tip of her tongue glides over her bottom lip again, and I want to grab her by the back of her head, pull her face to mine, suck her tongue into my mouth. Hold it Jesse, my swirling head warns. You could be hooking up with a lot more than this girl who's sitting beside you, opening her heart, her legs. You could be hooking up with some crazy kind of emotion you're just not ready for. Something you've been saving for another girl. The one that's always tucked into the darkness of your damn dizzy head. The one whose lips scorched yours months ago on a dark country road, and you just can't get the taste of those beautiful lips, that soft, warm body that was pressed against you, out of your fucking head. My focus returns to Kirby and my mind warns: No substitutes. No ties. Free sex, but no promises with eyes, bodies, actions, definitely not with words.

I haul in a breath, slow my heart, and let out another chuckle, but after the discussion my mind has just had with itself, this chuckle is casual, confident. "Drive," I say as I pluck the tip of her nose. "That way." My change in attitude, and I guess the friendly nose pluck, clears the glaze from Kirby's eyes. The sexy grin from her pouting mouth.

She lifts a brow and smirks, reaches over and flicks my ear with a fingertip. "Dick."

I laugh and shake my head. "Life is complicated. No commitments, okay?"

"No."

Her reply is flat. Startling. "No?"

"No commitments." Her laugh is as odd as her tone. Tossing her head she stares through the windshield. The engine turns over, she runs a hand through her hair, shifts into gear, grips the wheel with both hands, and eases the car onto the main road.

Rush hour is over. Traffic is light. While Kirby drives, I mess with the radio, find a rock station, then scrunch into a comfortable position, resting my head on the seat back. After a long day, and letting someone else do the driving for a change,

I begin to doze off.

"Hey," Kirby's voice cuts through my relaxing wave. "Nice to know how much my presence excites you."

Straightening in the seat, I run my fingers through my hair and stifle a yawn. "Not you, babe. It was a long day."

"Well I hope your nap energized you." She giggles and pokes my side.

"Don't worry. I'm recharged and ready for–" I stop myself. Play nice but … *Don't lead her on.* "Hey, hang a right here." I motion to a side road weaving through a grove of trees.

"I know." She's indignant as the car slows and the tires crackle on the gravel road.

As we approach the parking lot a few cars pass in the other direction. "Turn down that side road, nice and easy, it's bumpy.

"Mmm. I like bumpy."

I chuckle "Slow down."

"Mmm. I like slow."

I laugh. "You have a one-track mind, Kirby. Pull over."

"Why? Something wrong with my driving?" Her nose wrinkles with confusion.

"Nope. Rather than tell you … I'll show you."

"Show me what?" She pulls up on the grass and slides the shifter into park, leaving the engine running. "Nice things I hope?" Reaching across the seat, her hand grips my thigh.

"You'll see." I tug her across the seat and onto my lap, push the passenger door open and slide us out of the car. My feet hit the ground first, so I steady her, then position her ass to my front, and with my arm stretched over her shoulder, I point out the horizon. "Behold."

"What's going on? You brought me here to stare at the sky?"

"Trust me." My breath brushes her neck. "It gets better."

She whirls around and her brows go up. "Sounds intriguing, but why did we stop here? Did you get us lost?"

I wrap a lock of her hair around my finger and tug. "I know my way around, Kirby."

"This I'm learning. But tell me more."

"I have my own private parking lot."

She appears to enjoy the grin sweeping over my face. I watch her reaction and laugh. A real laugh, not a cover up, and it feels damn good.

Standing before me, she presses against my chest, and for a moment we stand close, not exchanging a word, just watching the setting sun light the lake on fire.

"Amazing, isn't it? The treed backdrop, orange and purple sky. Christ what colors. I could paint this right now."

"If you think this is amazing, you should watch a Miami sunset on the beach."

"Tell me about it." I tip her face to mine. "Convince me this job you keep talking about is going to change my life." My mind whirls with possibilities. "Make my dreams come true."

There are no words, just that damn longing in her eyes, and in seconds, her lips reach up to crush mine

There's no stopping the rush of adrenaline, testosterone, or whatever the fuck is firing through me. And this pent up energy is getting the better of me. I scoop her into my arms and carry her down the knoll to an area where we can do whatever we choose, where the outside world is just that – outside. We're in our own private place. Just me and Zoe. Zoe and me. *What the fuck just shot across my mind?* Thank God thoughts don't magically transform into words. Kirby is a nice girl. I shouldn't fuck with her. Just fuck her. That's what she wants. Her eyes, her arching body, everything about her in this moment is telling me that's what she wants.

"Ah, a perfect spot, right beside the lake," I say dropping to my knees where I set her down softly onto thick grass. "You think?" The moment I release her, she stretches out before me, like a lazy kitten waiting for her belly to be scratched. So I lie beside her, propped on an elbow and my fingers trace the side of her body, from breasts to thighs.

Lifting her face to mine, "Yeah, I think so," she purrs, "but I'd rather not think, or talk." There's that tongue again, teasing her bottom lip. Me. "Actions speak louder than words." Her fingers weave through my hair. "Show me some of that energy." Her voice is a hoarse whisper.

My fingers drag through her hair, trace her neck, glide over her breasts. "So, show me yours and I'll show you mine." My teasing words sound more husky than intended.

I gaze down at her, and for a moment wonder why I'm here, about to hook up with this girl I don't really have feelings for. I tell myself what I'm experiencing is the effect of testosterone. Deprivation. Combined with a fucked up life. My sex life hasn't been exactly thriving lately, not like in the past when I was Jesse. Who the fuck am I now?

I guess most guys would take advantage of the situation without a second thought, but I'm giving this a third and fourth consideration. I'm not like Jamie or Trent. I need to experience a twinge of emotion other than lust; which occurs almost instantaneously when Kirby's fingers grasp my crotch. What she's doing to me feels so good, good enough for me to roll onto my back and let her take care of me without moving a muscle; well maybe just one. I'm lazy. I'm selfish. I'm not in love with this girl. Not even in like. But I don't want to lose myself in her hand.

Think about something else, Jesse. Put yourself in another time. Another place. And enjoy this. Let it last. No girl. No emotions. You don't know when you're gonna get lucky again with someone willing to play around without committing.

So I force myself to think of stuff other than my throbbing dick, which unintentionally brings me back to the first time I jacked off when I was about twelve. I was home, in my dad's garage, searching for my hockey skates, when my fingers came in contact with a magazine, naked women, hot naked women, hmmm interesting. Once my eyes made contact, all thoughts of hockey with my team flew out the window. I felt that twinge – kind of like a butterflying sensation deep down inside, not like the intensity Kirby's touch is creating right now, but titillating just the same.

I rolled the magazine up so only the cigarette ads on the back were visible, not the sexy girl on the front cover – she was inside the roll, my head, my groin, and within minutes inside my room, alone with me. With heavy breath, I flipped through pages of sexy girls – then I found the centerfold. Miss January nearly gave me heart failure. My dick bounced to life – greater than any morning wood a guy at that tender age could have imagined. Wearing a fluffy red scarf around her swan neck, mittens and booties, she wore nothing else but a fur cap that sat cocked on her full head of jet black hair. Her eyes held pure sex. Her lips were red and plump and pouty. And her eyes – holy shit, her eyes were staring straight into mine.

Without much thinking, and with very few strokes, I lost it in a wad of paper towels. The surge was so intense, my face burned and I thought my heart would pound out of my chest. It was over in about five minutes.

Kirby is unzipping my fly, yanking my jeans down, and her fingers are working expertly. It's hard to concentrate. Difficult not to come. I'm caught between two worlds, thinking how fucking good this girl is stroking my dick, enjoying every selfish moment that I let her pleasure me while I stretch out, hands above head, ass sinking into a bed of grass. I don't want this to end, so I slip back into the past and I'm that kid again. I'm remembering a variety of emotions ranging from master of the universe to fear that my mom will find my balled up wad in my room. As soon as my face cooled, and my pulse returned to normal, I cracked my door open, checking both sides of the hallway. When I was certain no one was within earshot of my tiptoeing feet, I flew down the hall, petrified Jamie would see me and scream to the world, "My brother just beat off," as he rolled into a ball of hysteria.

The coast was clear so I headed for the kitchen where I dropped my wad on top of someone's half eaten sandwich, pulled the bag out and zipped it closed.

The tap on my arm startled me. "Jesse," Mom looked surprised, "what a little sweetheart you are. You didn't have to take it out." She was referring to the trash, but my mind flipped back to how I whipped *it* out so fast I almost destroyed the fly of my jeans.

Kirby's voice breaks into my reverie. "Jesse," she sounds so fucking horny. I know she's ready. She'd like to come with me. "Feel good?" she whispers.

"Yeah, baby," I whisper back. "Feels so good, don't want to come yet. Wanna make you feel this good." I'm in the clouds and my voice is just as distant.

Not long after the trash can incident, Dad tapped me on the shoulder. "I think it's time for us to have that talk now."

Fuck. I can't help but remember his warning. "Don't be like your brother. He's a hound dog. Respect the ones your with and they'll respect you."

And now I'm about to disrespect the hell out of Kirby, because her mouth has a death grip on my bulging dick and I can't take much more.

Along with her lips, her fingers are doing some wild things, stroking and probing, so I decide it's time to exit my coma and join the party.

By Kirby's moans, her writhing hips, and the glazed look in her eyes, she's in the early stage of euphoria.

"Come on, baby," I whisper, "roll over."

Instantly, she releases me and spreads out on the grass beside me. My fingers slip beneath her skirt and she begins to pant, buck her hips wildly. Now and then she lets out soft moans. Leaning in, I kiss her parted lips, devour her tongue. She wraps her arms around my neck, but I bring her wrists over her head, hold them while I lick the side of her neck, kiss her throat, and slowly run a palm over her breasts before lifting her shirt. "Let's lose this bra, babe." While I knead her breasts, I slide her panties down and my fingers dive right in. Kirby starts screaming, gasping as though she can't get enough air.

I grope my jeans for a condom and in moments we're pumping like there's no tomorrow. We're not like lovers; we're like two animals, engaged in a vicious struggle, and we're about to reach a brutal end. We claw, we pant, we gasp and it's over. But not before Kirby lets out a bloodcurdling scream.

"Jesus Christ," as I fall off her and onto my back, I let out a series of moans ending with, "Phew."

"Amen to that," she rasps as her outstretched arm comes down hard on my heaving chest. "Is this why you have your own private parking spot?"

I'm great at avoidance and denial. Along with changing the subject when I'm feeling uncomfortable enough to run. The story of my life, when things get complicated, run.

"This part of the lake is great for fishing."

She laughs and her elbow hits my rib cage. "Liar."

"No really. I come here because it's peaceful. To think."

She lets out a snarky laugh. "Think, huh?"

Out of nowhere I blurt, "Have you ever missed something you've never had?"

Kirby is up on all fours, straddling me.

"Are you becoming philosophical, Jesse? Or are you about to tell me you're missing someone who obviously is not me because I'm your right here freshly fucked girl of the day."

Her eyes are like jade stones, slanted like a cat's, narrow as hell, probing for answers.

"Would it matter?" Turning my head, I watch a breeze ruffle leaves that fall and scatter.

She blows out a breath that hits the side of my face and collapses beside me. "I guess not."

"Do you have someone in Florida?" I'm talking to Kirby but facing the darkening sky.

"Would it matter?" she says unenthusiastically.

"Probably not," I reply without much thought as I yank up my jeans. "It's getting late."

"Yeah. I might miss my flight."

"Not with me driving."

"Are you talking shit about my driving again?"

"You're a wonderful driver. Your car is a testament to that." I laugh. "Come on. Get dressed. I'll take you to the airport. Bring your piece of crap back to the garage. Keep it there till you get back."

"How do you know I'm coming back?"

"Because I have your car. Which I'll have towed if you don't return."

"So you're not coming?"

My body is still cooling, my throbbing cock trying to settle down; Kirby is on her knees; I watch her fit her breasts into her bra and snap it. "Still in the thinking stages." My words sound slurred.

"Don't think too long." She squeezes my abused crotch.

"Ouch," I swat her hand away. "Why do you want me down there so bad?"

I'm up on my feet, zipping my fly. Jumping to her feet, she gets right in my face. "For one thing, you won't be a thousand miles away. Like the look in your eyes the entire time I jerked you off, while we fucked, like right now. Where are you Jesse?"

Time heals. Externally, anyway. My cuts and scrapes are gone, so I don't need to plaster makeup all over my face anymore. I've fallen into a routine. I never thought it would happen. Adjustment. Resignation. Whatever, it makes existence more bearable.

Nina catches me in the hall between classes. "Let's cut. Go over to Coney."

My backpack is slung over my shoulder. "No can do," I say without looking at her, because my eyes follow my hand that's rummaging inside my bag for my English homework. "I have a test this period."

Annoyed sigh. "Fuck the test."

When I lift my eyes to study Nina's determined expression, my stare jerks past her. Several guys are grouped in front of a row of lockers, watching us. This is not unusual, however, one particular dude is staring me down. Or at least trying to.

"Who's that?" With my stare locked on the tall dark skinned guy, I cock my head and ask Nina. Normally I'd look away. But there's something about this guy – his eyes – magnetic. Even from the distance, it's obvious they're crystal green. Amazing. Mesmerizing. Familiar.

After a quick glance over her shoulder, Nina snips, "Who, those brothers?"

"Yes, those brothers. Especially the one trying to burn a hole in my head."

"You have a way with words." While she bursts out laughing, she swings herself around and waves to them, her smile snarky. "We don't hang with them, but the geeky gawking one is Nolan Royce."

"Gawking yes. Geeky? You're out of your mind. Far from it." For the first time, my eyes inch away. "What are *we* too good for them?" I ask, peering over her shoulder at the captivating dude whose eyes are communicating all kinds of things: interest, warmth, passion.

"Not hardly," she says with sarcasm, "they're the brainy bunch."

I'm taken aback. "So, we're the dummies?"

"Honors and degenerates don't mingle." Her voice is flat. This reminds me of my old school, only there I was the honors. Boy have the tables turned.

This is the first time I'm confronted with the possibility that I might be considered a degenerate. A chill runs down my spine. What would my parents think of their honors daughter if they could see her now? At the thought, I cringe. My eyes wander back to the guy who continues to stare, only now, a small smile creeps across his full lips and it's not fading. It looks a bit tight, however, which calm my butterflies – well kind of.

"Listen," she says, "stop eye-fucking him."

"What? I'm not ..."

She pitches a hip and slides a stick of gum between her lips, sucking the sweetness before chewing. "You want to meet him? Ah, how about if he comes with, will you go to Coney then? I don't think girls like us are their thing, but hell, it's worth a try."

"Girls like us?" I'm shocked that Nina considers me to be

the same as her. "No. I don't want to meet him." Before she can move, my fingernails dig into her arm.

Shrugging me off, she marches toward them, with me tagging along, harshly whispering, "I was just looking, Nina!" At the thought of talking to him, my knees go weak. "It's not like that…"

Stopping in her tracks she spins and faces me. "Are you into him or not?"

I feel the rise of a flush which I'm sure is plastered across my face. "Holy shit, Nina. Will you lower your voice? You're making a scene."

"I'm losing patience," she snaps before her gum wrapped tongue pokes through her lips and pops a bubble. "I'm trying to help. So make up your mind before the bell rings."

"No. I'm not into him." My palm is covering half of my mouth. If I could shrink, make myself invisible, I would. Then I could just stand here and gape at him. "There's just something about him. He looks different." How can I explain to my caustic cousin that along with stunning, I find his eyes warm and kind, which strikes a chord in my heart. There's a familiarity about the way he watches me. It's not romantic. He reminds me of home. Comfort. Things I left behind. Things I might be able to have again.

"He's not like the others around here," I mumble. "Did you ever see someone you felt you knew? Or maybe wanted to know? Because maybe they'd add something pleasant to your shitty, boring life?"

"Okay, that's it." She yanks my arm, and before I know it, I'm standing face to face with Nolan Royce.

Grinning up at him, my heart starts thumping. I try to cool my cheeks.

His lips curl into a warm smile, so I jump right in, "Hi. I'm Zoe. Want to come to Coney Island?"

His eyes flick over his friends who openly stare, then cut

back to mine. "Sure," he chuckles, "Coney Island sounds a hell of a lot better than chem lab."

I'm shocked that Nolan has agreed to cut class. We pile into Nino's car and head for Coney Island. It's a perfect day to be outdoors. Sun is shining, and once we're on the parkway heading out to Brooklyn, the breeze turns into ocean air scented with emissions – not fresh and sweet as the breeze at home – but this is life in the city. My heart begins to sink, then I dare sneak a peek at the guy sitting beside me in the back seat and my problems slip away. We're both plastered as close to our doors as possible. It's almost comical; I've found a guy who might be as timid as I am. Well maybe he's just a gentleman. Maybe this is what attracts me to him. Him to me. But oh, those eyes. I turn to speak to him and I'm lost in his eyes.

"What year are you?" I ask.

"Junior. You?"

"Sophomore."

"Oh."

Nino yells over the back seat. "Hey Royce. I thought you rich kids went to private schools. What are you doing in hell hole?"

I'm taken aback by Nino's rudeness and stammer, "Don't pay attention to him. His bark is worse than his bite." I know I sound silly, but Mom always used that expression when referring to Dad's bad moods, and I guess it stuck. I don't mind sounding like my mother. She'll always be part of me.

"This is your first year here," Nolan states, as if he already knows. Which must mean he's noticed me.

"Yup. Did you always go to this school?" Nino has me wondering why he mentioned private school to Nolan.

"Yep."

"Do you live near the school?" I ask.

"Not really. Do you?"

Nina rolls down her window way down, which forces me to

move closer so I can hear Nolan. "I live with *them*." I hitch my head to the front seat and shoot him a mock scowl, then we both laugh and the mood lightens.

"Why would Nino say that to you about our school?"

Nolan inches closer, turning those crystal eyes on me and I lose a breath. "Private school?" He chuckles. "I live uptown. My Dad's a doctor, but he was born and raised in Queens. My mom wanted me in private school, but my Dad wanted me to experience life the way he did. Maybe come back to the neighborhood to practice medicine, like he did."

"A doctor. Impressive."

"Hey you two," Nino bangs on my window, and for the first time I realize the car isn't moving. We're stopped in the parking lot. "Coming out today or would you rather sit in the car and miss the fun?" He guffaws.

Nolan and I exchange glances; my mouth scrunches, his grin creates a dimpled cheek. We slip out of the car and walk side by side. Occasionally, our arms brush. Nina and Nino walk ahead of us, clowning around. Now and then I hear them cursing. By the time we reach the boardwalk, Nina has landed at least a half dozen blows to Nino's side.

The park isn't crowded during the week, especially at this time of day. The first thing we do is buy tickets for the Cyclone Coaster.

"You gonna go on?" Nolan asks, pulling out his wallet.

"I've been on the Dragon at Rye–" I'm dizzy just staring up at the height of this coaster which appears to reach almost to the sky. "But never on anything this big. I might not go on."

"Why?" Nolan asks.

"It's so high. So fast. I might get vertigo." I get even dizzier when I watch the Cyclone in action and my stomach lurches when I hear the thunder of the cars on the tracks and the screams of the people flying past us.

Nina and Nino are already on line for the ride. "Come on, Zoe," Nolan coaxes. "You won't get vertigo. And if you do, I'll get you some Dramamine." His chuckle is soft. It's the kind of chuckle a guy makes when he thinks a girl is cute. Innocent.

"Phew," I let out a sigh, "I guess. But if I throw up on you–"

Nolan laughs. "We'll sit in front of your cousins, so anything will blow back on them."

His smile is contagious. His laugh, and his comment, brings on a bout of laughter.

"I could imagine that," I say. "But really, don't say I didn't warn you. And I apologize in advance if I freak out."

Our first physical contact is when his arm goes around me as we settle into the car. When I face him, he quickly withdraws it. So, we're shoulder to shoulder, Nolan snaps down the bar, the ride starts, and my heart is in my throat.

While the pulleys move us around a bend and up the first slope, Nolan says, "You don't remember me, do you."

My head swings around and I stare. "I knew I recognized those eyes." I suck in a breath. That was you. You're the guy I almost knocked over the first day of school."

A big smile breaks across his face. "That was me. By the look on your face, I knew you felt like you'd just entered the twilight zone."

I roll my eyes. "That bad, huh?" Then for some ungodly reason, I blurt, "I was so entranced by your eyes that I guess the rest of you didn't make that much of an impression."

His eyes bulge. "This is the first time anyone, especially a girl, has ever told my how unremarkable I am."

"Oh no," I say much too brash, because the couple in front of us turn to gape. "You are impressive. All of you. I meant your eyes are just so stunning."

His face softens and he laughs. "I know what you meant. I'm just teasing."

I feel the momentum as the car climbs and gasp. "Oh crap, Nolan." I manage to peel my fingers from my eyes. "Look! We're at the top!" A rush of adrenaline causes my heart to pound and I want off this ride. "I don't think I can do this." I believe I'm whimpering, but Nolan must hear me because he replies.

"You can do anything, Zoe, but you'll never know unless you try." His arm goes around me. "Here we go." He's filled with excitement, pulling me closer. "Hold on tight!"

My stomach leaps to my throat as we plunge. As if a switch in my chest has been flipped, my heart is light. Could I be having fun? There's no future; I remember no past; the world is lost in my screams, the thunder of the coaster, and we fly like a cast of falcons through the screeching wind.

Read the twisting, explosive conclusion of *Agony of Being Me* in *Finding You*, available on Amazon in Kindle and Paperback.

About The Author

I'm Victoria (January) Valentine, a New York writer and indie book publisher. I've been writing for most of my life in one form or another: poetry, short stories, song lyrics, children's books, adult novels. *Agony of Being Me* is my sixth novel.

My favorite genres to read and write are horror, thrillers, and contemporary romance. Besides being inspired by my family, I owe a shout out to Robert C. Wilson, author of *Crooked Tree*, and Robert McCammon, author of *They Thirst* and other fabulous books. The moment I read their novels, I knew I wanted to write horror.

Besides writing and publishing for others, I blog and when time permits, I host Away With Words on Blogtalkradio on Wednesdays @ 6:00 PM EST USA, where I pimp indie and traditionally published authors and their amazing books and careers. Our gabfests are a blast.

Thank you for reading *Agony of Being Me*. A writer would be nowhere without the support of readers and fans. I treasure each and every one of you and would love to hear from you!

Indie publishing is not always easy, but it's a blessing. Dear readers ... Thank you from the bottom of my heart for supporting me and my efforts. Right after I started Agony, my husband was diagnosed with incurable sarcoma. He passed away on May 6th 2015. Agony has had as many ups and downs as its author. During the writing process, the manuscript grew so long, I felt splitting it into two books would be best. There is so much to digest in the lives of these characters, and you may need a breather! I sure do.

For me, writing Agony has been exhausting. I've relived some of the past, some good, some not, but in the end it all turned out as God planned. Tom went home, and I finished my story. Stay tuned for *Finding You*, the conclusion of *Agony of Being Me*.

www.ingramcontent.com/pod-product-compliance
Lightning Source LLC
Chambersburg PA
CBHW051228260626
47162CB00002B/320